Bard

TAM DERUDDER JACKSON

Print ISBN number 978-1-7342666-6-5
Ebook ISBN number 978-1-7342666-7-2

Editor: Nikki Busch Editing
Cover Design: Steamy Designs
Formatting: Damonza
Distribution and POD: IngramSpark

For Coleene Brookshier Torgerson
If not for you, the Talisman Series would not exist

And for Dodo Rosling
In memoriam and with gratitude

"Only the story lasts. Heroes pass into the next life. Monuments erected in their honor fall and crumble into dust. The story endures. The story lives forever. We must tell the story the way we want it remembered."

—Griffin Walsh

CHAPTER ONE

THE BELL OVER the outer door to her office chimed, shattering Fallon Graham's concentration on her screen.

"Is this where I can buy season tickets for football?" asked the gorgeous blond man on the other side of her desk.

A scene flashed through her mind as Fallon stared at him, transfixed.

He rested his forearms on the counter, and she blinked back into the moment. "I'm sorry. Maybe you didn't hear me." His smile mesmerized her. "I was wondering if I could buy season tickets here." The melodious baritone of his voice washed over her, rippling through her chest.

Her face heated. Clearing her throat, she tried to regain control of herself. "Um, yes. Yes, it is. How many tickets do you need, and in which section of the stadium would you like to sit?" Attempting to recover some professionalism, she pulled her computer closer and called up the requisite ticket program. With the receptionist out on her break, it fell to Fallon to cover general foot traffic and telephone calls.

Normally, selling game tickets to a hot guy was ample

compensation for doing extra work. Dealing with this particular man was more like hazardous duty. That he was a warrior she had no doubt. No way could he look like the man whose fate had just slashed through her mind and not be a warrior. After all, she wouldn't have had a premonition about a civilian, would she? What she couldn't understand was why his story raced through her head at all, specifically his death. Unable to stop herself, she sneaked another peek over the top of her computer.

"I'll need three—make that four in the upper deck above the student section if you have them. Maybe I'll have a date when the season starts." He winked.

Judging from his height and the breadth of his shoulders, the man could know a thing or two about football from playing the game. Or maybe he put an inordinate amount of time into warrior training. Either way, he was sex on a stick. Certainly, he wasn't coming on to her, was he? "Let me see what we have," she said as she studiously applied herself to fulfilling his request. Those shoulders, and the fact that she'd just seen them naked when his fate flashed through her mind, kept distracting her though, and she struggled to keep her mind on her task.

While the woman studied her computer, Seamus Lochlann studied—Fallon Graham, according to the nameplate on her desk. He was used to having an effect on women, especially civilians. The pretty blush on this lady's face told him she wasn't immune to him. *Damn, she's hot. She might not be my usual preference—tall, leggy, blonde—but this woman is gorgeous. What color are her eyes— Green? Blue? Golden brown? And that mouth. So damn kissable.*

The flustered way she acted in his presence amused him. He grinned broadly at her when she sneaked a glance at him, an action that deepened her blush and caused her to lose her place in her task. *Must not laugh*, he admonished himself at the way he so obviously got to her.

When she found four seats together in the upper deck of the stadium, she swung her computer around to let him see his choices.

"I'll take the seats in this section here," he indicated with his index finger brushing the screen of her computer, and she sucked in a breath.

Seamus liked that she sounded unsteady when she said, "Super. Let me grab those for you."

She walked over to the other desk in the office to grab the tickets, giving him an uninterrupted view of her shapely athletic legs—beneath the fitted pencil skirt she wore—her tight, rounded ass, and slim waist. Thick auburn hair cascaded down her perfectly curved back. Involuntarily, he flexed his hands. *What I wouldn't give to plunge my fingers into all that hair.* When she returned with the tickets, he appreciated how her blouse didn't hide her generous curves. The way she moved radiated sexy.

Yeah, I'd like to know Fallon Graham a whole lot better.

As she handed him the tickets, he automatically attempted his sign on her, but instead of deftly tracing his Celtic trinity knot on her right wrist as he took the tickets from her, a piece of armor masquerading as a bracelet stymied him. She frowned at him and jerked her hand away.

"Anything else I can do for you?" she asked, her tone professionally polite.

He didn't miss that she pulled her hands behind her back. "Yeah. Will you show me your bracelet?"

She blinked at him and lifted her hand for him to inspect her jewelry.

"Interesting piece of armor you're wearing there. A remnant from your Wonder Woman costume at Halloween?" he teased.

"Something like that."

Then he noticed the triskele. *If this woman is a talisman, I can't ask her outright to remove her bracelet. I need to find another way to try my sign on her.*

"So, Fallon—that's your name, right?"

"I see you can read," she said with half a grin.

He didn't miss a beat. "One of my many talents." Taking a step closer to her, he said, "I'm Seamus Lochlann, and I was wondering what you're doing tonight."

Chapter Two

FALLON'S HEART SKIPPED a beat when Seamus asked her out. The logical response would be to accept, but she knew better than to date a single warrior. Her parents had drilled into her that her job as a talisman was to be available to a warrior to try his sign on her, but never to date one if he didn't belong to her. Too many warriors and talismans had been lost over the years to relationships determined by mortals rather than by the gods. Though Seamus Lochlann sent butterflies into flight through her insides, she knew better than to spend time alone with him. After having seen him naked in her mind a few minutes ago, she doubted she'd have any self-control on a date with him.

"You work fast, don't you?"

"Only because you're gorgeous." He leaned his arms on the counter above her workstation.

"That's a great line. Bet it works all the time." Stepping behind her chair, she folded her hands neatly on the back of it and stared back at him. Inwardly, she cursed her auburn hair and the fair skin that came with it as heat crept up her neck on its way to her face.

His eyes danced. "Is that a yes?"

That grin really should be outlawed for the mental health of women everywhere.

"I don't think so. I have plans for tonight. But thanks for the invitation."

"What about tomorrow night?"

She crossed her arms over her chest. "I'm going out of town for the weekend."

"Seriously? Or are you letting me down easy?"

"Yes."

"Damn. I must be losing my touch." He fished a card from his wallet and handed it to her. "Maybe you'll change your mind and give me a call."

"I doubt it, but thanks," she said with a small sad smile. Turning down a date with such a handsome man who possessed a sense of humor and a dose of humility was, no doubt, a terrible decision. Yet believing him to be a warrior and likely not hers left her no other choice.

Seamus quirked a brow. Before he could try again, the bell on the outer door to Fallon's office chimed.

"Thanks for your help with the tickets. I hope you'll change your mind and call me," he said with a nod toward her hand holding his business card. He turned toward the door, gifted the older woman who entered a huge smile, and walked out.

"Oh my! Now that is one good looking man. Did you get his name—or better yet—his number?" Dorthea asked as she slipped out of her linen jacket and hung it on the coat tree behind her desk.

"No, no, I didn't." Fallon surreptitiously tucked Seamus's card into the pocket of her skirt. "I sold him some football tickets is all."

"That's a darn shame. Beautiful young woman like you should

appeal to every red-blooded young man who walks into this place. I can't believe he didn't at least ask you to coffee or something."

Fallon changed the subject. "How was lunch with your son?"

Dorthea Jones, the receptionist for the athletic department, didn't look fifty-five, but her mothering skills could only have been honed as sharply as they were through a lifetime of experience. Fortunately for Fallon, most of Dorthea's energies focused on her thirty-year-old son Micah who seemed determined to spend his life in college, which didn't leave her much time to mother Fallon too. Not that she didn't try occasionally.

Dorthea sighed and dropped into her chair. "Exasperating, as usual. That boy can't decide what he wants to do with his life other than be a perpetual college student. I'm going to have to give him an ultimatum soon." She stared out the window. "At least this time he's talking about biotech, something he can apply some of his premed credits to."

"That sounds positive." Fallon sat down at her desk. "We've almost sold out season tickets for football. I'm going to work up a little internet push to sell them all. There's a stack of messages for you on your desk."

"Thank you, dear. I so enjoy the atmosphere around here when our teams are winning, but their success translates into mountains of work for us." Dorthea slapped her hands on her desk. "Right. Best get to it." She reached for the stack of messages.

"What are your plans for marketing the last of the tickets for the football season?" Alan Tremaine, their boss, demanded as he walked out of his adjoining office. As director of athletics, he believed his time to be of far greater value than any mere staffer's, which meant he often disregarded social pleasantries such as greeting a receptionist and asking if she'd had a nice lunch.

Fallon fought her immediate reaction to sit up straighter. "I'm adding a push on our website and in the weekly alumni and student e-letters. Did you have something specific you wanted to include?" She injected her tone with a politeness she didn't feel. She knew he didn't have any kind of plan. The eye roll she caught her colleague making behind their boss's back told her what Dorthea thought of Tremaine's rather ham-handed objective of controlling all behavior in "his" department.

"I have some ideas, but I'll wait to see what you work up. Will you have something before the end of the day?" he inquired neutrally.

Fallon loved the marketing aspect of her job, and she enjoyed working with Dorthea, the coaching staffs of the various sports teams the university supported, and the student athletes. However, she did *not* enjoy working for Alan Tremaine. Though he was about Dorthea's age, his ideas about women belonged to another generation that grew up during another era, like maybe the Dark Ages.

It occurred to her that Tremaine would never have made it in the time of the Celts when it was as likely a woman would be the chieftain and warlord of a tribe as would a man. In Celtic times, no man would dream of questioning her judgment or gainsaying her decrees let alone try to control her conversation while she worked her job. She'd made it a year and a half in the Athletic Director's office, about six months longer than her predecessor, but soon, she, too, was going to have to make a change.

Belatedly, she realized she hadn't responded to her boss when he bristled. "Are you there? Will you have something to show me by the end of the day?"

Frost stung her tone. "Of course." She needed more sleep if she had any hope of dealing with her boss's nastiness.

"If you can manage not to get lost in space," Tremaine said sarcastically, "you can bring your ideas to my office when you finish with them." He turned on his heel and stalked into his office.

Over the top of her computer, Fallon smiled lamely at Dorthea and went to work on her marketing ideas.

Her efforts paid off when she was able to knock off early

on Friday afternoon after Director Tremaine left the office for a weekend of meetings. Earlier in the morning, she'd launched her marketing push on the athletic department and alumni websites, her ideas entirely intact as she'd expected when she'd taken them to Tremaine the day before.

Her boss's absence meant she could gain a head start for the out-of-town getaway she'd mentioned to the blond-haired warrior she couldn't stop thinking about. She'd read about a new section of trails opening on the side of the valley opposite the downhill ski area and decided to take a backcountry hiking trip to explore them. The new trails promised spectacular scenery on the way to a secluded lake. From what she'd read, the lake's shore was ideally suited to camping. She could hardly wait to hit the trail, forget about her job, and hopefully not think about an incredibly handsome warrior who wasn't hers.

Seamus Lochlann was out of sorts. With his best friend Rowan Sheridan finding and marrying his talisman, Alyssa Macaulay, not only was he out a roommate but also a buddy to pal around with on the weekends. Rowan's brother Rio discovered that Ceri Ross, Alyssa's best friend, was his talisman, and they married in Scotland right after Samhain. It irritated him that he'd missed out on the monster battle Morgan organized to take Rio before he could marry Ceri and seal yet another loophole in Morgan's mercilessly unfair war against warriors. Lately, it seemed, the Sheridans were having all the fun.

Then there was Fallon Graham. The more he thought about her, the more he believed she was a talisman. Yet she'd firmly turned him down for a date, so how was he going to figure out for sure? Trouble was, she'd seemed sad about turning him down. Something definitely was going on with the woman. To his surprise, he wanted to know what.

It dawned on him as he sat in his broken-down recliner in his basically bare apartment that he should have tried reading her mind. If he could have read it, he might know several things. Like if she was a civilian and why she seemed sad about turning him down. If he couldn't read her mind, that meant she had a shield, confirming his suspicions that she was a talisman. Being able to try his sign on her would have gone a long way toward figuring her out as well. That damned bracelet she wore impeded his ability to determine her status, pissing him off and adding to his bad mood.

Why in hell am I sitting in my apartment alone on a Friday night brooding about a certain hot redhead when I could be out meeting someone, maybe even my talisman? He decided to put on his party face and go out, have a beer or two, and at least enjoy a civilian woman if tonight was not the night—again—for him to discover his fated mate. He reckoned he'd shook hands with at least a thousand women in the five years since he'd turned twenty-one. His sign, tracing a Celtic trinity knot on the inside of a woman's right wrist, was so easy to do that it became automatic for him. Yet not discovering his talisman after so many tries had started to grate on him.

While his best friend struggled to find his mate before the terrible deadline of midnight of his twenty-eighth birthday, Seamus had been unfailingly optimistic about both of them finding their talismans before Morgan could take advantage of the unfair rules she'd underhandedly applied to warriors a millennium ago. When Rowan found Alyssa, they'd fulfilled a thousand-year-old prophecy and lifted the age restriction, returning it to forty-two as the gods had intended when the warrior class came into being. The added time to find his mate should have cheered him. Instead, being the last of his family and friends to find his talisman had the opposite effect. Finding his talisman had become a pressing priority.

Dragging himself out of his morose thoughts, he pulled on his jacket, grabbed his keys, and headed out to the bars.

You're losing your touch, old son, Seamus scolded himself as he glanced around the bar one last time later that night. Not only had he struck out with Fallon Graham on Thursday afternoon, but he didn't meet anyone interesting at the bar either. *I need a break from this town and from women in general.*

As he considered his options, he remembered he'd promised his sister that he'd restock the family cabin with food and firewood and make sure no critters had invaded it during the spring. Besides, he needed a change of scenery after he'd been left behind to mind the store, literally, while Rowan took Alyssa for a mini-break to mark the end of her teaching term. The Sheridans ran Security Consultants Unlimited, a home security firm where Seamus had worked since he graduated college. The branch office he and Rowan opened two years ago served as a great cover for warriors who could be called anywhere at a moment's notice to defend civilians or aid other warriors in Morgan's ceaseless battles. For the last week, however, he'd been left tying up loose ends on a major security system installation in a local congressman's new monstrosity of a home.

After deciding a backcountry excursion might improve his attitude, Seamus showered in the twilight dawn of Saturday morning and packed gear in the framed backpack he used for backcountry trips. Since he'd only have one night at the cabin, he packed light on clothes to leave more room for food and sundries to carry into the family getaway. Once he'd stowed his pack in the back of his four-wheel-drive pickup, he headed to the twenty-four-hour grocery to load up on supplies before setting off to the trailhead and the cabin.

❧

The day dawned clear and brisk, though being June, no doubt it would be a scorcher by midafternoon. It was a perfect day to hike, and Fallon relished the chill air and gorgeous surroundings. She needed this outing if she was going to have any chance of regaining a sense of normalcy in her life. After a full day of hiking and taking photos—her new favorite hobby—she hoped she'd fall into a quiet dreamless sleep in her tent.

Thinking about sleeping arrangements led her directly to Seamus Lochlann, and not for the first time in the last two days did she second-guess her decision not to go out with him. His midnight blue eyes twinkling with mischief drew her in. The plaid shirt he wore struggled to cover the breadth of his shoulders. Surely one date with him wouldn't have hurt anything. His business card nearly burned a hole in the pocket of her skirt for the duration of Thursday afternoon, and she couldn't stop looking at it in odd moments at home on Friday night. He said he wanted her to call if she changed her mind, but did he mean that, or was he trying to save face?

Yet, the flash of a story the first time she saw Seamus played on a loop in her head. The terror and sorrow that ripped through her simultaneously told her she'd made the correct decision not to go out with him. If a goddess had him in her crosshairs, he was going to need his talisman. Which meant Fallon had no business distracting him from his duty in finding that woman.

Still, her natural inclination to help him nearly overwhelmed her good sense. If she'd revealed the scene that flashed through her mind, she couldn't imagine he'd thank her for it. What warrior would want to have his dignity and honor torn away in the throes of sexual congress with a goddess intent on killing him in her bed? No, she'd been right to walk away from him even though he was the sexiest man she'd ever met.

Of course, after the intensity of her nightmares the previous night, she had no doubt Seamus was the warrior whose story now invaded her sleep. Experiencing his anguish in Maeve's bed bolted Fallon upright, sweat drenching her body. After talking herself down, she checked the time. Four-thirty a.m. With a sigh, she threw herself back onto her pillow and stared at the ceiling. It was close enough to daylight she might as well shower, dress, pack up her gear, and head out on her trip.

Once she was on the trail, she was glad she'd made such an early start. After a long, gradual climb along a tree-lined path, she stepped out onto a relatively flat section flanked by soaring palisades of sheer granite that rose from the valley floor to scrape the sky. She couldn't remember witnessing a more beautiful scene. Pulling her camera from her backpack, she snapped several photos.

My best friend would love this. I'll have to make sure Sloane makes the trip with me next time. After returning her camera to its protective pocket, she pushed ahead on the trail. The private landowners who'd opened this trail to recreation had to be some of the most generous people on earth, and also some of the most responsible. The kind of scenery she was enjoying should be shared with as many people as possible, if for no other reason than as an advertisement for preserving it. She laughed at herself for thinking like a marketer rather than a backcountry enthusiast whose sole purpose for being there should have been enjoyment purely for the sake of it.

With her thoughts wandering, she didn't notice the graying of the sky, but the fat drops of rain splattering on her face grabbed her attention. Increasing her pace, she focused on finding shelter in the trees at the base of the palisades, but the wind and rain seemed to intensify proportionally to her efforts. Thunder cracked overhead. In the back of her mind, she wondered if Taranis was having a random temper tantrum or if he'd unleashed this thunderstorm on purpose. Though she spent a lot of time reading old Celtic stories, she couldn't remember any involving the taking a talisman across the ford of the river of death due to dying in a storm. Morgan could only escort talismans across her river of blood if they died as a result of helping a warrior in battle. Of course, the way the goddess played fast and loose with the rules, Fallon guessed anything was possible.

Pushing aside her morbid thoughts, she increased her pace in an effort to reach the tree line. She thought she must be close to the lake, but she needed to find a suitable camping spot before the sun completely disappeared. The black clouds and ropy rain of the storm would probably bring on night far earlier than she'd anticipated when she'd set her pace along the path.

The storm and the falling darkness forced her to seek out a camping spot along the trail rather than at her lakeside destination. Peering into the gathering dusk, she spotted a light not far off the path. Light meant shelter, and she set off toward it. Picking her way through the trees surrounding what appeared to be a small cabin, she made steady progress until she found herself at the base of the steps leading up to a front porch that was well stocked with firewood. Perhaps the inhabitants of the cabin wouldn't be averse to sharing some of that firewood or better yet would offer her shelter inside rather than leave her to her own devices in her soggy tent.

She climbed the two wide steps up onto the porch and took a deep breath before knocking on the door. Fixing a bright smile on her face, she braced herself for whoever opened the door and hoped the person was friendly or at least sympathetic. Her smile froze on her lips when the occupant of the cabin answered her knock on his door.

CHAPTER THREE

EAMUS HAD MADE the trip to his family's cabin in record time that afternoon, something he was grateful for after he stacked the last of the wood he'd split. When he'd checked the weather on the satellite before leaving town, he saw a storm was due midweek, so the lowering skies and fat raindrops pelting the windows of the cabin surprised him. Good thing he'd packed in about sixty pounds of food, most of it canned or dried. He also congratulated himself on successfully packing in a carton of eggs and a loaf of bread without breaking or squashing any of it. He could make himself a bacon and cheese omelet for dinner, scrambled eggs and toast for breakfast, and peanut butter and honey sandwiches for the trip out tomorrow, leaving all the rest of the food for his sister and brother-in-law when they made their annual trip to the cabin in July.

Siobhan Lochlann MacManus had been born a druid into a family of warriors, something of an anomaly in their community. She'd married a warrior, a choice definitely outside the norm for their culture. To be fair, Duncan MacManus's talisman, Jennifer Carlin, and he hadn't bonded though she still served him in battle as his talisman. Siobhan's enchantments had gone a long way toward keeping all three of them safe from the evil machinations of the wicked deities bent on their destruction. Her skills extended to the family cabin, which she enchanted every year as one of the several protected residences his family used to stay ahead of the war goddesses. Seamus was on his own in his apartment, a circumstance that never allowed him to sleep deeply. The cabin was different. Here he could let down his guard and truly rest.

As he slipped out of his hiking boots and hung up his coat on a peg by the door, it occurred to him he should have taken off work early yesterday and skipped the fruitless Friday-night bar scene for an extra night at their mountain retreat. He stoked the fire he'd started when he arrived and finished unpacking his back-pack, humming to himself as he refilled the tin canisters in the pantry with flour, sugar, and pancake mix. Next, he neatly stacked cans of stew, chili, vegetables, and fruit and rotated forward the foodstuffs Siobhan and Duncan had packed in when they skied in toward the end of the winter. Siobhan mentioned they were running low on spices, so he'd brought along an extra jar of the Italian herbs he liked as well as pepper, salt, cayenne, onion, and garlic powder. He smiled to himself. An army could probably stay at the cabin for a long visit and not go hungry.

As an extra treat, he'd brought along a fresh red pepper, an onion, a bag of spinach, mushrooms, and a pound of bacon, having decided his menu for the weekend while he shopped. He'd started frying the bacon and was in the process of laying out the vegetables for his omelet when the hairs on the back of his neck stood up. Hesitating in his dinner preparation, he listened intently, trying to discern what had disturbed him. It sounded like someone was climbing the steps to the cabin.

"What the hell?"

The knock at the door confirmed his suspicions.

He fingered his claymore then slowly opened the door. The

light from the lamps he'd lit in the cabin spilled out onto the porch, illuminating the face of the woman who'd kept invading his thoughts over the last two days. For a minute, he stared dumbly, wondering if he'd conjured her up.

Fallon recovered first. "Imagine meeting you here," she said with an awkward laugh. "I seem to have been caught out in the storm, and I was wondering if I could set up my tent by your fire pit and use some of your wood for a campfire."

"What are you doing out here?" he asked with equal parts confusion and surprise.

"Taking a backcountry hiking trip. Listen, I have everything I need except for firewood, and I see you have rather a lot of it stacked up here." She glanced at the mound of wood on the porch. "I'll pay you for what I use."

The rain had plastered her auburn hair to her head, and she should have looked like a drowned rat instead of like an enchanting fairy come to visit. The light playing over her face not only revealed rosy cheeks but also the tick along her jawline where she clamped her teeth to keep them from chattering. Why she'd even suggest spending the night in a tent when she could sleep comfortably inside a warm cabin was a problem he'd ponder later. Right now, he needed to coax her inside.

"I'm fixing an omelet. We can figure out the wood rations over dinner," he said as he stepped away from the door, silently inviting her inside.

"I-I don't want to impose on you. I really do have s-supplies and a winter camping tent and thermal sleeping bag." She nodded toward the rather large pack strapped to her back. "The plan was to tent camp at the lake at the end of the trail, so I'm prepared except for dry wood."

"You're also freezing, and I'm starting to catch a chill myself standing here with the door open. Can we continue this conversation inside?"

Like all warriors, Seamus possessed superhuman speed, and he wasn't above using it to get what he wanted. Lightning fast, he reached out and snagged her backpack off her person before she could protest, leaving her no choice but to follow him inside.

"How? How did you do that?"

"What?" he asked as he set her pack on a bench beside the door.

She looked from him to her pack, and he shrugged. "What can I say? I'm quick. And your hypothermia is slowing you down. You can leave your shoes on the mat."

Yep. That kind of speed left no doubt the man was a warrior. But with the rain intensifying outside, and the cozy warmth of the cabin enveloping her, Fallon decided to stay for dinner. Drying out a bit before returning to the deluge outside was too tempting to let a little thing like ethics stand in the way.

She stood on the rug in front of the door and looked around. The cabin was surprisingly more spacious than it appeared from outside. An efficiency kitchen, complete with a refrigerator, stove, and sink, lined the wall to the left of the front door. A double door to a closet-sized pantry stood ajar beside the sink. A pine dinette set separated the kitchen from the rest of the room. After his sneaky move to draw her into the cabin, Seamus had retreated to the stove from where the heavenly smell of frying bacon wafted through the air.

Fallon took two steps into the living room where two matching chairs and ottomans flanked a red plaid couch with a low pine table sitting in front of it. She smiled at the bookshelves stuffed with paperbacks and board games resting between two doors along the back wall of the room. Between the bookshelves, a ladder rose up to a loft jutting out over two-thirds of the living area.

Involuntarily, she gravitated toward the delicious heat of a

cheery fire blazing in a river-rock fireplace. Lamps that were strate-
gically placed on a small table near the fireplace, on a table beside
the couch, and hanging from a hook above the sink bathed the
room in light. She wiggled her toes over the braided area rug in
shades of brown, tan, and green that covered most of the smooth
pine floor. From the corner of her eye, she caught Seamus watching her as she took in the room.

*If one of those doors opens into a bedroom, I might be safe shar-
ing this cabin with him since one of us could sleep in the loft. Or I
could spend the night on the couch.*

"Nice place you've got here."

"Yeah. We like it."

We? "Are you sure I'm not intruding?" Fallon asked as she
glanced surreptitiously at the closed doors.

"Not at all. I needed a break and hiked up here this afternoon.
I wanted to restock the place and get it ready for my sister's visit
at the end of the month," Seamus said with an easy smile.

"You're alone?" she asked, then clamped her mouth tight.

"Not anymore." He grinned. "Come on, take off your coat
and stay awhile."

*It would take a far stronger woman than me to resist the lovely
warmth of this cabin*—she shrugged out of fleece-lined Gortex
jacket and hung it on a peg by the front door—*or pass up the
opportunity to sleep in a soft bed or the company of a man as incredibly handsome as Seamus Lochlann.*

He returned to the kitchen, and she saw him add more bacon
to the pan. Walking back to the warmth of the fireplace, she
shoved her hands into the back pockets of her jeans and watched
him cook while she counseled herself. *I'll be hiking out alone in the
morning. It's not as though we're a mated pair or anything.*

On the pretense of taking in the cabin, she studied her host
as he deftly flipped bacon before he diced vegetables. He wore his
dark blond hair long enough to curl over the collar of his charcoal

gray flannel shirt. The shirt itself, though generously cut, still pulled taut over his massive shoulders. *Like Atlas, he could hold up the world with those*, she mused. Because he'd tucked his shirt into his jeans, she could ogle the perfect taper of his torso from his shoulders to his slim waist. He didn't wear a belt, probably because he didn't need to. His well-worn jeans fit him like a second skin over a nicely formed ass and long legs.

Since he'd rolled the sleeves of his shirt halfway up his forearms, she could see a light dusting of blond hair and the heavy bones of a man who used his body hard. His big hands gracefully made short work of peppers, onions, and mushrooms. *Damn, but it's fun to watch him cook*. When he moved to check the bacon, she caught her reflection in the small window above the sink in front of him. Glancing up, he caught her eye and winked. A full body blush spread over her skin at being caught admiring him so openly.

"Like what you see?" His wicked smile sent her heart skittering.

She cleared her throat and tried to cover her embarrassment. "You have a cozy place here. Um, I was wondering, does the indoor plumbing extend past the kitchen sink?"

"The head is through there." He gestured with his knife at the door to the right of the kitchen and didn't bother to hide his pleasure at her embarrassment.

"Thanks." Cursing herself for being an idiot, she hot-footed it past him to the bathroom.

She closed the door behind her and leaned against it, trying to quiet her heartbeat. Admiring the warrior in the other room was one thing; being caught doing it was something else entirely. He must think her certifiable for checking him out so thoroughly after she'd turned down his date the other day. No doubt he could see how attracted she was to him, which made their current situation more untenable. Unless he was an utter and complete gentleman, there was no way she could spend the night under the same roof with him. He was far too tempting.

Damn. If it hadn't been for those scenes flashing through her mind, she wouldn't be in this predicament. Likely, she would have gone out with him the other night, had a great time, and discovered to their mutual chagrin they didn't belong to each other, but at least it would have been honest. The premonition she'd seen complicated everything. How did one go about telling a man she'd seen him naked, watched him pleasure a goddess, albeit against his will, and witnessed the act the second she met him? She blew a breath at the ceiling. How did she broach the subject of having seen his death?

Pushing herself away from the door, she glanced around a room that, like the kitchen, was built for efficiency. A warrior-sized shower took up one side of it while a small sink and toilet faced the door. The entire room was fitted with aqua-green ceramic tile with a bluish charcoal grout, giving it a spa-like atmosphere. She washed her hands and splashed cool water on her still-hot face before schooling her features into something bland and exiting the room.

"Anything I can do to help you with dinner? Set the table or something?" she asked brightly as she walked back into the kitchen.

"Sure. Plates are in here." He nodded toward a cupboard beside the window. "Silverware is in the drawer below it. Your timing is perfect. I'll be ready to plate these omelets any minute." Though his voice was even, the look he gave her sizzled with desire, and it was clear he wasn't going to let her be. *No doubt I'll be spending the night trying to keep dry in my tent.* She tried not to sigh.

⌒

While Fallon hid out in the bathroom, probably gathering herself after he caught her looking at him like she wanted to eat him for dinner, Seamus entertained some rather vivid thoughts himself. All of which he needed to keep in check. If she was a talisman but didn't belong to him, he had no choice but to leave her alone. He'd give her the bedroom since the door locked. Not that a mere lock would be enough to keep him out if he truly wanted to be in there with her. But it was enough to remind him of their obligations to other people, obligations that would absolutely preclude acting on the desire drawing them together.

On the other hand, if he was extra lucky and she was a civilian, all bets were off. The ultimate good fortune would be that she was his talisman. Yet the idea that his own talisman had walked up and knocked on his door late one stormy afternoon seemed too coincidental for any sane warrior to believe.

It was obvious she had good manners or she wouldn't have offered to help with dinner when he could tell what she truly wanted to do was run. It wasn't lost on him that she chose to do something to keep herself as far from him as possible in the small space. In the two encounters he'd had with her, he'd observed she held herself tightly in check, and he wanted to know why.

After she set the silverware on opposite sides of the dinette, she slid the plates onto the counter near the stove. "Where do you keep your condiments, and which ones do you want?" she asked from somewhere behind him.

"I like ketchup on my eggs. You'll find that in the fridge. There's also jam for the toast," Seamus said as he plated the omelets and set them on the table.

"What's your preference for a beverage?"

"It's a special occasion. How 'bout we break out the wine?"

"What occasion would we be celebrating?"

"The occasion of our first date." He waggled his brows at her.

"This is not a date," she said with a cute little huff.

"It isn't? Dinner, wine, two people who are attracted to each other—sure sounds like a date to me." He grinned.

"We're having dinner together out of necessity. I haven't agreed to drinking wine with you, and the attraction must be one-sided. Thanks for the compliment." She put her adorable nose in the air, but her voice dropped several notes.

"It's your story. Tell it however you want." He smirked. "Of course, it doesn't explain the way you were watching me earlier." He pulled two wineglasses from the cupboard and filled them with white wine before setting them on the table and seating himself.

For several seconds, Fallon hovered over her chair. Squaring her shoulders, she walked over to the cupboard, removed two water glasses, filled them with icy water from the tap, and set them on the table. As she seated herself across from him, the corner of her mouth turned up slightly.

Pouring a generous dollop of ketchup on his still-steaming omelet, he said, "Tell me again how you're out here in the woods all by yourself on a Saturday night during a rainstorm?"

"I took a week off from work to do some hiking and back-country camping. The forecast for the week said I would avoid the big storm. Maybe I'd have to put up with a mountain shower or two. This hurricane blowing in came as a complete surprise." She spread a thick layer of huckleberry jam over a piece of toast. "Actually, I was trying to find a place to set up camp when I saw the light from your cabin and hiked over."

"Do you go backcountry camping often?" He forked a mouthful of omelet and tried to concentrate on his food as he listened to the honey of her voice.

"Oh, yes," she said with enthusiasm. "It's one of the few aspects of my train—" She swallowed and started over. "It's one of the few activities I ever did with my parents that I actually enjoyed."

"Your parents taught you about backcountry camping? That's interesting." He stared meaningfully into her eyes. "So did mine."

Fallon reached for her wineglass, downed a big swallow, and

changed the subject. "These omelets are fantastic. Are you a chef or something?"

"No. My roommate got married last summer, forcing me to learn how to cook. Since I started doing it, I've discovered I enjoy it. But anyone can make an omelet." With mulish stubbornness, he didn't let go of her errant comment. "You were saying something about training?" he continued as she spoke over him.

"Where do you work?"

"I'm a security consultant and an installation expert for Security Consultants Unlimited, but—"

"Why do I know that name?"

Sighing, he gave up his probe for the moment and indulged her. "Maybe because we recently finished an installation on the congressman's monster house, which hit the papers last week after some cub reporter discovered it. Now the congressman's got egg on his face—no pun intended," he said gesturing to their plates with a smirk, "because he campaigned on the safety of the county under his leadership, yet he spent several thousand dollars on a state-of-the-art security system for his new house."

She raised a skeptical brow. "How did a cub reporter discover the security installation?"

He shrugged. "I'm not sure. Maybe a glitch in the code when the congressman came home drunk one night after a fund-raising dinner, something that set off an alarm at the local police station." He sat back in his chair and savored a mouthful of wine.

"You didn't." She laughed. "I love it when hypocrites like the congressman, like my boss"—she sighed—"get their comeuppances. Public ones are especially delicious when they expose sanctimonious public 'servants,'" she added with air quotes.

"Who says I had anything to do with it?"

She waved her fork at him. "You said you installed the system."

"Yes, but how was I to know he'd forget the sequence and trigger a chain reaction that found its way onto police scanners whose frequencies are picked up at the local newspaper?" He couldn't resist batting his eyes at her.

"I think I like you, Seamus Lochlann. We share a sense of justice." She laughed before downing the last of her wine.

He didn't bother to hide his desire for her as he rested his hand on the table, one finger playing dangerously close to her hand.

"Since you made dinner, I'll clean up." Abruptly, she pushed her chair from the table and walked her plate and utensils over to the sink. "Dish soap under here?" She bent down to peer into the cupboard beneath the sink, inadvertently giving him a rather nice view of her sweetly rounded ass. Stretch jeans hugged her curves in exactly the right way, and his hand was halfway to sliding over those curves before he caught himself and pulled it back to stack his utensils on his plate.

"Yeah, but you're my guest. You don't have to clean up." He stood and placed his dishes on the counter beside the sink.

"My mama didn't raise me to be waited on. Here it is!" She produced a bottle of dish soap from under the sink and proceeded to fill the basin with hot water. "Your cabin is pretty remote. How is it you have electricity and running water out here?"

"My family has owned this property for fifty years. My great-grandpa built the original cabin a little distance up the trail. Then a forest fire passed through and scorched it. My dad decided rather than try to repair the old place, he'd build a new one, and this is it." He leaned back against the counter so he could see her face, which she studiously angled down at the sink.

"The trail you hiked in on is actually a private road. Sometimes when we're feeling adventurous, we tax the hell out of our trucks and drive up here."

She glanced up at that.

"Dad had a well dug, septic put in, and power cabled out here. This place is meant to be a getaway, but we do like our creature comforts."

"Please don't tell me you have telephone, Wi-Fi, and satellite TV," she said with a groan.

"Okay, I won't tell you."

Pulling a face, she asked, "Some of it, or all of it?"

He smiled. "None of it. It's a getaway. We don't even have cell service. The point of coming here is to be off the grid."

She blew out a breath. "What a relief. That's why I hike and backcountry camp. It's the only way to go completely off the grid."

Picking up a towel, he started drying dishes as quickly as she rinsed them. He was enjoying the rather tranquil domestic rhythm into which they'd fallen when she tensed and gasped in a breath.

Seamus felt a jolt zap through him simultaneously with Fallon's gasp. He stopped drying midplate and tried to read her mind, but he discovered she had a shield, and it was securely in place. At least he had confirmation she was a talisman, a problem considering how beautiful and sexy he found her. Not to mention, when she let down her guard a bit, she shared his sense of fun.

Whatever thought passed through her mind sobered the atmosphere in the cabin in a breath. He tried to catch her eye, but she resolutely kept her attention on her task. Wordlessly, she let the water drain from the sink and rinsed it out before drying her hands and heading for the front door of the cabin.

"What gives?" Seamus asked as he walked directly behind her.

"I truly appreciate you sharing your supper with me, but I'll sleep outside," she said, her jaw tight as she reached for her coat.

Placing his hand firmly on the door, he said, "What the hell? Nothing has happened. Nothing is going to happen unless you want it to. What kind of man do you think I am?"

She struggled to pull the door open, so he grabbed her wrists and pinned her against it with her hands beside her head.

Her chin came up. "Words and actions."

"Answer me, please." He held her firmly, but not painfully. The tone of his voice, however, brooked no argument.

"You seem like a perfectly decent sort of guy." She glanced at her pinned hands. "It's me, all right? I need to put some distance between us because of me."

Crying out in pain, she let down her shield for a second and he saw her vision—a scene of himself in complete agony rather than orgasmic release inside an auburn-haired woman. At that moment he knew, even without trying his sign on her, Fallon was his. More than that, she'd known him before they met, considering her vision included the two of them making love. He shook his head. That couldn't be it, or he wouldn't have been in pain.

Though he couldn't understand what was happening, he knew one thing—he needed to find out for sure if she belonged to him. He stole a glance at her wrist. Mercifully, she wasn't wearing that enormous bracelet. Staring at her face, he traced his sign on the inside of her right wrist and watched in wonder as her eyes flew open. With a growl, she tried to pull her wrist away from him.

"Restraining me isn't enough for you? You think you have to brand me as well?" she ground out as she struggled against his hold.

"No restraint, no marks, but you are well and truly branded." His eyes bored into hers.

An earlier thought he'd had ripped through his mind again. No sane warrior would believe his talisman would walk right up and knock on his door on a rainy evening. But the gods were never predictable, and the craziest thing had just happened to him.

Chapter Four

OR GOOD MEASURE, Seamus stared intently into Fallon's eyes and retraced his sign on her. Instinctively, she tried to jerk her wrist away from him before her eyes widened from disbelief to understanding. He anticipated the tension going out of her. Instead, she vibrated with even more anxiety.

"You're a warrior," she stated, her voice barely above a whisper. Then even less audibly, "You're my warrior."

I always thought when I met my talisman, we'd both be relieved, certainly, but also a little happy about it maybe? "It appears I am. And you're my talisman." A slow smile spread over his lips. "And we were already attracted to each other before we discovered that happy fact. So your sleeping arrangements no longer include a tent. Do I have your word on that?"

"Yes, all right." Her voice remained soft. "I'll spend tonight inside the cabin." Her eyes slid to their hands. "You can let go now."

Reluctantly, he released her and stepped back, giving her space. She sucked in an unsteady breath and simply stared at his chest as he stood before her.

"Seamus Lochlann is my warrior. What the hell does that mean?"

He stared back at her. Did discovering their relationship somehow allow him to breach her shield? Or had she lost it momentarily? And why was she so worried about him being her warrior? Before he could ask, she stepped away from him.

Staggering over to the nearest chair, she sagged against it. Seeing her distress, he scooped her up in his arms and carried her to the couch to lie down.

"When I envisioned meeting my talisman, at the very least I thought she'd be as glad of our meeting as I knew I would be." He laid her on the cushions before sitting down beside her. "From your reaction, you're not thrilled about our pairing." Settling himself deeper into the cushions, he stared into the kaleidoscope of her eyes. "The way you were looking at me before dinner had my hopes up for tonight. What's changed?" he asked softly. "Does it have to do with that vision you had when I stopped you from leaving?"

He had positioned himself as her pillow. While he rested one arm along the back of the couch, he stroked her incredibly soft auburn hair. At the mention of her vision, the hair-trigger tension she showed him earlier once again stiffened her body.

"Wh-what did you see, exactly?" Her voice quivered as she scrambled to sit up straight.

He slid his hand over her shoulder and coaxed her back to her prone position. "It looked like the two of us were making love, but I didn't appear to be enjoying it much, which frankly I can't imagine. You had my attention the minute I walked through the door of your office the other day." He smoothed a fingertip over the frown forming on her brow and continued. "When you showed up here in those tight jeans that about wore me out, it's surprising I didn't need to use the first aid kit multiple times while I wielded sharp knives as I made supper." He smirked. "Since I couldn't keep my mind focused on my business."

Fallon smiled weakly at him before she sat up carefully and faced him. To his consternation, she scooted to the other end of the couch.

"*We* weren't making love. *You* were dying in Maeve's bed."

His heart spiked. "What the hell? What are you saying?"

Her beautiful eyes with their ever-changing colors filled with sorrow. "When you walked into my office, your story flashed through my mind." She wrapped her arms around her middle. "I saw Maeve take you over and over again. Each time was more agonizing for you than the last." She wrung her hands in her lap. "Desperately, you tried to deny her your passion, and you didn't give her your heart or your soul even though she kept promising to release you sooner if you would." Fallon's bottom lip quivered, and she closed her eyes tight. "You fought the passion she insisted on arousing in you."

Leaning forward, he rested his forearms on his thighs, clasped his hands between his knees, and tried to get a handle on what Fallon was saying.

"Yet she compelled you to take her as she demanded all of your life force until she spent you completely and laughed as Morgan escorted you across the ford in shame." She sucked in a breath and let it out slowly.

"Jesus."

She nodded, her eyes filled with unhappiness.

Thinking he'd heard the worst of it, he reached for her hands. When he discovered how icy they were, he scooted closer to her and warmed them in his own. But she had more to say.

"When you walked into my office the other day and shook my hand, you touched my bracelet. At your touch, it became so hot I nearly had to take it off. I knew you must be a warrior, and somehow, I'd seen your death."

Seamus sagged back against the couch.

"Is that why you turned me down for a date?"

"I... yes." She cleared her throat. "I just told you I've had visions of watching you die, and all you're worried about is that I turned you down for a date?"

He shrugged. "By the way, where is that piece of armor that stopped us from discovering each other sooner?"

"In my backpack. It gets in the way of climbing over rocks or trees when I hike, so I have to take it off. Why?"

"It's enchanted, isn't it?"

She nodded.

"May I see it?"

"What does my bracelet have to do with everything I told you?" She stood and walked over to her backpack to retrieve the piece of jewelry.

"My sister is a druid. When I attempted my sign on you the other day, I also noticed heat when I touched your bracelet, which made me think you might be a talisman." He cleared his throat. "It annoyed the hell out of me because it kept me from trying my sign on you."

She handed him the bracelet as she sat back down on the couch, annoying him again when she put distance between them.

For several minutes he said nothing as he studied her bracelet. The triskele stamped on the top was a Saint Brighid's cross, patron goddess of women, poetry, and inspiration. Almost unconsciously, he traced the triskele and whispered, "Dark the bitter winter, cutting its sharpness, but Bride's mantle brings spring to the land."

When he unclasped the bracelet, his eyes widened at the sight of the chain of Celtic trinity knots in the same size and style as his sign. Holding it out to her, he said, "Put this on, please."

Her brows knitted in silent question. Still, she took the bracelet and clasped it on her wrist.

"Now give me your hand."

A question in her eyes, she obliged him and gasped as they both felt the bracelet heat up where he traced his sign on it.

"Take it off."

Again, she followed his order. Both of them stared wide-eyed at the glowing trinity knot on the underside of the bracelet. Carefully, Seamus turned over Fallon's wrist, and they saw the mark the tracing of his sign over her bracelet had left on her body. When he lifted her wrist to his lips and brushed a kiss there, she jerked in his hold. Her crossed legs told him exactly how he'd affected her.

He arched a brow, but she said nothing. It didn't matter. The leap in her pulse as his lips touched the mark on her wrist told him she was well and truly his.

"Who gave you this bracelet, Fallon?"

"What?"

She stared at the mark on her wrist.

"Fallon?"

Blinking up at him, she said, "My aunt. Keela. She's a talisman, but she married a druid, so my family ostracized her."

The way she tossed off the comment set his teeth on edge.

She didn't seem to notice as she talked on. "Her husband made this for me for my twenty-first birthday. Keela told me to wear it or have it with me always since I didn't have the protection of a warrior or the enchantments of a druid. Something about my special powers." She shrugged. "But I'm only a talisman, so I don't know what she was talking about." She covered her face with her hands. "Wow, that didn't sound anything like a sophomore trying to impress the senior quarterback, did it?"

Seamus gently pulled her hands from her face and smiled. "Your aunt was right, you know. I'd really like to meet her and find out how she and her husband figured out the sign you'd respond to when you met your warrior." He slid closer to her. "It's something no talisman is supposed to know until her particular warrior tries it on her. Your family protected you and made sure that when I found you, I'd mark you with my sign." He looked deep into her eyes. "That means something. As part of our bonding, we're going to have to figure out what."

As he spoke, he set the bracelet on the table in front of them.

"I thought you'd be angry."

He stared unblinkingly at her.

"Upset at the very least at the fate the goddess has in store for you."

"You thought I'd take that anger out on you?" He returned to touching her hair, wrapping a strand around his finger, savoring its silkiness along his skin.

"Um, maybe. I don't know. I don't know you yet."

"We need to remedy that," he said quietly as he slipped one arm around her and used the index finger of his free hand to trace the contours of her face. "You've given me a gift. Why would that make me angry?"

Confusion flitted over her features. "The vision I saw is a gift?"

He smiled. The light tracing of his finger on her skin coupled with the easy massage he was giving the back of her neck beneath her hair had made her mind go blank. He'd checked.

"Yes. Now I know who my most dangerous enemy is and what she plans for me. That gives me an advantage. Tell me, in your premonition, did you see all of me?" he asked as he leaned in to kiss the corner of her mouth.

Her breath caught when his lips touched her skin. Using his nose to move her hair, he kissed along her jaw to her ear and whispered, "In your vision, did you see me naked?"

He traced the shell of her ear with his tongue, and she rewarded him with a full-body shiver and a little sigh as she relaxed into him.

"Yes."

Abruptly, she pulled away, her cheeks blooming in a lovely shade of rose.

"Hey, hey, come back here. I know you weren't spying on me or something equally perverted," he said laughing.

"That's right, I wasn't spying on you," she said, her tone huffy. He kind of liked it… liked baiting her. "I didn't even know who you were," she continued. "Plus, your story flashed through my head fast, so things were indistinct. I saw your skin, and from the activity in the vision, I knew you were naked, not so much from looking at you…" Her hands flew to her cheeks. "That didn't come out right."

Seamus didn't try to hide his amusement. "So you're saying that not only have you seen me naked, but you've observed my technique? What did you think?" he teased as he pulled her closer to him.

"It—it wasn't like that!"

A flustered Fallon was too cute to let up easily. "You took a shine to me right away, I take it."

"You were struggling and in pain. Maeve was killing you in bed." In a whisper she added, "And watching you die was killing me."

That sobered him.

"You were so strong, so noble, and you didn't want to die that way. You wanted a chance to fight honorably. It was awful watching Maeve enjoy your distress so much." Her eyes filled with tears, deepening them into shimmering pools of emotion.

"That vision is serious magic. It's important that you shared it with me. But I have to confess to a certain need to hear you say you want me because I want you. So much." He toured her face with his eyes, letting her see his desire for her.

With the heels of her hands, she dashed away the tears threatening to fall. "You couldn't figure that out after you caught me ogling you before dinner?"

"Hmm, I think there's a way to assuage our curiosity about each other." He grinned and waggled his eyebrows at her.

With a shaky laugh, she said, "What might that be?"

He stood and reached a hand down to her. "Come with me, and I'll show you, my Dream-girl."

For a split second, Fallon stared at his outstretched hand, keeping him in suspense. Closing her eyes, she took a deep breath and held it for a second. Looking up at him, she carefully placed her hand in his, and together they walked to the edge of the point of no return.

⁓

With Fallon's hand in his, Seamus opened the door to the bedroom and walked in ahead of her. He strode over to a table beside the bed and switched on a lamp before letting her go and stepping around her to close the door. In the soft lamplight, she took in a king-size bed, the frame carved from pine, the mattress covered with a quilted comforter in a tree of life design. The bed was fit for a warrior.

It occurred to her that she should be nervous. After all, she and Seamus had only met two days before. But she'd been watching him for so long in stories that popped into her head at random times before they'd met. She knew him to be an honorable man, a man she could count on. She also knew what was expected of her as a talisman. The first time his story flashed through her mind, he'd thrilled her, which she'd kept to herself out of embarrassment rather than spite when he'd been fishing for the compliment.

When he came to her, he took her face in his hands, holding her still for his kiss. At first, he went slow, tasting her. But the firmness of his mouth and the sweet hint of wine overwhelmed her as he deepened the kiss, his tongue tracing the contours of her lips. On a sigh, she opened for him. He plunged his tongue into her mouth, and she met him thrust for thrust, as eager to know him as he wanted to know her. Tracing a path along her jaw and down the column of her throat with his lips and tongue, he kissed and licked and set her skin on fire. A faint manly scent of sweat and outdoors filled her nostrils, and the heat radiating from him warmed her fingers as she ran her hands across his chest and up over his shoulders to meet behind his neck where she pulled him closer.

Wrapping her in his arms, he kissed her as though he couldn't get enough of her. Tugging at her sweater and the layer of clothes beneath it, he pulled them from her. His strong hands sketched her skin and fired her desire, leaving her wanting. He slid her garments up to her shoulders before tearing his mouth away from hers long enough to remove her clothes.

When he bent down to resume kissing her, Fallon put her hand on his chest. "I seem to be ahead in this game. Your turn."

He grinned as she busied herself unbuttoning the front of his flannel shirt. Finding the top of his jeans a barrier to the completion of her task, she unbuttoned them as well, the backs of her fingers grazing the sensitive skin around his navel, and he sucked in a breath. Thrilling at his response, she ran her fingertips up the length of his torso before sliding her hands over his shoulders and down his arms, removing his shirt in her exploration of his body. Obviously, he'd trained often, and she gazed at him with appreciation, palming the sculpted muscles of his chest, shoulders, and arms.

When she started to slide her arms around his neck, he stopped her. "It appears I've moved ahead now."

She questioned him with her raised brow, and he gestured to the black sports bra she still wore before he slid his fingers underneath it and pushed it up off her full breasts. "Jesus, Fallon. You're incredible," he murmured as his eyes drank in the sight of her taut nipples.

"So are you." She couldn't seem to touch enough of him as she ran her hands over the heavy muscles of his chest and the wide expanse of his shoulders.

He pulled her into his embrace, flattening her breasts against the solid wall of his chest, and she relished the feel of his hard body against her soft one as he took her mouth once more. This time, there was no holding back. Fallon gave as good as she got, demanding his tongue, his lips, his very breath. Before tonight, before this minute, she'd had no idea a kiss could be so all-consuming. With Seamus, she discovered all she wanted was to consume and be consumed in the heat of their mouths, the fire of their bodies.

At last, he tore his mouth from hers, his breath sawing in and out of him. "We aren't finished," he said, his voice hoarse as he slid his hands to the waistband of her jeans.

She heaved in a breath. "I certainly hope not."

Fumbling for the zipper of her jeans, he lowered it, and tugged them off her, pushing her socks off her feet along the way. Lightly, he retraced his route over her legs with his fingertips as though he was learning the contours of her body. She couldn't control her shivering as her skin responded to his touch, nor could she stop the little moans that escaped her lips as he explored her. He feathered his fingertips over her ankles, up the hearts of her calves, and along the convex lines of the backs of her thighs before he smoothed his hands over her ass. She cried out in surprise and delight when he planted a searing kiss through the lacy material covering the apex of her thighs.

"You're really something, Fallon Graham. I am one lucky warrior." He smiled up at her from his place on his knees in front of her.

"I think I've moved ahead again," she whispered.

He laughed. "That's all right. I like the view from behind." Slipping his fingers under her panties, he pulled them to her ankles in one smooth motion.

"Seamus."

"Open for me Fallon. There are parts of you I haven't kissed yet."

As he stroked her with one long finger, she closed her eyes and fought for air. He cupped her with the palm of his hand while he pleasured her hard nub first with his thumb then with the teasing tip of his tongue. When she arched toward his mouth, he sucked her hard while he stroked her tight channel first with one finger, then two. A spasm of ecstasy overtook her, and she moaned his name.

Gripping his wrist, she panted. "You need to catch up. Stand up and let me help you."

The desire smoldering in the midnight blue depths of his eyes was at odds with the deliberate way he stood. Taking her hands, he held their bodies at the edge of touching. Regaining a bit of her equilibrium with her hands in Seamus's grip, Fallon smiled up at him. "It really is your turn." Eyeing his jeans and the boxers peeking out above the waistband of his pants, she said impishly, "You have a ways to go before you're caught up."

He pulled in a breath, let it out slowly, and smiled at her. "All right. My turn."

She knelt in front of him and carefully lowered the zipper of his jeans, stopped, and glanced up at his face. The open need intensifying his features as he watched her grasp both the waistband of his jeans and his boxers gave her courage, and she divested him of his clothes in one go. Torturing him, she mimicked his slow exploration of her body, feathering her fingertips over his ankles, along the solid muscles of his calves, up the backs of his thighs to knead and test his ass in the palms of her hands before sliding her lips and tongue the length of his impressive cock.

"Fallon," he groaned. "I think this race ends in a tie."

"Only if we're truly lucky," she replied with a saucy grin as she stood before him.

Taking her in his arms, he kissed her until white lights danced in her head, showing her what was to come as he walked her backward. When her knees gave way at the edge of the bed, she didn't let go of him, and they fell together onto the mattress. Still, he kissed her while he palmed her body from her shoulders to her hips. His touch drove her crazy, and she moved to encourage more from him.

Seamus grunted when she took him in her hand, stroking him and guiding him to her. With a moan, he sank his entire length into her and cried out as she tightened her inner muscles around his cock and held him. Vaguely, she registered they were a perfect fit, and she lifted her hips to urge him to move inside her. Slowly, he pushed in and retreated, pushed in and retreated, his rhythms deliberate. Delicious. She clutched at his shoulders and arched her body to meet his, desperate to feel all of him. As he increased his pace, the white-hot heat of his lovemaking seared through her, and she lost herself in it.

Afterward, Seamus rested his whole weight on her. Fallon reveled in how she'd thoroughly satisfied so virile a warrior. It didn't matter that she couldn't quite pull in a full breath.

"Damn it. I'm sorry, Fallon."

He tried to rise, but she tightened her arms and legs around him and whispered, "Not yet. You're the only thing anchoring me to the universe."

She sensed his smile on the skin of her neck. "Definitely a tie." A chuckle escaped him. "Usually, I like to win, but I've discovered I like racing to a draw with you."

"Mmmm," she hummed as she began lazily gliding her hands up and down the expanse of his back, savoring the feel of him still inside her, his weight on top of her, his sweat-slicked skin smooth and taut over thick muscles and heavy bones. Experiencing his lovemaking was infinitely better than watching it. Giving him pleasure was incredible. No wonder her parents warned her so strenuously against becoming involved with a warrior who wasn't her own. Bonding with her warrior was the ultimate experience.

"The ultimate experience, yeah, I like that," Seamus murmured into her neck.

She stiffened and bucked against him, trying to push him off.

"What?" he asked, confused.

"What do you think you're doing sneaking into my thoughts?" she demanded.

"No sneaking needed. You were thinking rather loudly, and your shield was completely down. If I'm not mistaken, that's supposed to happen between a talisman and her warrior when they bond." His tone was mild while he used his significant size advantage to pin her right where she was, apparently right where he wanted her.

"Why didn't I hear what *you* were thinking?" she asked, suspicion roughening her words.

"Probably because I wasn't thinking. I was too busy feeling to think." He smiled at her. "You're right, though. There's a reason why a warrior doesn't involve himself with any talisman but his own." He traced his thumb over her cheek and smiled into her eyes. "I'll say it again. I. Am. One. Lucky. Warrior."

His kiss was enough to ignite the smoldering fires of their passion, and they took each other again before they fell into a soul-deep sleep, Fallon resting easily on Seamus's chest, his arm protectively sheltering her through the night.

CHAPTER FIVE

FALLON AWOKE DISORIENTED. Since it was still dark outside, the night wasn't over. Yet she felt strangely awake and refreshed like she'd experienced a full night's rest. Memories flooded her mind. She and Seamus had bonded for most of the night. His big warm body felt familiar beside her, familiar and safe. She smiled. Now that they'd met, perhaps she'd no longer have premonitions of him. But how did his death in the bed of one terrifyingly lusty goddess fit in? And how was it she had so much in common with Maeve's physical form? Auburn hair, curvy body? The goddess had left her alone during the night only to interrupt her happiness in the morning. With a groan, she tried to push away her morbid thoughts.

Seamus interrupted the troubling images swirling through her mind. "Good morning."

His rich baritone voice rumbled beneath her cheek. She rubbed her face over the soft dusting of blond hair covering his pecs before lifting up to smile at him.

"Good morning to you, but are you sure it's morning? It's so dark."

"My stomach's positive it is." As if to punctuate that fact, his stomach rumbled. Loudly.

She smirked. "We should do something about that."

Playfully, she kissed his belly and rolled away from him and off the bed before he had a chance to protest. She paid for that when her skin registered the profound lack of heat in the room. Shivering, she looked for her clothes and spied Seamus's generous flannel shirt, which she slipped on as she searched for her socks.

"You know, it's a lot warmer in here." He lifted the blankets, inviting her back to bed.

"I know it is, but I have other needs at the moment. Where did my socks end up?"

"Couldn't tell you."

She bent over to sort through the jumble of clothes on the floor, offering Seamus quite a view as his shirt rode up over her ass. Not that she cared at the moment.

"Aha! There they are." She waved the errant pair of socks in triumph and sat on the chair beside the door to put them on. "Maybe you should get up and start a fire or something."

"Maybe I am up, and if you came back to bed, I could start a fire right here," he said in a grumpy morning voice.

She batted her eyes at him as she opened the door.

"Brrr! I think I can see my breath in here!" she said on a mad dash through the great room to the bathroom.

Shit, I forgot to bank the fire last night. Wonder how I could have forgotten that? Seamus grinned to himself and rolled out of bed, the freezing air in the room effectively cooling his libido. He slipped on his jeans and walked out into the shock of the frigid great room. While Fallon occupied herself in the bathroom, he shrugged on his jacket, slid his bare feet into his boots, and stepped onto the porch to grab an armload of firewood.

Out on the porch, he discovered why the cabin seemed unnaturally dark. Rain had set in overnight, and the deluge dripped steadily through the trees, drenching the ground below. Tiny rivulets of water flowed away from the slope where the cabin sat. With the cabin nestled in the trees as it was, it didn't sustain the brunt of the wind that mainly harried the treetops, creating an eerie roar high up in the trees while near the ground there wasn't much wind at all. Puddles filled every depression in the earth. Seamus thought Fallon might have been washed away in her tent had she actually spent the night in it.

As he backed in through the door, he heard her exit the bathroom. When he turned and saw her, he nearly dropped the load of wood in his arms. Her long auburn hair fell over her shoulders in waves like molten fire. With his shirt hitting her at midthigh, he could see her shapely legs and remember how perfectly they wrapped around his waist when he thrust deep inside her. The rolled-up sleeves of his shirt exposed her delicate forearms and beautifully formed hands, her slender fingers capable of touches that drove him wild. It was her eyes, however, that mesmerized him. Their changeable color arrested his attention first, but there was something so deep and knowing in them. The knowledge, the stories hidden in their green, blue, and gold depths attracted him most of all.

"Look at all that rain. It's pouring outside," she said as she looked past him to the world beyond the cabin door. "How are we going to make it out to the trailhead in that today?"

Registering that she meant to return home so soon after they'd discovered each other grated on him. He caught the door with his heel and slammed it shut harder than he intended.

"Something I said?"

"No." He strode to the fireplace and set the wood on the hearth.

"Are you sure?"

He said nothing as he stirred the coals in the hopes some heat was left in them.

"Are we rained in?"

"Possibly. Is that a problem for you?"

He couldn't look at her. Not if she had no intention of staying.

"Wait," she said. "Do you *want* to be rained in with me?"

"Is *that* a problem for you?"

Finally, he faced her. The smile playing over her lips let him take a breath.

"Depends on how much food you have in this place. I only came prepared for one person for one week. Lots of granola, energy bars, and jerky."

"We could eat pretty well for a month with what's in the pantry." He nodded toward the kitchen. "Plus what you brought in your pack," he added as an afterthought, which he spoiled with a smirk.

She grinned back at him before she sobered. "I wonder if Sloane is trying to reach me." Worry swirled in her eyes. "You really don't have cell service up here?"

"Spotty and probably nonexistent in this storm." He sat back on his haunches, arranging wood and kindling over cold coals. "Who's Sloane?"

"My best friend. We look out for each other." She rubbed her hands up and down her arms, reminding him to hurry in his task.

"Do you have your phone with you?"

"No. Did you bring a phone?"

"Anyone I want to talk to I can reach telepathically, so there's no need to have it here." He cribbed lengths of wood in the fireplace and added more kindling before standing up to grab the box of matches that rested on the mantel.

"I should have thought of that." She smacked her hand on her forehead with a chuckle. "I'm going to contact Sloane, make sure she knows this rain hasn't drowned me."

Seamus nodded and struck a match, setting the flame to the kindling on the grate. Fallon grabbed the hand-tied blanket off the couch, wrapped it around herself, and sat in the corner, drawing her knees beneath her. Closing her eyes, she held herself still, and he had to remind himself of all the reasons why he must let her have her privacy when all he really wanted to do was listen in on her conversation, see how she explained her current situation to her best friend.

When the flames started licking the wood to his satisfaction, he glanced over to see a dreamy expression on her face. He certainly hoped it had something to do with him. Rather than indulge in the unethical behavior he craved, behavior his friends often berated him for when he breached their shields when he had no business in their heads, he hung up his coat, slipped off his boots, and went into the bedroom for fresh socks and another shirt. It would be awhile before the fire chased away the chill that had settled in the cabin.

✺

"Open up, Sloane. It's your favorite friend." Fallon couldn't keep the laughter out of her head. Sitting quietly, she tried to envision what her friend might be doing in the early hours of a Sunday morning. Hopefully, she wasn't interrupting Sloane entertaining a certain civilian grad student.

"I'm not entertaining anyone at the moment. Where the hell are you?"

Fallon jumped. It seemed her friend shouted at her so loudly she could be in the cabin with her.

"I'm stranded in a cabin in the woods somewhere off the trail I was hiking up to the lake. What's wrong? Why are you shouting at me?" Her concern overrode her initial annoyance at her friend's reaction.

"The news is calling the rain a once-in-a-century storm. I was so worried about you, I was about to call Search and Rescue."

"That won't do at all." Fallon tightened the blanket around herself.

"Why not? You can't visualize yourself back to town through this downpour. It's too dangerous."

"No worries. I'm not coming back to town until the storm quits." A smile played over her mouth.

"Spill."

"What?"

"You heard me. What's going on?"

"I really am stranded in a cabin like I told you. And we started bonding last night, so the storm is kind of a bonus." She didn't even try to keep the joy out of her voice as she snuggled down into the cushions of the couch.

"Come again? You're stranded in a cabin in the woods with a war-rior? With your warrior?" If it were possible to squee in her head, Fallon had no doubt Sloane definitely would have done it.

"That about covers it." She attempted to sound matter-of-fact. After all, she knew her shield was good, but she didn't know how much of her conversation Seamus could hear. Best not to give him a big head if she could help it. He had enough swagger as it was.

"Deets, girlfriend." Sloane sounded impatient. *"Give me details."*

"Wrong time. Wrong place. I'll say only this: everything we were taught about the bonding of warriors and talismans can't touch the actual experience."

"Wow." Silence fell between them for a beat. *"Can I at least know his name?"*

Fallon laughed at Sloane's wheedling tone. *"Seamus Lochlann. I stumbled in on him at his family's cabin. We'll be here until the storm blows itself out."*

"I've heard that name before. I'll have to think about where."

"You do that—after you let everyone know I'm safe but unavail-able for a few days. And no trying to breach my shield to assuage your ridiculous curiosity," Fallon warned.

"Fine." Even across time and space, the word sounded like a snort. *"I'll let you be. But only because your warrior found you first. When my warrior finds me, I'll expect the same courtesy."*

"Consider it done. Thanks, friend."

She was still smiling when Seamus walked back into the room. "That's some conversation you're having," he said.

"We finished a few minutes ago. Apparently, my friend was on the verge of calling out a search party for me."

He quirked a brow.

"She won't now," Fallon added hastily.

"Could be more than a day or two the way Taranis is behaving right now. Can't imagine what set him off this time." He sat on the couch, crowding her.

Tilting her head down, she eyed him from beneath her brows. "What makes you think this is Taranis's doing?"

"Even with my shirt and jeans on, it's pretty chilly in this room. Mind sharing some of that blanket? It'll be much warmer when we share body heat," he said, his expression the epitome of innocence.

He chuckled as she gifted him an arched eyebrow before she grudgingly unwrapped herself from the blanket.

"Why do you think Taranis is behind this storm?" she persisted while he took more than his share of the blanket. "Hey! You're far more dressed than I am. Give me some of that back."

He smirked and slipped his big hands beneath her legs to drag her onto his lap. Over her squeals of surprise, he said, "I checked the weather on the satellite before I headed up here yesterday morning. A small mountain thunderstorm was due midweek. This sucker coming in so fiercely and unexpectedly has Taranis written all over it."

"But why would he storm like this? He wouldn't have been trying to..." She couldn't finish the thought.

"Bring us together? I don't see how. The only gods who are

privy to the pairings of warriors and talismans are Danu and the Dagda, and no way are they telling Taranis."

She swallowed. "I wasn't thinking that."

He raised his brows and waited.

"I was thinking maybe he was trying to kill one or both of us." Though she tried to remain relaxed, she couldn't control the way her body tensed.

"That's a scary thought." Seamus tightened his arms around her. "He'll have to bring more than a little squall like this to take us," he said. "Even separately, we could have made it through this storm alive. Together, it's a lock. We have plenty of food and wood. Of course, we can stretch out the wood supply by spending lots of time in bed." He waggled his eyebrows. His comical expression as he leered at her sent Fallon into a fit of giggles, and she relaxed.

But his comment lodged in the back of her mind. If Maeve had set her sights on him as Fallon's premonitions insinuated, perhaps Taranis was involved in their current situation somehow. The thought scared her even more than death.

"Since I built the fire and cooked dinner last night, I think it's time you did something to pull your weight around here."

"What did you have in mind?" she asked a little breathlessly. He'd been rubbing her back as they talked, and his strokes had made their way perilously close to the base of her spine and the cleft in her ass. She held her breath as she tried to decide if she wanted him to discover that particularly sensitive part of her at this moment or not.

"Breakfast. I'm going to need fuel for the late-morning festivities."

"Late morning festivities?" she echoed.

"Yeah. You know, when we take a tour of each other's sensitive spots."

"You're a terrible person," she huffed. "You breached my shield again."

"Only for a second." He fingered a strand of her hair before he tucked it behind her ear. "You were so serious, I had to see what had you all wound up."

She pushed away from him and struggled to stand up. Deliberately, Seamus tangled her in the blanket in the guise of helping her out of it, which only fueled her anger.

"You have some nerve. There's a little thing called trust. We need to build it, which means only going places we've been invited." She fought her way out from under the blanket. "I haven't attempted to breach your shield even once since we discovered each other, yet you've helped yourself to my thoughts several times already." Planting her hands on her hips, her chest heaving, she faced him. "If you want to know something about me, how 'bout trying to discover it the conventional way—by asking."

Finished with her tirade, she turned on her heel and headed for the bedroom and the long johns she knew to be hiding somewhere in her pile of clothes.

"You're a touchy little firecracker, aren't you, Red?"

As she stalked out of the bedroom and crossed to the kitchen, she sent Seamus a withering look. "There are two things you need to know about me. One, I am not a firecracker, and two, I do not answer to the name Red." She slammed open a cupboard door. "Those stereotypes do not fit me. At. All." The pan hit the burner with a bang. "And I do not appreciate them. Now you know your first fun facts about me."

She jerked open the door to the small refrigerator and stared down its contents for breakfast ideas.

From the corner of her eye, she caught Seamus leaning against the back of the couch, his arms crossed over his massive chest. "I'll keep that in mind, especially the part about how you don't conform to any of the stereotypes about redheads. For example, I've noticed you have a serious lack of passion." The smirk on his face contradicted the grave tone of his voice.

"I have observed you are rarely serious at all," she said, imbuing her comment with as much disdain as she could muster. Gracelessly, she pulled eggs, onions, and peppers from the fridge, setting them none too gently on the tiny countertop beside it.

"I'm serious as a heart attack most of the time. Ask my family or friends," Seamus deadpanned.

Like all warriors, he could bend time, allowing him to move at incredible speed. Which meant he had no trouble sneaking behind her to wrap his arms around her. With her back to him, Fallon thought he was still standing beside the couch. When he touched her, she sucked in air and stilled while her heart fluttered in her chest and threatened to fly out of her throat.

"Leave some air in the room for me too," he said with a chuckle.

"Very funny." She hid behind sarcasm while she worked to regain some of her composure. "It's obvious you don't believe in following the rules."

"What do you mean?"

"You know what I mean. You're only supposed to use your special skills in defense of others or yourself."

"I *am* defending myself. You were attacking my character and my breakfast. Eggs are fragile, you know." She sensed his grin against her neck, and her anger evanesced in the warmth and laughter she was discovering to be Seamus Lochlann.

"You know what I've noticed?" The question was rhetorical since he didn't give her a chance to respond. "I've noticed you keep your shield up when you're worried and only let it down when you start feeling aroused."

Her hands stilled.

"Of course, I can try to keep you in a near-constant state of arousal, but that will require a lot of breakfast."

In a hundred lifetimes, she couldn't have stopped the laugh that escaped from her throat.

Giving in, she leaned back into Seamus's big strong body. "Scrambled Denver-style eggs work for you?"

"Whatever you're cooking works for me, but make a lot. I'm going to need massive amounts of energy today." He punctuated his comment with a hot kiss right below her ear. The simple caress sent a jolt of desire through her that lodged low in her belly, but before she could give in to it, Seamus let her go and stepped around her to start the coffee.

Fallon had the uncomfortable notion that he deliberately wanted her off-balance. *He must be testing me somehow,* she thought and then checked to be sure she had her shield firmly in place. Determined not to let him gain the upper hand, she carefully let her thoughts go blank and only considered the task at hand: chop the peppers and onions, break and scramble the eggs, heat the pan and the pat of butter to cook the meal.

∽

As was his wont, Seamus attempted to breach Fallon's shield to see where his teasing had taken him. To his chagrin, she seemed to be onto him, her shield firmly in place.

It was clear she'd learned from a master how to keep others out of her head since one of his specialties was breaching the shields of nearly everyone he met in the warrior community. The only people who could keep him out consistently were his best friend Rowan Sheridan and Rowan's dad Owen, both of whom were master warriors. Still, he could console himself. She'd let the thing down when he touched her, when he aroused her, and didn't pay attention to shielding him when she felt safe. It seemed a good start for them. Even if at the moment she deliberately baited him.

There would be paybacks.

He grinned to himself as he plotted them.

Chapter Six

IDLY, TARANIS RECLINED in a Moroccan leather chair fit for a god. If he weren't so magnificent, Maeve would have asked another god for assistance. Instead, she paraded herself in front of him, showing off her assets in human form. When she turned to him and took a breath, she jutted out her full breasts and erect nipples exposed by the thin silk of the sheath dress she wore. She took note of the way his rain-silver eyes glowed with desire as he watched her. Though she disguised her delight behind an air of indifference, she tuned into the way his body seemed to hum in anticipation of the night she had planned for them when he'd unleashed his latest storm. It had definitely been too long since they'd enjoyed each other.

Still, she needed to make him understand his role.

"Honestly, Taranis, I don't know what you're thinking. A torrent when I had plans to incite a small turf war here in LA, something that would grab Seamus Lochlann's attention?" Her chest rose on the breath she pulled in to start her rant. "First, you abandon Morgan in the middle of a battle for a pair of civilian women when she summoned you to Scotland to help her best the Sheridans, and now you thwart me with an unscheduled storm?" Giving him the once-over, she waited for a response. When none came, she continued. "I thought we were a team. I thought we worked in concert to create havoc in the warrior community."

Taranis ignored her implied question and glanced around her stronghold. "You've made improvements since my last visit. I like the leather furniture." He skimmed a long-fingered hand over the arm of the chair in which he sat. "The Oriental rug covering your new walnut floor is exquisite." He stood and strolled over to the floor-to-ceiling smoked glass windows looking out over a rather magnificent view of the city regardless of the fact she'd located her stronghold in the warehouse district of East Los Angeles.

She was vain enough to indulge his appreciation of her stronghold.

"I take it the single malt Scotch whiskey suits you?" Even though she was one angry goddess at the moment, she prided herself on her impeccable taste and manners.

He saluted her with the tumbler he held before he downed half the fiery liquid in the glass.

"I helped Morgan. I called up a mist, confused the warriors, made a few civilians vulnerable to her attacks as well." He gazed at the amber liquor as he swirled his glass. "As I recall, I tried to take two talismans belonging to the Sheridans, but a meddling old druid interfered and presented me with civilians who were only too willing to share my bed." He slanted her a look.

"At least I showed up to the party, which is more than you can say for yourself, Maeve. Since that warrior you're so hot for stayed behind, you did too. Which begs the question of why you are calling me out?" His voice rumbled like thunder, putting her off-balance as she tried to decide if he was merely annoyed with her or truly angry.

"I wasn't needed in Scotland at Samhain," she said with a

haughty sniff. "And now I must wait to have my way with that very delicious Seamus Lochlann, thanks to you." She stood before him with her fists planted on her hips. "Sometimes you forget yourself. Morgan and I are two powerful aspects of the triple goddess, and as such we outrank you. When we require your help, we expect you to give it." She dialed her eyes up to full power as she stared him down.

Taranis smiled lazily at her. "If I'm so far beneath you, why is it you depend on me so much? Hmm? Perhaps I should excuse myself and spend my time blowing zephyrs in the Caribbean or the Mediterranean, enjoy a civilian or several, and leave you triple goddesses to it." He sipped his drink. "I have noticed that Macha hasn't been involved at all in the vendetta Morgan and you have with the Sheridans and anyone associated with them. Perhaps she would *appreciate* my help with a project in Ireland."

He drained his whiskey and stared her down. His full height in his human form was an impressive six foot five, and Maeve eyed him up and down appreciatively. With a raised brow, he gazed steadily back at her through his storm-gray eyes and waited.

Changing her tone, she said, "No need to sulk, Taranis. You might find a way to atone for your interference and help me take my mind off the delay in my plans." She walked her fingers up his chest.

"Maeve," he drawled. Leaning back against a chair, he quirked a brow. "What did you have in mind?"

"It has been awhile since you entertained me in my bed. If you are exceptionally good this time, I may be able to forgive you for thoroughly irritating me."

Setting his empty glass aside, Taranis took her roughly into his arms, setting the tone for their tryst from the outset. He ground his mouth down on hers before reaching up to the back of the neck of her dress and tearing it in half with one swift, sure stroke. She shivered and nipped his lower lip hard. Teasing him further, she licked the silver blood she'd drawn, and they both laughed at her eagerness before Taranis scooped her high into his arms and strode to her bedroom.

She adored sex with Taranis. He gave as good as he got, and it took days for her to wear him out.

"You'll probably need to rest after a day or two this time, Taranis." She grinned in challenge as she slid her foot up the side of his leg, eventually hooking her calf over his hip. "Morgan has been so stingy with the warriors she has allowed me to use up in my bed. I hope you have the stamina to satisfy me for a while."

In the heat of her lust, she didn't consider the consequences of keeping Taranis so occupied. The deluge he'd conjured to annoy her into taking him to bed raged on unabated in the mountains of southwestern Montana.

⋘

Seamus banked the fire. "Judging from the way the storm is screaming outside, Taranis is in a real state. I have no idea how long his mood is going to last, so we better be as conservative with wood as possible."

Fallon glanced up from the book she'd been reading when he turned back from the fireplace. From the look on his face, she didn't need telepathy to know exactly what he was thinking. If his wolfish grin didn't present enough of a clue, the desire shining in his blue eyes and turning them nearly obsidian told her exactly what was on his mind.

"Seamus," her tone warned. "It's not even lunchtime. You aren't thinking…" Her voice trailed off as he purposefully strode to her.

"The hour of the day or night doesn't have anything to do with anything, Fallon. What matters is how incredibly sexy you look in my shirt and the fact that I know you have nothing on underneath it."

Sitting down beside her on the couch, he relieved her of the book she'd been reading. He didn't pay any attention to the volume of Celtic stories he laid on the coffee table. Fallon, however, needed a minute to pull her mind into the present.

Wanting to give her full attention to Seamus and the incredible way he made her feel when he touched her, she closed her eyes and willed her mind to go blank. The sad story of Diarmuid and Grainne she'd been reading certainly didn't serve as an aphrodisiac. Though her body heated at Seamus's gaze, her mind refused to cooperate. She kept seeing Diarmuid dying from the wound he'd sustained from the boar he'd been tricked into fighting and Grainne's anguish at the loss of her love, a man who had led a life as a "charmer of women" until he met her. Something in Diarmuid's story triggered a vision, and suddenly, her head throbbed like it would burst with the pain of it.

Seamus's ardor left him in a breath as he watched his talisman struggle helplessly with something her mind couldn't control. Without a care for ethics or her demand for trust, he breached her shield and wished for once he would have restrained his impulse.

He only saw the part where Maeve denied him the dignity of dying on the battlefield before Fallon regained enough control to block him from her thoughts. It was enough. For the second time since she'd arrived at the cabin, she'd had a premonition of him in the goddess's bed, and each time he died there. Whatever was going on with his talisman, it was clear they needed to work together to discover what they could of the fate the goddess planned for him. More importantly, they needed to devise a way to thwart her.

Seamus gathered Fallon onto his lap and held her. Instinctively, he knew he couldn't interfere with the vision she was experiencing, but the anguish he sensed in her nearly undid him.

In the space of a day, she'd become so important to him he would do anything to protect her. But the one place where he couldn't protect her was in her own mind.

Finally, she came out of it. When she blinked her lids open and looked at him, what he saw chilled him to the bone. Entire worlds swirled in the changeable colors of her hazel eyes. It seemed like he could read eons of human anguish but also human triumph there. The depth of her understanding overwhelmed him. Then she blinked and was Fallon again, silent tears spilling down her cheeks.

With deliberate care, he dried her tears with the pads of his thumbs, cupping her face as he waited for her to share what she'd seen. When she lowered her lashes and tried to turn her face away from him, he held her fast and whispered, "Part of bonding is discovering what the talisman's skill is, the way she's best suited to aid her fated warrior. Your premonitions concerning me have something to do with your particular skill. For us to discover it, you need to share them with me."

At her dubious expression, he quirked his own brow. "All of them. In their entirety."

She sniffed back her tears and shook her head. "It's too cruel for me to be the bearer of such terrible news, especially since I can't see how you could want anything to do with me once you know all of it."

"And you want me to want you."

She ducked her head and nodded.

Seamus tightened his arms around her. "You've already figured out I don't have much for scruples when it comes to breaching someone's shield." With his index finger, he smoothed the frown from her forehead. "You're quite adept at keeping me out of your head, but when the visions start, your shield falls away, so I've seen parts of the two you've experienced since you arrived at my cabin."

Her eyes saucered.

"Then you reconstruct your shield and close me out, so I haven't seen all of it. You need to share it, Fallon."

"But then you won't want me anymore." Her voice was so small, she broke his heart.

"You're wrong there, Fireworks."

She pulled a face, and he grinned.

"I've tasted the delights you have to offer. The tiny sample I've had so far has only whetted my appetite for a full course meal, one that's going to require a very long time to enjoy. Decades, hopefully." He held her in his eyes. "Now tell me what you saw."

Her throat worked before she gave him a watery smile. Sucking in a breath, she began. "Not long after Samhain, I started having visions about a certain devastatingly handsome warrior."

Seamus smiled. "Do go on."

She rolled her eyes. "At first, I thought he was making love with me because I only saw the woman from behind, and her long auburn hair and her size and shape looked like me. One time, though, the woman turned and stared straight at me, and I realized I stared into the terrifying eyes of a goddess. Not just any goddess, but Maeve, the supremely lusty sister of the Washer of the Ford." Fallon smoothed the hem of his shirt where it brushed the top of her thigh.

He rubbed his thumb along her neck then cupped her nape in his hand and waited.

"In the horrible triumph of her smile, she paralyzed me." A shiver rippled over her. "Then I saw the warrior—you—lying propped against thick pillows on this huge bed outfitted in green silks." She glanced up at him through her lashes.

He fought to keep his face impassive even as thoughts tore through his mind. *Why is Morgan seen as the supreme bitch in that unholy trio? Based on Fallon's visions, Maeve could take a run at her.*

Instead of voicing his thoughts, he inclined his head, and she continued. "She'd tied you, hands and feet, to her bed with silken cords of gold." Fallon swallowed hard. "Though you fought her with every ounce of will you possessed, in the end, she took what she wanted. She's a goddess. No mortal can resist a goddess."

She slumped into his chest and hiccupped back a sob. "She spoke to me, telling me you were even more of a man than she anticipated, and you had pleased her well. Now I had a choice of pleasing her too by letting her watch as Taranis enjoyed me before I accompanied you on our shameful journey across the ford." She grabbed a handful of the front of his shirt and held on. "Or I could return to the mortal world." Her voice cracked. "I could live out my days knowing I should have been able to save you from your fate, but I didn't."

She wrapped her arm across his chest and burrowed in, as though clinging to him gave her comfort. He hoped it did since her words scared the hell out of him.

"It's always at that point that I come out of it. On Thursday, I met you in person, and now the visions are like previews, like the movie trailer for the end of our lives." She pulled back enough to catch his eyes. "Seamus, I can't stand watching her take you over and over, hearing your screams of anguish even as she gives you ecstasy, feeling your desperation not to let her win."

Fallon's tears fell in a steady stream down her beautiful face. Tension vibrated everywhere their bodies touched. "I can't imagine how I can help you prevent your fate. Having shared your bed and bonded with you, I can't imagine how much more agonizing it would be to be forced to watch as Maeve takes you over and over." With both hands, she hauled him closer to her—like that was possible at the moment.

"You can't imagine it because it's not going to happen."

She continued as though she hadn't heard him. "Probably the reason I've never seen myself make the choice between a life of purgatory on earth and a quick death betraying you in

Taranis's bed is because I won't have to make the choice when the time comes."

"What are you saying?"

"I'll probably die from enduring the sight of your agony and my inability to help you fight the goddess." She sniffed back tears, regained her composure, and continued. "Honestly, Seamus, death would be a welcome release from the torture Maeve has in mind for the two of us. Either way, Morgan will escort us across the ford in our shame while she and Maeve revel in their triumph."

Seamus wrapped Fallon in his arms and held her for a long while as they both thought about her premonitions. Smoothing his hand up and down her spine, he plotted how best to discover his talisman's skill so he could put it to use to frustrate the goddess and deny her the opportunity for her evil plans to come to fruition.

Though he liked to tease and came across as a person who took nothing seriously, the reality of the way his mind worked contrasted sharply with his devil-may-care manner. His ability to examine and plan was a contributing factor to his fast friendship with Rowan Sheridan. The fact he could see, analyze, and act in the moment had saved both of them numerous times on the battlefield when Morgan came to call. His abilities saved Rowan's talisman Alyssa Macaulay from the torturous fate to which Morgan and Maeve had subjected her last winter. His skills contributed significantly to the battle Rowan and Alyssa won that restored some of the balance of power between warriors and the gods. Perhaps Fallon didn't know it yet, but she had a determined and formidable protector in the warrior the gods had chosen for her, a man who had no intention of pleasuring any woman—or goddess—but Fallon Graham for the rest of his days.

CHAPTER SEVEN

EAMUS'S MIND RACED back through every encounter he'd had with Fallon that had included a premonition. In each case, she believed she was under some kind of duress. Except this time. This time, she'd merely been sitting on the couch reading. It occurred to him perhaps something in the book triggered a vision. Reaching past her, he grabbed the book off the table. *Celtic Myths and Legends.* His lip quirked. "You didn't get enough of this in your training as a kid?"

"I didn't get much of it at all. My parents were very strict about keeping the lines clear between the races in our community." She sighed and repeated as if by rote. "Warriors and talismans stay together. Druids stay together. Each race does its job and stays out of the other race's way."

Seamus scowled. *What kind of messed up logic is that?* But he didn't interrupt.

"My Aunt Keela, who I told you about, encouraged me when I showed an interest in storytelling early on, but my parents forbade me from studying our legends or our mythology, fearing that somehow I might not be a talisman or something."

"What the fuck?"

She shrugged apologetically. "Keela, who is my father's younger sister, married a druid named Griffin Walsh. After that, my parents disallowed me any contact with her, which meant my studies of our bardic traditions and the heritage of our Celtic legends formally ended when she was forced out of my life when I was twelve."

"What the hell happened to your parents that they have such a deep prejudice against druids?" He knew he sounded harsh, but he couldn't help it.

She stiffened, her eyes saucering. Pulling in a deep breath, he deliberately relaxed.

"I have no idea," she whispered. "I was too afraid to ask." Her eyes traveled back to the book. "But I couldn't leave the stories behind, so I sneaked books into the house and read them behind my parents' backs. I've loved all the old tales ever since I first discovered them."

"Yeah?"

She nodded. "When we were kids, my best friend Sloane MacIntosh and I would act out the tales in her bedroom. Of course, we both always wanted to be the heroes, but we figured out how to compromise and take turns." Settling back into him with a little wiggle, she reached for the book, smoothing her hands over the cover. "After a while, we discovered I could embellish the stories in ways that gave us both opportunities to save the day." A wistful smile curved her lips. "Those became our favorite stories."

Carefully, Seamus asked, "You don't harbor your parents' prejudices against druids?"

She slanted him a look. "Of course not. Otherwise, I wouldn't be so partial to my bracelet you call body armor. In fact, I kind of think you're right."

He arched a brow.

"Uncle Griff meant that bracelet to protect me when my

parents forbade druidic protections. My parents thought I needed to take care of myself and get on with the business of finding my warrior." A frown marred her pretty features. "Honestly, I think they were disappointed when the Sheridans bested Morgan last winter and gave fourteen years back to warriors and talismans."

"You have no druidic protections other than your bracelet? Unbelievable!" Seamus wanted to hit something—like Fallon's dad. "That's one of the duties of druids, to devise protections for warriors and talismans regardless of whether or not they've found each other. In fact, if it hadn't been for the powerful protections of a shrewd old druid, Rowan would have never found Alyssa, and the playing field they leveled would have remained out of balance for eternity."

Fallon gaped at him then snapped her jaw closed. "I keep forgetting you know the Sheridans personally."

Seamus placed his forefinger beneath her chin and gently raised it. "Rowan Sheridan is my best friend." He smirked. "And supposedly my boss at Security Consultants Unlimited."

"Right. I think I remember you saying something about that."

Sitting up a little straighter, he said, "I helped him rescue his talisman Alyssa Macauley from Maeve's stronghold in Los Angeles last winter." He couldn't help but enjoy her response to his revelations. He'd never received credit in the warrior community for being intimately involved in Alyssa's rescue, but the fact the Sheridans deeply appreciated his contribution to that little party more than gratified him. Still, it made him happy that he could impress his own talisman.

"You'll definitely impress my parents when they meet you. You're every warrior's hero."

In the glow of her genuine smile, a profound warmth spread through his chest.

Sobering, he said, "I will, and I won't. You see, my sister is one of my all-time favorite people."

Fallon smiled.

"She's a druid."

Fallon gasped, and he talked over her. "She's also married to a warrior who pursued the hell out of her *after* he found his talisman." The look he gave her dared her to say something offensive.

"Why didn't your sister's husband stay with his talisman?"

At her curious—rather than censorious—tone, Seamus jacked himself down. "They didn't bond. Sometimes that happens." He shrugged. "For the record, Siobhan, my sister, resisted Duncan for nearly a year before she finally gave in to his advances." A slow grin crossed his face. "He wore her out chasing her."

"What do you mean, they didn't bond? You mean they didn't…" Fallon colored the rose blush he liked so much.

"They slept together, but there was no attraction, no chemistry. They tried. They really did. They lived together, they trained together, they liked each other, but they never truly bonded. It's rare, but it happens." Of their own volition, his fingers found her silky hair, and he played there as he spoke. "Jennifer Carlin, Duncan's talisman, lives next door to Siobhan and Duncan. Siobhan has enchanted both of their houses separately and together, so they're well protected. Jennifer does her duty to Duncan as his talisman in battle, and they're actually a good team." He wrapped his arms tightly around her. "Not as strong as a bonded pair but still effective. It's worked for over five years now."

"Wow. Your family sounds—tolerant. If only my family…" She squeezed the forearm he rested across her chest. "Well, Keela and Griff have made it work too, for twelve years so far. I have no idea about Keela's warrior. We never had a chance to talk about him."

A thought struck him. "If your parents forbade you contact with her, how did she give you the bracelet?"

"On my twenty-first birthday, she surprised me by sneaking a visit with me. Since my parents planned to visit me too, my time with Keela was necessarily short, only long enough for her to wish me well and to give me the bracelet with instructions to keep it with me always. Or at least until I found my warrior." She gazed into the flames of the fire crackling in the fireplace. "Now that I think about it, Keela was adamant I do my best to find my warrior. We didn't have time to talk of much else. I don't even know where she lives." Fallon's voice trailed off.

Her sadness at her estrangement from her aunt tugged at his heart. "So Keela introduced you to the legends and stories of our community?"

She nodded. "She was my teacher for that part of my training."

He studied a strand of Fallon's rich auburn hair that he'd wrapped around his finger. "There's something with the stories, the gap in your training, your uncle's uncanny choices for your protection bracelet, and your aunt being a talisman *and* a storyteller. If we can figure out how the puzzle pieces fit, we may be on to your skill," he said, thoughtfully. "You said something earlier about changing the stories so both you and your friend could be heroes. That fits into this somehow too, I think." He shifted, settling her even closer to him. "We might have to contact Rowan's mom Sian. She spends much of her time studying family trees and relationships between warriors and talismans and such. She might be able to help us."

He rubbed his cheek over her hair before pushing it aside with his nose to kiss her temple. "But before we let others intrude on our newly discovered partnership, there are one or two things we need to do to strengthen it."

He slid a hand from Fallon's knee up her thigh to a point tantalizingly close to her center. She shivered at his touch, and a little sigh escaped her. With a smile, he lightly traced a pattern on her thigh and watched as her eyes widened in recognition even as her entire body rippled beneath his fingertip.

"You mentioned something about exploring each other's

secret, sensitive places. I know you're sitting on one of yours, but I think I just found another." A lazy grin spread over his face.

"I didn't *say* anything. You breached my shield. Oh!" She exhaled in midprotest as he traced the pattern again.

"I wonder…" He slid his hand back down her thigh to a spot above her knee where he traced the pattern again. She rewarded him with an answering quiver of her leg. "You respond to my sign wherever I trace it, Fallon. I think that's unusual too."

"Not to mention that it does wonders for your ego," she said, her voice breathy.

Seamus traced another trinity knot along the inside of her thigh. Her skin heated beneath his touch, and she wiggled and squirmed on his lap like she wanted to escape and mold herself to him at the same time.

Gently, he pushed her down into the cushions of the couch and traced his sign on her flat belly. Closing her eyes, she sucked in air.

"Is he going to make me come with just his fingers tracing patterns on my skin?"

"That's the goal, Fireworks."

"Stop breaching my shield!"

With a laugh, he ignored her protest and traced his sign over her erect nipples. Her breathy moan of pleasure told him all was forgiven—or at least forgotten.

"Maybe your special skill is making me feel ten feet tall and bulletproof," Seamus said with a smile as he slowly undid the buttons of the shirt Fallon wore, exposing her creamy flesh. For long minutes he looked his fill while in his mind he heard her thoughts willing him to touch her again. At last, he gave her what she craved, tracing his sign over her exposed skin.

At his touch, she surged up, took his face in her hands, and kissed him hungrily, her tongue plunging into his mouth, taking him in some measure the way he'd taken her with the touch of his fingertips. His little experiment resulted in a mindless need for him she couldn't seem to control.

He was anything but immune to the responses he elicited in his talisman. The knowledge that he could bring her to such an all-consuming desire with a touch of his finger on her body fired him in ways he'd never experienced before with any of the civilian women he'd pleasured in his past. Fallon owned his body as much as it appeared he owned hers. The uninhibited way she kissed him sent him straight over the edge.

Without breaking the kiss, he freed himself from his jeans before he pushed her back into the cushions of the couch. Reaching between them, he positioned himself and entered her with one hard thrust. She grabbed handfuls of his shirt over his shoulders and clung to him while their mouths mimicked the activity of their bodies, Fallon's thrusting tongue encouraging him to give her more of himself. Though he feared he might hurt her, and he tried to hold back, her insistent urging, the heels of her feet digging into his ass to push him deeper into her, wouldn't allow him to give her anything less than everything he had to give. Her silent demands rendered him powerless to deny her.

Tightening her inner muscles as she came, she milked him until both of them could take no more. They soared into heaven with cries torn from the deep places inside them. An eternity later, each of them finally became coherent enough to speak, the world righting itself after it fell off its axis.

"I had no idea…"

"That really just happened…"

Each spoke over the other before they stopped and stared into each other's eyes. Seamus shivered involuntarily at the worlds he glimpsed shimmering in Fallon's changeable eyes before she blinked and hid them away. As much as he desired her body, a desire that overwhelmed him, what he really wanted was her essence, that unexplainable something she revealed for a nanosecond that made her Fallon. Instinctively, he understood if he could touch that part of her, she would be forever his—this intriguing woman who defied her parents for the sake of a good story, who hiked in the woods alone without fear, who responded to him without inhibition, who wanted more than anything to protect him from a fate worse than death. In the short space of a day, he'd fallen in love with her.

Griffin Walsh was a druid of the highest order. His skills as a prophet had saved many people in the warrior community, but he hadn't been able to save an arrogant and headstrong warrior bent on besting Morgan before he could discover and bond with his talisman. Taking on Morgan's civilian army of gang members after they'd murdered a popular pro football player in downtown Denver seemed a foolhardy demonstration of a power the warrior didn't understand was incomplete. What Griff had failed to see when the man asked for his prophecy the night of the fight was the rogue warrior hidden among the gang-bangers. The young warrior didn't stand a chance, which thrilled Morgan when she confronted Griff after the battle. In that moment, he experienced a vision of Keela Graham, the warrior's talisman. As a self-imposed penance, he chose to tell her of her warrior's fate himself.

When he met her, she was in a park with a beautiful little auburn-haired talisman he later learned was her niece. They were telling each other stories, and Griff to his surprise and chagrin, fell instantly in love. Keela was sunshine and laughter, patience and goodness personified. However, her niece drew him like a magnet when he sensed her incredible power. She was one of the special ones, talismans with druidic skill, and highly sought after both by the gods and by the warrior community. Trained appropriately by a warrior and a druid, she would be able to rescue warriors from death at the hands of the Morrigan with the power of her stories.

He took his time approaching them, wishing he had some other task to fulfill than to tell this stunning woman she was destined to spend her life alone.

Keela took the news of her warrior's death better than he'd expected. During her training with her older brother, she'd discovered her special gift of prophecy. She could see the future of her warrior and help him create strategies to alter it—if she met him in time. Several days before her warrior's death, a prophecy had come her. Though she couldn't see his face, she knew intuitively that the warrior she watched die fighting a rogue warrior aligned with a civilian gang was her warrior. What she couldn't predict was where and when the event would occur so she could be there to stop him.

Surprisingly, Griff's news didn't steal Keela's spirit. It turned out she'd had another prophecy of a second man who would come to her, a man who would face incredible obstacles to claim her. Keela assumed the man to be a warrior, but the man in her vision was the druid who stood before her telling her the news of a warrior she'd never have the chance to meet.

The battle with her family when he came to marry her was epic and brutal, the weapons were words of such prejudice and hate they penetrated his psyche like red-hot knives. Before he met Keela's family, he thought such inexplicable hatred of another race of people only existed among the unenlightened or civilians. The Grahams were exceptionally trained and highly educated warriors. Their prejudice had no discernable basis, no reasonable explanation, no business in the warrior community.

While Griff took a willing Keela away from the ugliness of her family's beliefs, he despaired of her niece. Little Fallon would grow up with only half her training, half her education, and none of the druidic protections she of all talismans needed. Determined to protect her, he and Keela settled down to live near Fallon without his in-laws' knowledge, both of them keeping a watchful eye on her. When she moved from Colorado to Montana, they transferred their civilian jobs and moved with her, careful never to let her know they were nearby. Remaining out of Fallon's sight spared her from confrontations with her parents about having a relationship with her "dirtied" aunt and her aunt's hateful lover.

Though he'd never seen Fallon's warrior in any of his prophetic rituals, he'd been able to predict her warrior's sign. With that knowledge, he engraved the sign into the bracelet he enchanted for her twenty-first birthday. Sensing that she wore it faithfully cheered him as nothing else in his stunted relationship with her could have. What he hadn't foreseen was how he and Keela would respond to Fallon's warrior discovering her. When that event occurred, Griff and Keela simultaneously experienced prophecies that seared their brains with such intense pain neither of them could focus on the pictures they were seeing, the visions reduced to nebulous outlines of shifting scenes and indistinct edges like a sick fun house version of the aurora borealis. After the prophecies ended, a red-hot desire they were compelled to sate with each other assailed them.

By Sunday night, both were exhausted from worry about their niece and wonder at the intense bonding experience neither ever expected to have. The certainty that Fallon remained with her warrior did little to assuage their anxiety for her since they both understood her lack of training. They also understood that Fallon and her warrior were on a collision course with disaster if Keela and Griff didn't reach her before the gods put them to the test.

CHAPTER EIGHT

WHILE SEAMUS STOKED the fire, Fallon rummaged in the pantry for something tasty for dinner, settling on a large can of beef stew. She decided to jazz it up with some of the spices she'd also discovered and pair it with a spinach and pepper salad. An afternoon of bonding hadn't brought them any insights into her special skill, but it left them both ravenous.

Thoughts of the way she responded to Seamus's sign as he traced it all over her body left her hot and bothered, so she worked to think of anything else instead. Glancing out the window above the sink, she saw the weather outside didn't seem to be letting up. Good thing she'd taken off an entire week off from work. Negotiating slippery trails while trying to keep her sense of direction in the midst of a torrential downpour held little appeal. Especially when the alternative was spending time in a cozy cabin with a hot warrior who just happened to be hers.

That thought led her to trying to puzzle out how her uncle had known to put Seamus's sign on her bracelet. She knew Griff was a druid and a prophet, but she hadn't been allowed enough time with him to understand his powers. Then again, maybe the pattern on her bracelet and Seamus's sign were coincidences. After all, trinity knots were ubiquitous art choices throughout the ages. Even the civilians had co-opted them into their religious practices and everyday lives.

Yet her response to Seamus contradicted the notion of mere coincidence. Something powerful was at work with them, and her gut told her they only had the time allotted by the storm to figure things out. More than anything, she hoped Taranis had some monumental distraction going on to keep him from quieting the tempest he'd unleashed. They needed time to sort out her premonitions and figure out her special skill. Once Maeve found out Seamus had discovered his talisman, Fallon harbored no illusions the goddess would be generous and give them time to learn to work together to thwart her terrible plans. Morose thoughts concerning her warrior tumbled through her mind as she set about putting a meal on the table for them.

❧

While Fallon busied herself in the galley-sized kitchen, Seamus contacted his best friend and "boss" about his pending absence from work.

"Hey buddy. You busy?" Seamus hoped Rowan didn't have his formidable shield in place. Since it was dinnertime, a prearranged time for them to communicate if they needed to, he figured he had a decent shot at reaching his friend.

"What's up?" Rowan answered immediately.

Relieved he wouldn't have to resort to sneaky tactics like breaching Rowan's wife's shield to get his attention, Seamus replied, *"Oh, this-n-that. I won't be in to work for a few days. I seem to be stranded at the cabin with my talisman."* The faux nonchalance of his tone belied his excitement at being able to relay his news.

"Hello, what? You found your talisman? Awesome! When did that happy little event happen?"

"Yesterday afternoon." The smile on Seamus's face carried through time and space and echoed in Rowan's laughter.

"Let me guess. She's a tall, leggy blonde with killer blue eyes and a sly sense of humor."

"Not quite. She's a bit taller than Alyssa, auburn-haired, with the most amazing hazel eyes. I never know what color they're going to be. But she does share my sense of humor." His eyes drifted to the woman in question as she chopped peppers beside the sink.

"You never really had a type anyway, old son. You liked all the girls." Distance and telepathy didn't dampen the sound of Rowan's mirth.

"Not anymore. Bonding with my talisman is so much more than we were told to expect in our training. Now I get why you're so devoted to Alyssa." He knew he probably sounded like a sap, but he didn't care.

"Having a talisman brings every man, even Seamus the lady-killer, into the fold." Rowan chuckled. *"Glad to hear your experience is better than your brother-in-law's. She's bonding to you too, isn't she?"*

"Oh yeah." Seamus grinned. *"We discovered something interesting that I hope your mom or your wife can figure out. Fallon responds intensely to my sign no matter where I trace it on her."*

"Yeah?"

"And get this, she has a bracelet her druid uncle made for her. The inside of it is an unending series of trinity knots. When I traced my sign over it when she was wearing it"—he pulled in some air—*"I branded her. She still carries the mark."* The circumstance of branding his sign on Fallon's wrist bothered him.

"Whoa, buddy. That's definitely weird. I'll ask Mom and Alyssa about it. Have you discovered her skill yet?"

When he huffed out a sigh, Fallon slanted him a look. He smiled reassuringly at her before returning to his conversation with his friend. *"Still working on it. Between needing to discover her skill and not being able to visualize ourselves out of here in the storm, you can understand why I won't be in to work for a while. There is one thing though—Fallon's had several premonitions of my death."*

"Ouch! Harsh, man. How does Morgan plan to take you?" Rowan's concern resonated in his tone.

"In shame after Maeve spends me in her bed while Fallon watches."

"Kinda fitting considering your reputation—"

"Hey!"

"But not the way any of us wants to go. You say your talisman has premonitions? Maybe she's a prophet like Ceri," Rowan suggested in reference to his new sister-in-law who also happened to be his wife's best friend.

"Her vision never changes. There's also this weird thing with her eyes. Sometimes when she comes out of a vision or wakes up from sleep, I catch a glimpse of another world going on in there, but she blinks and it's gone. Ask your mom and Alyssa about that too." Though he knew Rowan couldn't see him, he stood up and stretched, the smells of dinner making him ready to end the conversation.

"Anything else before I rejoin my beautiful talisman for dinner?"

"If you're fishing for details, I already told you enough when I mentioned Fallon's response to my sign."

Rowan chuckled. *"She'll appreciate you don't kiss and tell."*

Seamus scowled.

"By the way, what's Fallon's last name?"

"Graham. Why? You know her?"

"Nope, but finding out something about her family might give a clue to her special skill."

Seamus shoved his fists in his pockets. *"Not people I want to meet just yet. I'll fill you in on that later. Have a nice dinner."* He reerected his shield and stepped over to the kitchenette to check out the source of the delicious smells wafting through the cabin.

"I'm assuming you like anything I find in the pantry," Fallon said as he reached around her to grab a spoon to taste test the dinner cooking on the stove.

"Yeah, but this doesn't smell—or taste—like canned stew. What did you do to it?" He dipped the spoon back into the pot for another sample.

She smiled. "I also assumed you liked the spices I found, so I added a few. It works, I take it."

"Definitely. Of course, with the appetite you worked up in me, I'd probably find tree bark tasty." He peeked at her from beneath his brows.

"Nothing's stopping you from helping yourself to whatever tree bark you dropped by the fireplace," she retorted with a sniff before she set the plates none too gently on the dinette.

Bingo.

Seamus couldn't hide his grin. "You're too easy, Red."

"I *told* you, I do *not* answer to Red." She jerked open the silverware drawer.

"I noticed that," he replied sardonically, his grin blooming into a full smile.

"You. Are. Insufferable!"

"*You* are beautiful." He pulled her into his embrace. "Teasing you is a bonus." Before she could sputter a reply, he planted a smacking kiss on her mouth.

When he finally let both of them up for air, he added, "By the way, your stew is delicious. Let's eat it before it gets cold."

Fallon glanced at the stew still bubbling gently on the stove and sighed. "You make it very hard to stay mad at you."

He patted her ass, and she rolled her eyes at him, but her lips twitched into a smile.

As they tucked into their dinner, she asked, "Who were you communicating with earlier?"

He savored the bite of stew he'd shoveled in, swallowed, and said, "Rowan. I needed to let him know I won't be at the office for a few days."

"If we're lucky."

He set his fork down.

"Seamus, I have a bad feeling we only have until Taranis gets over his latest tantrum to figure out my skill. Ironically, I think the storm is keeping us safe."

"That and my sister's enchantments. Believe me, Fallon, this cabin is like a fortress. My sister is especially skilled at protection spells." Reaching across the table, he squeezed her hand.

"That may be, but we'll have to leave here sometime. What then?"

He took her other hand in his. "Rowan's mom studies warrior and talisman pairs. It's a hobby of hers."

Fallon tilted her head and waited.

"I asked Rowan to ask her about us, see if she has any suggestions for things we can do to discover your skill. Rowan's wife Alyssa is an associate professor in Celtic studies at the university, so she may have some ideas as well."

"I was reading Celtic stories before you interrupted me this afternoon," she reminded him.

"Which led to you suffering your endlessly repetitive premonition. Does it ever change?"

"No. That's why it scares the hell out of me. I watch helplessly as Maeve ends your life," she said, her pretty mouth turning down.

Seamus rubbed his thumbs over the soft skin of her hands. "She's not going to win, Fallon. Trust me. Because of you, I know exactly who my worst enemy is and what she plans, so I can prepare a strategy to stop her."

"She's a goddess, Seamus." Fallon pulled away from him. "What makes you think she's going to fight fair or give you any kind of chance to use a strategy?"

"She won't, but that won't stop me from devising one. Besides, we have a very powerful goddess on our side too."

"Who?"

"Scathach."

"Seriously?"

He didn't even try to keep the pride off his face. "She was right in the middle of things when Rowan and I rescued Alyssa from Morgan and Maeve last year. She hates to lose warriors she's spent her personal time training. Besides, she likes me." He waggled his brows and let a grin tug at the corner of his mouth.

"You know Scathach personally? You've trained with her?" Awe filled Fallon's voice.

"Don't sound so shocked. Remember how I told you Rowan Sheridan is my best friend?"

She nodded.

"Scathach has a special interest in the Sheridan family. They're like her own personal army against her sister goddesses. Since I'm tight with them and not a bad fighter either"—he gave her a pointed look—"she trains me as well."

"Which makes you even more irresistible to Maeve." Fallon's expression said she was more worried than impressed as he'd hoped she'd be.

Her glum response to his showing off surprised him. Then again, he hadn't been experiencing regular nightmares of his death.

"We'll figure it out in time, Fireworks. I believe in us." He took her hand again and rubbed his finger over her wrist. "Take your response to my sign. If we aren't meant to make it together, what explanation can there be for the mark I left on you or the way we both react when I trace my sign anywhere on your body?"

At the mention of that particular perk of their bonding, color suffused her face, a response that had Seamus puffing out his chest.

"See. All I have to do is mention it, and you're thinking about dessert."

She squeezed her eyes shut and pulled in a deep breath like she was trying to summon patience. Then she exhaled, opened her eyes, and stared at him. "If we're going to discover my special skill, we're going to have to do some work outside the sack,

Seamus." Her tone reminded him of his perpetually scolding second-grade teacher.

"Nice try, but your blush tells me you want the same dessert I do."

"Dessert comes last on the menu for a reason, Seamus. Before we can have any, we're going to have eat our lima beans." She flashed him a little grin and finished off the last of her helping of stew.

"Jeez, you have yet to meet my mother, and already you sound like her. Fair warning, I've always found a way around her."

She lifted a delicate auburn eyebrow, the challenge in her eyes unmistakable. Though Seamus understood the importance of uncovering his talisman's particular skill, he certainly wasn't above distracting her occasionally with some fun. Especially when that fun included her over-the-top responses to his newly discovered technique as her special lover.

The little bombshell Seamus delivered to his best friend reverberated throughout their immediate corner of the warrior community. Having Seamus's permission to share details about his talisman with the others close to them meant the cell phone towers in certain parts of Montana nearly glowed red-hot with the news of this most recent pairing and its ramifications, and more importantly, what Seamus's talisman's vision meant to him and to his family and friends.

First on Rowan's list was Siobhan MacManus, Seamus's sister.

"I do understand why Seamus contacted you first. It's only that I—"

"You don't understand why he didn't contact you as well," Rowan finished for her.

"Well, yeah. He's my brother, and you know how close we've always been. I thought when he made his happy discovery, he'd tell me right away," Siobhan said, the sadness in her voice almost palpable.

Rowan scrubbed a hand over his face. "It's not a slight to you that he let me be the bearer of his good news. Bonding is like that for most warriors. Some don't tell anyone for days or weeks depending on how long it takes to determine their talismans' skill or if they feel relatively safe from Morgan while they're getting to know each other." He shifted the phone to his other ear. "The circumstance of needing to report in to work probably had more to do with Seamus's choice of confidants than anything."

"Like civilians, druids have a choice in mates, so we don't experience bonding like warriors. I trained with my brother, so I get it on an intellectual level, but the whole emotional, physical aspect eludes me, I guess."

Siobhan's tone tore at Rowan.

"I don't need to breach your shield to know that you're thinking about your husband. The bonding experience with his talisman didn't work for them, and he adores you. Obviously, something important happened between the two of you emotionally and physically. He didn't miss anything," Rowan said. "Anyway, Seamus is asking for all of our help in determining his talisman's skill. Apparently, since Samhain, she's been having premonitions about his death."

Siobhan gasped.

"I know. But we have to consider her premonitions as positive. Something we can work with."

"Could she be a prophet?"

"He doesn't think so. He told me Fallon's vision never changes."

"That's significant. Anything else?"

"If I have this straight, she has other worlds swirling in her eyes, then she blinks, and everything clears. Seamus doesn't think she's even aware of what her eyes reveal," Rowan said.

"That's weird. I'll do some digging, as I know you will. I assume Alyssa is involved as well."

"You know what a caretaker she is, and she adores your brother. If not for him, I'd probably still be utterly obnoxious about sneaking around in her head," he said with a snort.

"Seamus did you both a favor," she said, and Rowan could almost hear her eyes rolling. "Now it's time for all of us to help him."

CHAPTER NINE

"ER SHIELD IS closed, she's not answering her phone, and she's not at her house. I don't know how to reach her." The anguish in Keela's voice unnerved Griff.

"They have to be close, or we wouldn't have felt the shift in the cosmos when she met her warrior," he said, giving her shoulder a squeeze.

"Doesn't matter how close they are if we can't reach them." She sat heavily on the plush sofa in their living room.

"We'll reach her, Keela. We will. You have to have faith." Griff sat beside his wife on the love seat and pulled her close.

"Have you seen anything of her warrior? You must know something since you were so adamant about his sign." Her tone accused him of keeping things from her.

Another man might have taken offense, but Griffin Walsh understood even better than his wife the importance of their niece in the warrior community. Her anxiety was well-founded. "I haven't seen her fate, if that's what you're asking."

"I want to know who her warrior is. If we can find that out, we might be able to contact him or his people. Warn them about Fallon's special gift."

"You know I've tried every spell I can think of to conjure even a name with no success." He threaded his fingers through hers to stop her trying to rub a hole in the top of her jeans.

Keela sighed and leaned into him. "I know you have. I really do know that." She covered his heart with her palm. "It's—I feel so helpless, so useless. What good is it to live close to her if we can't help her when she needs it most?"

Griff glanced at the rain running in sheets down the window. "Perhaps when the storm lets up, we'll have a chance to contact her. Of course, our inability to contact her could also have something to do with the bonding experience she's having." He brushed a kiss over Keela's temple.

"I understand, but that doesn't stop me worrying. I'm going to keep trying to reach her telepathically."

His stern expression warned her.

She huffed out a breath. "I know it's dangerous both with the gods and her parents, but she needs to know what she is, what she brings to her warrior before the gods discover them."

Griff knew he'd have no luck distracting his wife from her singular mission to keep Fallon safe, so he gave up on his half-hearted attempt and settled back to hold her close and let her get on with it. Too bad she hadn't had more time with her niece when she gave her the bracelet three years earlier. Perhaps she would have thought to tell Fallon to contact them as soon as she could after her warrior found her. As it was, they had no reasonable expectation of meeting the man before it was too late and the gods engaged him in battle. Not that Griff would mention that to Keela. For now, they could only keep trying to reach her and hope.

∾

Fallon sighed. Loudly. "Somehow, I thought the answer to discovering what my skill is might be in the old Celtic myths."

Seamus tangled his fingers in the fire of her hair. "But—"

"But the only stories that are calling to me are the tragic ones where a beautiful woman caught between the loves of two equally powerful men suffers the terrible fate of seeing her lover die."

"Such as?"

"Such as the one where Conchobar tricks Naoise into returning to Ireland from Scotland just so Conchobar could turn his champion loose to kill Naoise while Deirdre watched."

Seamus tried to suppress a shudder and failed.

Fallon shot him a side-eye and continued. "Guenevere caused a civil war after Mordred caught her with Lancelot. Grainne watched helplessly as Diarmuid died of his wounds while his best friend Fionn stood by and did nothing when he could have saved him." Her mouth turned down. "Deirdre chose to jump from a chariot and dash her brains out on some rocks rather than be sold off to the champion who killed her love."

"Babe—"

Seeming not to hear him, she went on. "Like my dreams, none of the stories has a happy ending. Guenevere spent the rest of her life doing penance as an abbess. Grainne threw herself off a cliff rather than wed an old man who stood by and did nothing while her lover died." She glanced up at the ceiling. "The only plus I can hear right now is the steady patter of rain on the roof of this cabin. The longer it rains, the more time we have."

"Then let's hope Taranis is in a piss-poor mood that takes a long time for him to get over," Seamus said, his lips curving slightly.

Holding her close, he shifted his attention to the unnatural darkness outside the window. As he stared out at the rain, he worked on devising strategies to outwit the lusty goddess bent on his destruction. He thought she'd attack him while he fought in a battle contrived purely for the purpose of drawing him away from his talisman and his companions. So he was going to need some powerful protection spells and additional training with Scathach to avoid his fate. When Fallon picked up the book again to read stories in the hopes of discovering her skill, Seamus decided to talk to his sister.

"Siobhan, are you open to conversation?" He barely began before his sister responded.

"Seamus! I've been hoping to hear from you all evening. Rowan called with the happy news. He said you're 'stranded' at the cabin."

He winced at the hurt he heard in her voice. *"Siobhan, I'm sorry you weren't the first to know. If not for the fact that I happen to work for the Sheridans, I probably wouldn't have told anyone yet. Fallon and I haven't discovered her skill, which means we have work to do before we venture out into the world."*

"I'm sorry. Somehow I thought I'd sense when you met your special lady."

"Or I'd tell you pretty soon afterward," he finished wryly.

"Something like that." He relaxed at the smile in her tone. *"Anyway, you didn't contact me to tell me what I already know. What's up?"*

"Fallon, my talisman, has been experiencing premonitions of my death since Samhain. She's seen me, *not some faceless warrior, dying quite a nasty death in Maeve's bed."* He shifted, the thought drawing him up uncomfortably. *"When Maeve finishes with me, Morgan escorts me across the ford."* Siobhan's gasp echoed through time and space, but he talked past it. *"Much as I've always loved women, I can't think of a worse way to go than in Maeve's bed."*

"Your talisman watches while you die?" Siobhan's concern ripped through him. *"How can she let you go like that?"*

He glanced at Fallon. Even the direness of his situation couldn't dampen the warmth that spread through him when he looked at her. His mouth turned down. *"She can't help me. Maeve forces her to watch then gives her a choice of betraying me in Tara-nis's bed while Maeve watches or living a long mortal life with the knowledge she didn't save me. Fallon always comes out of it before she makes the choice, but she knows we both cross the ford together."*

"Ouch, bro. That's a terrible fate. What can I do to help you?"

"I was hoping after the storm you could come to the cabin and chant some protection spells over me. If you can come up with some spells to alert me to danger or to make it difficult for Maeve to get near me, it might buy others time to come to my aid before she can take me."

"I'll consult my books and find something to help you, I promise. But Duncan and I will have to interrupt your bonding in order for me to chant over you, you know." She didn't try very hard to keep the mischief from her voice.

He grinned. *"There's room in the loft for the two of you. Bring earplugs."*

"Seamus Lochlann, you have no shame! Wonder how your talisman will feel about a family visit during your bonding."

"She'll adjust." He sobered. *"Actually, Sis, she's pretty down about the possibility of us besting Maeve. I think she'll be open to any help we can get even if we discover her special skill before you arrive. Give us tonight, then come out tomorrow."*

"We'll be there. Take care of yourself Seamus. You're the only brother I have." The catch in her voice was clear even via telepathy.

"You too, Siobhan."

Seamus reerected his shield and turned his attention to Fallon who, by the downturned expression on her face, was lost in morose thoughts. As usual, she wasn't letting him hear them. Stubborn woman. He needed to help her learn to trust him.

"What's bothering you, Fireworks?"

"What? Oh. Sorry. I was thinking about how sad it is that in so many of our stories and myths there are love triangles that never end well."

"At the risk of sounding insensitive—duh. Love *triangles* usually have no other outcome, Fallon."

She gave him a long look. "I realize that, Seamus. What I meant was the women involved always seem to be promised to the wrong men in the first place. If those in power would have been patient or less greedy, several people, and in the case of Deirdre and Naoise the whole Irish county of Ulster, would have been spared their terrible fates."

As she presented her case, he shifted, sitting up straighter and facing her. "Our situation is kinda similar, only the person in question is a man."

She quirked her eyebrow in a gesture that was becoming familiar to him.

He stood and paced to the fireplace and back, stopping to stand in front of her. "Hear me out. The fates decreed I'm your warrior, yet a greedy goddess with too much power has decided she wants me too. And she's willing to destroy us and probably anyone who helps us to get what she wants."

"Go on."

"What's in the stories that we can reverse? How can we use the scenario to beat her?"

Fallon sank lower into the cushions of the couch. "I don't know. In every case, the principle players die or live the rest of their lives in exile. Like I said, there are no happy endings."

"We'll have to work out a strategy to make one." He slid her a cocky grin. "I've already started."

She sat up and laid the book she'd been reading on the table, giving him her full attention. "What's your strategy?"

"I think Maeve will stage some sort of pseudo battle to draw me out. If I don't let her isolate me from you or from my warrior buddies who come to our aid, she won't be able to take me easily."

"But how can you ensure she won't be able to isolate you?"

When he saw her mouth turn down, he hurried on. "I've

invited my sister and her husband to join us here at the cabin as soon as they can get here. Siobhan is an expert at creating protection spells, so I want her to enchant us."

She scooted to the edge of the cushion. "I've never experienced a protection spell."

He raised his brows skeptically, staring pointedly at her wrist. "Oh."

"I'm also going to ask Scathach for her help." Pleasure surged through him at her quick intake of breath with this pronouncement. "No doubt she'll have some ideas for how to keep me in the thick of battle and away from Maeve."

"Scathach. Wow." She blew out a breath. "It's hard to wrap my head around you training with a goddess." Her pretty eyes clouded. "But if you're in the middle of the fighting and I can't help you because I don't know my skill, how will you survive?"

"The same way I always have—outfight the other guy. The thing about rogue warriors is they lack character." Stuffing his hands in his pockets, he rocked on his heels. "Morgan and Maeve suck out any character the rogues may have had, so I know they'll always fight dirty. Which means I don't feel any remorse at what happens to them. It frees me to fight the way I know I have to."

Returning to his seat beside her, he took her hand, stroking his thumb over her soft skin. "The zombies the evil ladies send back to the battlefield have no souls, hearts, or brains. They know one thing—keep moving until a warrior divests them of some vital body part like a head," he said with a smirk. "Scathach's training sessions always focus on how to take on and kill Morgan's zombies. Since she tends to reincarnate mythological beasts and villains, we already know how to kill them. We reenact the zombie warrior's last battle or a close approximation and take it out again."

Fallon trained her eyes on her fingers as she picked at the buttons on her shirt. "Sometimes Morgan wins. If she didn't occasionally take some warriors across the ford, she'd stop fighting," she whispered.

"True. But she's not going to win this time because we have a plan. It might not be a bona fide prophesy, but your premonition does give us an advantage."

When her gloomy demeanor didn't change, he cupped her cheek and stared deep into her eyes. "Fallon, honey, have a little faith. I know you haven't seen me in action, but I really am a formidable warrior." He pulled her close and pressed a kiss on her forehead. "Think about it. If I didn't have some skill, Scathach wouldn't bother with me. Maeve isn't going to have her way with me—but I'd like it if you did." He flashed her a grin and waggled his eyebrows suggestively.

A slow smile tugged at her lips before she sobered again. "Maybe if I hadn't been fighting sleep for months, I'd have more confidence. Or if I knew what skill I bring to the table."

"Hey, hey, Fireworks, how are you going to take advantage of me from way over there?"

"What are you talking about? I'm right beside you."

"And not nearly close enough. Come here."

"I couldn't be any closer to him unless I sat in his lap."

"That's a good spot."

"What are you doing in my head?" She blinked at him.

"Trying to talk you into two things—one, trusting me, and two, taking advantage of me."

He stroked his fingers through her hair on the way to palming the nape of her neck. "The gods fated us to be a team, Fallon. We play for the same side, and we have the same goals—to take on the evil gods of the pantheon and best them." The warm satin of her skin drew him closer to her. "We want to live long happy lives with people who matter to us. That's why our mother goddess designed our bonding ritual to be so intimate." He ducked his head to catch her eyes. "Even though my brother-in-law and his talisman aren't a bonded pair, they still care deeply for each other. And they don't shield each other when it's really important," he finished pointedly.

Her unhappy expression tore at him.

"I'm sorry Seamus. But I learned the hard way that letting down my shield meant serious consequences. It took me until I was nearly sixteen to figure out how my parents knew I hadn't given up our mythology after they demanded it of me." She wrapped her arms around her waist. "My punishments were regular and severe. After a while, I realized if I had an impenetrable shield, they couldn't mess around in my head and punish me for my thoughts and interests." She let out a breath. "My shield became my only defense." As she fiddled with the hem of his shirt, he summoned some patience, waiting her out, for once.

At long last, she said, "I know I'm supposed to keep my shield open where you're concerned, but it's so hard when I'm expecting you to think something terrible of me when you get inside my head."

"What kind of home life did you *have*?" Though his anger was directed at her parents, she flinched.

Seamus took a deep breath and tried to rein in his emotions. Reacting wasn't going to help her overcome the serious lack of trust her parents had instilled in her.

"I'm sorry, Fallon. But I can't understand how or why your parents could harbor such hate for half our race. Maybe because I grew up with one, I know firsthand how incredibly important druids are in our community. How could your family avoid the worst of Morgan's attacks without the help of druids?"

"We kept a very low profile. Not communicating much via telepathy, not socializing often with other warrior families, not becoming involved in many battles kept us under Morgan's radar."

"It also denied you freedom and the opportunity to contribute in any meaningful way in our community." He traced his forefinger along the contours of her cheek. "Yet I see empathy in you that completely contradicts the way you were raised. You desperately wanted to help me even before you met me. You wanted to help me when you didn't believe I was your warrior. You're stronger than your parents, Fallon." He cupped her jaw and held her gaze. "You can be stronger still if you learn to trust me."

"I trust Sloane," she said, crossing her arms defiantly over her chest.

"That's a good start. Now you have to learn to trust me. Open your shield, please."

Closing her eyes, she took a breath, deliberately relaxed, and opened her mind.

"Beautiful Fallon, it's your turn to lead."

He heard her breath catch, but otherwise the only sounds in the room were the comforting crackle and pop of the fire in the fireplace and rhythmic patter of rain on the cabin's roof.

"What do you mean?"

"You know exactly what I mean."

Her eyes flew open.

He cocked a brow and didn't bother to hide his intense desire for his woman.

"Oh." For several long seconds, she stared into his eyes. At last, she nodded and hoisted herself onto his lap. "I still don't know how having dessert is going to help us discover my skill, but I think I've had enough lima beans for one night." A tiny smile curved her plump lips.

"Definitely time for dessert. What did you have in mind?" he asked as he began stroking her fall of long hair with one hand, entangling his fingers in its glossy softness while he teased her by drawing part of his sign above her knee with his other hand.

Shivering at his touch, she shifted on his lap, straddling him. "I wonder what happens if I trace your sign on you? Like here," she suggested as she pulled up his sweater and bared his chest.

First, she traced his sign with her finger on his bare skin. When his breath caught, her eyes twinkled mischievously at him before she leaned forward and traced his sign in the same place—with her tongue. Seamus sucked in air, his heart hammering into overtime at her touch.

His response fired her confidence because she kissed her way across his chest, openmouthed kisses she alternated with tracing his sign on him with her tongue.

"This is in the way," she insisted as she tugged at his sweater. "Lift your arms."

Fallon's clever little mouth was driving him wild, making him more than happy to indulge her. "Whatever you say, Fireworks."

She shot him a look, and he half shrugged a shoulder, daring her to contradict him.

Her desire won. After divesting him of his sweater, she took her time exploring his shoulders and chest with featherlike touches of her fingertips. "Your size should intimidate me—"

He tilted his head.

"But I think you're thrilling."

"Yeah?" He grinned.

"Uh-huh." Smiling coyly back at him, she said, "It's time to explore other sensitive places. So far, I've discovered your chest is quite responsive. I wonder about here." She leaned forward and tasted the column of his throat, which shot fire straight to his groin. He lifted his chin to give her more access, and she kissed her way to her favorite spot behind his ear where she licked him delicately and blew on his skin. With a growl of pleasure, he settled his hands on her round ass and squeezed.

"What do you think you're doing? This is my show, warrior," she warned before she grabbed his hands and pulled them above his head. "You did mention it was my turn to lead." She ruined the severity of her tone when she tipped forward to lick and nip along his jaw.

Fallon's deliberate attempt to keep her attention on his upper body was driving him wild. He wished she'd share that part of her body with him.

"Is that what you want? I can arrange that." She leaned back on his lap and took her time to divest herself of his shirt, unbuttoning the buttons with excruciating slowness while she stared deeply into his eyes.

At first, he smiled and kept his eyes on hers, watching the colors change from gold to green to deep blue. But in his peripheral vision, he could see her coming close to baring her breasts, and finally, he could no longer deny himself the pleasure of gazing at her naked beauty. Breaking eye contact, he watched intently as she undid the last button before she let his shirt slide off her body with agonizing deliberateness.

"My chest is especially sensitive to the touch of your breasts, in case you were wondering." He unleashed a slow, wicked smile.

"Like this?" She nearly drove him out of his mind when she barely brushed his pecs with her erect nipples.

"For a start."

He tried to be cool about it, but his blood heated exponentially at her touch, his heart rate ratcheting up like he was chasing her.

Fallon gave him fuller contact as she flattened herself against the wall of his chest, wrapped her arms around his neck, and took his mouth in a whisper-light touch of her lips before she slipped her tongue inside and traced his sign on his tongue.

At her kiss, Seamus lost his mind. Wrapping his arms tightly around her, he held her to him and followed her lead, his tongue mating and tracing with hers until coherent thought was a thing of myth.

Eons later, she tore her mouth from his to drag in air. "Am I still leading?"

"Oh yeah, Fireworks. You're definitely in charge," he said, panting.

"In that case, I think it's time I took you to bed."

She slid backward off his lap and headed to the bedroom. When he didn't follow immediately, she half turned and crooked her finger at him. Grinning at her flirty gesture, he leaped off the couch and stepped up behind her.

"That little move is such a cliché," he said with a laugh.

Her eyes danced. "But it works every time." She grabbed his hand to lead him to bed.

Seamus tried hard to let Fallon have her way, but her tormenting slowness with undressing him and then herself nearly sent him over the edge. When at last she straddled him on the bed, he worried he'd come the second she sheathed him inside her. Clenching his jaw, he worked to regain some control over his hypersensitized body. That was when she dragged sleek strands of her fiery hair along the sides of his belly and up over his chest before she lightly rubbed her nipples over him as she made her way to kissing his mouth.

Against his lips she whispered, "You seem to have lots of sensitive spots on your beautiful body, Seamus Lochlann."

Surprising him, she pulled back and settled herself between his legs, using her clever little tongue to trace his sign on his stiff cock. At her touch, he surged up off the bed.

"Fallon!" he cried out hoarsely, his body radiating sparks from his groin outward.

Without thinking, he grabbed her high on her waist, pulled her up, and flipped her on her back. She exhaled a startled cry as Seamus thrust himself between her legs and filled her completely.

Once he started to move inside her, the welcome wet heat of her body drove him wild. He only realized how out of control he was after he came back down to earth from the incredible orgasm she gave him. When she tightened around him in her own release, to his utter shock, he came again.

It took several minutes for him to regain his equilibrium and his breath. "Fallon, I'm sorry. I didn't mean to lose control like that. Are you all right?" he asked, his throat raw from shouting his pleasure.

"Mmmm, terrific," she murmured contentedly as she smoothed her hands over and down his shoulders and back.

"Are you sure? Here let me—"

When he tried to lift his weight off her body, she tightened her arms around him, holding him to her. "You took the lead for a few minutes, but I think this is still my show. And I'm not ready for you to go anywhere yet," she said into his neck before kissing him there.

Aware of how much bigger he was, Seamus didn't completely rest himself on her body. When his arms began to shake, she hugged him closer to her, silently insisting he lay on her fully.

"I'll squish you," he protested.

"You want me to trust you, but you don't give me any credit for knowing my own strength. Relax. I like your weight on me."

He gave in, his body and Fallon leaving him no other choice.

I truly love touching this man, having him touch me. Before meeting Seamus, I never would have thought such a huge man would appeal to me. Now I can't imagine not having him in my life.

Seamus smiled at Fallon's unguarded thoughts.

She stiffened beneath him.

Noting the change in her body, he sent her a counterattack. She began tracing his sign across his back, first with her left hand then with her right, flowing and intertwining patterns over his skin. The effort seemed to hold her premonition at bay until he grew hard inside her again, and she wriggled and shifted, pulling him deeper inside her.

"This sign of yours seems to have lots of interesting uses with some rather promising results," she commented casually as he began to move slowly inside her.

"You've noticed that too?" he asked almost matter-of-factly before she tightened her inner muscles, and he sucked in air.

"Yes. It seems to make me forget to think about anything. Just feel." She countered the guilelessness of her smile with rhythmic contractions of her sweet channel that shot electric fire up and down his spine, an even greater pleasure than when she used his sign on him.

"You are so much woman." He matched his rhythm to hers.

Shutting both of them up, he kissed her deeply, sharing the same breath. As he loved her, he recognized he'd become one with his magnificent talisman. Then he stopped thinking altogether.

CHAPTER TEN

HEN HE OPENED the door to his guests, Shanley and Alaisdair Graham, Rowan Sheridan greeted them with, "Seamus has found his talisman."

He was glad the continuous rainstorm didn't deter Alyssa and him from hosting their regular Sunday night dinner. In what was becoming almost a ritual, they hosted Alyssa's best friend Ceri Ross Sheridan's Aunt Shanley and her new husband Alaisdair. Rowan's dad had offered Alaisdair a job in his security firm after he and Shanley married. They needed the help while Rowan's brother Rio and his new wife Ceri spent a required year in Shanley and Ceri's ancestral home in Scotland. Most of the time, Seamus joined them for this meal, so the Grahams expressed surprise when they arrived and didn't see his big black truck parked in the drive.

"They're bonding right now?" Shanley asked as she joined Alyssa in the kitchen.

"I imagine so," Rowan said with a grin.

"I take it they're enjoying this experience with a little more privacy than some of us had." Shanley blushed and trained her focus on helping with dinner.

"Och, lass, we both had tae wait such a long time fer our moment. Surely ye dinnae want tae begrudge me some braggin' rights with the likes o' the Sheridan clan?" Alaisdair stepped behind his wife and wrapped his arms around her.

"Hmmph." Shanley sniffed.

Rowan smiled as he watched her relax into her warrior husband's embrace.

"They're at Seamus's family's cabin up the mountain from here, so yes, they're enjoying some privacy," Alyssa said as she tossed a handful of cherry tomatoes into the salad she'd been preparing when their guests arrived.

"Who is she, d'ye know?" Alaisdair asked.

"Her name is Fallon Graham. Get this—she's been having some damn scary premonitions about Seamus since Samhain," Rowan said as he pulled beers from the fridge, popped the tops off, and handed one to Alaisdair before he sipped from the other one.

"What did ye say her name was?" Alaisdair asked.

"Fallon Graham. Why?"

"Dae ye know her parents' names by chance?" Alaisdair leaned his forearms on the island. But there was nothing relaxed in his expression.

"Seamus didn't talk long. All he told me was her name and that she'd been seeing flashes of him in her mind for most of this past year." Rowan took a contemplative pull from his bottle of beer. "There was something strange though. When I asked about her family, he said they weren't people he was in a hurry to know. Something's up with that."

"Ye have nae idea if she's a member o' the American branch o' my side o' the family?" Alaisdair asked, the tone of his voice betraying worry.

"You think Seamus's talisman is a danger to him?" Rowan set

his beer on the island. "You know, one of my uncles lost his life because of his talisman's lack of character."

Alaisdair cocked a brow. "I donnae know that she is, but if she's a part o' my clan, her family may be a problem, what with Seamus's sister bein' a druid," he said without telling them anything.

Alyssa set the bowl of salad and a bottle of dressing on the island. "What does that mean?"

"It means there are some warriors who descended from Fianna Conlan from her first marriage who believed she betrayed her warrior husband, especially after she took a druid fer her second one." Absently, he patted Shanley's hand where it rested on his shoulder as she stood behind him. "Many o' them moved over here tae America and did their best tae weed out any druids among them. If I knew the lass's parents' names, I could tell ye if she's a distant cousin tae me and tae the Conlans."

Rowan scowled. "If she is a part of that bunch, there are serious complications in Seamus's relationship with her before they even deal with the nasty ladies. With what he told me Maeve has in mind for him, their plates are full to overflowing as it is."

"What's Maeve planning, and how do they know?" Shanley asked.

"Fallon sees Maeve spending Seamus in her bed." Rowan shuddered and stepped closer to Alyssa.

"Och, I wouldna wish such a fate on my worst enemy," Alaisdair said. "She makes a mockery of our bondin' when she does such a thing tae a warrior."

"Is Fallon a prophet?" Shanley asked.

Alaisdair pulled her around to sit on his lap since everyone knew what she was asking.

"Seamus says no. Her vision never changes. I believe yours and Ceri's do, don't they?"

Shanley nodded. "A prophet can foretell a possibility of the future, so yes, our visions change."

"There's something else," Rowan added. "Fallon's got a druid uncle by marriage who made her a bracelet bearing Seamus's sign. Seamus said when he traced his sign over it while she wore it"—he pulled in a breath—"he branded her. What do you make of that?"

"I'd say there's powerful magic going on with this pair. We need to figure out how we're going to help them when the time comes," Alyssa said, staring meaningfully up at her husband.

"Knowin' who his talisman's people are would be a good place tae start," Alaisdair said.

"I'll try to reach him after dinner," Rowan said. "If we need to involve ourselves with them, we'd better hope it's not at the cabin. The road will be accessible with four-wheelers at best, but in this weather, probably only on foot. For some reason, Taranis is in a mood right now."

They all stared glumly out the window at the torrential rain. Though Rowan and Alyssa had worked together to create a delicious chicken cacciatore dinner, the group's collective worry for their friend dampened everyone's appetite and their usual teasing and boisterous mood. They pushed their food around on their plates and made inconsequential small talk until Rowan couldn't stand it anymore.

When he abruptly stood up and walked down the hall, Alaisdair took a long pull from his beer. "About time."

Rowan stood in the study of the home he shared with his wife. Along one wall she'd hung a tapestry of the three patron goddesses of warriors—Scathach the warrior trainer, Brighid the healer and bard, and Rhiannon the patroness of freedom. Perhaps it was the magic Alyssa's druid grandmother wove into the tapestry as she created it. Perhaps it was the reminder of what these goddesses had done for warriors over the years. Perhaps it was the way the colors seemed to move in the design in the cloth—whatever it was, Rowan always felt calm and centered when he stood before this particular tapestry. During dinner, the tension in the kitchen had reached such a crescendo he needed the serenity the tapestry gave him before he reached out to his friend.

◈

"What gives? I already checked in, dad." The incredible experience Seamus had shared with Fallon must have left him vulnerable. It was the only explanation for how Rowan could breach his shield so easily.

"Yeah, I know, son." Rowan chuckled. *"But it seems we may have found an additional complication in your pairing with Fallon."*

Rowan's grave tone put Seamus on high alert. *"What do you mean?"* He tugged the sleepy woman in question even closer to his body.

"What is it?" she asked.

"I'll let you know in a minute."

"What's Fallon's dad's name?"

Seamus smoothed his hand over the velvety skin of Fallon's waist. "Time for family history. What are your parents' names?"

"My dad is Clancy Graham and my mom is Ivori Ferguson Graham. Why?"

"The family wants to know," Seamus replied with an eyeroll before passing on the information to Rowan.

"Is your sister working on something?" Fallon asked.

"No, but Rowan and Alyssa are, apparently. His timing sucks. I was about to float away into a beautiful nap," he said as he stroked Fallon's thick, silky hair. "By the way, I like when you lead." He smiled and she relaxed, resting her cheek on his chest.

"As I remember it, you sort of took off out in front about halfway through," she teased.

"I did, didn't I? Guess we'll have to try again, see if I can contain myself a little better next time."

"What would be the fun in that?" Peeking up from beneath her brows, she batted her lashes at him.

"Now you're getting it, Fireworks," he said, his voice deepening as his body anticipated another intensely pleasurable experience with his talisman.

Rowan interrupted again. *"Alaisdair and Shanley are here for dinner. It seems your talisman is related to Alaisdair. Her family has had a singular goal of denying druids for generations. Something to do with an unfounded belief about the matriarch of their line betraying her warrior husband to marry a druid. Sorry to be the bearer of bad news."*

"You've only given me details to facts I already knew. Fallon's parents disassociated themselves from her dad's sister when she married a druid. It left a big hole in my talisman's life." Unconsciously, he stroked his palm up and down Fallon's arm.

"She doesn't share her parents' prejudices?"

Seamus knew his friend too well to miss the caution in those words.

"No. Is there anything else?" he asked and didn't try to hide his impatience.

"Yeah. What's her aunt's name?"

"Keela Walsh. Her husband is Griffin Walsh, but Fallon doesn't know where they are. The last time she saw her uncle was when he married Keela about a dozen years ago. Now can you let me get back to something important?"

Rowan laughed, a sound Seamus could hear in his own head. *"Oh yeah, payback's a bitch, ain't it, buddy? I seem to remember a friend of mine sneaking into my head at a rather inconvenient time when I was bonding with my talisman."*

Seamus couldn't help but smile at the memory of being able to breach Rowan's formidable shield right after he found Alyssa. *"Touché."*

"I'm not going where I have no business, trust me. But it would be good if you at least kept your shield lowered a bit in case we find out something that will help the two of you. Alyssa thinks there's

powerful magic in your pairing to explain how you branded Fallon with your sign."

"All right. I'll let you in occasionally. But if you're having trouble, consider your timing blows and give up for a few minutes."

He could hear Rowan's laughter through time and space.

"Deal. Let us know if you discover Fallon's skill—or if you're in trouble with the goddesses."

"What was that all about?" Fallon asked.

"It seems you're related to some good friends of mine. Alaisdair Graham discovered that my friend Ceri Ross's aunt was his talisman when they were all at the Conlan family manor last Samhain," Seamus said. The bitterness of being left behind during the battle at Conlan Manor still lingered.

Beneath his arm, Fallon stiffened. "What about that is bothering you? Did you think one of them was your talisman or something?"

"I knew neither one was my talisman. I tried my sign on Ceri, and Shanley was forty at the time, well past the age of finding her warrior. Of course, Rowan and Alyssa reversing the curse on warriors and talismans opened the door for her to find her warrior. Alaisdair Graham was in hiding at the manor." Fallon sat up and stared at him. "He'd been on the run from Morgan for almost fourteen years when he discovered Shanley was his talisman after she arrived at the manor last fall."

"That's good for all of them, isn't it?"

He nodded.

"So, what's the problem?"

"The problem is I was left here to mind the store—literally—while the rest of them took on Morgan and Taranis and evened the playing field for the Conlans and their descendants."

"You're mad you missed out on the fight." She crossed her arms over her pretty breasts. "If you had been there, as the only warrior on the team without a talisman, you would have been especially vulnerable. Where would that have left us?"

He waved off her comment as a thought occurred to him. "If Alaisdair is right, you're a Conlan descendant too. I wonder if the protections Ceri and Rio's pairing gives to them and to Shanley and Alaisdair and their Scots cousins also apply to you."

Fallon slid back down beside him. "That would be nice. Unless there are druids involved. If my parents know about such protections but suspect a druid helped them to have them, they'll reject the help."

"That doesn't mean you have to reject it." Seamus held his breath for her reaction. She said she had no prejudices where druids were concerned, but her actions would tell the real story.

She lay very still.

"You're right, it doesn't." She buried her face in his arm. "You must think me so uneducated. I'm way behind on bardic traditions, and I haven't a clue about my family tree. Then, of course, there's my skill, which we haven't made any progress discovering." She traced the pads of her fingers over his chest. "I know you feel cheated out of the big battle your friends fought." Her voice dropped. "Probably, you wouldn't have been any less vulnerable had your talisman been standing right beside you."

Seamus had aimed for a commitment from Fallon, not this feeling of utter failure. He shifted so he could look directly into her eyes. "You are not responsible for your parents' failings because they cling to their prejudices. What matters is what *you* think, what *you* believe. Your insistence on learning the bardic side of our culture in spite of the obstacles your parents put up says loads about your character." He pushed a shiny strand of hair from her face and let his palm linger on her cheek. "And I have yet to meet a warrior-talisman pair who knew the talisman's skill when they met. We're going to be fine, Fallon. Better than fine if you are indeed related to the Conlan clan."

"I don't know, Seamus. But I hope so. I truly hope so."

Setting his lips on hers, he shared his belief in them with his kiss. In the space of that kiss, they forgot all about everything the outside world wished to press on them as they lost themselves in each other again.

❧

Alyssa's eyes saucered. "Keela and Griffin Walsh are Fallon's family?"

"That's what she said," Rowan replied after he rejoined the others at dinner.

"She doesn't know where they are?" Her voice rose on each word until she squeaked.

"What are you on about, lass?" Alaisdair asked.

"Griffin Walsh is the head of the folklore department at the university. He mentored me on my master's thesis—and he knew I was a talisman long before I did…"

Rowan sensed his wife's distress and snagged her attention with a look. *Stop worrying about what you didn't know at first. Your Grandma Afton kept you alive long enough for me to find you. I'll always be grateful to her for that.*

Alyssa nodded.

"Maybe they live here because Fallon is here," Shanley suggested. "Kind of like Finn Daly watching over you and your gram and Ceri and me all those years."

Silence descended on the group at the mention of their old friend who lost his life fighting Morgan at Samhain.

Rowan cleared his throat. "That could be it. But why would they watch out for her without her knowledge?"

"Seamus will figure it out," Alyssa said.

Rowan smiled at her. "After the way he trained you on shielding, you're always going to see him as a champion, aren't you?"

She arched a saucy brow at him and said nothing.

"Since ye know Griffin Walsh, Alyssa, perhaps ye could have

a wee chat with him taemorrow. See what he can tell us about Fallon." Alaisdair said, pushing his plate away. "One thing is sure. If Maeve wants Seamus, she'll stop at naethin' tae have him. Especially once she finds out he's discovered his talisman." He stretched his arm across the back of his wife's chair.

"I'll arrange to meet with Griff first thing in the morning. Hopefully, this rain lets up so we can reach Seamus and Fallon if we need to," Alyssa said.

"Having some knowledge and a plan has revived my appetite. Sorry, old man." Rowan addressed Shadow, Alyssa's Great Pyrenees who lay on the floor where the great room met the kitchen. "Guess there won't be scraps for you after all," he said as he helped himself to a another serving of chicken cacciatore.

They all laughed at the comical way Shadow let out a low woof as though protesting Rowan's pronouncement, the big dog's response cheering the evening.

CHAPTER ELEVEN

ONDAY DAWNED SOAKING wet and foul. Griffin Walsh couldn't remember a time so much rain had fallen in June in southern Montana. Apparently, Taranis was having more than an average tantrum.

From the open door of his campus office, he noticed Alyssa Sheridan shaking off her umbrella as she entered the foyer of the folklore department. The pensive look on her face told him she had something serious on her mind. They'd formed an instant bond when Alyssa joined the department. Of course, he knew immediately what she was even when she didn't know herself. When she discovered they were part of the same shadow community of warriors in a world of civilians, she'd dressed him down savagely for keeping that knowledge to himself. Being a druid who possessed incredible prognosticating skill, Griffin knew how Alyssa would respond when she discovered her true calling in the world. He'd been ready for her with a series of stories to help her understand why so many people had kept her ignorant of her true self for so long.

It took some time, but eventually, Alyssa had forgiven

them all, especially her beloved grandmother who had insisted she not know her actual place in the world unless and until her warrior found her. Alyssa's grandmother thought it was the best way to keep her safe from the fate her parents suffered at the hands of Morgan and her minions. Alyssa's love of Celtic mythology gave him the opportunity to become her master's thesis mentor, thus making it easy for him to watch over her. No one found it odd that she spent so much time with her professor—time Griff used to reinforce her grandmother's protections and surreptitiously cast his own protection spells over Alyssa.

Now they were colleagues in the civilian world of academics. Lately, however, their schedules and Alyssa's year-old marriage had afforded them few opportunities for conversation.

As she stepped through the door of his office, he smiled as her eyes inevitably veered to the human skull carved with interlocking Celtic knots sitting atop his desk. He'd placed it there to tease civilian freshmen—and to send a message to any druid or warrior who happened to be his college student.

"Someday, I want an office decorated like this one. I've always liked the built-in bookshelves lining your walls in here."

"Good afternoon to you too, Alyssa."

She laughed and dropped her coat over the chair in front of the massive oak desk he'd had to dismantle to move into the room.

His decorations sent messages. From the size and placement of his desk in front of the window between the two walls of books, to the pewter-blue rug swirled with mythical beasts—cranes, salmon, horses—all animals inherently sacred in Celtic mythology, to the two straight-backed chairs in front of his desk, he wanted anyone from the warrior community to know exactly who they were dealing with when they entered his space. The fact that it either amused civilians with his Celtic "eccentricities" or intimidated them was a bonus.

"To what do I owe the pleasure of this meeting? Have you

decided to pursue your doctorate so you can join my department full-time?"

"I'm considering it. But right now, that's not important." She closed the door and faced him.

Eyeing her warily, he said, "This isn't about your work is it?"

"It's about my friend Seamus Lochlann. Tell me, do you have a niece named Fallon Graham?" Alyssa sat carefully in the hard chair across from him as she dropped her little bomb.

Griff nearly leaped over his desk. "Is he Fallon's warrior?"

"He's a very dear friend of mine. As is Shanley Conlan Graham, Ceri's aunt. Perhaps you remember them? And remember that Shanley recently married Alaisdair Graham—from Scotland?" She tilted her head, and he had the distinct impression she was enjoy-ing knowing something he didn't this time.

It didn't matter. Only Fallon mattered. "There are warriors from the Conlan branch of my wife's family here?" Griff asked, falling back in his comfy leather chair.

"As a matter of fact, yes. You remember that my best friend is the heir of Conlan Manor? The reason I took a leave of absence at Samhain last term was to help her and my brother-in-law defend Conlan Manor from Morgan and her zombie warriors." Alyssa smoothed her hair down and settled into a more comfortable position on the chair.

"Of course, of course." He waved away that part of her story. "What has all this to do with your warrior friend?" Though he desperately wanted to know all the intricacies of the connections Alyssa presented, Griff's focus remained on his niece.

"While the Sheridans were in Scotland, Seamus stayed behind to run the family's business. He didn't take the assignment well, but everyone thought it in his best interest not to expose himself when he hadn't found his talisman yet."

Griff nodded. "Sounds wise not to let him go alone to fight the goddesses on their home turf."

"He's been a bit grumpy with us ever since." The corner of Alyssa's mouth quirked up. "However, yesterday afternoon, he let my husband know he wouldn't be in to work for a while. He'd found his talisman, a woman named Fallon Graham."

Griff narrowed his eyes at the confirmation that Fallon had indeed found her warrior.

"We usually have dinner with Seamus and our friends Shanley and Alaisdair Graham on Sunday evenings. When we shared Seamus's good news, Alaisdair had a few insights. Rowan interrupted Seamus, and we discovered some connections." Alyssa crossed her arms over her chest. "Fallon doesn't know you're here watching her, does she?"

"We don't want to force her to make a choice with her family," Griff said slowly.

"Even when her parents have demanded she make such a choice? She told Seamus she hasn't seen you in a dozen years. How do you do that when both she and you work on the same campus? How did she not see your name listed on course catalogs and faculty directories?"

"Alyssa," Griff intoned, "do you forget I'm a druid? I can cloak myself even on paper when I wish. It's not too difficult to hide in plain sight. By being near her, Keela and I can protect her. By not letting her know we're here, we keep her from having to lie to her parents to keep the peace."

She frowned. "How did you know Fallon had found her warrior?"

"Your curiosity while you were my student always challenged me." He smiled.

"That's no answer, Griff." There was steel in her tone. The way she eyed him as she slipped one foot beneath herself and relaxed more deeply into her chair told him she was in for the long haul.

Resignedly, he sighed. When Alyssa didn't know her heritage, it had been easier to put her off. Since she came into her own as a talisman, Griff discovered he couldn't withstand her tenacity when she truly wanted to know something. "You know I'm a prognosticator. I can choose the best times for battle and for rituals in our community. What you may not know is I'm also an accomplished metalsmith."

"Go on."

"After I had a vision of a warrior's sign before Fallon's twenty-first birthday, I fashioned a bracelet for her. Although I wasn't sure the sign belonged to her warrior, I knew it to be important for her."

"Uh-huh."

"Friday night, I felt a shift in the cosmos, and I experienced the vision again. That's when I suspected Fallon's warrior had found her." He left out the part where Keela and he had had their own bonding experience, simultaneously, he suspected, with Fallon and her warrior. "Now that we've established our mutual interest in this particular warrior pair, what is your real reason for coming to see me?"

Alyssa leaned her forearms on Griff's desk. "Fallon has been predicting Seamus's death since Samhain. The timing seems significant as well as the fact that her premonition remains constant, which indicates she's not a prophet."

He snorted. "Not surprising considering how carefully her family has tried to weed out any form of druidism for several generations."

"Which is surprising considering her Conlan relatives are prophetesses."

His eyes widened. "What does Fallon see of her warrior's fate?"

"Seamus dies in Maeve's bed while Fallon is forced to watch. Then Morgan wades in their blood as she escorts both of them across the ford."

He stood and paced between his massive desk and the wall of bookshelves behind it. "In order for that to happen, Maeve will have to take Fallon first and put her in a kind of limbo from which she can't escape. Something from which it will be nearly impossible to rescue her."

Alyssa sat up straight. "She tried that with me when she took me from Rowan and imprisoned me in her stronghold in Los Angeles. She breached my shield and tortured me with images until I nearly gave in and let Morgan escort me across the ford." She shuddered at the memory. "Seamus helped Rowan find and save me."

"She'll do worse to Fallon," he said with conviction—and fear.

Her head came up. "Why? How do you know? Morgan and Maeve had a specific reason for torturing me. They needed to keep Rowan and me apart in order to keep their curse alive. Beyond a momentary orgasmic pleasure, what do they gain by taking Seamus and Fallon?" The fear vibrating in her voice told him how important this particular friend was to her.

"At least as much if not more than they would have gained had they succeeded in taking you." He stared at the rain sheeting down the window. "My niece is probably the greatest talisman of your generation. She has powers beyond anything I've ever seen in the warrior community." He turned back to Alyssa. "Unfortunately, she's only half trained. Her parents' prejudice against druids could very well cost their daughter and her warrior their lives."

Alyssa's eyes saucered. "*What?*"

"Exactly. A great irony considering the esteem in which they hold the Sheridan clan and any warrior associated with them." He stopped pacing for a moment as a thought occurred to him. "I met Seamus Lochlann at your wedding, didn't I? He was your husband's best man, wasn't he?"

"Yes."

"He's a powerful warrior, but he has a sense of bravado that could be a problem."

"What do you mean?"

"He doesn't appear to take things as seriously as he should."

Alyssa narrowed her eyes. "You figured that out from meeting him one afternoon at a wedding no less? Really, Griff, for someone who professes to despise prejudice in other people, you're a touch judgmental where my friend is concerned."

"You must understand—Fallon is a very special talisman. At any rate, we need to interrupt Seamus and her. If we can reach them before Maeve realizes her prize is almost beyond her grasp, we may be able to derail her plans for them. Do you know where they are?"

"Yes, but in this weather, they're inaccessible. Unless you know a way to visualize yourself through a storm to a place you've never seen and manage to land there unscathed," Alyssa said. "Although it wouldn't surprise me at all to discover you do indeed have a way to bend time and space to move in a way that even warriors can't."

He would have laughed at her snark if the situation weren't so dire. "Are they nearby, at least?"

"They're at Seamus's family's cabin up the canyon from my place. It's on a mountain road that's little more than a hiking trail on a good day. After three straight days of nonstop rain, I doubt you could paddle your way up there."

His hands on his desktop, Griff leaned toward her. "You've been there? You could visualize yourself there?"

"Not today. If I tried to visualize myself through this storm, I'd probably land in a cave under a waterfall in Argentina. We have to be patient." She crossed her arms back over her chest. "I came to you for help, but instead you're kinda scaring me."

"We need to sort out a plan to save Fallon before Maeve finds her. May we meet at your place this afternoon?" It wasn't a request, which Alyssa's raised eyebrows told him she understood perfectly.

"Who else do you want to be there?"

"Your husband, your friends the Grahams, anyone else who

is associated with your friend Seamus. Does he have family in the area?"

"His sister Siobhan and her husband Duncan live nearby. Are you going to invite Fallon's parents?"

"If I thought they'd actually put aside their differences with Keela and me long enough to help their daughter, I would. But that would mean them allowing me to give Fallon a crash course in the bardic training she should have had growing up, and I can't imagine them allowing that." He blew out a breath. "So, in answer to your question, no."

She nodded. "Something you should know about Seamus is he's extremely close to his sister." She stared deep into his eyes. "Who is a druid. She's married to a warrior whose talisman is alive and well and an integral part of their lives."

"The gods truly do know what they're doing when they pair warriors and talismans," he said with a chuckle, and for the first time since Alyssa walked through his door, he allowed himself a tiny moment to relax before he started making plans for saving his niece and her warrior from the terrible fate the goddesses planned.

❧

"Check," Seamus said, his eyes glittering triumph.

"Not so fast, warrior. I still have a move."

"Admit it, Fallon. I have you exactly where I want you."

"Do you now? Exactly where you want me?" she asked as she considered him from beneath her brows, her eyes flashing mischief as she undid the top button of her shirt with one hand.

When Seamus's eyes followed her hand on her shirt, she surreptitiously slid her king over one square with her other hand.

"Exactly where I want you," Seamus whispered in her ear from behind her as he imprisoned her hand.

"You're cheating!" Fallon squeaked.

"No more than you are, Fireworks. Since we're both such

cheaters, what do you say we call it a draw and move on to a different game?" He stroked one long finger seductively over the back of her hand, and she shivered.

"What did you have in mind?"

"Something that's clothing optional." He pushed her hair behind her ear so he could trace the shell of it with his tongue.

She felt his smile on her skin when she shivered at his touch. He tasted her again and whispered, "You in?"

She turned her face to him. "Only if you are."

Seamus laughed at her innuendo before he scooped her out of her chair at the dinette and carried her to the couch, settling there with her on his lap.

"You know what I think?" He started leisurely undoing the buttons on her shirt.

"What do you think?" She fisted her hands so as not to reach up to help him with his task.

"I think we would have found each other even if we weren't fated to be together."

The implications of cheating at chess were one thing. Cheating fate ventured far beyond the pale. She tensed at the ramifications of his comment. Sitting up straighter, she said, "I don't think so. I turned you down when you asked me out after we met because I knew you were a warrior, but I didn't think you were mine."

"Relax, Fallon. That's not what I meant." He smoothed his palm up and down her arm. "I meant, if we were only two civilians, we would have found each other. Think about it." He shifted beneath her. "We're made for each other."

His comments distracted her from his true intention until the pads of his fingers tickled the bare skin of her belly. "The sex is *supposed* to be mind-blowing Seamus. It's part of the way the gods try to guarantee we bond." Fallon tried to sound prim even as her skin rippled and shivered at his touch, her core tightening in anticipation at where that touch would lead.

"Mind-blowing, eh?" He nuzzled her neck and gave her an openmouthed kiss in the hollow of her throat, leaving her momentarily speechless. It stunned her how quickly he'd discovered her most sensitive places.

"Like your ego needs more stroking," she whispered when she could speak again.

"I enjoy you stroking any part of me."

She sensed more than heard his mirth, and her own laughter bubbled out of her even as she tried to suppress it. Seamus didn't need more encouragement for his wit or his sexual prowess.

"I'm a lucky man, Fallon Graham. The more I get to know you, the more I see how perfect you are for me—even outside the sheets." Waggling brows accompanied his sexy grin. "Though I do like you between them too."

She smiled back at him, and he blinked.

"You have a dimple in your cheek."

She nodded.

"How did I miss that before?"

As he kissed her there, the outside world intruded on them with a deep rolling thunder that gained momentum and decibels as it neared the cabin. When it cracked overhead, the house shuddered on its foundations.

The lovely mood Seamus had been creating shattered in the moment as Fallon nearly jumped off his lap. He pulled her back down and said, "Whatever has Taranis's shorts in a knot is out there. We're safe in here, I promise."

"Sorry, Seamus. I can't help it. This whole weekend I've had this weird dread that when the storm ends, our problems are going to begin. I don't think Taranis is serving notice that his tantrum is intensifying. I think he's letting us know that our time is almost up."

Seamus lightly stroked her thigh. "Fallon, your sense of

foreboding is so tangible I think I could almost gather it up and put it in a bag." He chuckled at his own joke, but she didn't.

"If only it were that easy."

He sighed. "Since you didn't grow up with them, it's understandable you don't trust the druidic protections Siobhan places on this cabin regularly. But you need to trust in them—and me—if we're going to have a snowball's chance in hell of denying Maeve and Morgan their prizes."

She snuggled into his chest. "You have to know that I'm trying."

"As soon as this storm lets up, we'll hike out of here and head up to the Sheridans' compound on Flathead Lake." He kissed the side of her head. "They have a training room where we can practice scenarios and maybe even train with Scathach. We'll figure out your skill before Maeve puts us to the test." He hugged her close. "Your premonition is a possibility, not a fact. Have some faith."

She relaxed a fraction when a series of sonic booms tore up the atmosphere, followed seconds later by lightning strikes that lit up the interior of the cabin like klieg lights. Something had Taranis in a towering temper. Tangling her fingers in Seamus's shirt, she curled into a ball on his lap.

"This isn't the first time I've appreciated my sister's skills with protection spells, especially in light of Taranis's bad attitude."

The hairs on Fallon's neck stood up as she clung to Seamus and hoped he was right.

CHAPTER TWELVE

"MAEVE, ARE YOU even concentrating?" Taranis demanded. Though he was buried to the hilt inside her, she sensed his mood strangely bordered on surly. "When I share pleasure with you in your bed, I expect to be the center of your attention. This experience is proving—mechanical."

"We're having sex. Of course I'm concentrating," Maeve retorted as she rocked herself on him. "Why are you in such a mood?"

"Because you are pleasuring me but you are not all in. I don't want your honor or faithfulness to me," he sneered, "but I would not mind your *focus* on me when you are riding my cock."

"Are you jealous?" Her lips stretched in a smile. "How delicious. Is that why you are expending unnecessary energy on storms wherever you have unleashed them when you could be directing all that power inside me?" she taunted him and tightened her inner muscles in a vicelike grip around his member.

Taranis drove up into her again and continued to press his point. "I am not jealous. I'm a god after all. No mere warrior can satisfy you the way I do." She relaxed her grip on him slightly as he thrust more deeply into her. "But I do appreciate being the only male in the room—in every sense of the word—when I am with a female, goddess or mortal. I need more from you than going through the motions."

"I think I like you when you are being petulant, darling." Her dig produced the desired effect when he roared and surged so deeply inside her his momentum bordered on pain. Just the way she liked it.

"I. Am. Not. Petulant," Taranis gritted out, punctuating each word with a hard thrust deep inside her. He gripped her hips, effectively taking away her control and demanding she return his pleasure.

Smiling ferally at him, she palmed her breasts and plucked her distended nipples, using her hands to bounce her breasts even more than Taranis's mighty thrusts were doing. Watching her through narrowed eyes, he clamped down on her hips even harder—had she been mortal, he would have left bruises on her body—and finished in a frenzy.

"Wretched wench," he said panting. "That cost me the lovely monsoon I'd unleashed on Indonesia." He glared at her. "You know I dislike it when other gods dictate my play."

"Taranis, my pet. You are too easy." When he pressed his thumb to her clitoris, she shrieked. "Do you think to test me, my lord?"

Taranis paid no attention to the fire in her tone as he stared smugly into Maeve's eyes. "You see. It's always better when you concentrate, Maeve." His eyes bore into hers as he deliberately lifted her off him and dropped her unceremoniously beside him on the bed so he could stand and stretch. His actions indicated a dismissal that enraged her. She flew off the bed and grabbed him by his chiseled arms.

Quick as a thought, she bound his wrists with the silken cord hanging from the massive oak bedposts. "We are not finished here, *my lord.*" She nodded at the cord that magically wound itself around the post, pulling Taranis back to the bed where he sat down with a thump.

"It is fine for you to ignore me when we are in the middle of things, but you do not appreciate the same treatment, Maeve?" Taranis taunted her as he spread his legs wide, inviting her to enjoy him again, though he regarded her through wary storm-silver eyes.

"If it were not for the fact you please me so well, I think I would banish you to some outer planet where your storms would have no consequence," Maeve said as she lowered herself to her knees in front of him. Letting her glorious auburn hair fall forward to veil her face, she hid her carnal reaction to Taranis's undeniable invitation.

"As if you could." He snorted. His tone belied the telltale tensing of his muscles beneath her hands where she rested them on his thighs.

"Never underestimate me, Taranis," she whispered before she sheathed his erect phallus in her mouth.

Intending to teach him a lesson about the extent of her power, she teased him by denying him her whole mouth after her initial promise. When she sneaked a peek at his face, she smiled at the beads of sweat dotting his forehead and the ruddy color riding high on his cheeks from the exertion of withholding his climax from her. The tenseness of his jaw as he gritted his teeth in an attempt to control his body's responses encouraged her, and she rubbed and rolled his balls then feathered her fingertips over his cock from base to tip. He rewarded her with a pearlescent drop she lapped up like a cat at a basin of cream.

Triumph surged through her when at last Taranis ground out, "However you plan to take me this time, Maeve, do it *now.*"

She stood up, turned around, and backed up to position

herself over him. As she impaled herself on him, Morgan strolled through the door of Maeve's elaborate bedroom.

"Oh dear. It appears I am interrupting. Pity." Morgan's tone implied she was anything but sorry about walking in on them.

Taranis took advantage of Maeve's momentary focus on Morgan to surge deeply into her.

She emitted a rather unfeminine grunt as she took all of him inside her, clamping down on him in a most pleasurable fashion.

"Of course, Taranis. Of course, you should continue what you are doing. It is so much more important than impeding a warrior from finding his talisman in time. Your recent tantrum in a certain northwestern state has contributed rather effectively to the bonding of a warrior Maeve particularly prizes," Morgan said airily while she selected a chair from among several plush choices and settled in to watch Maeve and Taranis together.

Maeve enjoyed an audience to witness her pleasure. She knew Morgan also enjoyed watching, especially when Maeve took a civilian or a warrior since Morgan knew she would enjoy her own orgasm afterward when she escorted the mortal across the ford. With her focus on the satisfaction Taranis was giving her, and on showing off for her new audience, she didn't pay much attention to what Morgan was actually saying.

Taranis interrupted her thoughts. "I do enjoy Maeve's lusty pleasures. However, if you want to join us, Morgan, that would please me too."

He must have sensed the shift in her mood because he drove hard and fast into her, determined to come. In her distracted state, she recognized his intention a fraction too late, and he went off like a fountain inside her.

"Bravo, Taranis! Bravo! You know of course it may take her years to forgive you for what you did just now in this room and for what you're doing in the mountains of Montana," Morgan said, an evil grin spreading over her features. "After the way the two of you abandoned me at Samhain, it is only fitting you are engaged with each other while a certain warrior Maeve covets bonds with his talisman."

The beginnings of a tantrum vibrated through Maeve, but Morgan apparently didn't care because she kept talking. "After all, if I cannot have my prizes, I do not see why you should have yours."

With her attention on Morgan, she forgot about the silken cords with which she bound Taranis, and they slipped from his wrists. Carelessly leaving her unsatisfied, he lifted her off himself, stood, stretched, and walked purposefully over to her dressing room where he retrieved a plush robe of charcoal-colored velvet. She might have appreciated the way the nap of the fabric caught the light and resembled a gathering storm cloud whenever he moved except for the throbbing ache of unrequited lust between her legs and Morgan's bombshell.

Facing him, she demanded, "Have you deliberately distracted me while I missed out on a mortal prize?" She fisted her hands on her hips, her breasts heaving as angry breath sawed in and out of her lungs. In the moment, she couldn't make up her mind where to direct her rage. At Taranis for not letting her finish? At Morgan's disturbing news? At Taranis's ill-conceived storm that allowed a warrior a chance to escape?

An otherworldly scream tore from her throat.

"What is the matter, dear? You seem to be having trouble responding. I, too, have had Taranis, but as fantastic as he is, I do not remember him leaving me incapable of coherent thought." Morgan winked at Taranis. "Then again, it has been awhile for us, has it not, Taranis?"

The storm god regarded Morgan from beneath hooded eyelids and said nothing.

Morgan gave a bored wave of her hand toward the dressing

room. "Maeve, darling, put something on. It is rather tiring the way you like to show off."

"Oh, I don't know, Morgan," Taranis drawled. "The sheen of sex-induced sweat illuminates her curves rather beautifully."

In spite of her anger, Maeve couldn't help but preen at his compliment.

He glanced at the wall where a series of paintings of couples in various states of coitus hung. "Like the art in this room, I would rather Maeve remain in her current state of undress. Her mortal body should remain on display for the enjoyment of others—especially me."

After the way he'd left her hanging, his comment made her spitting mad, but she directed her vitriol at Morgan. "Where in Montana did you say Taranis unleashed a mighty storm?" The passion of her tone had the desired effect on the other two deities in the room, causing both of them to pause their taunts.

At last Morgan answered. "In the mountains very near that blasted Rowan Sheridan's residence." She leaned back into her chair.

"Are you saying to me that *Seamus Lochlann* has discovered his talisman?" Maeve asked. Though her voice dropped even lower than a whisper, its intensity carried her words to every corner of the room.

"In a word—yes," Morgan replied. The glee in her smile was obscene.

Maeve flew at Taranis, pounding her fists on his massive chest in an otherworldly rage. "How could you do this to me? You were sooo jealous. You could not stand it that I lusted after a mortal warrior. You think him inferior to you, but I want him!" She stomped her bare foot rather ineffectually on the thick carpet. "I want him! I will kill him in my bed eventually, so it is not like I am replacing you. You are so selfish, Taranis!"

It took Taranis several seconds to grab her wrists and hold

her away from him to stop her bruising onslaught. "I am most definitely *not* jealous of a warrior, madam. The big monsoon I unleashed on the South Pacific did not drain off enough energy. So, I turned some rain loose on the Rockies for the hell of it." He shrugged. "Montana is not the only area enjoying a display of my power. If we had not been so rudely interrupted"—he sneered at Morgan—"I may have had to shift my energy from my storms in the Rocky Mountains to other, more interesting pursuits."

"Now you are blaming me for your screwup? That is rich, Taranis," Morgan scoffed. "However, I am rather surprised you chose to interfere with Maeve's plans for Seamus Lochlann."

Taranis sighed, creating a gust of wind that rattled the windows of Maeve's warehouse stronghold. "For the last time, I did not deliberately create a storm to help Lochlann or any warrior find his talisman." He glanced up at the ceiling and muttered, "Too bad goddesses are such a pain in the ass outside the sheets. Eternity is a long time to spend with a pair of carping harpies."

"What did you say?" Morgan asked.

Maeve had more pressing concerns than Taranis's insults. "When did Seamus discover his talisman? Have they bonded completely?"

After scowling at Taranis, Morgan returned her attention to Maeve. "I believe they have only been together a few days." She plucked a grape from the bowl on the table beside her chair and popped it into her mouth. "However, there is powerful magic associated with this particular talisman. She comes from the Conlan clan on the warrior side, but she possesses the traits of a druid."

"Are you saying she might be a bard?" Maeve's voice climbed an octave on the last word.

"It appears she might be exactly that," Morgan replied casually as she fingered a chocolate truffle on a tray beside the bowl of fruit.

Maeve threw her hands into the air and paced the room. "I

truly do not understand what Danu was thinking when she created mortals with the ability to change history with a perfectly structured story. Once they discover their particular skill, they become insufferable."

Taranis seated himself in the chair across the table from Morgan. "You mean, they stop you from having your fun," he corrected as he perused the sensual treats on offer, selecting a delicate strawberry and taking a jaw-snapping bite of it.

Maeve stopped pacing directly in front of him. "Do you think it acceptable that a mere mortal can function at the level of a god, Taranis?" Her tone barely concealed her rage.

"Do not put words into my mouth. I am merely pointing out that if Seamus Lochlann is bonded to a bard, you may have your opportunity to enjoy him, but you will not be able to spend him in your bed unless you take his talisman or render her incapable of using her skill before you take him."

"Where are they, Morgan?" she asked as she donned a silken robe of deep purple trimmed with black sable.

"In a heavily enchanted cabin in the mountains of south-central Montana. Quite near the Sheridans." Morgan spat out that last part.

"We will need to lure them out of it." She tied the sash tightly around her tiny waist. "Once they are beyond the safety of the enchantments, they will be easy to target." She tapped her chin. "A gang war here in LA worked to bring the Sheridans to us in the past. Perhaps we need another." She glanced at the storm god. "You might think about returning to my good graces, Taranis, by ending the storm you unleashed in the Rockies." She was not making a suggestion.

Taranis stuffed his mouth with a chocolate-covered caramel.

"You do remember the outcome of that little gang war distraction, do you not, sister?"

"Well, then, we will have to devise a different plan," Maeve snapped at Morgan as she planted her fists on her hips.

Morgan's tone was sly. "Taranis could draw them out with a mist. There is a lake located conveniently near the Lochlann cabin that would do nicely for such a trick." She helped herself to another of the ambrosial truffles on the tray between Taranis and her.

"That is a rather low suggestion, do you not think, Morgan?" he asked. "While I too enjoy besting mortals, it is more fun when they have a sporting chance to succeed." Very ungodlike, he licked chocolate from his fingers, and in spite of herself, Maeve felt her body quicken as she watched him. "Even monumental storms like hurricanes and blizzards offer courageous and enterprising mortals a bit of a chance to survive. A mist of the kind Morgan suggests ensures the mortals' failure."

"For a god of your proven ferocity, Taranis, you sometimes worry me with your soft spot for warriors. Your performance at Samhain is a prime example," Morgan said, returning to her insufferably favorite topic. "When I needed you to call the mists, you were busying yourself trying to lure talismans to your bed. When they did not fall for your ruse, you settled for a couple of civilian mortals and completely neglected your promise to help me."

"I called up the mists, Morgan. When I saw that your zombies were not up to the task of taking the Sheridans, I sought my own entertainments." His tone was lazy as he directed his attention to the bowl of fruit. "Had I been successful with the talismans, you would have had your victory after I finished pleasuring them to death. You conveniently forget that part." He popped a cherry into his mouth.

Stretching out his legs, he allowed his robe to fall open, drawing Maeve's attention to his crotch. "Exactly what happened between the two of you at Samhain? And do you intend to let your problems with each other interfere with my plans for Seamus Lochlann?"

Taranis shrugged while Morgan shot daggers at him with her eyes.

Changing her tack, Maeve stepped over beside his chair and ran one finger down his bicep. "Taranis, I hope you have decided to end the storm you unleashed. I am sure the good people of Montana have had enough of your tantrum for the moment."

He cocked his head and shot her the side-eye. "I will only let up if you promise not to banish me from your bed for the foreseeable future, madam."

She fisted her hands at her sides, giving up all hint of pretense. "I see how it is with you. If I insist on taking some of your power, you will insist on having some of mine. Very well. However, I cannot guarantee you will *enjoy* yourself in my bed."

He smiled. "I always enjoy myself in your bed, *my lady*. Now if you will excuse me, I have a storm to tend." On that parting note, he disappeared into a silver-gray shower of raindrops that evaporated almost immediately.

CHAPTER THIRTEEN

"*WHAT IS IT, Sloane?*"

"*We need to talk, girlfriend. Is now a good time?*"

"*Actually, yes. It'll take my mind off the fact that I think Taranis is trying to kill us.*" Fallon didn't even attempt to hide her fear. The storm god's terrifying display had shaken her to her core.

"*What are you saying?*"

She could hear Sloane's concern through time and space. "*A few minutes ago, he sent a lightning bolt through a tree beside the cabin. Half of it fell only a couple of feet from the steps of the front porch. Thunder has been crashing ceaselessly over the cabin for the last half hour. We are* not *having a good time here.*"

She glanced at Seamus who was inspecting the ceiling for possible leaks.

"*Hang tough, girl. The cavalry is massing as we speak. There's a whole group of warriors, talismans, and druids coming to the rescue if you can hang on through the night.*"

Fallon's pulse kicked up as she sank her fingers into the cushions of the couch on either side of her. "*Please tell me you're not coming. This is too dangerous a place for a lone talisman whose warrior hasn't found her yet."*

"Yeah, the others thought so too. I'm staying behind to man the fort, so to speak. But I thought you'd like to know that your bonding time will be cut short. By the way, Griff and Keela are part of the rescue party. Nice people. I like them a lot."

Fallon shot off the couch. *"Griff and Keela are with you? How? What? How did that happen?"*

"Apparently your warrior's friend's wife is one of Griff's colleagues at the university."

"Hello? Griff works at the university? The same one we attended? The same one where I work? *How can that be?"* Without thinking about what she was doing, she walked into the bedroom and retrieved her bracelet from the nightstand where she'd left it.

"He's a druid, Fallon. You know they're capable of all kinds of sleights of hand. Anyway, I wanted to warn you so you didn't freak out when everyone arrives sometime tomorrow. They're leaving at first light no matter what the weather is."

Fallon slipped the cuff bracelet onto her wrist and returned to the living room where she found Seamus's midnight blue eyes studying her intently.

"Who all is coming here tomorrow?"

"Your aunt and uncle, Seamus's sister and her husband, and Seamus's friend Rowan and his wife Alyssa. As cavalries go, you're lucky to have such a good one."

"That doesn't leave us much time to discover my skill," she communicated to her best friend, but her eyes were on Seamus.

"You haven't managed that yet? Wonder why." There was mischief in Sloane's tone.

"Knock it off, Sloane. I'm not giving you any details, at least not telepathically." Her exasperation with her friend was only a momentary distraction before she returned to the subject that troubled her. *"I have no idea how to go about figuring out my skill."*

"Your warrior's sister says there are lots of books at the cabin. Maybe you should try reading the stories of Rhiannon. Remember how you used to change her story with a hero—me—stumbling in on the maids as they disposed of her son's body? Think about that," Sloane suggested.

"You think that will help?" Fallon's tone wavered between sarcasm and hope.

"Couldn't hurt, unless it gets in the way of all the bonding you seem to be doing." The smirk in her friend's voice was clear.

"Your turn's coming. I hope I can remember to be nice."

Something changed, and Fallon heard it in the sobering of Sloane's tone as she said, *"Give it a try, will you? Maybe it will help you, maybe it won't, but trying the stories is a place to start at least."*

"Yeah, yeah, all right. I'll give it a go. Thanks for the suggestion."

"Good. I'll talk to you soon."

✄

Seamus pulled Fallon down onto his lap in the big chair by the fireplace. "Who's had your attention for so long?" Though she lay quietly in his arms, the tight coils of her muscles made her anything but soft and pliant.

"Sloane. She said the cavalry's coming tomorrow no matter what the weather is." She looked into his eyes. "Aunt Keela and Uncle Griff are among those who are coming. They've been living near me in town, and I never even knew it." Her voice drifted away on her last words.

He massaged the nape of her neck, as much because he needed to touch her as because he wanted to reassure her. "That bothers you?"

"Yeah." She blew out a breath. "I know they don't want to cause problems for me with my parents, but I'm an adult now. I guess I can socialize with who I want."

He let that go. "You said the cavalry. Who else is coming?"

"Lots of people. Most of them I don't know."

Seamus cocked a brow. "Excuse me for a minute. I need to know."

Closing his eyes, he opened his shield to his best friend. *"Hey buddy, you there?"*

Rowan must have been waiting for him because he responded immediately. *"Yeah. We're plotting your rescue."* Laughter colored his voice.

"Rescue from what? I'm enjoying weathering one helluva storm with my beautiful talisman in the safety of an exceptionally enchanted cabin. No rescue needed—or wanted," Seamus warned.

"I was pretty sure you'd react that way. Seems I had a similar reaction." The laughter left his voice. *"But like Alyssa and me, there are forces greater than you at play here, and you're going to need some help, probably sooner rather than later."*

"What are you talking about?"

"Can't give you too many details—unless you've discovered Fallon's skill?"

He cuddled the woman in question closer to his chest. *"Not yet, but what does that have to do with anything? We've only been together a little over twenty-four hours. Even you didn't figure out Alyssa's skill that fast."*

"You need to concentrate your efforts on discovering her skill, old son. The bonding will still be there once you've done that."

He didn't miss the concern beneath the teasing words. *"You know something about Fallon. Say it."*

"Can't, at least not without jeopardizing your connection with her. Like the rest of us, you've got to figure this one out together— like now."

"Thanks for the comforting words." Fallon shifted on his lap, her expression one of question, but in her eyes, there was fear. Seamus changed the subject. *"Who's coming with you tomorrow? Fallon said something about the cavalry."* Rowan's urgency had him

more than spooked, but he didn't want to alarm either his friend or his talisman.

"Alyssa and me, and Siobhan and Duncan, of course, and Fallon's aunt and uncle. You met them at my wedding, Griffin and Keela Walsh. Griff was Alyssa's master's degree mentor. Alaisdair and Shanley are staying behind with your talisman's friend Sloane but will be ready reinforcements if we need them."

Seamus couldn't help himself. He wrapped an arm tightly around Fallon's waist and squeezed her thigh with his other hand. *Reinforcements if they needed them? What the hell?* But Rowan wasn't finished.

"By the way, it appears you're about to become related to the Grahams since they are distant cousins to your talisman. Alasdair and Shanley want to send some of their Conlan protections to Fallon and you."

He sighed. *"This is serious. I wish you'd tell me what's going on."*

"Wish I could, buddy. Maybe by the time we arrive, you'll have it figured out. While you're working on Fallon's skill, you might consider giving her some extra training on shielding. Remember how Maeve used Alyssa's incomplete shield against her?" Rowan asked.

Even though he knew his friend couldn't see him, he nodded. *"See you tomorrow."*

"Yeah."

Unconsciously, Seamus rubbed his palm up and down Fallon's thigh. The two of them must be the epicenter of yet another curse or enchantment the nasty ladies wanted to keep intact. What the hell could it be?

"Maybe we'll find the answer in the myths," Fallon suggested.

"Now *you* are invading *my* head? Were you listening to my conversation with Rowan?" he asked, finding himself less than happy to have the tables turned on him.

"I only tuned in when I felt your body relax a little, so I was pretty sure you were the only one in your head." She shrugged.

"Hmmm. You didn't like it much when I breached your shield?" she asked, her expression mischievous.

"Point taken." He smirked. "Maybe we should train on that some."

She grinned back.

"According to Rowan, the cabin is going to be full tomorrow night. Which means we don't have much time to try to figure out your skill. Any ideas?"

"Sloane said I should read the old myths, especially the story of Rhiannon. Is that somewhere on your bookshelves?" She stood and walked over to the cabin library lining the back wall of the great room.

He unfolded himself from his comfortable place in the chair and joined her in perusing the spines of the books his family had left there. "Can't imagine it's not here. Siobhan can't be anywhere where she doesn't have her books to consult." He spied an intriguing tome. "Here's a copy of a history of warrior and talisman pairs. Maybe we'll find something in it that will help us." He pulled the book from the shelf and settled himself on the couch to read it.

"Found it. *Myths and Legends of Albion, Eire, and Wales,*" Fallon announced as she pulled a fat hardcover from the shelves.

Snuggling between Seamus and the back cushions of the couch, Fallon lay back against his shoulder. Both of them opened their books and began to read.

⌘

Seamus put down his book and turned his head from side to side, rolling his neck and shoulders. "Find anything yet?"

"I've reread this tale three times, and I can't figure out what Sloane was trying to tell me by suggesting I read it. Have you found anything?"

"Not yet. But I did notice the fire has burned down. I'll take a break and stoke it. How 'bout you fix us something to drink?"

"Hot chocolate suit you?" She stood and stretched. Only when she was no longer reading did she notice how stiff she'd become after lying on the couch for hours.

"Hot chocolate's fine," he called over his shoulder as he headed out the door to the woodpile.

Padding over to the pantry, Fallon noticed the rain had let up. When Seamus came back inside the cabin with an armload of wood, he exchanged a look with her confirming her observations.

"Taranis is backing off. How much time do you think we have?" she asked.

"Like I said before, I don't think Taranis's tantrum has anything to do with us. The time we have is dictated by our well-meaning but meddlesome family and friends, not the gods."

"I hope you're right. Especially since our family and friends seem to know things about us that we don't know yet." Though she tried, Fallon couldn't keep the bitterness out of her tone. Uncle Griff and Aunt Keela would have some things to answer for when they arrived.

As Seamus banked the fire, he said, "Maybe the answer isn't in the story itself. Maybe the answer is in your experience with the story. Is the Rhiannon story one you and Sloane used to read together when your parents didn't know?"

"Yes," she replied slowly as she pulled two mugs from the cupboard. "More than that though. We used to act that one out. I used to have to change it a little so Sloane and I could both be heroic."

He walked over to the kitchen and leaned against the counter. "What do you mean, 'change it a little'?"

"I'd retell it the way we wanted it to be rather than the way it was. Sloane would watch as the maids disposed of Rhiannon's son, and then when I, playing the part of Rhiannon, would protest my innocence before my husband, the maids would tell their lies to implicate me, and Sloane would step in and save me." She reached around him to grab a spoon from the drawer. "I'd punish the maids, resurrect my son, and fly away from my husband who had so little faith in me."

"Did your stories always have happy endings?" he asked with a smile.

"For the characters we liked." She smirked. "Those we didn't like suffered even more in my retellings than in the original stories."

Seamus crossed his arms over his chest and waited.

"For example, the maids stood in for Rhiannon and knelt in the muck of the courtyard to be mounting blocks for the heaviest of the warriors until they could no longer remain on their hands and knees. They were trampled into the mud and left to rot."

"Vicious. Remind me not to piss you off in any serious way," he said, laughing.

"Exactly right, bucko, and don't you forget it," she replied, punctuating each word with the teaspoon she'd used to measure chocolate mix into the mugs.

He grabbed the spoon from her hand, set it on the counter, and took her into his arms. "How long until that hot chocolate is ready?"

"When the teapot whistles. Why?" With her hands braced on his chest, she looked up at him suspiciously.

"Then we have time to make out. Rowan suggested I should save bonding time until after we've discovered your skill, but he didn't say anything against a little kissing and touching." Seamus buried his face in Fallon's neck, kissing a trail from the base of her ear to her collarbone and back up.

She shivered at his touch. "Why does your friend think he can dictate our bonding for us?"

"Don't know. Something about us being in the middle of another situation that's not going to sit well with the goddesses when we best them again," he said as he ran his hands down her back, caught the hem of her shirt, and slipped them underneath it to caress her naked skin.

The tea kettle whistled shrilly, tearing apart the web of desire Seamus was trying so attentively to weave.

"Damn! I thought I had more time. Doesn't it take water longer to boil at this elevation?" he asked, glaring at the teapot.

"It appears even inanimate objects are siding with your friend. Wonder if there's a conspiracy here," Fallon said with a grin as she disengaged herself from her warrior and set about pouring hot water over the chocolate powder in the bottoms of their mugs.

Seamus heaved a dramatic sigh. "Guess it's back to the old grindstone. But I'm giving you fair warning—I'm not spending the rest of the night with my nose in a book. Somewhere before we're rudely interrupted tomorrow, we're going to enjoy some naked time." He punctuated his "threat" with a hard kiss on her mouth before he carried his hot chocolate back to the couch and their books.

CHAPTER FOURTEEN

ONDAY DAWNED WITH an annoying drizzle as family and friends met at the Sheridans' mountain home. After loading Rowan's black crew-cab pickup and Griff's Range Rover with their laden backpacks, the Sheridans, the MacManuses, who had been joined by Duncan's talisman Jennifer Carlin, and the Walshes waved good-bye to Sloane MacIntosh and the Grahams who were staying at the Sheridans' home during their absence. Shadow, Alyssa's Great Pyrenees, pushed between Alasdair and Shanley at the front door and yipped once for his mistress before retreating inside the house.

Alyssa said, "I hope he's saying 'good luck' not 'watch out,'" as she climbed in beside Rowan who would lead the party to the trailhead.

He reached over the console and squeezed her knee. "Have a little faith, Pixie-girl. We're the good guys, remember?"

She shot him a side-eye as she buckled herself in.

A short drive later, the company arrived at the trailhead where Rowan saw only two vehicles parked in the lot—Seamus's SUV and a sedan that must have been Fallon's.

"That's a good sign, their cars parked together here," Keela said after the crew gathered in front of their vehicles.

"You're a romantic, my love." Griff gave his wife a one-armed hug before he headed to the back of their rig to retrieve their packs.

As he unlocked the tonneau cover on the bed of his truck and lowered the tailgate, Rowan listened to their conversation.

"The gods know what they're doing when they pair warriors and talismans," Keela said.

"This pair makes me wonder if there isn't some payback here on Danu's part for both Morgan and Maeve seducing the Dagda at one time or another," Griff added as he handed Keela her pack.

"Or some atonement on the Dagda's part for succumbing to those seductions," she replied.

"Maybe they want to create parity for warriors who have to take on unscrupulous immortals with nasty agendas and ancient vendettas," Rowan said as he buckled on his pack.

"Only if we best them again, which is going to take serious skill and a bit of luck. We're pushing the odds this time, I think." Duncan said as he walked around the front of Rowan's truck after he helped Jennifer with her gear. She'd been a late addition to the party, but one the MacManuses had insisted on. Duncan strapped a folding cot to his backpack to accommodate her when they reached the cabin.

"Point taken," Rowan replied as he helped Alyssa shrug on her pack.

Siobhan's anxiety for her brother manifested in her impatient pacing in front of the turnstile that opened the way onto the trail. "I've got a great idea—how 'bout if we speculate as we hike? Taranis has nearly blown himself out of here, so my guess is we're on borrowed time we can't waste."

"Hey, hey, hey, sweet girl, slow down. Nobody is wasting time here," Duncan said as he walked up to his wife and gave her a swift kiss. "We're all anxious for Seamus same as you are. Go on. Lead the way."

Whatever retort she had in mind, Siobhan blew it out in a huffy sigh, turned on her heel, and zig-zagged through the turnstile, setting a punishing pace up the trail. Though she was a druid, she trained with warriors and talismans regularly, including Rowan and Alyssa on several occasions. Her fitness showed in her seemingly effortless, ground-eating strides. Whatever Morgan and Maeve had in mind for her brother, it was obvious to Rowan that she was determined to stop it.

⸙

Fallon woke up alone in bed, Seamus's pillow cold to her touch. Not hearing any movement inside the cabin told her she was there alone. Her terrible vision flashed in her head for a second. In a panic, she bounded out of bed to hunt for her clothes.

"Hey, hey, Fireworks. What set you off?"

It took her a few seconds to register that Seamus was in the room and speaking to her. Tangled in her sweater, her long underwear stuck at her knees, she must have looked ridiculous. She stopped moving and peeked out from the folds of her sweater to see him leaning against the doorframe, massive arms crossed over his chest and grinning at her alarm.

"You're here!"

His grin flipped into a frown. "Of course, I'm here. Where else would I be?"

"You could have woken me to let me know you were going out to get wood." Her breathless response made her sound petulant to her own ears rather than indignant, so she settled on glaring at him.

"Why would I do that? You were so beautiful sleeping there, all that gorgeous auburn hair spread over the pillow, your face relaxed, a smile playing on your pretty mouth." He pushed away from the door and stepped farther into the room. "Honestly, I spent quite some time staring at you until I remembered I hadn't banked the fire again before we went to bed last night." He traced her cheek with his index finger. "Actually, I was hoping to wake you slowly—and pleasurably this morning. Since you're not quite dressed"—he indicated her nakedness between her chest and her knees with a nod of his head and a waggle of his brows—"maybe I can still rouse you the way I planned."

"What if our family arrives when we're—"

"You know how long a hike it is back here. We have hours yet before they arrive." He pulled her into his arms.

Fallon tried to sidestep him, but her long underwear around her knees tripped her up, and before she knew it, Seamus had lifted her high in his arms and carried her back to bed.

"What about working some more on trying to discover my skill?" she asked on a puff of air when Seamus dropped her onto the bed.

"What about it? I'm bonding with you. Seems a much better use of our time than poring through old books looking for answers." As he spoke, he tugged Fallon's long underwear off her legs. When she sat up to stop him, he grabbed the hem of her sweater and yanked it up off her arms, leaving her naked before him.

"Bonding hasn't helped us either," she said, desire pooling between her thighs as she watched Seamus shuck his jeans and flannel shirt.

"Maybe not, but bonding brings us and keeps us close to each other, and that's gotta be a good thing."

He demonstrated by climbing on top of her, wrapping his arms around her, and rolling them both over so she lay atop him. Before she could form the idea of sliding off him, he took her face in his big hands, stared deeply into her eyes, and opened his mind to her. *You're everything to me. I don't know how that happened so fast, but there it is. Stay with me, my beautiful Fallon."* He guided her mouth to his and kissed her gently, his lips brushing hers before he increased the pressure. Then he touched his tongue to the seam of her mouth, a silent plea to be allowed in.

His words, his trust, his touch overwhelmed her, and she knew two things: one, she couldn't resist him, and two, she didn't want to resist him. When she relaxed and opened for him, he traced her lips with his tongue, and she sighed in surrender.

CHAPTER FIFTEEN

"WHAT DO YOU plan to do, sister?" Morgan asked as she irritated Maeve by reclining indolently against the arm of the chaise lounge in Maeve's great room. "Staging a gang war here with a bunch of civilians and some rogue or zombie warriors is not likely to draw in your prize. He has been down here for that too many times in the past."

"I *know* that, Morgan. Somehow, I have to lure him out of that enchanted fortress his conniving sister made of that old cabin. Truly, I cannot understand why Danu and the Dagda gave so much power to mortals that they can keep us out of their homes," Maeve complained.

"Taranis stopped the mountain storm after he left here last night. Perhaps they are on the trail out of the cabin even now."

Maeve stomped her foot. "Do you know something else I do not?"

Morgan waved her hand lazily. "Not at all. Merely speculating. Why don't you look into your cauldron to see exactly what they *are* doing?"

Maeve didn't trust her sister, but the suggestion was

sound. Trying not to appear too eager, she glided gracefully from the room and forced herself to saunter languidly down the hall to her conservatory where she kept her magic cauldron and the plants she needed to feed it. She sensed Morgan standing up to follow her and realized her sister wanted to know as much as she did about what the warriors were doing.

With studied care, Maeve selected two long brown beans from her castor bush, several leaves from her nightshade plant, and a lovely fat berry from the belladonna she grew in pots around the room. She added these ingredients to the cauldron she kept in a continuous roiling boil and waited with outward patience for the bubbles of the brew to reveal the secrets she wished to know. Like the spell churning in the cauldron, she seethed at the turn events had taken. If she'd acted on her first impulse a year and a half ago, Seamus Lochlann would be a distant, albeit pleasant, memory rather than the current irritating itch she desperately wanted to scratch.

Morgan glided up beside her and gazed into the brew with obscene avidity. "What do you see, Maeve?"

"Nothing yet. Perhaps I need to add another belladonna berry," Maeve said though she never took her eyes from the frothing concoction.

In time, a fat bubble floated above the popping and spitting contents of the enormous pot, and Maeve willed herself into a trance to watch what went on in another part of the world. What she saw made her blood boil almost as hotly as her cauldron. Seamus Lochlann had indeed found his talisman, an auburn-haired woman with intriguing hazel eyes. Her body moved sensuously as she rode Seamus in his bed inside his family's cabin. The smile on his face revealed more than his physical pleasure. This woman, with a body not unlike the one Maeve preferred in her mortal state, not only controlled Seamus Lochlann's body, but also his heart.

Quelling her initial jealousy of the talisman in Seamus's bed, Maeve turned her thoughts to her own pleasure. She too would ride Seamus in a tormenting re-creation of the scene she now witnessed. She would ride him until he looked at her the way he looked at the inferior mortal, and then she would release him to Morgan to take naked into the mists. If his stamina proved to be as great as his battle prowess implied, she could look forward to at least two or three days of him in her bed.

A gasp beside her brought her out of her reverie, and she remembered rather waspishly that she was not alone. "What is it, Morgan? What have you seen that causes you to interrupt my plotting so rudely?"

"Rowan and Alyssa Sheridan are exposed on the trail to the Lochlann cabin." Her eyes glowed red. "They are in the company of Siobhan and Duncan MacManus, Jennifer Carlin, and Griffin and Keela Walsh. The trail is muddy and slick from Taranis's tantrum, and they are burdened by large packs. It seems your dilemma for luring out your prize has solved itself."

"What do you mean?" Though annoyed with her sister, the scene Morgan described intrigued her.

"Perhaps Taranis helped us after all. The ground is soft, wet, and slick. It will impede the warriors in battle. If we can talk Taranis into adding to the mists left over from his storm, we can use them to hide our rogues and zombies from the warriors and their talismans. I can unleash one or two of my zombie champions, something of the *Nephilim*, say Gorm and Cormoran, perhaps even Bolster, the Cornish giants who caused so much havoc in their day." Morgan rubbed her hands together with undignified relish. "Seamus will have no choice but to come to the aid of his friends."

Suspicion lodged itself in Maeve's chest. "Why are you so eager to help me when yesterday you were only too willing to leave me on my own after you thought I 'slighted' you on Samhain?"

"I was perfectly happy to leave you to your own devices, but that was before the Sheridans became involved. No matter how you lure him, you will derive the greatest pleasure from Seamus Lochlann, and I will have only his leftovers. With the Sheridans in the picture, I have a chance both at revenge and additional blood in the ford as I escort them into the mists." Her feral smile bared her evil anticipation. "Who knows, maybe Owen and Sian Sheridan will join the party when they realize their children are in peril, and my orgasmic traverse through the ford will exceed even your own delight."

Maeve glared at her.

"Since when did this little party become about you, Morgan?" Maeve planted her hands on her hips and faced her sister goddess. "You've had your chances, and while I like this battle plan to attack along the trail, the focus is on capturing Seamus Lochlann and spending him in my bed. Taking the Sheridans is *not* the priority here." When she watched Morgan's eyes narrow, she softened her tone. "You can have Seamus's talisman. I doubt she will want to live after she sees Seamus give himself to me completely."

Morgan crossed her arms and sneered at Maeve's suggestion.

Maeve didn't budge. "Give me your word that once I have Seamus, you will call off your zombie giants." Squaring her shoulders, she added, "Besides, if you take the Sheridans all at once, who will you have left to pursue? Even an orgasm as drawn out and intense as one that involved wading through the blood of so many warriors, it would be a finite experience, one you'll need more warriors to re-create. Take a Sheridan if you can, but stop the battle once I have captured Seamus."

Morgan huffed out a breath. "You are correct. If I take the entire group at once, I will deprive myself of future fun." Idly, she ran her fingertips over various poisonous plants as she paced the room. "Then again, if I take Rowan and his father, perhaps the

Sheridan twins, Rio and Riley, will expose themselves foolishly and I will be able to enjoy their defeat as well."

In a fit of pique, Maeve stomped her foot, dropped her silky manner, and snarled. "I will find another way to take Seamus if you are going to insist on making this attack about you this time. You demand all the war gods on Tara always do your bidding. Taranis and I and Macha, who confines her mischief to Ireland and Scotland, and Arawn who loves revenge more than any of us and whom you must summon to release your champions from the Underworld—you insist that all of us always aid you in your desires." She stared down the tall, regal goddess. "Sometimes, it would be good of you to remember that we are all-powerful deities in our own right. We are not required to cater to your dictates with no return compensation."

Morgan directed a long-suffering glance at the ornate ceiling, obviously pretending to admire the swirling battles waged in perpetuity in oil paint.

Maeve was having none of it. "If you will recall, I staged the skirmish to lure one of your favorite targets, Rowan Sheridan, into battle. I tortured his talisman in an attempt to help you take both of them across the ford. All of that took place here in this fortress." She stepped into Morgan's space. "The fact you were not successful that time has nothing to do with my aid. I wanted Seamus Lochlann then, but I refrained from taking him in deference to helping you achieve your goal. Now it is your time to return the favor."

Maeve deliberately changed the purple of her eyes to black, and her stature grew with anger. Morgan nodded demurely and gave in. "Fine, I will call the zombie giants for as long as it takes to draw Seamus and his talisman from their protected lair. However, if any of my champions are successful, I will leave the battlefield to escort my prize across the ford." At Maeve's raised brow, Morgan added, "Whomever it may be. Will that suit you?"

"Very well. Position your champions in the clearing near the cabin. It is rocky and boggy there. With the added slickness and deep puddles left by Taranis's torrent, your Cornish giants who were used to fighting in such conditions during their lives will have the advantage." A smile curved Maeve's lips. "The warrior party will have no choice but to call for Seamus's help—or he may even see them and come of his own accord. His loyalty is his curse." She chuckled with evil delight. "He will have no choice but to come to the aid of his friends."

Any entity other than a fellow immortal looking at the pure evil radiating from Maeve's face likely would have suffered a fate like a person gazing on the Greeks' Medusa. Maeve could almost feel Seamus's torment between her legs. She touched herself lightly over the silk of her gown and shivered in vicious anticipation.

"Is it me or is it weird how the sky is such a pure intense blue while the last of the mists still hangs in the trees?" Alyssa asked as the warrior party rested on slabs of rock near the trail.

"I don't like it. It smacks of Taranis's involvement in Fallon's affairs," Griff said.

"I don't think it has as much to do with Fallon as with Seamus. If her premonitions are correct, Seamus is the target," Siobhan said, the acid in her tone directed at her fellow druid. Apparently, she still smarted from the promise Griffin had extracted from everyone the night before, the one requiring all of them to agree to save Fallon at all costs, including Seamus's life if necessary. Rowan had to admit, he didn't like that part of the plan much either.

"No doubt you're correct, Siobhan. Forgive me. Fallon has yet to show her skill, if indeed she's even discovered it. But as Seamus's talisman, she's still in danger." Griff knocked back a long swig of water.

Duncan shifted beside Siobhan, and Rowan saw him try to

catch Keela's eye. When she looked up from her coffee, he cocked an eyebrow. Rowan's prowess with breaching others' shields while keeping his own intact had served him well on several occasions. Duncan gave him a nearly imperceptible nod, and Rowan tuned into the telepathic conversation between Duncan and Keela.

"Can you encourage your husband to stop antagonizing my wife? She's been known to cast some pretty vindictive spells when she's upset."

"I hope that's not a threat. You have no idea how compelling a druid Griffin is." She shrugged. *"Besides, we have an idea of the sheer power of this pairing based on how we realized Fallon's warrior had found her. No doubt that's contributing to Griff's tunnel vision."* Keela's face perceptibly pinkened.

"There's a story there I'd like to hear when this is all over." Duncan smiled. *"But for now, we need to be a team, and Griff isn't doing much to encourage my wife to play nice with him."*

"I'll see what I can do."

Rowan raised a brow in Duncan's direction. While Duncan and Keela exchanged telepathic pleasantries, Siobhan had remained single-minded in her need to protect Seamus.

"We're all in danger right now. I propose we call up a spell to shield the warriors from the mists Taranis has left behind. That way Morgan and Maeve can't surprise us easily."

Griff seemed distracted as he listened to Siobhan. He hesitated before he agreed with her plan. "Shielding our warriors from Taranis's mists is a good idea, Siobhan. Shall we chant now or wait until we're a bit farther along the trail?"

Siobhan blinked when Griff agreed with her. Rowan followed her gaze when she looked up at the mists swirling menacingly in the tops of the trees. "Now seems a good time to cast protection spells. Who knows when that mercurial god will decide to work himself into another outburst."

Rowan wrapped his arms around Alyssa and watched Siobhan as she opened her backpack to pull a packet of herbs from it.

"What are you using?" Alyssa asked.

"The powerful protection of herbs of Midsummer Night."

On a stone slab she used as a table, Siobhan laid out chamomile and cinquefoil leaves, figwort, and juniper and dogwood branches. She also produced a full bottle of mead, balancing it carefully beside the herbs. Griffin carried his backpack over to her "table" and added to her druidic assortment an unopened bottle of water and his oak staff, which he'd been using as a walking stick as he hiked along the trail.

"I collected this from the well at Slieve Gullion in the Irish county of Armagh when I last visited," he said as he set the water down. "This is pure water that will impart supernatural knowledge and powers."

No one needed an explanation for the oak staff since they all understood it to be necessary to any ritual the druids decided to perform in the middle of a pine forest devoid of the trees basic to Celtic life.

"Do you intend to drink it, share it, or pour it over the herbs?" Siobhan asked, her tone curious rather than combative for once.

"We'll cut the mead with it at the end of the ritual and all share it. We're going to need every weapon at our disposal for this battle. Druids and warriors will have to come together as one in a way we may have never done before," Griff said, catching the eyes of each member of their little band individually.

"Good thing this group is already so interdependent, what with a warrior married to one druid, a talisman married to another, and yet another talisman who is the granddaughter of a powerful druid," Alyssa said, snuggling closer into Rowan's embrace.

"Another reason we thought it best not to involve Fallon's parents in this battle. The combination of warriors and druids is fitting though, considering what she is," Griffin said.

"And considering her warrior descends from a line that includes druids in it." Siobhan glared at him.

Right when Rowan thought he'd have to run interference between the druids, Griff acquiesced. "Exactly so."

Rowan disentangled himself from his wife and stood. "All right you two, we need to end your little standoff right now. What Alyssa was trying to say was that we're all committed to this enterprise, and our interconnectedness should make us stronger." He glanced from Siobhan to Griff. "Our goal is to help *both* Seamus and Fallon, and if Fallon is half the woman Seamus implied to me she is, I doubt she'll stay on this side of the ford if Maeve and Morgan take Seamus. Enough already." He blew out a breath. "Cast your enchantment, and let's get going."

Jennifer cracked up at Rowan's frustration. Soon, the entire group was laughing, and the tension between them lifted like Taranis's latest storm.

"Please, Siobhan, cast your enchantment over the warriors and talismans gathered here," Griff said after everyone settled back down.

Siobhan nodded and began mixing ingredients in a Connemara stone mortar she'd brought along for such a purpose. "Griff, would you please purify the area around this table with the juniper branch?" she asked, her request a metaphorical olive branch that allowed the group to let go of the breath they'd collectively held since they stepped onto the trail.

Without comment, Griff took the juniper branch and began enchanting the area Siobhan had selected as the site for the ritual. Instinctively, the others stepped inside the circle he made. "Powers of the East, source of abundance, give us wisdom and solidarity." He saluted the direction with the branch. "Powers of the South, source of our Mother, Earth, give us the strength of stone." Another salute. "Powers of the West, source of illumination, give us intelligence and logic." Yet another salutation. "Powers of the North, source of leadership, give us courage."

As he chanted, Griff brushed the earth in the four directions and wafted the branch on the breeze around the circle, the intense juniper scent energizing the warriors and talismans gathered in the center of it. Finishing the first part of the chant, he laid the juniper branch beside Siobhan and took up his oak staff. Stepping to the center of the circle, he struck his staff into the soft earth and intoned, "Powers of the Center, source of the life-giving tree, give us balance and mastery over ourselves and our battleground."

No one spoke as echoes of Griff's bass voice drifted away on the wind. All knew the importance and power of a druid's spell, but the ancient enchantment cast with the resonance of Griff's voice seemed to lend the spell additional potency. Siobhan, caught up in her own chanting as she assembled the herbs in her mortar, seemed the only one oblivious to Griff's authority. However, she turned from her work at exactly the right moment, struck a match, and dropped it into the contents of her mortar, which she offered to the sacred tree represented by Griff's staff.

"We call to you, Mother Goddess, source of all strength in earth and sky,

"We call to you to protect us in the waxing hours to Midsummer.

"We call to you to protect us from dark influences.

"We call to you to protect us from dark influences.

"We call to you to protect us from dark influences.

"We call to you to preserve us in health.

"Great Mother Goddess, we call to you," Siobhan chanted as the contents of her mortar evanesced into sweet smoke wafting around and among the warriors.

Griff produced a silver goblet from his backpack, and together, the druids combined the sacred well water with the fermented honey mead and offered it to each warrior and talisman in turn. The water added a crisp, sweet introduction to the bubbly champagne-like quality of Siobhan's mead. Rowan watched as each person in the group experienced the surge of physical strength he'd felt upon being first to partake of the potent drink.

Finally, Siobhan and Griff took their turns tasting the contents of the goblet. As a talisman, Keela could still give aid in battle even though she didn't have a warrior. Rowan decided that must be the reason Griff only sipped at his share and extended the rest to his wife. With that one gesture, Rowan understood the depth of Griff's commitment to Fallon and her family. He did and said what he did out of a profound belief in the necessity of saving his niece. That could be the only explanation for a druid giving up an opportunity at acquiring the profound strength offered by ingesting the sacred water.

The ritual completed, Griff retrieved his staff from the earth, and everyone silently packed up to resume their trek to the cabin. Siobhan let Duncan lead the way for this part of the hike, pulling back to converse with Griff.

"You gave your wife an extra taste from the goblet at your expense. Why?"

"I think you know the answer to that."

"I think I do, but I want to hear you say it," Siobhan said.

"Keela has never blamed me for what happened to her warrior, not even in the face of her family's accusations that I deliberately withheld information from him that put him at a fatal disadvantage in the battle that took his life. You see, I was his prognosticator, but she dreamed his death too. Without knowing who or where he was, she couldn't help him. As his druidic protector, it was my job to prophecy for him until he found her."

Rowan and Alyssa fell in step behind Griff and Siobhan.

"I warned him not to fight on the day he died. It haunts me still, though recent circumstances have led me to believe the gods intended for Keela and me to be together."

Rowan exchanged a look with Alyssa, but before either of them, or Siobhan, could ask, Griff continued. "Still, she has a skill, and I must do what I can to help her put it to use. I don't know which, if any, of the assembled warriors she can help, but if she can help even one, even at great cost to me, then my sacrifice is worth it."

Rowan squeezed Alyssa's hand as they watched Siobhan soften toward Griff.

"I'm sorry I've resented you. Until I saw you give most of your share to your wife, I thought your true motivation was to train the woman you feel is the most powerful talisman in a generation." Her lips quirked up in half a smile. "Now I see your commitment is to Keela and her family." Her voice dropped, low and urgent. "I, too, am committed with my life to protect my family."

"That's why our joint performance of the ritual will give our warriors the ability to succeed against whatever Maeve and her sister decide to throw at them. Thank you for allowing me to be included."

Rowan nearly plowed into them as Griff stopped to extend his hand to Siobhan.

When Siobhan took Griff's hand, a visible current flowed between them. For several long seconds, the two enchanters seemed to glow in a silver light emanating from their joined hands. Rowan stared transfixed as the druids seemed to become one entity. When they let each other go, the look they exchanged told Rowan that from now on, the druids were a team. He let out a breath he hadn't realized he held, tugged at Alyssa's hand, and continued up the trail.

CHAPTER SIXTEEN

ALLON YAWNED AND stretched, deliberately arching her body along Seamus's side. "It's almost summer solstice yet we still need a fire in the great room."

"Only when you insist on doing something other than bonding," Seamus said with a scowl that immediately flipped into a grin when she narrowed her eyes at him.

"By something, do you mean cooking and enjoying a meal once in a while? I'm finding it takes a lot of energy to maintain my stamina with you."

Tapping his chin, he feigned deep thought. "As I recall, you started it this time when you went all crazy and tried to go looking for me before you were completely dressed. I had to rescue you from injuring yourself."

She rolled her eyes, and he grinned. "Of course, the little display you're putting on at the moment is purely about waking up from a nap, isn't it?"

After a stretch, she'd molded herself to Seamus's side, her bare breasts flattened against his ribs, her hand "idly" tracing patterns of half of his sign over the powerful pectoral muscles of his chest before sliding suggestively lower over his abs. Glancing flirtatiously up at him from beneath her lashes, she smiled. "I'm sure I have no idea what you mean. I was talking about food. Specifically, I was thinking we should go out to the kitchen and find some. I'm starving."

"So am I—for you," he said before he rolled her over onto her back, took her breast in his hand, and flicked her taut nipple with the tip of his tongue.

Understanding she'd teased him too far—she honestly had wanted some brunch—she tried half-heartedly to push him up, but when he closed his mouth on her nipple and sucked, she forgot all about anything but her warrior's touch and how insatiable her need for him had become. Perhaps in his bed, she'd assumed the mortal incarnation of Maeve who couldn't be satisfied with anything less than everything he had to give.

As soon as that thought slipped into her mind, a searing pain lanced through her head. She cried out and rolled away from him, curling up in a ball of agony. Incoherent, vague, terrifying visions assailed her, and though she couldn't make out distinct pictures, the feelings emanating from the images threatened to tear her beating heart from her chest. Caught in the coils of her pain, she couldn't draw in a breath, and she clawed at her throat for air.

Eventually, her body superseded her mind, and she passed out, allowing her lungs to breathe. From somewhere very far away, she thought she heard Seamus calling to her, and she tried to call back, but when she started to regain consciousness, the vision threatened again, and she retreated into oblivion.

Seamus panicked as he tried in vain to reach Fallon. Several times he'd attempted to breach her shield, finding to his increasing agony that her shield was stronger than anything he'd ever encountered other than with a god. He held her, he called to her, he whispered his love, but after she passed out, she refused to wake up. Whatever she'd seen had sent her straight into shock, and he didn't know how to help her. Gathering her inert body onto his lap, he tugged her close as he rested his back against the bed frame. In vain, he attempted to break through her shield, but that part of her held firm. Either that, or Maeve had succeeded in penetrating Siobhan's formidable enchantments to take over Fallon's mind. Unconsciously, he traced his sign on her skin while tears ran unchecked down his face. "Fallon, Fallon baby. Wake up. I'm here. I've got you. We're safe. Wake up," he chanted over and over.

Time slipped away as Seamus worked to reach his talisman. About the time he grew conscious of feeling cold, he also noted a strange ripple in the air, like the electric calm before a huge storm breaks. He glanced out the window, glimpsed a clear blue sky, and wondered what the feeling meant. Then Fallon stirred in his arms, coming awake with a gasp.

Her eyes were huge, and horrifying images formed and evanesced in their depths for long seconds, long enough for a new kind of fear to grip Seamus low in his gut. With a blink, she dissolved into a torrent of tears as she wrapped herself around him and clung to him like a Titanic survivor to a life preserver.

Holding her close, he whispered soothing nonsense to her, trying to calm her. After a while, she hiccupped and relaxed enough in his arms for him to look into her face. "Hello, Fireworks. Welcome back," he whispered. "You want to tell me about it?"

"There's not much to tell this time."

"Right," he said, drawing the word out. "That's why you disappeared for about an hour and couldn't come back the several times you tried to." He tipped her chin up to stare into her eyes. "We're a team, Fallon. You have to trust me." He tried not to let his hurt show, but she caught on anyway.

Smoothing his hair from his forehead, she leaned up and brushed a light kiss over his mouth. "I'm not holding back,

Seamus. While it's true I had a vision, I have no idea what it was, only I've never felt so afraid in my life. Something beyond evil entered my head—"

"What was it?"

"That," she swallowed and started again. "That somehow I was the physical incarnation of Maeve come to steal your life force." She brushed a hand over her face. "Once that thought sneaked into my mind, pain seared through my head, and indistinct images started swirling. I couldn't make out any of them clearly, only that they meant something horrible was happening—something I'm powerless to stop." She cuddled in closer in his lap.

"You scared the hell out of me. No matter what I did, I couldn't get inside your thoughts to help you, and you didn't hear me call out to you physically either." He rested his chin on top of her head and stroked his hand up and down her back to soothe both of them.

"I didn't keep you out on purpose. Honestly, Seamus, all I could think about was the pain you were in." She turned her face into his neck, and though he enjoyed her kiss, he shoved all thoughts of sex to the back of his mind.

Running his hand over her hair, he said, "Rowan mentioned yesterday we might want to work on shielding. Because I'm a master at building, and, as you know already, at breaching shields"—he smiled when she pulled back to glare at him—"I didn't actually want to work on that because you're already adept at keeping me out of your head most of the time." He blew out a breath. "But after what you went through for the better part of the last hour when I couldn't breach your shield to help you, I have to put away my selfish desire to keep your shield a little thin for my own interests and help you build something strong enough to keep Maeve and her visions out of your mind."

Fallon pulled the covers higher over herself and him, and he could see she planned to stay in bed rather than face the training they both now understood she needed.

"Come on, Fireworks." He pushed the covers back down. "Let's get dressed and grab something to eat. After that we can go to work on denying Maeve her vicious desire to steal your sanity."

She nodded, and he hugged her close and kissed her reverently before lifting her off his body. When he gave her a look meant to reassure her of his deep feelings for her, he saw a fleeting glimpse of her terror vision in her eyes. As she closed her eyes and shook her head, he hoped she was accepting his view and not whatever she'd seen in the dark places inside her mind.

After he rolled out of bed and started dressing, she didn't follow him, so he tossed her sports bra and his flannel shirt at her before he pulled his jeans on over his boxers. He stole a peek at her to gauge her reaction to his playful gambit and saw she still sat there with his shirt on her head. When he thought he might have lost her again, she raised her hands and held his shirt to her face. With his shirt draped over her head, she noisily inhaled his scent before dropping the shirt into her lap long enough to put on her bra. She looked up and smiled at him, a smile that told him that she was safe—for the moment.

"I'll rustle up some grub," he said, gratified when his lame imitation of some old-time mountain man stole a chuckle out of her. "What are you in the mood for?"

"Whatever you set in front of me," she replied with some semblance of her typical sassy self.

"You're tempting me again, woman."

"Food, Seamus, food. Something I put in my mouth"—she paused and shot a naughty grin at him—"with a fork."

"Ouch!" He rested one hand over his heart in a long-suffering gesture while the other hovered over his crotch. "All right already. I think we have some eggs and bacon left. Guess we'll eat that. Wouldn't want anyone fighting over the fresh food when the whole team shows up today."

At the mention of the people who would be descending on them soon, Fallon jumped out of bed and raced to pull on her panties and hiking pants. "Omigosh! I forgot about them. Seamus, we need to clean this place up, or they'll think all we did was—" She blushed the lovely rose color he found so adorable.

"They know all we did was—" Seamus almost finished for her, waggling his eyebrows as he laughed. "They're all bonded and married, so they won't think anything. We're supposed to be doing what we've been doing, Fallon love."

He pulled her into his arms and held her close. Again, she sucked in a long breath, almost like she was trying to draw his essence inside her. Standing there in his arms, breathing in his smell, she relaxed and hugged him back before slipping from his embrace.

"At least I can tidy up this room, make the bed or something while *you* fix my food." She ducked her head while simultaneously raising a brow at him, and he grinned at her not-so-subtle hint.

"You know, you're really not as big as your appetite. Just sayin,'" he teased.

"You have no idea." She gifted him with an arch look. "Now go on, Cookie. Hustle your sweet ass out to the kitchen and make me some food." She emphasized her words by turning him toward the door and sliding her hand across his ass to give him a gentle push.

When he glanced over his shoulder and pretended to glare at her, she added, "Remember, a talisman's job is to direct her warrior in battle. I guess it's time you started getting used to taking orders, mister."

"Uh-huh." He cocked a brow. "You're going to pay for that, Fireworks."

Leaving the bedroom door open, Seamus walked across the

great room to start cooking. Though he was happy to have his talisman back, at least for the moment, he couldn't help sneaking glances at her to make sure she didn't slip away from him when he wasn't looking. For the first time in his life, he worried that Siobhan's powerful enchantments might not be enough to keep him safe in his own home.

⤫

"Be alert," Rowan warned the team as they approached a series of hairpin turns on a steep ascent of the trail. They'd have to cross a boggy meadow to reenter the tree line and reach the cabin. Sensing the ripple in the air, he looked around for the danger he anticipated it would bring.

In a low tone, Griff said, "That felt vicious and purely evil, but it didn't feel like rogues arriving or zombie champions materializing. What do you make of it?"

Beside him, Siobhan shivered. "I hope it doesn't mean we're too late." Her eyes were wide and fearful. "Do you feel how it pulses, like waves piling up on shore after some huge object has crashed into a lake?" Stopping, she crossed her arms over her middle. "It's making me nauseous. It has to do with Seamus, but he hasn't called out to any of us. I think we still have time." She doubled over, resting her hands on her knees as she panted in a breath.

Duncan, who had been leading, heard his wife's distress and doubled back to join her. "Sweet girl, are you all right? You're looking a little green. Do you need to rest?"

"No!" she snapped before she hissed a breath through her teeth. "No, babe, I don't need rest. There's no time for rest." Her increasing breathlessness belied her words.

Rowan exchanged a look with Duncan.

"If you're feeling sick, we can take a break, grab some water," Duncan said, his tone gentle.

"She's not feeling the effects of the hike. Your training with your wife has her in the shape of a highly skilled talisman. Rather, she's having an acute reaction to a pulse in the cosmos, something we druids feel occasionally," Griff said.

Duncan's eyes narrowed. "Why aren't you affected then?"

Griff put up a conciliatory hand. "Don't you worry. I'm feeling it plenty sharply, but I think it has to do with her brother specifically, so Siobhan's reaction is more pronounced. The pulse tells us evil is near, so she's right, there is no time to rest."

As they talked, the others stopped and returned to the little circle surrounding Siobhan.

With a weak smile, she said, "I can do this. Let's keep going."

Closing her eyes, she pulled in a long breath before she resumed the hike, increasing her pace after the initial pulsing wave washed over them. Duncan raised a dubious eyebrow at Rowan before falling into step beside his wife.

"You know the way to the cabin as well as I do, Rowan. How 'bout if you lead for a while?" Duncan asked.

Ignoring her husband's suggestion, Siobhan took back the lead on the trail. Duncan shook his head. Two strides later, he joined his wife at the front of the rest of the group.

Rowan and Alyssa allowed Jennifer Carlin to fall in beside Keela Walsh in front of them. As they walked, the women's conversation carried through the unnatural stillness of the forest.

"It's strange having a skill the gods intended you to use for one man, yet you find you have nothing else to offer him. Still, that doesn't impede your usefulness in a battle," Jennifer said to Keela.

"Your warrior lives. I never met mine, so I've never determined my skill." Sadness colored her words. "We've always believed I was a prophet based on the vision I had of my warrior and given my family tree. If I'm called upon to help someone in this battle, I'm not sure what I'll have to offer." She hitched her backpack higher up on her shoulders. "I've often felt I somehow cheated the warrior community by not actively contributing to it with my skill, whatever it would have been."

"You're a talisman. Whatever skill you possess, you'll discover in battle."

Rowan exchanged a look with Alyssa. Jennifer didn't judge, which was one of the reasons everyone liked her so well. That and the exemplary way she served as Duncan's talisman.

"Since your husband will have other duties, I think it best you stay near me. I know where Duncan needs me to move at any given moment in a battle, but I stay on the edge. I've found the old adage 'out of sight, out of mind' works well where zombie warriors are concerned. They're sensorially deficient as it is." A smile ghosted over Jennifer's face as she glanced over at Keela.

"At the risk of sticking my nose in where it doesn't belong, why didn't you bond with Duncan?" Keela asked.

Though he knew the story, Rowan still found himself quite interested in Jennifer's answer to that question.

"Probably for the same reason you would not have bonded with your warrior had you met him," she said.

Keela stumbled, and Rowan reached out to catch her. Ignoring his outstretched hand, she focused her attention on Jennifer. "What do you mean? You can't know that I wouldn't have bonded with him if I had met my warrior," she insisted, her tone indignant. Her outburst drew the attention of Siobhan and Duncan walking in front of them, but Jennifer smiled and waved them on.

"As the odd woman out, I have ample opportunities to watch other people. You and Griff are no exception. The two of you operate on a level like a bonded warrior and talisman pair." She turned to look back at them. "In fact, you look a lot like Rowan and Alyssa when you're together."

Rowan smiled at Jennifer before turning to his wife whose silver eyes twinkled back at him.

Jennifer nodded. "Exchanging charged looks, unconscious

touches that have meaning, anticipating the other's needs." Rowan chuckled, and Jennifer returned her attention to Keela. "Regardless of whether your warrior would have lived, you and Griff would have found each other." A self-satisfied expression crossed her face.

Keela returned to the original question. "So, what happened between you and Duncan?"

"We met, he tried his sign on me and discovered I was his, and we tried to bond." Jennifer laughed. "Boy, did we try to bond"—she shuddered—"but nothing happened. There was zero chemistry. We discovered my skill in a battle with some rogue warriors, and luckily for us, I sort of came prepackaged with my skill completely intact from the first time I was called upon to put it to use."

The small band of warriors and talismans encountered a short, steep section of trail, interrupting Jennifer's narrative. Once they crested it, Rowan studied the deepening forest while Jennifer continued her story.

"When we realized our relationship was more like a brother and his sister than a warrior and his talisman, we approached Scathach about it during a training session at the Sheridan compound."

At the mention of the warrior goddess, Keela gasped. "You've worked directly with Scathach?" Her voice rose nearly an octave on the question, frightening some ravens into flight above them.

Rowan couldn't help but chuckle at Keela's surprise. Jennifer ignored him and forged on with her story.

"The Sheridans are her particular favorites. As a consequence of being very close friends of theirs, we share some of the benefits of Scathach's direct interest in them."

"Impressive." Keela sneaked a peek back at him, and Rowan grinned. Turning back to Jennifer, she prompted, "You approached Scathach with your dilemma—"

"Yeah, and she said that for reasons of their own, Danu and

the Dagda don't always match warriors completely to their talismans. Something about keeping the mortals from becoming too powerful. Scathach gave us her blessing to remain committed to each other in our warrior capacities, but to pursue love wherever we found it. Not long after that, Duncan met Siobhan who led him on a merry chase before she finally gave in. I was 'best woman' at their wedding." Her tone carried her smile.

"But if Danu and the Dagda don't want mortals to become too powerful, why did they allow for the possibility of bards like my niece?"

"Now *that* is a million-dollar question."

The trail widened, and Griff took the opportunity to fall into step beside Keela and Jennifer. "Perhaps Danu and the Dagda don't wish for lesser immortals to abuse their powers over mortals. Bards offer an opportunity for mortals to balance the power," he said.

"So do certain warrior and talisman pairings. We discovered that with Rowan and Alyssa about a year and a half ago," Jennifer said as a shiver overtook her. "I owe Seamus for that one. I hope I can return the favor this time."

Alyssa glanced over at Rowan, a similar shiver blowing over her too. He reached over and squeezed her hand. "Us too," he said.

With Griff's addition, the conversation crescendoed, and Siobhan said over her shoulder, "Everyone in this party owes Seamus. It's why we're bound by honor, not just by love, to rescue him from Maeve's terrible plans for him."

Griff cleared his throat, but Siobhan wasn't finished. "Without Seamus, Fallon can't develop her skill to its full potential. As a storyteller, she needs her warrior's involvement in events to practice. She needs Seamus to remain alive."

Griff stopped and stared after Siobhan. Behind him, Rowan and Alyssa stopped walking too. Something in the druid's expression alerted him, and Rowan cast his ethics aside, breaching Griff's shield to listen in on his thoughts.

With his eyes closed, Griff communicated telepathically. *"Put on the bracelet, Fallon. Put on the bracelet and ask Seamus to trace his sign over it. Over all of it. Please, Fallon.*

"Brighid, goddess of bards, watch over our precious niece," he prayed. *"If Scathach took such an interest in the Sheridans to train them personally, perhaps you would do the same for Fallon?"* Opening his eyes, he resumed the hike, smiling reassuringly at his wife as he caught up to her.

Griff's last thoughts before Rowan slipped back out of his head made him wish he'd followed his better nature and stayed out of Griff's mind.

"Every step we take closer to this battle, it becomes clearer this fight is the biggest one we've ever faced. I hope we're up for it."

CHAPTER SEVENTEEN

"I SHOULD HAVE GUESSED by the incredible shape you keep yourself in that you'd train like a demon. Can we please take a break? I think I've sweat out every spare drop of water in my body," Fallon complained. She'd long since discarded Seamus's shirt and thought about sliding out of her pants as well. Who knew shielding training could be so strenuous? Nothing she and Sloane had ever practiced came near to the exhausting workout Seamus had subjected her to over the last several hours.

"You're a quick study, Fireworks. You remind me of Alyssa, only you had a much bigger head start."

"What do you mean?" She couldn't help the edge that crept into her voice. The way Seamus talked about Alyssa Sheridan sometimes left Fallon envious, which she hid by filling two glasses of icy water from the tap.

"She had no shield when I met her. When I discovered how Rowan was exploiting that fact, I spent an afternoon with her like the hours we just put in. When we were finished, she could keep him out of her head when she wanted to most of the time.

Thanks." He took the glass she handed him and downed it in one long gulp. "You already knew how to shield your thoughts and had created a pretty solid shield before we met."

She quirked a brow and glanced at him over the top of her glass before she took another swallow, relishing the icy water as it slid down her throat.

"After what you showed me today, I doubt anyone, not even the real master, Rowan's dad, can penetrate your mind if you choose to keep him out," Seamus said, pride resonating through his gorgeous baritone voice. As she handed him another glass of water, she beamed at his praise.

"That means you're going to have to be on especially good behavior if you expect to wander around in my head from now on." She batted her lashes at him with a saucy smirk.

"I can manage that." Seamus's midnight blue eyes twinkled with mischief. "But remember, two can play that game. You'll have to be an exceptionally good girl to take a stroll through my thoughts."

Her laugh pealed through the cabin as she headed for the couch on her way to a well-earned break. As she walked past the door where her backpack hung on a peg, she stopped cold. For some inexplicably urgent reason, the need to put on her bracelet compelled her to reach into the front pocket of her pack, pull the cuff out, and clasp it around her wrist.

"Why did you do that?" Seamus asked, his tone drained of its previous flirtatiousness. "You're safe inside this enchanted cabin—with me."

"I had a sudden feeling I needed to put it on," she said, confused by the idea she didn't have complete control of her thoughts. When she looked up at Seamus, he enfolded her tightly in his arms, like he feared losing her to another of her terrible premonitions.

"It's all right, Seamus. I'm not going anywhere. I'm not experiencing a premonition. It's more of a sensation. They're not the same." Still, she burrowed farther into his warm, massive chest. As they held each other, another thought entered her head. "I need you to do something for me."

Pulling back from his embrace, she held her armored wrist out to him. "Trace your sign over the entire bracelet while I'm wearing it."

His gorgeous eyes clouded. "You know what happened the last time I traced my sign over your bracelet while you wore it. I don't think it's natural for a warrior to brand his talisman."

"I don't know why, but I have this intense impression you need to do this. Please don't fight me, Seamus."

At the look he gave her, she changed her tactic. "I'll let you into my head. We'll experience this together. Please." She held her wrist out to him. "Though I don't understand why, I know it's super important for you to trace your sign over my bracelet."

Stubbornly, she held her wrist out to him. Taking her forearm with his left hand, Seamus held Fallon's right hand in his and traced his sign in its customary place on the underside of her wrist. When she sucked in a breath, he stopped, and she heard him tuning in to her thoughts to discover how much pain he was causing her. His eyes widened as he heard her desire instead.

"Don't stop, warrior. Trace over all the trinity knots on the inside of this piece of jewelry." She closed her eyes and fought not to cross her legs. *"Oh, wow, Seamus. Oh. Wow."*

"At the risk of sounding crude, Fireworks, are you creaming your jeans?" He continued tracing his sign over her bracelet as she'd asked, a laugh playing in his voice.

"I'll let you know after you've finished." Even in her mind, she couldn't suppress the sigh his touch elicited.

She blinked her eyes open to find him smiling as he sensed the softening of her body. "What kind of supernatural power is in this piece of metal?" he asked aloud before he switched back to telepathy. *"I think you should leave this on for the foreseeable future, Fallon. There's something special about it."*

"Mmmm."

Once he completed a circuit of the bracelet, Seamus gazed at Fallon's face, her eyes closed, a tiny smile playing over her generous mouth, and he had to kiss her. She melted into him and kissed him back, slowly, savoring their kiss, like they had all the time in the world to enjoy each other. He lost himself in her. Sometime later and not completely aware of how he'd accomplished it, he found himself entangled with her on the wide couch. His water glass, which he'd unthinkingly placed on the armrest when he was tracing his sign on her, tipped off and hit the thick rug with a soft thump when he kicked off his jeans. Her hiking pants disappeared somewhere between the cushions along with the lacey panties he was so happy she preferred.

Straddling him, she smiled as she lowered herself over his ready body, sheathing him in her hot, wet center before she slowly removed her bra. Folding his hands behind his head, he lay back and enjoyed the show. When she started moving over him, he willed himself not to lose control, even though she looked so sexy palming her breasts like that and smiling down at him. Her velvety body felt so good he knew he could spend himself inside her in a red-hot second if he didn't pay attention.

Stretching her arms above her head, she covered her braceleted wrist with her free hand and held on as she rode him. Taking her time, she rode him deliberately, her inner muscles clenching around him as she moved over him, her slick heat gliding enticingly over his hard length. When his need became too strong, he unclasped his hands from behind his head and smoothed them along her sides from the lovely hollows above her hip bones, to the soft curve of her waist, over her ribs and back down to settle on her hips. Her languid lovemaking drove him wild. Eventually, he took control, holding her still while he thrust up deep inside her, and still, she held herself in her taut position above him.

"God, Fallon, your strength is amazing. You are so much woman."

She gasped and tightened her inner walls around him as pleasure washed over him. Before he could fully appreciate what he'd done for her, his own orgasm started at the base of his spine and burst through him up into her. Crying out, he unconsciously clamped his hands on her body, holding her in place as he came hard inside her.

An eternity later, Seamus relaxed his grip, and Fallon settled her torso, like a gracefully falling flower petal, on the taut abs and chest he rigorously worked to maintain. She rested her cheek in the hollow of his neck while her hands fluttered down to his shoulders. She puffed out a tiny sigh, and he could feel her smile on his skin. Wrapping her in his arms, he held her loosely to himself, all of his strength sapped for the moment in the power of their lovemaking.

Nearby on the trail leading to the cabin, an otherworldly golden warmth enveloped Griffin Walsh. He stopped for a step to thank a goddess for hearing his prayer.

Ahead of him, Siobhan and Duncan neared the part of the trail opening out onto a marsh. They stopped so abruptly, the others nearly piled into them. "We need to make a plan for crossing the exposed area of the marsh," Duncan said. "We're going to be the most vulnerable to attack as soon as we leave the cover of the trees."

Rowan started to speak when a red and gold shimmer flickered in the air on the trail ahead. Scathach, the great warrior goddess herself, materialized before them.

"You were wise to hike in rather than to try to visualize yourselves here. I am afraid my fellow goddesses quite forget that I have trained you personally, so you are not as likely as other, more rash warriors to act before you think." She nodded approvingly. "Well done, Duncan, to stop before you exposed yourself on the battlefield."

All warriors and talismans in the party bowed in deference to the goddess as she spoke, but Griff and Keela, having never encountered an immortal face-to-face, stared in awe.

"I was hoping to see you here milady," Rowan said familiarly, as though speaking to a friend. "We had an idea this boulder-strewn bog would be Maeve and Morgan's choice for their minions to engage us. Your help will, as always, make the difference."

"You are smooth, Rowan Sheridan. I hope you are also sincere."

"Of course, milady." Rowan said as he shot the goddess a cheeky grin. "Even I know the only warrior you allow to tease you is my brother Rio."

Siobhan stepped in front of him. "Truly, Lady Scathach, I am relieved you've come to join us. I fear my brother is in real danger of crossing the ford this time."

"We are not going to let that happen. I have spent too much time training him to lose him to Maeve's endless lust. She can slake herself with the rogue warriors she and Morgan have stolen from me." Scathach's impatience with the other goddesses manifested itself in a trembling ripple in the earth beneath their feet, an action that Griff noticed even sobered up Rowan, who had been grinning at his patroness since she appeared before them.

Griff's awe in the presence of the goddess rendered him uncharacteristically impolitic. "You're aware of what Maeve has in store for Seamus Lochlann?"

"Of course I'm aware! I am a goddess after all," Scathach snapped. "One would have thought that as a druid, you would be better versed in the powers of immortals than to suppose I do not suspect what my sisters plan."

"I'm sorry, Lady Scathach," Griff said, bowing in deference and embarrassment.

Coming up beside him, Alyssa whispered, "She scares the hell out of me too, and I've trained with her on more than one occasion."

He nodded.

"I certainly hope I scare you, Alyssa Sheridan. I hope I scare all of you enough to follow my every direction and to use all the skills I have taught you," Scathach said, staring down each of the assembled warriors and talismans in turn.

In the silence that followed, the whole party tensed at the change in the air signaling the arrival of Maeve and Morgan, or at least some manifestation of their evil. Scathach threw back her battle-sculpted shoulders, lifted her chest, and commanded the attention of her war party with her battle stance. "The time for conversation is over. When we step out of the cover of the trees, the battle will be engaged. I suggest the talismans spread out and melt into the tree line as close to the edge of the marsh as safely possible." She walked around the group, directing each of them. "Siobhan and Griffin, you must follow the warriors and wait on either side of the trail where it clears the trees. Let the rogues or the zombies Morgan has called focus their attention on you rather than on the talismans. That way the talismans can do their jobs with fewer worries of being taken."

"Yes, milady," Siobhan said.

Griff echoed her.

"Keela, focus your attention on Duncan, at least at first. If you discover your skills are better suited to helping another warrior—either Rowan or Seamus—move to help him. But to begin, stay near Jennifer and help Duncan. Alyssa and Jennifer, you know your jobs. Do not let emotion impede the delivery of your skills." She gifted Alyssa with a charged stare, and Griff noted how Alyssa glanced away. A story for another day—if they survived this one.

"Siobhan and Griffin, weave a spell to keep yourselves safe

and to create barriers between the rogues and the warriors. If Duncan, Rowan, and Seamus can concentrate on the zombies without having to watch for rogues, we can level the playing field more quickly."

"You expect Seamus to fight in this battle, milady?" Siobhan asked, her tone revealing her great fear for her brother.

"Seamus's loyalty is his greatest asset. Since you all came to help him and his talisman, my sisters choose to bring the battle to him."

Siobhan's mouth turned down. "His greatest asset now becomes his greatest liability."

"Not if we do our jobs and help him, which is exactly what we are going to do," Scathach said, her voice softening for the first time since her arrival. Tipping her face to the sky, she sniffed the air. "I sense a presence nearby. We have no more time to talk. Stow your gear nearby and prepare for battle."

Following her pronouncement, Scathach disappeared into a red and gold mist, leaving the warrior band to follow her dictates to the letter. Siobhan embraced Duncan tightly before slipping behind him to follow him to the clearing. Alyssa turned to Rowan and placed her hands on his face, looking deeply into his eyes. Anyone watching them, even a civilian, would know their communion was of souls, their eyes were locked so fiercely on each other. Then Rowan pulled Alyssa into his arms and kissed her soundly before he fell in behind Duncan. Alyssa melted away into the trees to the right of the trail.

Jennifer nodded to Keela who took one last savoring look at her husband. Griff reached out and squeezed her hand tightly before she followed the other talisman into the trees. He stared at the spot where Keela disappeared before he followed the others up the trail. The moment each dreaded and anticipated was upon them.

Seamus came awake in a rush. During the short nap he'd dropped into after his latest bonding experience with Fallon, he'd dreamed of them both taking on a zombie warrior, something like a Fomorian, but it didn't make sense. Morgan summoning a fallen Fomorian would be like Poseidon deliberately freeing a Titan. What a weird dream.

When he reached for Fallon to tell her about it, he found her fully dressed and seated at the end of the couch staring at him, concern written large on her face.

"What is it? Why are you all the way over there? And why are you dressed?" he asked.

"Can't you hear it?"

Seamus calmed his breathing and listened. What he heard made his blood run cold. Somewhere beyond the cabin, a battle raged, the clanging of swords rang through the valley to echo off the mountains surrounding their hideaway. It could only mean one thing: Maeve and Morgan knew where they were and had brought the battle to them—before he and Fallon had had the chance to discover her skill. The expression on his talisman's face tore at his heart.

"You know it's our families out there fighting for us," he said.

"You have to go to them," she said, her eyes filled with sorrow. "She brought the battle to you so you'd have no choice but to expose yourself. She gambled that I haven't figured out how to help you, a gamble that's going to pay off."

Her despair radiated off her in waves that threatened to drown him.

He stood and pulled her to him. "We are not giving up before we've even waded into the battle, Fireworks. My brother-in-law's talisman didn't figure out her skill until she and Duncan engaged in their first battle together. Perhaps that's how it will go for us too." He kissed the top of her head. "Even if it doesn't, we'll be that much closer to discovering what your skill is."

She squeezed him tight enough to cut off his air, almost. "In time to save you from Maeve?"

"I'm not letting her take me, Fallon." *Especially not now after I've found you and fallen for you.*

She inhaled like she was trying to breathe him inside her. "I'm not letting her take you either."

Following one last squeeze, she stepped out of his embrace and gifted him a watery smile. "I know our ancestors preferred to take on the enemy naked, and some of those zombies may very well be in that state, but I think you're going to be better off in your jeans, leather jacket, and hiking boots."

Glancing down at his nakedness, he laughed. "I think you're right."

He'd just pulled on his pants when a red and gold shimmer hovered in the air in the great room before Scathach stood on the rug in front of the hearth and surveyed him in his half-dressed state.

Without the mundane preamble of a greeting, she said, "The battle has begun, Seamus. I know your loyalty. I know you believe you have no choice but to join it, but before you do, I want to know if the two of you have discovered your talisman's skill." Turning to Fallon, she continued. "I appreciate your awe and surprise at seeing me, and normally, I would enjoy your discomfiture, but there is no time for that now, Fallon Graham."

Fallon snapped her gaping jaw closed, swallowed, and stammered, "Y-you know who I am?"

"What is it with you American Grahams? First your uncle and aunt and now you. I am a goddess. Of course, I know who you are," Scathach growled. "Now, answer my question."

"We haven't discovered her skill yet, milady." Seamus stepped over to his talisman. "In answer to your next accusation, we haven't spent all our time together bonding either," he added with a grin.

He winked at Fallon who blushed deeply and stared at the floor. "Seamus," she hissed. "You can't talk to a goddess in that tone of voice. Especially the patron goddess of warriors. You sound like you're teasing your mom."

Throwing an arm over her shoulders, he pulled her close and kissed her on the tip of her nose.

"What *have* you done besides bond with your talisman?"

Seamus's attitude changed to all business when he heard the edge in Scathach's question. "We've done some serious shielding training since it appears Maeve is determined to mess with Fallon's mind using visions. At her friend Sloane's suggestion, we've read nearly everything in the cabin concerning old Celtic stories, thinking something in them would give us a clue about Fallon's skill. Then there's her bracelet—"

"What about it?"

"The inside of it is stamped with a series of Celtic trinity knots like my sign. We discovered when I trace my sign over the bracelet, it marks her skin."

Scathach motioned toward Fallon's right wrist. "Is it painful when Seamus marks you?"

"No, milady." She cleared her throat. "It's quite—pleasurable."

His favorite rose blush rode high on Fallon's cheeks, and he couldn't help the surge of ego he experienced knowing he'd given her that pleasure.

He did his best to hide a smirk, but Scathach missed nothing. "So of course this marking led to other things not necessarily helpful to discovering your talisman's skill." Her tone left nothing of her displeasure to the imagination. Seamus sobered up fast.

Fallon slid a look at him before she addressed the goddess. "I felt like I was being directed to have Seamus trace the sign over me while I wore the bracelet. I don't know how to explain it. It was like a golden glow guiding us."

He laced his fingers with hers and waited.

"While it did lead to bonding"—she stopped and swallowed, her embarrassment nearly palpable under the goddess's severe gaze—"it also led to a closer connection between us, something beyond physical. Perhaps that's a good thing?"

The hope on her face tugged at his heart.

"A golden glow, you say?" Scathach tapped a finger on her chin.

"Yes, milady."

"That changes things."

Warrior and talisman exchanged a puzzled look.

"It appears I may have an ally this time when we face my sister goddesses. A very powerful ally."

"If you don't mind my asking, who do you think is joining you?" Seamus asked.

"That, my boy, I cannot reveal until I am certain. Ready yourself in case you're needed in the marsh."

"They're fighting in the marsh? How can you let that happen? Fighting there is all to Morgan's advantage!" He raced into the bedroom to grab a shirt, pulling it over his head as he strode purposefully across the great room to the bench beside the door where he sat down and pulled on his boots.

As Seamus reached for his thick leather jacket, Fallon grabbed his arm and tugged him around to face her. "Seamus! How can you leave the protections of this cabin, protections you've been bragging about practically since I arrived? How can you put yourself in a situation you know is a trap, especially when you know what Maeve plans if she can get her claws on you?" Her wild-eyed expression tore him in two.

"I can't let my friends fight for me and give them no aid. My sister and my best friend are among those who are fighting. I can't stay here in safety while they risk their lives to give us time, to give us a chance. I have to help them." He held her face in his palms. "Because if we lose any of them, what does that say of our chances together?"

His kiss showed her how much she mattered to him.

"This is why a goddess would take such a personal interest in him. He's so loyal. I'll die if anything happens to him."

Seamus broke the kiss. "And I'll die if anything happens to you. Stay here where it's safe and protected."

Stepping away from her, he shrugged on his leather jacket and grabbed his claymore from a hidden compartment in the tongue-and-groove paneling of the wall beside the door. "If you're a prophet like my friend Ceri or a dreamer like my friend Alyssa, you won't need to be right on the battlefield to help me. If you're something else, we may discover your skill with you safely here inside the cabin. Promise me you'll be here when I return."

He wasn't making a request.

"Seamus, I don't want you to go out there alone," she said, her tone pleading.

"I won't be alone, Fireworks. One of the best warriors on the planet is out there, and so is my brother-in-law, all of us trained by Scathach herself, who by the way is part of this party in case you hadn't noticed," he said with a wink.

"I will watch your back until you reach the others, Seamus," Scathach said before turning her gaze to Fallon who seemed to shrink from the goddess's intensity.

Seamus stepped out of the cabin, took a deep breath, and wondered for a second if he should have been more careful about what he wished for when he was wishing he'd been with his friends in Scotland last fall. There was no time for speculation, though, as the clashing of swords and the cries of men assailed his ears. The battle song crescendoed in his blood. Following the direction of the sounds, he slipped into the woods with the idea of flanking the battleground and entering the battle beside his friends. If Maeve wanted a fight, he'd give her one.

CHAPTER EIGHTEEN

"FOMORIAN? *SERIOUSLY?* HOW the hell did Morgan manage that?" Duncan panted as he and Rowan took on the Titan-like creature together.

"More importantly, what does raising one say of her powers?" Rowan said on a jagged breath as he feinted to give Duncan a chance at an unobstructed blow.

"Or her common sense? Did she forget how dangerous the Fomorians were to the *Tuatha Dè Danann?* How they nearly over-ran Scotland? How difficult it was to defeat them in the first place?" He danced away from the giant's fist. "Wasn't she on the Dagda's team against them way back when?" He succeeded in hamstringing their common opponent who swung a mighty arm in his direction. A Fomorian, a creature of limited agility in the first place, coupled with its current existence as a zombie, gave Duncan relatively little trouble causing an injury that opened a clear opportunity for Rowan to down their foe with a straight jab between the giant zombie's ribs through what passed for its heart.

"Apparently, she's become desperate after the recent losses we've dealt her. She can only raise her old zombie champions like the Morhaus so many times before they're defeated for good," Rowan said as he pulled his sword from the downed monster. Before he could catch his breath, he saw five rogues break free of whatever enchantments Siobhan and Griff had managed to hold them. "Here comes more trouble, and these guys look like they've had some practice."

"You must take these rogues before Seamus arrives to help, Rowan. He's in serious trouble from them if you don't," Alyssa communicated to him.

"Is Seamus coming? Do you see him?" Rowan asked, worried for his friend as he awaited their enemies with his back to Duncan.

"We haven't seen him, but Keela had a prophecy."

"We'll do all we can," Rowan said.

The five rogue warriors descended on Rowan and Duncan, their vacant eyes like sharks, their intent deadly. The clashing of swords and the grunts of men assaulted the quiet of the mountain meadow.

Like commanders in the field, the talismans had to pay attention to the enemy's tactics and try to counter them successfully. Rowan could sense Alyssa's concentration on a huge man who stood half a head taller than he and outweighed him by at least fifty pounds. Then it clicked. He'd taken on this particular rogue once before. Judging from his tactics, the rogue had done some intense training since the last time Rowan had engaged him.

"Rowan, try to attack the big warrior's left side. He's favoring it," Alyssa said.

"I'm on it. Thanks."

Using their supernatural skill at bending time and space, Rowan and Duncan appeared to switch places in the blink of an eye, but when Rowan attacked the rogue as Alyssa had told him to, the wily devil grinned evilly and switched his grip on his claymore. Obviously, the rogue knew Rowan's talisman was nearby observing the fight and helping him. Now the rogue also knew how Rowan's talisman helped him, a distinct advantage for the rogue.

As the rogue changed his tactics, Rowan could hear Alyssa's gasp. *"I'm so sorry Rowan!"*

"It's all right, Pixie-girl. Look for something else, something not so obvious. Or ask Siobhan to conjure up a distraction."

What he'd discovered was the rogue's acting ability. Intentionally favoring his left side to draw Rowan there had been a ploy, his left side being his dominant side. He sought to wear out his opponent using his weaker side before finishing him with his dominant sword arm, a tactic he'd never seen a rogue use. Surely this man had never benefited from Scathach's training, had he? Rowan had no time to ponder the situation as he tried to take out his other opponent while playing defense against the huge rogue and the fifth attacker who seemed to trade off between Duncan and him at regular intervals.

Their enemies had Rowan and Duncan pinned against a boulder when something happened to the ground immediately behind the rogues. Rowan saw the druids, and though he couldn't see what the druids did, he intuitively understood they gained an advantage if they could push the rogues back onto the ground behind them. So intent were they on their prey, the rogues didn't see the druids creep up behind them and chant over the grasses at the perimeter of the fight.

Exchanging a glance with his partner, both Rowan and Duncan redoubled their efforts, driving their attackers backward. The rogue assigned to harass them went down first, his feet seeming to sink into the earth. Two others fell, one on top of the first, the other beside him. They cried out in frustration and fury before Rowan finished off the two who landed atop each other. Though he couldn't stand up, the third downed rogue escaped the two warriors' swords as his allies, realizing the danger, came at Rowan and Duncan from the sides.

Now the odds were even, and Rowan had little trouble dispatching his opponent. Duncan, however, sustained a deep cut to his sword arm and was weakening fast. As Rowan turned to help, Seamus appeared from behind the boulder, and the rogue left off his battle with Duncan to take on the newcomer.

"The guest of honor has finally arrived. I have strict orders to take you alive though I can't understand why," the rogue growled as he engaged Seamus.

To his consternation, Rowan suddenly couldn't reach the rogue, and Duncan, who was closer to the action, seemed barred from the battle his brother-in-law now fought. An invisible barrier impeded their attempts to help their friend. A keening wail from the vicinity of the trees where the talismans hid rent the air at the same time the two warriors discovered they couldn't help Seamus. The downed rogue caught in the enchanted grass nearby laughed hoarsely. He wouldn't live, but he and his comrades had succeeded in their assigned mission. Furiously, Rowan turned on the rogue and buried his sword in the man's throat, cutting off the derisive laughter that signaled the failure of his party's mission. Seamus wouldn't die at the hands of the rogue warrior, but Maeve had secured her prize.

At first Seamus was so intent on taking the rogue warrior who threatened his friends that he didn't notice Rowan and Duncan hadn't joined him. He attacked ferociously, taking out all his pent-up frustration at being left out of the festivities in Scotland the previous fall on the dishonorable specimen before him. When he wounded the rogue's sword arm, the man merely switched hands and kept fighting. Seamus marveled at the man's skill and durability, vaguely noting the rogue's response looked something like a tactic Scathach had taught him. Then he didn't have time to think as the rogue redoubled his attack.

By the time he realized the rogue had maneuvered him behind the boulder into a hollow between a rock and a towering pine, he knew he was in trouble. His friends were nowhere to be found, and the rogue's skill and stamina belied the battle Seamus believed his friends had engaged with him. By rights, the rogue should be so tired, coupled with his profusely bleeding wound, that he should be easy work for Seamus. Yet the man persisted, an evil grin playing about his lips.

"She promised not to kill me in her bed. Just let me taste the delights of her mortal body and her immortal technique. I've been training with her for nearly a year," the rogue boasted as he pushed Seamus farther into the hollow.

He didn't need to be enlightened about who "she" was. Maeve had been planning this attack for a long time. When did Fallon say the premonitions started? Samhain? He couldn't think about it as he tried to assess the danger while staving off the rogue's increasingly intent attack.

"She'll kill you with your own lust, you fool. Then Morgan will march you across the ford in everlasting shame. Run away now, and you can return to the field when you're healed and die with some semblance of honor," Seamus gritted out before dealing a blow to the man's shoulder, rendering his right arm useless.

"Perhaps, but it's too late for you," the rogue taunted as he danced out of range of Seamus's claymore.

When he stepped forward and raised his sword to finish the rogue, his progress abruptly stopped, his body trapped in an invisible net. When he tried to move, the net cinched more tightly around him, and too late, he realized why his friends hadn't come to his aid. The area had been enchanted by a malevolent goddess determined to have her way. He looked around and saw her lounging indolently on top of the boulder where the battle had taken place.

"The others will exact their revenge on you if you don't run quickly," Maeve said to the rogue who smiled expectantly up at the goddess.

It took the man some seconds to understand what the goddess said to him. When he turned to run, he found himself flanked by Duncan and Rowan. In his weakened state, they had no trouble finishing him off.

"Rowan! Over here!" Seamus called out.

"He cannot hear you darling. I have seen to that. He will be able to watch, however, when I take you with me. I do not want there to be any question about who won this particular battle." She flicked a glance at the downed warrior. "Pity about my pet. I would have enjoyed him as an appetizer to the main course. Alas, Morgan insisted I let her have the rogues, even the one I trained especially for this battle, in exchange for taking you first. It seems a small price. Drop your sword. Where we're going, you'll only need the one you were born with." She laughed obscenely at her own joke.

Seamus struggled to hold on to his claymore, but a force beyond his control had other intentions. Sweat poured from his body as he valiantly fought to retain his weapon, but ultimately, his hands lost their grip, and his sword clattered against the rocks at his feet. The sound alerted his friends to his location, and they ran to his defense only to watch helplessly as Maeve appeared beside him, wrapped her arms around him, and jerked him through time and space.

Her premonition assaulted her, rendering her helpless in its intensity. Maeve had succeeded in taking Seamus from her. Fallon's knees buckled, and she wrapped her arms around her middle as waves of sorrow washed her. She'd lost her warrior without even discovering how she could help him. She'd fallen so hard for him so fast, exactly as the gods desired, but she'd let him down. When it mattered most, she didn't do her job, didn't even know what her job was. If only she'd had some way of changing the story for Seamus and her, give it a happy ending, one where they took on Maeve and won. He would need his claymore for that, she thought idly.

The powerful warrior goddess Scathach had abandoned her to help Seamus in the fight, yet even the help of a goddess hadn't been enough to save her warrior from his fate. Through her tears, she gazed around the small space and knew she couldn't stay inside the cabin another minute. Every inch of it held a memory of Seamus. They'd packed so much emotion and physical intensity into such a short time. The feelings crashing down on her threatened to drown her in sorrow and despair, but somewhere inside her a tiny light flickered, urging her to move.

Sleepwalking her way around the cabin, she gathered her few belongings and haphazardly stuffed them into her backpack. Formulating some sort of plan escaped her, but somehow her subconscious prompted her to take along trail mix when she found herself staring at it in the pantry. After she pulled on her hiking boots, she absently dragged a sweatshirt over her head, one Seamus had left hanging on a peg by the door. Out of habit, she centered her backpack and anchored it with the clip at her waist. When she stepped through the door and stood on the porch, she braced herself for sounds of battle.

Hearing a distant keening cry like a raptor circling high overhead but no sounds of fighting, she knew beyond any doubt that Seamus's friends had failed to save him. She thought she should join them anyway and set off on the footpath leading to the trail back to civilization. A long walk later, she discovered herself in another place altogether.

Rowan watched in horror as his friend disappeared into a purple and black mist in the arms of the terrifying goddess. Oblivious to their own danger, Duncan and he ran to the spot from where she'd taken him, intent on trying to gain some idea of where they might look for him. As they spun in circles trying to discover a clue, Scathach arrived.

"What do the two of you think you're doing rushing into the area of Maeve's trap like th—?" she demanded, her red-hot anger pulsing around her.

When the goddess arrived to harangue them, Duncan stopped right as he reached for Seamus's claymore. He blinked up in surprise when it disappeared from his grasp, stunning even Scathach whose rant ended in the middle of a word. For several seconds, the three of them stared at the spot where Seamus's claymore had lain.

With her arms crossed over her chest and a sour look on her face, Scathach glared at the bare space left behind by Seamus's weapon. "Certainly, Maeve has no use for Seamus's sword."

"Indeed, milady, she took great glee in forcing Seamus to let it go before she swallowed him up in her purple and black mist," Rowan said. "We could only watch his agony as he fought to maintain his grip on it, but we couldn't come to his aid. Maeve erected some sort of invisible barrier between us and him."

"We can be reasonably certain Maeve did not change her mind. I cannot imagine what this means," Scathach said as she paced impatiently over the battle-pounded earth.

While the three of them tried to make sense of the disappearance of Seamus's claymore, the rest of their party joined them. In two seconds, Siobhan realized Maeve had succeeded in taking her brother, a keening cry rising from her as she ran into Duncan's arms.

"We didn't have a chance, did we?" she cried into her husband's broad shoulder.

"Have a little faith, Siobhan. We rescued Alyssa from that evil witch's terrible dungeon"—Rowan wrapped an arm around his wife's shoulder—"and we'll rescue Seamus as well. We can reasonably guess she'll take him to her stronghold in Los Angles since it's her closest lair, which means we should make plans to attack her there." He reached out and patted Siobhan's shoulder. "Fortunately, I have an idea of the layout of the place, as does Alyssa—and Seamus for that matter. We have advantages this time we didn't have before."

"We do need to deal with the complication of Seamus's missing claymore," Scathach reminded him.

Griff stepped forward. "What are you talking about, milady?"

"Maeve forced Seamus to leave his claymore behind. A minute ago as I tried to retrieve it, it disappeared from my hand," Duncan said.

"We have no time to lose. How far are we from the cabin?" Griff asked.

Rowan blinked at him. "Less than half a mile. Why?"

"We must get to Fallon. Now."

Scathach snorted, a sound Rowan knew from experience didn't bode well for Griff. "Druid, you are beginning to irritate me. She was perfectly safe under Siobhan's enchantments in the cabin when I left her." She nodded in Siobhan's direction. "Also, I may have erected a barrier at the door to keep her inside after she insisted on accompanying Seamus to the field even though she is not yet aware of her skill."

Griff's eyes pleaded with Rowan for assistance.

"Milady, Griff believes Fallon is a bard. If that's true, she's in as much danger as Seamus, maybe more if Maeve and Morgan figure it out before we can rescue him and reunite them."

"That explains the sword."

The warrior goddess ignored her warrior band's quizzical looks. "Grab your gear and go to the cabin as quickly as possible. I'll meet you there."

CHAPTER NINETEEN

HOUGH DEVASTATED BY the turn of events they had fought so hard to preclude, the warriors wasted no time hiking the short distance to the cabin where they found Scathach alone on the porch in a towering temper.

"She is not here." The goddess's aura flared red. "Some other deity has decided to interfere."

"We have to find her," Griff insisted, his fear vibrating in his voice. "If she's alone out there, she stands no chance against Morgan and Maeve."

"Obviously." Scathach's sarcasm seared the charged atmosphere like acid.

"We didn't pass her on the trail on the way here," Keela said.

After glancing around the cabin, Scathach said, "She did have the good sense to take her belongings with her, so wherever she went, she has her gear. Somewhere along the way, she had some training." Some of her anger visibly dissipated as her red and gold aura toned down from blazing to pulsing.

"Why would she take her gear? Could Maeve have suborned her the way she did that rogue?" Jennifer asked.

Keela rounded on Jennifer. "Of course not! How could you even consider such a thing?"

Rowan stepped in to quell the brewing argument, which was already wasting time while his best friend's life hung in the balance. "How 'bout we try to find her? We'll split up into two teams. The MacManuses, Jennifer, and Keela in one group. Griff, Alyssa, and me in the other. Griff and Keela can stay in telepathic contact while the rest of us keep our shields up. That way we're harder for the nasty ladies to detect." He looked around at each member of the team. "No doubt Morgan is out there somewhere planning another attack while Maeve imposes her torture on Seamus. We can't afford to waste time here."

"As usual, you show wisdom, Rowan Sheridan." Scathach cast her eyes on the rest of the warriors. "You will do as Rowan suggests."

With the goal of ensuring more speed and stamina while they searched, they left the bulk of their gear at the cabin. Griff and Siobhan shouldered their druidic satchels containing the necessary herbs and objects for certain spells they might be called upon to cast. The talismans carried only water while the warriors traveled with nothing but their claymores.

The MacManus group headed out along the main road and, as arranged, turned off at the first spur trail while the Sheridans continued on toward the lake on the main road. None of them dared call out for Fallon for fear they'd alert their common enemy to her whereabouts and vulnerable state if she were acting on her own.

"Keela can't reach Fallon. She must have her shield firmly in place," Griff whispered as they labored to hike the trail the rains had left too slippery for the team's pace. "Keela is struggling."

"What do you mean?" Alyssa asked, her quiet tone fearful.

"The longer we go without being able to reach Fallon, the lower our chances of discovering her unscathed."

"We're all worried, Griff. But more than anything, we can't lose faith, right Pixie-girl?"

Alyssa placed her hand on Rowan's back as he led them along the trail. "Never lose faith," she said.

To Rowan's ears, it was as though she'd whispered volumes.

◈

The trip through time and space in the goddess's net was more wrenching than Seamus believed visualizing could be. When at last Maeve released him, he discovered he'd landed in a castle like something out of a fairy tale—or a nightmare. Its atmosphere of unreality almost made him question his own consciousness.

Maeve had left him in some sort of great hall. The floor looked to be made of slate tiles, but waves of shimmery light indicated the surface might not be quite solid. Cautiously, he knelt and ran his palm over the tiles, discovering the coarse texture, like hewn stone but somehow lacking the stability of natural rock. Something wasn't right. He laughed at himself. *Of course, it's not right, dumbass. This is one of Maeve's playhouses. Nothing about it is real—except for her plans for you.*

That thought sobered him instantly. He studied the space with an eye toward escape. Yards and yards of fine golden silk draped the walls, the fabric secured with broad brass medallions near the ceiling. The ceiling itself appeared to be sculpted plaster. As his eyes adjusted, he observed the sculpture depicted sexual acts, including bestiality with centaurs and satyrs. If the scenes were intended to trigger his libido, they fell far short of the mark. Instead of turning him on, they left him nauseous. If the area in which he found himself was the foyer, and these were the scenes meant for "company," then the rooms where the real action took place must be beyond the sickest of fantasies. Intellectually, he understood that like every effective torture, the damage to the mind was the ultimate goal. Medieval inquisitors liked to display their torture devices in front of their victims—Maeve's ceiling sculptures apparently served a similar purpose.

Tearing his gaze from the scenes above him, he concentrated on finding a way out of the room, one that wouldn't lead him deeper into the fortress—or wherever he was. Finding the walls impenetrable and no doorways hidden behind the draperies, he strode back to the middle of the room and tried to decide which end of the hall would lead outside to possible safety and which would lead farther inside to Maeve's intended torture. Having no natural light in the room to guide him reduced him to flipping a mental coin and hoping for some good luck.

The two doors from which he could choose appeared to be made of heavy wood with brass doorknobs the size of dinner plates placed in exactly the same location in the middle of each one. Nothing about the doors themselves was remarkable or revealing. He chose the one to his right, took a deep breath, and without hesitation, grasped the knob, turned it quickly, and pulled the door open. Immediately, he saw his mistake. The door opened into another great room, this one empty except for a wide stair-case leading up to another floor. Before he could back out of the room, the door closed behind him and disappeared into the wall. Desperately, he tried to find a doorknob, a seam, some hinges—anything to indicate a way out. Instead, he found the same impenetrable material of the walls as in the previous room.

Sucking in a breath to calm himself, he scanned the space to determine if he had a choice in this room as well. Perhaps there was an option other than the obvious one of climbing the stairs to the terrible encounter Maeve planned.

On either side of the stairs, he glimpsed narrow passages and decided to check them out. Moving carefully around the stairs to his left, he found the passages came together behind and under the stairs. As in the first room, there were no windows, no natural light, yet this room glowed like it was its own light source. Moving back to the foot of the stairs, he allowed his eyes to roam up along the ornately carved banisters and discerned that the stairs stopped at a landing where he'd have to make another choice. Stairs angled up to the left and to the right of the landing, leading to two different wings of the castle.

The stairs themselves gleamed like they'd been carved from mahogany. An intricately woven rug ran up the middle of them. When he knelt for a closer look at the carpet, he saw that like the ceiling in the foyer, the runner depicted sex scenes. The distortion of the pictures created by laying the carpet over the steps enhanced their disturbing nature. Once more, waves of nausea swept through him.

He didn't look down as he ascended the stairs. Upon reaching the landing, his choices were mirror images of each other with no distinguishing characteristics to help him decide which way to go. After his experience with the door, he had the distinct impression if he chose poorly again, his other option would disappear like the door into this room, and he'd have no choice but to follow whichever corridor opened to him.

Slowly, he started up the stairs to his right before the hairs on the back of his neck stood up. He leaped back down to the landing and sprinted up the stairs on the left. When he reached the top and looked behind him, he saw that the other staircase, indeed the entire room, had disappeared. There was nothing there but a cloud of swirling gasses. The whole place imitated a carnival fun house, but Seamus didn't feel like laughing.

Hoping he'd made the right choice, and having no other option but to move forward, he wandered warily down a long corridor, which had suddenly opened before him. More than anything, he wished for his claymore. Scanning from one side of the hallway to the other, he noted what at first appeared to be doors leading off the corridor were merely paintings in shallow alcoves. In a cruel twist, each painting had a brass doorknob sticking out in bas-relief.

As he strolled along the corridor, the space never changed

other than to appear endless. His limbs fatigued, weighted down, like he'd hiked the corridor for days, and he wondered if that was part of the enchantment. The monotony of the painted doors wore on him as well. Action would be better than the interminable walk down the unending hallway.

The endless walking dulled his senses, and he traveled several paces beyond it before he stopped stone-still. One of the painted doors he'd passed was actually a window. Retracing his steps, he glanced out of it and determined that the castle, or wherever he was, hovered above the lake near his cabin. Maeve hadn't taken him very far, or her enchantments were especially cruel. Possibly both. With growing desperation, he searched for a latch or some way to open the window. The window was sealed shut, though, so he decided to break it. Pulling his hand back into the sleeve of his leather jacket to shield his fist from the glass, he punched the window hard, the shock of the blow reverberating up his arm for several excruciating minutes afterward. He swore and flexed his bruised fist. Though transparent, the window wasn't made of glass.

He shook out his pain before checking to see if he'd broken any bones. Somehow, he thought Maeve would be rather angry if he showed up to her chamber damaged. He laughed. "She's not interested in your hands, old son. Too bad for her. I'm rather handy with them." He laughed again at his bad pun. The pain in his fist felt welcome. Anything to remind him that he was still of the earth and possibly not as crazy as his laughter sounded echoing down the endless hallway.

Intuitively knowing the window was yet another torture, he still couldn't stop himself from gazing out of it. On the shore of the lake, the mists had burned off in the heat of the afternoon sun. The water lapped gently at the sand while the sun playfully glinted off the waves. He could almost feel the refreshingly freezing lake water washing over his skin as he remembered swimming in it countless times in his life.

A movement caught the corner of his eye, abruptly ending his reminiscence. Pushing his nose to the window to find an angle from which to see more clearly, he watched the movement coalesce into a person, and his blood ran cold. Fallon stood alone on the edge of the lake, her distress evident in the tight way she held herself. He couldn't see into the trees from which she'd emerged, so he couldn't be sure someone—or something—wasn't chasing her. It didn't matter. He couldn't reach her from where he was, which was a form of torture that went far beyond sick erotica and mind-numbing imprisonment.

Pounding on the window, he cried out to her. "Fallon! Fallon! Go back to the cabin! You're not safe here. Go back, honey, please." His desperate voice echoed down the corridor.

She looked up when Seamus called to her, but she didn't seem to see him. Another torture. After unclipping the waist strap, she slipped off her backpack and laid it on the ground. In slow motion, she moved toward the water. A wave of bone-deep despair washed over him as he imagined her intent. Surely, she wouldn't walk into the lake?

"Fallon! Fallon! I'm here. I'm alive. Maeve hasn't touched me. Please, Fireworks, hold on. We're going to get through this!" Seamus cried out to her, but she didn't respond in any way. Her now-formidable shield seemed to be firmly in place. Either that or Maeve's enchanted abode served as a barrier to telepathic communication.

For hours-long minutes, Fallon stood at the edge of the water hugging herself. Seamus could feel the pain radiating off of her like scalding steam. Several times, he hurled himself against the window but only succeeded in bruising his shoulders and arms. He swore and once again wished for his claymore, even knowing it would do him little good for breaking free and reaching his talisman.

Suddenly, a fine iridescent mist started to form over her. As he watched in impotent horror, the mist enveloped her, forming a bubble around her. Once it surrounded her completely, the bubble lifted into the air and floated over the lake to hover beside the castle. From somewhere down the hall, Seamus heard Maeve's malevolent laughter, and he knew the terrible goddess had made sure Fallon would have a front row seat from which to view his torture. He crumpled against the wall as desolation washed over him.

⌇

Fallon woke up as if from a trance to discover herself hovering several terrifying feet above a lake. Fearful of moving, she scanned her space with her eyes only and figured out she floated inside a bubble. When it started moving, she lost her balance, landing on her knees inside it. A scream ripped from her throat as she struggled to keep from tearing the fragile membrane and crashing into the lake. The bubble bounced her back to a standing position while it glided toward some sort of castle suspended even higher above the water.

When she saw the castle, she forgot to be afraid of her own predicament and what it might mean that she drifted in a bubble above the dark waves rolling beneath her. Surely, both entities, the bubble and the castle, were the evil goddess Maeve's creations. Only she could create torture chambers so seemingly lovely as a floating castle and an iridescent bubble. Instinctively, she knew Maeve had trapped Seamus inside the castle, and neither of them could escape their enchanted prisons.

The bubble gently sailed to a spot directly outside a window of the ethereal edifice. Unlike the windows in a normal palace, the one before which the bubble came to rest resembled plate glass. It looked more suited to a discount chain warehouse store than to a delicate fairy-tale castle. Without having to peek into the window, she knew that behind it lay Maeve's bedroom, the place where she held Seamus and planned to drain him of his life force.

When she realized she was intended to have a prime view

of her love succumbing to Maeve's torturous delights, she began pushing desperately against the membrane in which the goddess had caged her. She preferred falling to her death in the freezing lake to watching Maeve's unholy plans for her love. She'd watched that particular scenario enough over the past months. She knew how it ended.

Though a bubble, her prison was made of something far more substantial than water. No matter how hard she flung herself against it, the membrane barely gave. It was too large for her to stretch and touch it diametrically with her hands and feet, so she had no leverage for pushing hard enough against it to burst it. Spying her backpack far down on the beach, she screeched in frustration at having no tools with her to puncture the balloon holding her against her will. With mounting fear, she flailed against her pretty floating cage until she had no more strength to fight it.

Sitting down heavily, Fallon wept in sorrowful resignation. The floor of the bubble didn't sag under her weight, a fact she barely registered as she stared at the castle, her tears distorting the scene before her but not washing it away. A black cloak of despair settled over her as she watched Seamus step cautiously through the door of the bedroom in front of her, spy the huge four-poster bed in the middle of it, and desperately try to back out of the now-nonexistent door.

CHAPTER TWENTY

RIFF AND THE Sheridans heard a scream and figured out Fallon must be somewhere ahead of them on the main trail.

"Keela, she's probably at the lake. Backtrack and meet us there," Griff communicated.

"Do you see her? Is she safe?" Keela asked, her frantic fear for her niece resonating from her mind to her husband's.

Electing not to alarm his wife more than necessary, he replied, *"We heard her. We're close. Hurry and join us on the main trail. And Keela, pay attention. We all could be walking into a trap."*

As Griff communicated with Keela, he, Rowan, and Alyssa reached the end of the tree-lined trail and cautiously stepped onto the rocky beach of a high mountain lake. The waters distorted the most beautiful and terrifying scene any of them had ever witnessed. Floating serenely above the unnaturally smooth surface of the water was multiturreted castle.

"What the hell *is* that?" Rowan asked, his voice barely above a whisper.

As they watched, the castle seemed to morph into a

manor house with lush green lawns flanking a long, impeccably graveled drive. After several minutes, the scene changed again to something like a medieval stronghold with massive round towers, a drawbridge, and a moat. The edifice so entranced them, they barely acknowledged their friends' arrival beside them on the lakeshore.

"What the hell is *that*?" Duncan asked, breaking the silence.

"Exactly what we'd like to know," Rowan said.

Griff's fear reverberated around the party as he explained. "That, my friends, is Maeve's playhouse."

"That? Look how it moves and changes. It's a mirage. How can Maeve hold Seamus in something so insubstantial?" Duncan scoffed.

"The same way she took a warrior at least once before."

"What do you mean?" Rowan asked.

"A long time ago, sometime in the mid-1860s," Griff began, "the local people marveled at the sight of a beautiful castle floating above the sea near Inishowen, Ireland, a short trip up the coast from Derry. As people gathered to watch, the castle changed to a manor house then to a magnificent multiturreted castle. The 'mirage,' as the local scientists and experts called it, lasted for well over two hours."

He turned from the scene above the lake to face the rest of rescue party. "The local papers called it 'the Phantom Island,' and people who saw it believed they were privileged to have seen such an enchanting sight," he continued. "What they didn't know was inside that ephemeral building a warrior was losing his life force to a voracious goddess who delighted in tricking the civilian population into thinking her incredible ugliness was something sublime."

"Jesus. She may be even more evil than Morgan," Rowan said as he wrapped a protective arm around Alyssa who hugged him back.

"She built the Phantom Island on the west coast of Ireland

away from the warrior's Scots family and friends to ensure no one would come along and find a way to interfere in her fun. Siobhan, would you like to tell the rest?" Griff asked, deferring to his fellow druid. Earlier when they had seen into each other's minds, Griff had seen this story of the agony of another warrior in another time, which gave him a greater appreciation for her desperation for her brother.

Siobhan swallowed several times. Eventually, she spoke, her voice rough with unshed tears. "We have a story in our family history of an ancestor, a powerful warrior also named Seamus, who encountered Maeve in a battle and disappeared. No one knows what happened to him, but there was evidence to suggest he was the warrior who succumbed to Maeve's terrible lust in an enchanted castle somewhere off the coast of Ireland." She blindly reached for Duncan's hand, grabbed it, and Griff watched her knuckles turn white as she finished the story. "Until now, I thought the castle was an actual stronghold. Now I see it's something even more terrifying because we have no way to assault it, to breach its enchantments and free my brother." Tears flowed unabated over her cheeks, her eyes riveted on the pulsating scene before them.

Duncan pulled her into his arms and held her while they all stared at the Phantom Island that had changed into a multistory castle with enormous windows, its fairy-tale quality morphing into something grotesque.

"She's not taking this Seamus, not if I can help it. There has to be a way inside," Rowan said. "I refuse to give up on saving my friend." He paced along the shoreline, staring at the otherworldly vision like he was trying to find a solid part of it where he could enter.

Rowan's impatient pacing drew their attention to a backpack lying on the beach. Rushing over to it, Keela cried out in horror.

"Oh no! I think Fallon is in that terrible castle too." She lifted Fallon's pack to show the others.

"No, she's not inside that place, but she's every bit as trapped. Check out the giant bubble hovering outside one of the third-story windows," Alyssa said as she pointed to a satellite with Fallon trapped inside.

As the team watched in fear and fascination, they determined that Fallon locked her concentration on something inside the castle, something only she could see from her vantage point. Based on what they knew of her premonitions, it didn't take much imagination to figure out what riveted her attention and why they'd heard her scream.

"Fallon, can you hear us?" Keela called out to her. "Fallon, darling, we're here with you. Look to the shore of the lake."

When she didn't respond to Keela's persistent calls, Griff grabbed his wife by the shoulders. "Keela, stop! Either that bubble is soundproof or her concentration on what she's seeing impedes her from hearing you. We don't know yet what other traps are here, traps intended to take more than Fallon and Seamus. We must be cautious." He sought to soften his remonstrance by enfolding Keela in his arms and whispering, "Clearly, we still have a little time."

After a beat, she nodded.

With Keela in his arms, Griff addressed the others. "We need a plan and we need it quick."

"I take it you already have an idea," Rowan said.

He nodded. "We should leave Duncan, Jennifer, and Keela watching from the trees at the edge of the beach and taking on any minions Morgan unleashes against us when we move to free Seamus." He tightened his arms around Keela when he sensed her protest. "Rowan and Alyssa, your job will be to circle the lake to try to find a way to reach him in that unnatural stronghold." They nodded. "Siobhan, you and I will work with Fallon, try to guide her to discovering her gift in time to save Seamus."

"At long last, druid, you are useful," Scathach interrupted as she marched out from the trees into the clearing.

"Thank you, milady," Griff said as he stepped away from his wife and sketched a bow to the goddess.

"If you can prove yourselves, you and Siobhan can expect some help from another quarter who is not yet ready to reveal herself. She has already stepped in to help Fallon by freeing her from my barrier at the cabin when she thwarted Maeve by returning Seamus's sword to him."

A tiny grin ghosted her face at the shocked surprise of her warriors at her news.

Rowan was first to recover. "What are you saying, milady?"

"When Maeve took Seamus, she forced him to drop his sword. You two saw that," Scathach said as she gestured to Rowan and Duncan. "As the three of us watched in wonder, Seamus's sword disappeared as you reached for it, Duncan."

The warrior nodded.

"In that moment, Fallon gave Seamus his sword. He has it with him even now. She has taken the first step toward changing Seamus's story, which was the sign a powerful goddess wished to see before she intervened in Fallon and Seamus's destiny."

Druids and warriors exchanged looks ranging from disbelief to wonder.

"By the way, Griffin," Scathach continued. "You were right to instruct Fallon to put on her bracelet and have Seamus brand her with his sign. The goddess approved of you relying on your 'instinct' to instruct your niece."

"*Branding* her? *What?*"

The goddess waved a hand at Keela's outburst. "Those marks physically link her to him, deepening their connection. Seamus's sign on Fallon's wrist will be Maeve's undoing, but only if you lot do your jobs instead of standing around waiting for Maeve to have her way." Scathach's stature seemed to grow in proportion to her impatience.

None of the warrior band needed further instruction. Duncan, Jennifer, and Keela headed back into the trees. Rowan took Alyssa's hand and led her along the lake in the opposite direction of their friends. Siobhan and Griff stayed where they were in sight of Fallon and determined how to breach either her shield or Maeve's enchantments. Scathach disappeared in a red and gold shimmer.

Oblivious to the help amassing on the shoreline of the lake, Seamus stared back at Fallon as she took in the scene unfolding in the massive bedchamber of Maeve's enchanted castle. Earlier when he saw the bubble encasing Fallon drift away down the exterior of the castle, he ran from the window up the corridor seeking another place from which to see it and hopefully to let Fallon see him. In his fear for his talisman, he didn't pay attention to his surroundings other than to find another window or an actual door facing outside, which led him to a small, nondescript door that, unfortunately, opened into the goddess's ornate bedchamber. Discovering his mistake, he tried to back out, but once again the door melted into the wall, and he was well and truly trapped.

Glancing around the room, he saw that Fallon could see him through the enormous window Maeve had obviously placed purely for Fallon's "entertainment."

As he bumped into the wall in his attempt to retrace his steps out of the now-nonexistent door, he felt the familiar heft and shape of his claymore. "What the hell?" he said as he reached behind his head for his sword.

Right as he grasped it, Fallon called out. *"No Seamus! She's coming! Don't let her see your sword."*

He blinked as Fallon breached his shield. Dropping his

hands to clasp them in front of himself, he stood at ease, nonchalantly facing the space where the door had been as he awaited the goddess.

⌀

Unable to see anything other than the room itself, Fallon had no idea how she knew Maeve was about to enter the bedroom, but she understood instinctively Seamus needed to hide his weapon from the goddess.

Clearly a master of the dramatic entrance, Maeve tossed open a hidden door, waited a few seconds for Seamus to give her his full attention, and stepped into the room. With a nod, she closed the door behind her. For several long minutes she stood facing him, letting him take in all of her because of course she had dressed specifically for the occasion.

With her ample chest pushed forward, one foot positioned slightly in front of the other, her knee subtly bent, her chin elevated enough for her to look down her nose at him, Maeve struck a pose. Her long red hair cascaded loosely down her back except for one fat curl that dropped tantalizingly over her shoulder to hang over and off one of her breasts. The gossamer dress hugging her curves like a second skin was so thin as to almost disguise its pale green color. She was more naked than dressed. Fallon gasped at the goddess's beauty before despair crowded into her mind. How could anyone, but especially a man as virile as Seamus, withstand such temptation? Though he stood with his hands clasped in front of him, his arousal was evident. The smile on Maeve's face as she gazed at her prey made Fallon's blood run cold.

Swallowing over the lump in her throat, she reached out to her warrior and hoped he could hear her. *"She's going to take you. Fight her as much as you can, but know she's going to win the first round. You mustn't feel guilty. It's how you'll learn how to best her. Trust me."*

"Fallon, I won't betray you. Don't ask that of me."

Her heart broke at the anguish she could hear in Seamus's mind.

"I can't see another way," she said, her agony as acute as her warrior's.

"Oh, I do hope those expressions crossing your face mean you are communicating with your talisman. I am sure she is going to enjoy the show." Maeve nodded in Fallon's direction, and her bubble prison kissed the window, sound penetrating like it had been piped in, making sure Fallon could hear everything going on in the room. "Too bad everything she will learn from me about pleasuring you will be for naught since she will never have the chance to use any of my techniques on you." The cat-with-the-cream expression on the goddess's face as she slowly advanced on him roiled Fallon's stomach. "You can easily see what I have to offer you. Now I wish to see what you have to offer me. Take off your clothes, Seamus," she demanded as she glided over to the bed and lay across it to watch her private striptease.

Seamus defied her. "I'd rather not, Maeve, if you don't mind. I have no intention of making anything that happens in this room easy for you."

"Pity. I do rather enjoy my paramours to be attentive to my needs—and commands."

With a nod of her head, the room rolled, and Seamus stumbled to the end of the bed. "As you can see, everything in this place does my bidding. You will too. Take off your clothes."

Fallon watched in horror as the room shifted again, forcing Seamus closer to the vicious goddess lusting for his body—and his life. Desperately, she wanted to change the scene, retell the story like she used to do with the old myths when Sloane and she were kids.

As soon as that idea struck her, she thought she heard Griff calling to her. Momentarily, she tore her eyes from the scene unfolding in the room behind the glass and blinked several times at her uncle who was frantically waving to her from the shore of the lake. He stood beside a striking blonde whose attention never wavered from Fallon in her bubble. *"Uncle Griff? What are you doing here?"*

"At last, Fallon." He sighed as he dropped his arms. *"Have you discovered your skill yet?"*

"Apparently not."

He smiled. *"Does Seamus have his sword with him?"*

"Yes. Why?"

"Maeve forced him to give it up when she stole him. Do you have any idea how he regained it?"

"No," she replied, perplexed.

"Think, Fallon. This is really important. Did any ideas about Seamus's sword occur to you today?"

As she thought back over the events of the day, she remembered being on the floor of the cabin as she came out of an especially brutal version of her premonition and thinking she'd like to rewrite the ending. Seamus would need his claymore to help them accomplish that. *"Um, yes, actually. Why?"*

"Was Seamus with you then?"

"He was at the battle. I thought about his sword sometime after I felt Maeve take him from me." She hoped Griff couldn't hear her anguish as she recounted her greatest sorrow.

"When you had that thought, you gave it back to him. You changed the story, Fallon."

On her guard, she asked, *"What are you saying, Uncle Griff?"*

The blonde standing on the beach beside Griff interrupted their conversation. *"Fallon, I'm Seamus's sister Siobhan. We talked to your friend Sloane MacIntyre who told us you used to like to change the old Celtic stories when you were kids. Have you had any thoughts about changing yours and Seamus's story?"*

For several long seconds, she didn't answer. She was too

stunned. How could this woman know what she'd been thinking only minutes before Griff had grabbed her attention?

"I can change Seamus's story?" she asked slowly, not daring to hope for a different ending to the terrible visions she'd watched for so long.

"You have that power, yes. But you have to use it carefully. You have to think through the story before you change it," Griff warned her.

"How can I do that?" Flattening her hands on the stretchy iridescent membrane of her floating prison, she stared down at the people on the beach.

Before Griff could answer her, she heard a warning shout from beyond the tree line. Griff and Siobhan had a fraction of a second to react before a massive giant man-creature crashed down the shore toward them.

Fallon screamed.

Now her attention was divided by Seamus trapped in Maeve's chamber and her family suddenly battling for their lives on the shore as she saw Keela step from the trees along with a warrior and talisman she didn't know. They seemed intent on distracting the giant from its attack on Griff and Siobhan.

As if sensing her distress, Griff called out to her. *"Pay no attention to us. We've taken on one like this already today. Direct your skills toward Seamus. Take care of your warrior."* He turned his attention from her to take on the new threat.

Emotionally torn in two, Fallon wrenched her gaze away from the scene on the beach and focused on her warrior. To her horror, she saw that while she'd conversed with Griff and Siobhan, Maeve had somehow forced Seamus into her unholy bed where she held him securely, his hands and feet tied to the four bedposts with golden cords. The sight of him lying there naked and erect, his agony etched on his face, debilitated her. Tormenting pain doubled her over and numbed her in the face of Seamus's and her shared torture.

Griff had said something about her having the power to change their story, but he didn't tell her how to do it. Though her enchanted prison kept her physically safe from the dangers her family faced, it served its purpose well and prevented her from aiding any of them, an exquisite torture she had no doubt the goddess delighted in inflicting. Maeve's plan was obvious as she stood at the window with the Morrigan, her flowing white hair and glowing blood-red eyes a dead giveaway as to her identity, as the two watched the battle unfold on the beach. Vaguely, it occurred to Fallon that all this time her vision had been incomplete. The goddess wanted more than Seamus. She wanted all of them. Seamus, Fallon, and their families. Somehow, she had to find a way to prevent Maeve from reaching her goal.

CHAPTER TWENTY-ONE

EARING DUNCAN'S SHOUT, Rowan and Alyssa doubled back to the area of the shore where they'd left Griff and Siobhan, their efforts in finding an entrance to the floating castle fruitless.

"Which one is this?" Duncan asked as he feinted toward a boulder in an attempt to draw the zombie giant into tripping over it.

"Alyssa? Ideas?" Rowan asked.

"I think it's Bolster, the Cornish giant. He had a penchant for young women. Rather fitting Morgan sends him when our party runs long on women," Alyssa replied sardonically. Then she reached out to Rowan telepathically. *"His death was caused by a cunning act of bloodletting. Let the talismans lure him to the lake where you'll need to slash his wrists."*

"Not too fond of the plan, Pixie-girl, since it puts all of you in danger," Rowan began before Alyssa cut him off with an exaggerated eye roll. *"But I know your expertise in Celtic lore, so we'll go with it."*

"Bolster! He-ey Bolster. We're over here. If you wish to

taste our charms, come sit on this rock with us and rest your hand near the water," Alyssa called as she, Keela, and Jennifer skipped along the shore, reaching a shallow creek that turned to churning foam where it fed into the lake.

The area Alyssa chose held as much danger to her and her fellow talismans as the zombie giant they lured to the water crashing against the boulders where the creek met the lake. Though he didn't like the perilousness of the plan, Rowan understood it couldn't be helped.

In her usual way, Alyssa sensed his unease. *"Saint Agnes tempted Bolster in exactly this way when she killed him by tricking him into slitting his wrist to fill a hole in the ocean. Though this giant no longer has any blood, I'm gambling that reenacting his death in the lake will kill him again with equal effectiveness."*

Rowan nodded, his claymore at the ready as he concealed himself behind a nearby boulder. The talismans carefully stepped from rock to rock as they climbed their way up the boulders piled along the stream. They gathered at a shallow dish carved into the top of one of the boulders. With coquettish gyrations and smiles, they beckoned the giant to come close. With the giant's attention focused on the women, Rowan and Duncan were free to follow and pick their time with no resistance from the giant himself. As Bolster neared the rocks where the women had positioned themselves, Rowan stepped forward and slashed the giant's wrist while Duncan, taking no chances, sliced the other one.

Rowan grinned. Bolster's intent to have the beautiful women rendered him senseless to danger. He blinked his vacant eyes, and a look of surprise crossed his face when his life force left him in a rush. He toppled over, disappearing beneath the steamy brown foam of the rushing stream making its loud and dangerous way to the lake.

The warriors knew better than to celebrate their victory. If anything, the giant's appearance and the relatively easy way in which they dispatched him indicated he was merely the vanguard of the troops Morgan intended to unleash against them.

⁂

Seamus struggled unceasingly against both the cords physically holding him and the unholy lust Maeve forced him to experience. As much as he wanted her, he knew that giving in to the demands she forced on his body would condemn his soul to everlasting torture as he walked in the mists among warriors who had given their lives honorably in battle in service to their fellow man. Keeping the shame of his demise in the forefront of his thoughts, he continued to look for a way to defeat his greatest enemy.

Sweat beaded his body as he glared at Maeve who eyed him like she meant to eat him whole.

"Keep it up, Seamus. I find that sheen of sweat especially enticing." Her tongue snaked out of her mouth as she licked her lips dramatically. Her move reminded him of a villain in a campy melodrama. If his situation weren't so desperate, he might have laughed at her over-the-top attempt at sexy. "Did you know that you are not the first of your family to entertain me in this way in this place?" Her malevolent tone warred with her sinuous movements.

His struggles manifested in the raspy sound of his voice. "What are you talking about?"

"A long time ago—in human terms—I took a fancy to one of your ancestors, a warrior also named Seamus." She touched a finger to her lips. "His surname was Gallagher I think. Anyway, I lured him into battle and spirited him away to this same enchanted fortress floating off the shores of Ireland where he pleasured me well for several days before he finally gave in and walked across the ford with my sister." She ran a finger up and down the cord near his right foot. "Sound familiar? His talisman was not as powerful as yours, however, so it was pointless to invite her to the festivities." She glanced out the window at Fallon still floating in her bubble that gently bounced against the enchanted glass of the castle. "Your talisman possesses certain skills that make it especially delicious for me to include her in our sexy little party."

Seamus had no idea what Maeve was on about. He and Fallon hadn't had a chance to discover her skill before Maeve stole him away to her terrible bed.

"Of course, I have my sister's wishes to consider." An angry expression darkened her features for a second. "She would like to have fresh blood to wade across into the mists, so your talisman and your friends and your family were necessary guests as well."

At the mention of his family and friends, Seamus fought his bonds even harder.

Her purple-black eyes lit up at the look of pure horror he couldn't stop from sliding across his face. Slowly, she peeled off her nearly nonexistent dress.

"How do you like to take your pleasure, warrior?"

Sensing that she wanted to invade his mind, he gritted his teeth and redoubled his shield.

She sniffed derisively before returning her attention to the window.

"Fallon, darling, I do hope you are enjoying the show. I would very much like to help Seamus in his current state," she paused to draw Fallon's attention to Seamus's erect member, "but he is vexingly uncooperative about telling me what he likes. Perhaps you can help me?"

"Don't let her in Fallon!" Seamus screamed.

It was too late.

Maeve grinned in evil triumph.

"Noooo!" Fallon cried as Maeve slowly crawled up the bed between Seamus's legs before she languidly pulled her own legs up to straddle him. Sinuously, she raised her arms above her head and stared into his eyes as she lowered herself inch by excruciating inch, sheathing him inside her.

Both Seamus and Fallon cried out in anguish as the goddess reenacted their lovemaking on Seamus's body. Every movement sent waves of breath-stealing pleasure-pain radiating from his center through his entire body. When he tore his eyes away from the goddess, fresh agony assailed him as he watched Fallon claw at her throat in a terrible struggle to breathe.

Maeve rode him harder while she tempted him to give in to her. "Come, warrior. You know you want to. You know how incredibly good it will feel to spill your life force deep inside the body of a goddess. In your heart, you know you want to give me what I want."

As Maeve rode him, she turned her attention to the other goddess in the room. "Morgan, the party is over here. You have an even better seat than that sad little mortal floating outside the window. Why are you not paying attention to our triumph?" She shifted over him, and he fought against the pleasure threatening to arrow down his spine. "Really, Morgan. Do you never tire of watching battle? Why don't you make yourself comfortable and enjoy a different sort of battle, single combat with one sword and one sheath?"

Seamus ground down on his teeth to keep from crying out, the battle between his emotions and his body the most excruciating pain he'd ever endured.

"I've unleashed the rest of the *Nephilim* on the warriors who wish to thwart us. Two warriors taking on two giants is quite entertaining. You should see it." Morgan's obscene concentration riveted on the scene unfolding on the beach, and a new pain shot through him as he worried about his family fighting for him.

Maeve settled for a second, giving Seamus a fraction of time to regroup, hold himself back.

Her sigh held all kinds of exasperation. "Morgan, how can

you get off only with blood ebbing and flowing around your legs? The real pleasure takes place between them." She increased her tempo on his captive body.

He fisted his hands, knocking them against the bedposts as he fought the pleasure-pain Maeve inflicted on him. Reaching out to his talisman, he pleaded, *"Find a way for us, Fallon. Find a way for us, please!"*

Tearing at her throat, Fallon fought to breathe. Her left hand unconsciously grabbed her right wrist, and electricity pulsed throughout her body. The direct contact of the inside of her bracelet to her branded skin where the metal aligned with the signs Seamus had traced on her abruptly shocked her out of the enervating trance the scene in front of her spun over her mind.

Without understanding how she knew it, she had the idea Seamus needed a new story. In her hubris, when Maeve had opened the sound barriers between the bubble and the enchanted castle to allow Fallon to hear the conversations going on there, her intention was for Fallon to hear Seamus voicing his acute suffering, or worse, his pleasure in the goddess. But now she also heard Maeve describing the fate of another Seamus at another time. She needed to tell a story of this Seamus whose story had a better ending.

Remembering her uncle's directive to think through every possible outcome to the story, Fallon closed her eyes and let her mind go blank. A picture of Seamus's claymore and how she returned it to him entered her mind. Studying Maeve's enchanted bedroom, she searched for Seamus's belongings. Spying his jacket and jeans on the floor beside the bed, she scanned that area more closely. When she couldn't locate his claymore, despair crowded in. Yet when her bubble shifted, she caught a glimpse of something shiny beneath his clothes. A tiny smile tipped the corner of her mouth. She needed every resource she had to win this battle, beginning with a mind open to a perfect possibility.

❧

"Now Morgan's just showing off," Duncan panted as he took on Gorm, the Gorge of Avon giant while Rowan battled with Cormoran, the Cornish giant first defeated by King Brute. "She brings the Celtic Titans from Scotland, England, and Cornwall against us all in one afternoon? That's a bit much, even for her."

"You're forgetting the big brute Fomorian we took on earlier today in the marsh," Rowan reminded him as he ducked an enormous blow Cormoran determined to land. When the blow didn't connect, the giant's momentum spun him into the soft silt of the beach, giving Rowan an open shot. Slashing his sword across the backs of the giant's exposed legs, he hamstrung the giant, ending his threat. Now he could give his attention to helping his friend take on the cannibalistic Gorm the Grim.

"Yeah, and the five rogues who appeared out of nowhere. Don't they have to visualize like we do?" Duncan asked, sounding perplexed.

"Morgan bends the rules for her minions. Like that's a surprise," Rowan said as he feinted to draw the giant's attention away from Duncan.

In his zombie state, Gorm relished the taste of human flesh even more, and he zeroed in on Duncan. Rowan could see the giant intended to back his friend into the lake, forcing him into the giant's range. Shouting and dancing in close, Rowan did his best to draw Gorm's attention away from his fellow warrior.

Through the din, he heard a desperate telepathic conversation between the two people least experienced in battle.

"Griff, Siobhan needs to come to the aid of her warrior. He's about to be taken either by the lake or by the giant he battles. You must help."

"Fallon is at a critical point. She's almost discovered her skill. We can't leave her now," Griff said.

"Her brother or her husband. Siobhan is going to have to choose." Keela's agitation and sorrow came through loud and clear.

The situation was spiraling out of control.

"Call your brother, Keela," Griff commanded.

For a split second, Rowan worried about Griff's idea. Then Gorm lunged at Duncan, and he decided he'd accept reinforcements from wherever they came.

Griff's conversation interrupted again. *"Siobhan, Duncan needs you. You must weave a spell for him, create a barrier between him and his enemy."*

"Fallon is about to discover her skill. She can save Seamus. I have to help her, too."

The anguish Rowan heard in Siobhan's voice stiffened his resolve, and he tried even harder to distract the giant from his intention to eat Duncan for lunch. A minute later, he marveled as he watched water plants rise out of the lake to climb and intertwine into an impenetrable wall between Duncan and Gorm the Grim. Siobhan had made her choice.

"Behind you!" Alyssa called out.

Forgetting that zombies have no feeling, Rowan thought he'd defeated Cormoran when in fact he'd only slowed him down for a minute. The giant clumsily pulled up from the hole he'd dug himself into and lumbered toward Rowan on legs made unsteady from Rowan's cutting blow. Facing the new danger, he saw he and Duncan were truly in dire straits. *"Call Alaisdair and Shanley. We need Alaisdair's sword, Alyssa,"* he directed as he swung his claymore, opening a gaping gash in the giant from his shoulder to his ribs. Still, the brute came on.

As he fought his own battle, from the corner of his eye he saw that the living barrier Siobhan had erected between her husband and the menace attempting to steal his life had reached a towering height. Like it could no longer bear its own weight, it toppled over on Gorm, entangling him in a mass of ever-tightening moss and long grass. With a furious scream, Gorm the Grim fell heavily to the earth. Duncan rested his hands on the pommel of his sword for a few seconds as he caught his breath.

Gathering himself, he walked within a sword's reach of the giant, warmed up his shoulders, and delivered a crushing blow right as Gorm broke free of the net. The mosses and grass stopped the head from rolling away from the body.

"Again, Duncan! Slice through the net and force the head from the body!" Jennifer shouted.

"Duncan! He's not dead. Strike him again!" Siobhan yelled as she ran along the shoreline toward her husband.

The shouting of the women alerted Cormoran to them, and he turned his attention to the nearest one, Siobhan running toward the battle. Forgetting Rowan, the giant lumbered toward his new target. Intent on reaching her husband, Siobhan kept running toward danger until Alaisdair Graham materialized in front of her, his claymore balanced and ready to deliver a devastating blow.

"Slow down, lass. I've got 'im," Alaisdair said as he drew the giant's attention away from Siobhan.

She skidded to a stop as Alaisdair feinted away from the zombie giant before stepping in to slice a gash across its belly to match the one Rowan had delivered to its shoulder. Then an unfamiliar warrior arrived and pulled her out of harm's way.

"The cavalry has arrived, Siobhan, and now I need your help," Griff shouted from down the beach.

She stumbled back to Griff and their assembled druidic accouterments. "What's happening?"

"Fallon's parents have arrived. Clancy Graham has joined his distant cousin in rescuing you from imminent danger."

Rowan's sigh of relief caught in his throat when Griff's next words made his blood run cold. "I just hope he doesn't turn on us when he realizes you aren't your husband's talisman."

It was all Rowan could do not to attack the new arrival who had helped to rescue Siobhan and give them reinforcements. Fallon's dad hated druids? *What the hell?*

As Griffin finished his not-so-private communication, Rowan noticed a fresh influx of rogues swarming in to aid the undead Cormoran.

"We've got more company coming, boys," he said. "Time to put this guy down once and for all before his reinforcements make it hard on us."

Together, Rowan, Duncan, Alaisdair, and Fallon's father descended on the giant. With no clear target, Cormoran flailed his arms uselessly while the four warriors together ran him through. For extra good measure, they beheaded him and rolled his body into the lake where, like Bolster and Gorm the Grim, he disappeared beneath the surface in a hiss of steaming brown foam.

CHAPTER TWENTY-TWO

EAMUS ALMOST LAUGHED when Morgan stomped her foot in a fit of pique. "Once again a Sheridan and his friends have defeated my zombie champions. It took a great deal of skill and energy to summon such a gathering." Her hands balled into fists. "A Fomorian and the Nephilim should have been more than enough to best these mortals, yet I find myself again without a prize to escort across the ford." She stared pointedly at Maeve's back.

Maeve sat still for a moment atop Seamus and regarded Morgan over her shoulder while she continued to torture him by fondling her breasts. "Another defeat, Morgan? Pity. Perhaps if you directed your attention to my conquest, you would feel better. You know you will have at least one of Scathach's champions when I have finished with him."

"Maeve, you are far too interested in that which does not matter. Watching you with a warrior or a god is mildly entertaining. The power you expend is barely worth noting. Whereas, the power inherent in directing a battle is an aphrodisiac beyond compare. The thin lifeless blood left over from the warriors you give me barely touches me." She sniffed, glancing down her nose at Seamus sprawled out beneath Maeve.

He might have taken offense if Maeve hadn't shifted, drawing his attention back to his cock. Over the roaring in his ears, he heard Morgan speaking, the dreaminess of her tone an obscenity on par with the way Maeve was using him.

"The full-bodied adrenaline-rich blood of warriors slain in battle nearly takes my breath away," Morgan said.

"Exactly. Which is why you are so frustrated at the moment. Because *your* power over the Sheridans and their friends is so great," Maeve taunted.

Turning her attention back to him, she licked a finger and ran it up the middle of his torso from the place where she joined their bodies to the divot in his collarbone. He hissed a breath in through gritted teeth and refused to cry out at the contact that singed him like molten metal. "You take my ministrations so well, warrior. Almost as well as one of my favorite lovers, Taranis. Of course, unlike Taranis, you give me your full attention. He is nearly always attending to some storm or other while he services me. I find it rude of him," she said as though her mind were elsewhere while she renewed her torment of his body.

"Perhaps you should call him and ask him to take care of your needs since he clearly satisfies you better than I can." He clenched his jaws so tight, his lips barely moved with his words.

"Oh, no. He is merely a plaything when I am not busy wreaking havoc with mortal warriors. As you have already noticed, I like to be in charge." She rocked her hips to prove the point, and he groaned in painful lust. "Even when I tie Taranis up sometimes, he only gives me what he wants to give me. It is most unchivalrous of him," Maeve said with a pout.

"Careful, sister. You never know where Taranis is lurking. If he hears you, he might stay out of your bed for years," Morgan warned. "Ah, there they are. This should be interesting."

"What are you doing now, Morgan?" Maeve demanded as she started moving over Seamus's body again, her rhythm intentionally slow to maximize the excruciating pain she intended to inflict both on the warrior and on his talisman.

He understood she intended for him to cry out, to beg for mercy or to shout in orgasmic pleasure, but he'd die before he gave her what she wanted. His abdominal muscles screamed in torment as he tried to pull his body deeper into the mattress and away from the clenching sheath of the goddess. All the while, he called out to Fallon who seemed to have slipped away from him. Tears he couldn't stop himself from shedding slid over his temples to intermingle with the sweat plastering his hair to his head.

∽

Beside the lake, Rowan, Duncan, and their reinforcements of Clancy and Alaisdair Graham faced a small army of rogue warriors. The men formed a square with their backs to each other to face their common enemy.

As they awaited the rogues' attack, Alaisdair said, "So ye're my American relative several generations removed, then." He glanced briefly in Clancy's direction. "I'm Alaisdair Graham late o' Conlan Manor in Scotland."

From somewhere to his left, Rowan heard Clancy's sharp intake of breath when Alaisdair mentioned their ancestral home.

"I'm descended from the druid line, in case ye were wonderin'," Alaisdair continued genially, the tone of his voice seeming to dare the other man to respond.

"I should have known that sneaky, classless, coward, druid brother-in-law of mine would entangle my daughter with lowlifes who will drag her down," Clancy Graham snarled.

Alaisdair's tone remained genial, a sure sign to anyone paying attention that the man was about to ruin Clancy's day. "May I introduce ye tae my friend Duncan MacManus, who is going tae be yer daughter's brother-in-law once we sort out this whole mess, and his friend Rowan Sheridan, the man responsible fer levelin' the playin' field fer all warriors last year."

To Rowan's right, Alaisdair shifted slightly. If they weren't facing an army of rogue warriors, Rowan would have laughed himself silly at the way Alaisdair entangled his relative in a web of his own ugly prejudices.

"I rather enjoy hanging out with these particular lowlifes." Alaisdair chuckled. "It's because o' the Sheridans that those o' us descended from the powerful *druid* who started Conlan Manor have special protections from the goddesses we're fightin'."

"Seriously? *The* Rowan Sheridan?" Clancy asked. Turning his attention to Duncan, he continued. "Weren't you with the Sheridans when they defeated the Morrigan that time?" The awe in his voice told Rowan that Clancy had forgotten he'd just insulted the lot of them.

"As a matter of fact, I did help out on that one, as did my wife Siobhan," Duncan replied.

"Your talisman is required to help you. As your wife, she would also *want* to help you," Clancy said, as though speaking to an imbecile.

"My *talisman* is Jennifer Carlin. She and I didn't bond though she serves me well in battle as you're about to see. My *wife* is a druid. At the moment, she's assisting your daughter as they try to rescue Fallon's warrior, my brother-in-law Seamus Lochlann." Duncan didn't pause or lose his focus on the coming rogues as he dropped his little bomb on Clancy Graham. Rowan nodded at Duncan approvingly.

Clancy, however, nearly dropped his sword. *"The Walshes have poisoned this warrior band against me, Ivori. Why did Keela summon us?"*

"You don't have much of a shield. You should work on that," Rowan said casually. "Ivori must be your wife? I believe Keela summoned the two you on Griff's orders. Something about it being appropriate that you help your daughter when her life and the lives of many others hang in the balance." He glanced at Clancy's sword. "I hope we can count on you because we're all about to be tested."

Conversation abruptly ended as the rogue warriors finally worked up the courage to charge the uneasy band awaiting them at the edge of the lake.

The clanging of steel on steel rang through the valley when the battle commenced. Several jays and a flock of chickadees vehemently protested the sudden noise before fluttering overhead as they decamped to a more peaceful part of the forest. The rogues descended en masse on the small band of warriors. With relative ease, Rowan, Duncan, and Alaisdair dispatched the initial onslaught while Clancy struggled with the first rogue who took him on. It was obvious to Rowan that Clancy had kept himself out of battle. His skills weren't on par with the others under attack. Though his sheer strength gave him an advantage that eventually caused him to finish off his enemy, it only took the rogues the first salvo to figure out Clancy was the weak link and to concentrate their attack on him.

"Tell me again why Griff thought bringing Fallon's parents in was a good idea," Duncan said as he dispatched yet another rogue who had zeroed in on Clancy.

"What are you saying?" Clancy responded indignantly as he wounded a second attacker who had accompanied Duncan's kill.

"It seems your wife and your sister are about to appear out of the trees on the business end of a rogue's sword. If you want to save them, you'd better not react," Duncan warned as he balanced on the balls of his feet ready for the next wave of rogues to attack.

Right then, the women appeared from the cover of the forest. The other rogues backed out of the fight to see which warriors would respond to the capture of their talismans. To his credit,

Clancy looked every bit as impassive as his fellow fighters. To her credit, Clancy's wife didn't let on about which warrior was hers. With other warrior pairs, their behavior would have been expected, but with these two loose cannons, Rowan had had his doubts.

"You must be here with someone. Which one is he?" the rogue demanded as he pushed the point of his sword into the middle of Clancy's wife's back enough to draw blood.

"Like her," the woman nodded in Keela's direction, "my warrior is dead. Unlike her"—she gave Keela a withering look—"my warrior died honorably. We're here to try to help our friends however we can."

"I told you I was here alone," Keela said in a long-suffering tone.

The rogue looked speculatively at the women before he addressed the warriors. "None of you claim these two? How convenient for us." He looked around at his friends who'd momentarily halted their advance with the arrival of the talismans. "Since we've never had the pleasure of bonding with a talisman, we can see what some of the fuss is about with these two. Unlike you lot"— he glared at the warriors—"we'll share."

If he hoped to draw out the talismans' warriors with his crude innuendo, he was disappointed.

Taking one step away from his friends, Rowan faced the rogue. "It appears we're at an impasse. These women, though valuable because they're on our side, understand that in a situation like this, they're expendable. Though your idea of sharing them sounds barbaric. Should have expected that from men who, when given the choice, chose dishonor over death." The last bit came out as a taunt.

The rogues apparently took exception to having the truth aired so bluntly, and several of them came at him. In that instant, Clancy bent time and space to take out the rogue whose sword tip had damaged both his wife and his sister while Alyssa and Jennifer seemed to appear from nowhere to pull Keela and Clancy's wife out of the way.

While their allies used their supernatural skills to take on the rogues, Rowan and Duncan faced five-to-two odds again. "This is becoming a tad old, my friend," Duncan deadpanned as he swung his claymore and sliced it through the sword arm of his nearest opponent who screamed and ran away toward the woods.

"Tell me about it, buddy. Where does Morgan keep finding these guys?" Rowan asked rhetorically as he swung his sword to parry a blow from one rogue, the momentum of which carried him into contact with the next one, a powerful blow that shivered up his sword arm.

"Keep them busy for a minute more, and Clancy will dispatch one of them, evening your odds, darling," Alyssa communicated.

Though the battle raged for several minutes, once the odds narrowed to one-on-one, the outcome was obvious. Seeing his wife keep her head when she faced such danger seemed to galvanize Clancy Graham, and he stood his ground against the opponent he chose after he killed the man who threatened his wife. Perhaps there was hope for the man yet.

After the last rogue either lay dead or had run back to the safety of the forest, it took the party several long minutes to catch their breath and gather themselves. Glancing around at the area, they noted the carnage of the afternoon. Rowan counted twenty dead rogue warriors bathing the earth with their blood.

"What are we going to do with them? We can't leave them out here," Duncan said, gesturing at the casualties of their battle.

"You will pile them together on the shore and set them ablaze as is the custom for warriors of course," Scathach said as she strolled up to the warrior party. "Though you might want to wait since there is still plenty of daylight, this being the summer solstice. Morgan is likely not finished here yet."

"Scathach?" Clancy's surprise came out on a gasp.

"Did you think I would be elsewhere when some of my best fighters are here trying to rescue one of my favorites from that witch Maeve?" she answered, disdain dripping from her words.

Clancy clamped his mouth shut and stared at the goddess in reverent silence before exchanging a glance with his wife.

"You are fortunate, Clancy Graham. Though you've chosen the coward's way out for most of your life, somehow the Dagda destined your daughter to be linked with some powerful and well-connected people."

Rowan understood the smile on Scathach's face. It didn't bode well for the American branch of the Graham family.

CHAPTER TWENTY-THREE

FALLON CAME OUT of her trance in a rush. Having considered the stories from her ancestors, stories that seemed to enter her head like magic, she knew what story she needed to tell about Seamus Lochlann, her Seamus, the one she could save.

She didn't know how long she'd been entranced, but she hoped the time in her head skipped at the speed of light and she hadn't lost Seamus right when she knew how to save him. Hazarding a look into the window of Maeve's torture chamber, she at first encountered blood-red eyes glowing in anger in Morgan's face. The goddess's attention was trained somewhere beneath Fallon, so she looked over her shoulder to see her friends, a warrior she didn't know, and her parents gathered beside the lake. Beyond them lay the carnage of battle. At the sight on the beach, bile rose in her throat. Then a sound assaulted her ears that rent her heart in two.

Swinging around so quickly she rocked her bubble cage, she fixed her eyes on the scene behind Morgan. Seamus remained tied to Maeve's bed, his body on full sexual alert, but the goddess had apparently given him a reprieve. Or she'd taken him once when Fallon had been away, lost in the possibilities for their story. Judging from the way Seamus moaned, Maeve had forced him to come for her. Crying out, Fallon smashed her hands against the impenetrable membrane of her prison before she crumpled to the floor and curled into herself in despair.

When Fallon hugged herself, Maeve laughed in triumph. Fallon accidentally pulled her bracelet into full contact with Seamus's sign on her wrist and inhaled his scent on the old sweatshirt she'd pulled on when she left the cabin earlier in the afternoon. The latter two events went unnoticed by the goddess, but they dispelled her despair, replacing it with courage.

She repeated the sequence, holding her bracelet to her wrist while simultaneously breathing Seamus's scent deep into herself. The action intensified her connection to her warrior and reminded her of his singular loyalty and valor. Though the goddess held him far from her, his touch lingered on her, which imbued her with his better traits. Her premonitions had told her Maeve would take Seamus at least once, but now she knew she could change the outcome of his story, the outcome of *their* story. As she made this discovery, a golden glow warmed her, an aura of calm safety that gave her the confidence to act.

Remaining in her fetal position, she feigned one who had given up. Since she'd tuned in again to the events playing out in the enchanted mirage, she could hear Maeve gloating. "You see, sister. Our plan worked. I have hopes Seamus will give me three or four climaxes before he runs out of life—and you have a battlefield full of dead warriors whose blood even now is filling the ford. Soon we will add Seamus's talisman and take back some of our power from these meddling mortals."

"They took all of my rogues, you twit," Morgan fumed. "Not one of Scathach's warriors sustained even a scratch. The battle is not going to plan."

Maeve yawned. "Bring in more rogues. Scathach's champions

are tired. They'll be easy to defeat after having battled a Fomorian, the Nephilim, and an army of rogues. They may have some supernatural powers, but they're still human, my dear." It was clear Maeve thought she could afford to be magnanimous. She stretched and said, "The sex with Seamus was even better than I had anticipated."

Fallon tried not to flinch—and failed.

Maeve talked on. "He truly is a magnificent specimen."

Fallon watched as the goddess trailed a blood-red fingernail between her breasts as she glanced over her shoulder at Seamus, apparently contemplating having him again. The goddess's terrible delight at torturing her warrior fired her resolve.

While the goddesses stood at the window and considered the scene by the lake, Fallon reached out to her love.

"Seamus, I know what to do. Listen to me. I'm going to tell your story. You must act in the way that I tell it. Do you understand?"

"Fallon, why did you leave me?"

Seamus's grief tore at her, but she had to ignore it and do her job. *"She didn't succeed in taking you, Seamus. Listen to the story."*

"What are you saying? She rode me until I couldn't fight anymore, and I came so deep inside her I thought she might swallow me whole from my cock outward."

It was all she could do to keep her own agony in check at the tears she could hear in Seamus's voice.

"She's going to mount me again soon, I know it, and I won't be able to hold out half as long."

"Seamus, I'm a bard. When I tell your story, it will be the truth. Your truth. My truth. In the story I will tell, you will conquer Maeve and her unholy lust. Listen."

Fallon's revelation stunned him. Seamus had heard of bards, of course. Living with a druid for a sister, he'd had no choice but to be immersed in the old Celtic tales. He knew the bards of old were revered among Celtic peoples at the same level as warriors. Bards told the stories that made warriors immortal. Without bards, no one would remember Cuchulain, or King Arthur, or Finn Mac-Cool, the great heroes of times long past.

In modern times, true bards were extremely rare. The gods didn't seem to appreciate the competition of mortals who could alter reality with their stories, change the truth of the cosmos with a well-told tale. Yet bards did exist. Vaguely, he remembered that. Fallon spoke to him again.

"Call your sword to you and cut your bonds. Though they're magic, fairies wove them of ordinary silk. Once the steel of your sword touches them, they will lose their power to bind you. Move quickly while Maeve is distracted. Your clothes are on the floor between the bed and the door."

In his hyperaroused state, Seamus didn't think he could follow Fallon's commands, but he discovered when he concentrated on retrieving his sword, his erection subsided a little. Cheered by that event and the heft of his sword in his hand, he made short work of the silken cords holding him captive on the bed. As Fallon predicted, the cords slithered away from the steel of his sword as though something terrible tainted them. Fairies and their wares had no power against steel.

"The goddesses are busy plotting their next move against our warriors. They won't notice you've left them until you pass through the door. Follow the stairs down to a landing. Turn left and descend another set of stairs. By then, Maeve will have discovered your absence. Open the door directly in front of you and step out. Do not think. Act."

Seamus bent time to dress and exit the room. The more distance he put between himself and his enemy, the more like himself he felt. Per Fallon's direction, he didn't think. He acted. It wasn't until he exited the enchanted castle on the opposite shore from his friends that he saw Fallon was still trapped. She'd rescued him, but at what cost to herself? Fear for his talisman gripped him, and he took a chance at being caught again in Maeve's web.

"Seamus? What the hell, buddy? Did she just let you go?" Rowan asked as Seamus materialized beside his best friend.

"Right about now, the witch is discovering I've escaped. And Fallon is in terrible danger," he said, his attention riveted on the bubble suspended above the lake.

"Are you Fallon's warrior?" a woman asked him, her voice quiet and trembling.

"Yes, and you must be her mother," he said before giving his attention to the man beside her. "You're her father, I take it?"

"It's an honor to meet you. You were with the Sheridans when they defeated Morgan a while back," Clancy Graham said, smiling and extending his hand.

Ignoring Graham's outstretched hand, he said coldly, "What the hell did you think you were doing to deny Fallon half her heritage? Now she's floating in Maeve's prison. Though she could tell the tale of my great escape from the goddess's chamber, she can't tell a tale to rescue herself. That's your doing." It was all Seamus could do to stop himself from taking a swing at the older man.

Maeve's spell of lust had fallen away from him now that he'd distanced himself from her torturous bedchamber. When he'd escaped from her enchanted fun house, he remembered everything Siobhan had ever taught him about bards. Having been enthralled with them since she discovered herself to be a druid, Siobhan had made studying bards and their special skills a hobby bordering on obsession. She even pulled Rowan's mom into her enthusiastic studies, creating a tight friendship between the two women. One thing he remembered was that bards needed extensive training with a druid in the art of storytelling, something Fallon's parents had not only denied but had expressly forbidden. Now he and Fallon faced the price of her parents' prejudice. He was in no mood to be civil.

Fallon's parents reacted as though Seamus had, indeed, slapped them.

Clancy's initial response gave way to anger in a breath. "Who do you think you are to tell us how we should have raised our daughter? Druids are inferior to warriors. As a warrior who has faced the evil of the war goddesses and won, you of all people should know that," he spat.

"Uh-huh," Seamus said with deadly calm. "'Course, I might have had a little help from my sister, who happens to be a druid. If not for her, no doubt Fallon and I wouldn't have had a chance to bond, considering we spent the time since we discovered each other inside the safety of our family cabin. My sister enchanted it so heavily Maeve had to lure us out of it to attack us." He barely kept his temper on a leash as he laid out facts for his future father-in-law.

"Your sister is a druid?" Fallon's mother asked.

"Yeah, and she's married to that guy." Seamus pointed at Duncan who executed a curt bow before crossing his arms defiantly over his chest. "It appears the one scenario you were so determined to shield Fallon from is the exact scenario the gods planned for her. Your ridiculous prejudices may cost her her life, and if that happens, you'll be sorrier than you can imagine." Neither of Fallon's parents could have missed the steel he injected into his words.

"In this mission, you'll do exactly as the rest of us say. No questions. No opinions. No arguments." He stared down at them. "You're in way over your heads, but you are Fallon's parents, so you may be of some use." His commanding tone brooked no rebuttal.

Staying quiet in the face of a direct order must not have been in Clancy Graham's nature. "Scathach, speak to him. Surely, as the goddess of warriors you see my point."

"You are as arrogant as your druid brother-in-law." Scathach glared at him, her aura veering dangerously close to full red. "The reason I favor these particular warriors and have gone out of my way to train them is because they revere the gods. They understand that even though they have supernatural traits, they are still mortal. Mortals need all the tools at their disposal. Those tools include druids, some of whom I personally have trained on occasion, eh, Alaisdair?" She winked at her Scots protégé.

"Aye, milady. One Fianna Conlan comes tae mind." A grin played about his lips as he glanced over at Clancy. "There's also my auld friend Hamish Buchanan. He's a druid o' the first order and rather handy with a claymore when he's of a mind tae use it. So is Davy Sutherland, Hamish's druid protégé. He trained with me regularly before I discovered Shanley tae be my talisman and moved with her over here tae America."

Seamus smiled as he watched Alaisdair enjoying Clancy's discomfort, probably a bit too much, but it was entertaining all the same.

"As a warrior, you will do your job and fight whatever Morgan still wants to throw at us." Scathach aimed her directive at Clancy. To Ivori, she said, "You will do everything you can to help your warrior without arguing with the others and putting yourself into unnecessary danger."

Summarily chastised, Clancy and Ivori nodded at the goddess, but the charged look they exchanged left no one in the dark as to what they truly thought of the situation. Warily, Seamus observed them before tucking away his attitude about Fallon's parents. The hairs on the back of his neck stood at attention, and instantly, he knew Maeve was coming for him.

For the first time since he escaped it, he looked at the enchanted castle floating above the lake and couldn't comprehend its ethereal beauty. How could something so lovely from the shore of the lake be such a nightmare inside? Ruefully, he answered his own question: Maeve and Morgan were inside that place. Their evil pulsated through it, and like a magnet, it held Fallon's delicate cage close to it. Too close to them. Too far from him.

⁂

"Look where your gloating has got you, sister." Morgan's lips curved in delight as she nodded toward Seamus standing fully dressed among his friends on the beach.

"*What?*" Maeve shrieked. She'd been contemplating the talisman's agony, but now she swung around to the bed, empty except for rumpled sheets and severed cords.

"How could he possibly have escaped?" Narrowing her eyes, she refocused her attention on her other captive floating in her iridescent bubble.

"She gave up. Look at her. She is curled in on herself, afraid to look at what I have done, what I have had with her warrior. One time, and like any weak mortal, she could not take it. Surely, *she* did not help Seamus escape," Maeve fumed, unable to grasp the idea that a talisman, a mere mortal, had stolen away her prize.

"Scathach is on the beach with her warriors. Perhaps she had something to do with his escape?" Morgan casually eyed her blood-red nails. "After the way you ignored my needs in Scotland at Samhain, I think this turn of events vindicates me."

"Scathach could not touch this place, and you know it. Somehow, Fallon Graham rescued her warrior. Let us see how she does with herself." Pulling her purple robe around her like armor, the goddess prepared herself for a new battle.

⁂

Fallon remained in her submissive position until long after she'd changed Seamus's story. When she hazarded a look at the bed in Maeve's chamber, what she saw made her blood run cold. Maeve's opulent chamber of lust had transformed into a dungeon. A giant boar whose tusks dripped yellow poison that hissed and steamed as it hit the floor fought against the iron chaining him to the wall. Its close-set piggy eyes were a blood-red match to those glowing in Morgan's face as she watched the battles she orchestrated. Its bristly black hair stood up on end as though it were frightened—or, as Fallon suspected, extremely angry. From the way the boar eyed her, she understood it would like nothing better than to eat her alive.

On the heels of that conclusion, she perceived her membranous prison had seemed to become thinner where it hovered dangerously close to the floating castle. In horror, she stared wide-eyed as her bubble docked with the enchanted building, though the membrane of her cage remained intact. This was the way Maeve intended to exact her revenge for Fallon's interference in Seamus's destiny? Like Diarmuid of old, she must fight Fionn, the boar? Could Maeve take on such a disguise, she wondered? In this twisted version of the story, would Seamus, playing the part of Grainne, watch helplessly as Fallon died from the effects of the boar's poison?

To confirm her suspicions, she glanced back at the shoreline where Seamus stood among several warriors and talismans riveted on the unfolding scene floating above the water. A soft pop like a kiss alerted her that her bubble cage had docked once again with the dungeon imprisoning her enemy. The ephemeral outer wall of the edifice remained intact, furthering her torture as she tried to figure out how long she had before she landed inside the room with the monster.

"Fallon! Open your shield. Griff and my sister can help you if you let them in," Seamus pleaded.

She gazed briefly at the beach but couldn't see Griff anywhere. Still, she did as Seamus asked and opened her shield a little more.

"We had to wait until you discovered your skill to be able to help you. Don't be afraid," Griff said, his tone soothing her.

"Where are you? I saw Keela on the beach, but I didn't see you."

She tried to hide her panic, but she'd detected the fetid odor ema-nating from the dungeon and knew she had little time before she faced the beast with nothing between them.

"We're hidden. We can't help you if Maeve keys on us. Whatever happens, pay no attention to the battles going on by the lake. They will come, but they're only distractions. Seamus won't be in any real danger. You're the ultimate prize here, and we're going to help you escape whatever terrible fate she plans for you," Griff said.

There was no more time for explanations as Fallon landed hard on the stone floor, trapped in a dungeon with an angry giant boar.

CHAPTER TWENTY-FOUR

FALLON'S SCREAM TORE the air. Rowan and Duncan jumped to restrain Seamus as he ran for the lake and his talisman. Before he could reach the water, they jerked him back and struggled to hold on to him.

"Whoa, buddy. How do you think you can help her from here?" Rowan asked as Seamus surged against their hold.

Duncan said, "Don't even think about visualizing yourself into that space. You of all people know it's not real. Hard tellin' where you'll end up."

"You have no idea what kind of evil Maeve can concoct." Raw fear roughened his hoarse shout as he fought to escape his friends' restraints. "Whatever Fallon is facing, she can't face it by herself!"

"I think we have a clue, old son. FYI, wasted heroism doesn't make it into the stories," Rowan said as he wrapped both his arms around Seamus's sword arm. "We have Siobhan and Fallon's Uncle Griff helping her. Remember? Didn't you just tell her to open her shield to them?"

Agony ripped through him. "But she's alone up there," he rasped out. "She and I are a team. She needs my help."

"According to Griff, she needs to tell a story. You have to let her do that." Glancing over his shoulder, he added, "Besides, we're about to have our own trouble. Look."

Rowan turned Seamus away from the lake as a fresh contingent of rogue warriors boldly walked up the trail to face them. Such a maneuver could only mean one thing—the good guys were badly outnumbered. Again.

"Morgan's tactics are becoming redundant. Maybe being immortal has sapped her of ideas with strategy or pizzazz." Rowan sighed. "It appears she thinks to beat us with numbers alone. Boring."

Seamus understood his friend sought to distract him. Still, he couldn't help but look back at the castle floating above the lake, where, to his horror, he saw Fallon's protective bubble had vanished completely.

"I can't figure out what Morgan's game is. A Fomorian, the Nephilim, and scores of rogues. She intends to wear us out, I think. She has to know Scathach is with us, so of course we're in fighting shape. This lack of imagination isn't like her. It makes me nervous." Rowan readied his claymore to face the new enemy.

Still holding Seamus, Duncan asked, "You are going to help us, brother. Right? You aren't going to bail out and do something stupid while we're fighting off a whole army of rogues?"

"They're a distraction for the real battle taking place. You know that don't you?" he pleaded.

"Like we said before, Seamus, you can't help her if you can't visualize yourself to where she is. And where she is ain't necessarily inside that pleasure palace floating above the lake right now," Duncan reminded him. "So far, she's done her job. Now it's your turn to do yours. Griff and Siobhan are training her on the fly, if you want to know how it is. I know it's hard, buddy, but you have to trust them—and Fallon."

Right as Duncan finished speaking, the rogues were on

them, and instinct took over as the party of warriors took on the new threat. Having no other choice, Seamus joined Rowan and Duncan, forming a tight triangle with their backs to each other, claymores at the ready.

"Seamus." Alyssa's voice entered his head.

Of course, she'd be able to breach his shield in his current state. Or maybe he'd subconsciously let her in after the intense connection the two of them formed back when he'd trained her to shield her thoughts from Rowan's unscrupulous prying.

"Fallon's Aunt Keela is standing in as your talisman. Open your shield to her please," Alyssa said before he heard her turn her attention to Rowan who was taking on two warriors by himself—as usual. *"Does he need to show off in every battle he fights?"*

Seamus would have laughed if the odds weren't so dire as to require his full concentration. Being down three to one tended to keep a man focused.

"We met at Rowan's wedding, Seamus. I'm Fallon's aunt and a prophetess. Maintain your concentration on the rogues who come at you. One of them harbors a lethal sword if you aren't careful."

He nodded and hoped his helper understood. From the corner of his eye, he saw Rowan slide his claymore cleanly through the abdomen of the rogue to his left before turning his attention to the rogue's friend. That they were friends was obvious when the man cried out in anger and pain as he watched his fellow slide bonelessly to the earth.

❧

Fallon fought for her life. She knew the outcome to the story of Diarmuid and Grainne. Fionn could have saved Diarmuid from the boar's poison if only he could have found it in his heart to forgive his former friend for stealing his woman. That the woman in question had never loved Fionn didn't figure into the equation. In the end, Fionn arrived with the sacred water too late to bathe

Diarmuid's wounds and thus save his life. Grainne threw herself off a cliff onto a field of sharp rocks rather than continue living without her love.

Like Fionn, Maeve would never forgive Fallon for rescuing Seamus. There was no longer any question that Maeve somehow knew Fallon had rescued him. How to survive the boar, whether the creature was Maeve herself or some monster she conjured, became the only thing Fallon could consider at the moment.

"Tell the story, Fallon. Tell your story."

She heard the unfamiliar voice from a distance, like a dream or an echo. Neither Griff's voice nor Siobhan's spoke to her. She worried the command came from the boar itself. Then the same golden glow she'd experienced before when she knew how to save Seamus settled over her, and she trusted it without question.

"The boar could not escape the irons holding it fast to the wall where the mighty warrior, Seamus Lochlann had chained it," Fallon began. "Its great head lolled from side to side, its terrible tusks dripping acid death. To escape her prison, Fallon Graham knew she had to skirt those lethal tusks and reach the door the boar guarded."

Her other possible escape route, ironically the bubble cage in which she'd spent most of the afternoon, had disappeared behind her, replaced by a solid rock wall. *Now what do I do? I have no claymore and no training with one even if the weapon miraculously found its way into my hand.*

"You don't have a claymore, Fireworks, but I do," Seamus interrupted.

"I just broke you out of this place. I certainly have no intention of inviting you back into it."

If the circumstances hadn't been so dire, she might have believed she heard Seamus chuckling at the huffiness she didn't even try to keep out of her thoughts.

"Change the place, Fallon."

The boar, apparently keying in on her fear, lunged at her, rattling its chains in a deafening fashion, and she jumped away in fright. With her hand pressed against her chest to still her beating heart, she continued the story. "Seamus Lochlann had chained the boar to a great boulder on the lakeshore near his family's cabin. The beast's red eyes glowed with hatred for the man and anyone connected to him," she said and waited for the enchanted space to change.

It didn't. Instead, the boar lunged harder at her, and she fell back against the wall behind her. Her heart raced like that of a rabbit hiding beneath a bush as a falcon flew overhead. Still, she worked to collect herself and face the beast like a warrior. Then she noticed that when the boar made his mighty feint at her, he dislodged the enormous screws holding his chains to the wall, and a new terror rushed through her.

Desperately, she tried again. "Seamus Lochlann had chained the boar to an outcropping near the lake above his cabin."

The scene didn't change. She remained trapped in the dungeon with the vicious beast. Clammy sweat trickled down her spine. The fetid odor of the boar's breath made her gag. She had to escape, but apparently her storytelling couldn't change her physical reality. She needed another tactic, but she had no idea what it might be.

Seamus reached out to her again. *"Fallon, tell a story to change your surroundings."*

"I tried. They won't change."

"I'm coming for you."

"No! No, Seamus! I'm in a different place. It's not the same as where she confined you. Please. Concentrate on winning your battle."

"I can't let you face your fight alone."

She could hear his desperation even telepathically. Perhaps even more so because it came through his thoughts. At once, she sensed a searing pain pulse through him.

"Seamus? What happened?"

"Was careless. Got a nick on my arm. Nothing to worry about."

"Saving you from Maeve was my job. I know that now. Whatever else happens, you must live."

Seamus roared as a new pain assailed his mind—Fallon firmly closed her shield to him. Her withdrawal stung infinitely more than the blow he'd sustained from his current foe. He cried out in anguish, a sound the rogue mistook for the pain of the strike he'd dealt Seamus, and unwisely, he lifted his sword above his head for a killing blow. Seamus took out his pain, his fear, and his frustration at not being able to help his talisman on the unsuspecting rogue, nearly splitting the man in two as he spun around and used his momentum to cut through the rogue's middle. The man died with a look of utter shock on his face.

Though the rogue lost his life, he succeeded in dealing the injury to Seamus's arm that Fallon's aunt had foreseen. Somehow, over the clanging din of the battle, he heard his sister's voice. "Seamus is hurt. I must go to him." He shook it off even as the excruciating ache from the gash in his arm heated up to a thousand on a scale of one-to-ten.

Siobhan and Griff had chanted themselves into a parallel time and place where they could see all of what happened to their family and friends both along the lakeshore and inside Maeve's enchanted palace. Such an arrangement gave them the chance to let Fallon know all the facets of the story she needed to tell.

"I know I insisted on saving Fallon first and foremost, but seeing what she did to rescue Seamus, I see now she'd only be a shell of her potential if we managed to save her and lose him," Griff said. "The connection between a bonded pair is too strong to allow one to function at a high level without the companionship and love of the other." He sighed. "Fallon made her profound love for Seamus clear the second she closed her shield to him to keep him from trying to reach her."

"Their union is what the gods intend," Siobhan said, patting his shoulder. "Make sure to keep your shield locked to me. We can't take a chance the goddesses will discover one or the other of us and attack Seamus or Fallon through us."

"Good luck, friend." In the short space of an afternoon, they had dispelled their doubts of each other and discovered that together they too were a formidable team.

Siobhan visualized herself to a place behind a tree near where her brother had taken on the rogue. Blood escaped the wound beneath the thick layer of his leather jacket. With her trained eye, she could see the purple-black tinge of poison marring the deep red of Seamus's blood, and she shuddered. She had no time to waste.

"Duncan, cover Seamus and me as I pull him out of the fight. The rogue he fought poisoned him, but I don't think he knows it yet," she communicated to her husband.

Duncan didn't question her. Instead, he fought his way through the three rogues between Seamus and him to stand shoulder to shoulder with his brother-in-law.

"You've got a nasty gash there, buddy. My wife is going to take care of it. Work your way to your left," Duncan communicated to Seamus. Unfortunately, the rogues they were fighting must have picked up on his wound too and redoubled their attacks on him.

Landing on the other side of Seamus, Alaisdair, along with Duncan, effectively created a human shield around him. Siobhan put herself in their midst and tossed a cloud of herbs over Seamus as she enchanted the space around him. Her diversionary tactic caused him to "disappear" from the rogues' sight, which had the desired effect of momentarily confusing them, giving Duncan and

Alaisdair an advantage they didn't waste while Siobhan pulled her brother away from the fray to a quiet place behind some nearby currant bushes.

"What the hell, Siobhan? I can't help Fallon. The least you could let me do is help my friends," he growled when he saw where he was and what she had done.

Acid, like the poison oozing from Seamus's wound, dripped from her voice. "You won't be much good to anyone if you die of the poison the rogue introduced into your system."

"What?"

"You're gravely injured. If you don't let me tend your wound, you may well lose your arm—or your life. I didn't come all this way and involve all these people only to see you die from an underhanded trick. Take off your jacket," Siobhan commanded.

With ill grace, Seamus tore off his jacket—and hissed a breath in through his teeth.

"That's even worse than I expected." She grimaced and pulled some herbs from her bag. "I can't take a chance on running to the lake for water, so I'm going to improvise a salve to clean that out," she said, nodding at the blackening blood that pulsed out of his arm with each beat of his heart.

He glanced past her as she rummaged in her satchel. "You're Keela, right? Griff's wife?"

The woman behind Siobhan inclined her head at him. "Yes. Fallon's aunt and your stand-in talisman for the moment." She directed her attention to Siobhan. "Griff thought you might need this and could see you were in no position to get it. Here." She handed Siobhan a thermos filled with fresh water from the creek.

"You're a lifesaver," Siobhan said without a trace of irony.

She set to work trickling the water over Seamus's wound. Puffing out his cheeks, he blew air to keep from crying out against the pain. "Damn! It feels like you're bathing my arm in battery acid."

"That's it, big brother. Grin and bear it. Cleaning out the poison is the worst part, I promise."

"I've heard that from you before. Do you torture Duncan like this too?" he gritted out through his clenched jaw.

"Only when he hares off with some goddess for an afternoon. Then I think he has it coming."

At the mention of his time with Maeve, Seamus's knees buckled.

Siobhan caught him on the way down. Though he was far too heavy for her to hold, somehow, she safely guided him to the ground. "Whoa, sorry. Bad joke. Really bad joke. I should have had you lie down to start, Seamus. Here," she said as she took off her jacket and stuffed it beneath his head as a makeshift pillow. "I'm going to need more water. I hate to ask it of you, knowing the risk and that you've already been attacked once by a rogue today."

Keela waved her hand dismissively. "We all have a job to do here, Siobhan. Do you have any other containers I can take along? From the looks of that wound, this thermos isn't going to be enough."

Siobhan ran her hand over Seamus's fevered brow. "Damn. I don't have time." Pulling on a pair of surgical gloves, the one concession to the twenty-first century that she kept in her bag, she used her hands to scrape away the welled blood along the length of his wound. Pain overwhelmed him, and he screamed.

CHAPTER TWENTY-FIVE

FALLON DIDN'T KNOW if Seamus experienced real pain or if the sound was another one of Maeve's tortures. Either way, his anguish debilitated her, and bonelessly, she slid down the wall. From this vantage point, she couldn't see anything beyond the giant, snarling beast fighting its chains to reach her. With a lurch, the wall behind her moved, and her blood ran cold. The room was shrinking. When she started her story about the boar, she must have made the chains so strong that even though the boar could loosen the bolts holding its irons to the stone wall, he couldn't completely pull himself free to attack her. Since he couldn't come to her, Maeve apparently decided Fallon should come to him.

The boar didn't have to kill her outright. All he had to do was gash her skin with his razor-sharp tusk, and his poison would do the rest. She recalled from the old Celtic stories that Diarmuid lingered in a cave for three days after sustaining his poisoned wound. She thought she'd experience at least that much torture.

Of course, in her enchanted prison, time was irrelevant.

Griff interrupted her morose thoughts. *"Seamus has*

been injured. You must escape and change his story. There's a way out. Devise it."

"*What happened?*" Her fear for her warrior superseded her fear for herself in her present danger.

"*He's been poisoned. Siobhan is treating him, but he's going to need more powerful magic than druidic medicine and chanting. He needs a story.*"

"*I thought his pain might be one of Maeve's tortures. Now I know it is.*" She pushed herself back to standing, bracing herself as the room lurched again and narrowed. "*I'm trapped with the giant boar between the door and me. I tried to change the venue, but my story can't do that.*"

As though to punctuate the point, the room narrowed another half a foot. The boar roared and snapped its teeth like it anticipated the tender flesh awaiting it.

"*You told a story to help Seamus escape. Now tell your story of escape.*"

"*As a warrior, Seamus has a skill I could exploit but which I do not possess. He can bend time and space. I cannot. Visualizing myself elsewhere is out of the question in this sick joke of a fun house.*"

Like living paint, she flattened herself to the wall behind her.

"*Why don't you try what other trapped maids before you have done with success.*"

"*Huh?*"

"*Sing to the beast. Put him to sleep with a song, then walk out the door.*"

Having no other inspiration, she decided to give Griff's suggestion a try.

"Trapped with a mighty boar in a remote tower of Maeve's enchanted palace, Fallon Graham desperately fought despair. As the room began to shrink, magically bringing her closer to the fate the goddess planned for her, she sang to comfort herself while she tried to devise a way out. An old song came to her:

'In high Midsummer, when all the leaves are green
The fields are fragrant with the promise of plenty.
The newborn lambkin skips in happy rhythm as
The maidens gather flowers of yellow and orange and pink;
Their baskets overflow with summer beauty.

They weave long garlands of perfumed splendor
As they sing their goodbye song.
They give themselves to save their people
Draping their pretty garlands
On the bull who demands their sacrifice
At the height of great Midsummer.'

"Fallon's voice lulled the beast. It fought slumber, its piggy eyes slanting shut only to open with a start before sliding closed again. Finally, it gave in to sleep before the last notes of her song whispered through the chamber. Knowing she didn't have much time, she cautiously skirted the boar in the room that had shrunk to half its size from when she'd been forced into it.

"When she reached the door the boar guarded, she spit on the rusted metal handle, correctly guessing it needed lubrication to unlatch from the jamb without noise. She forgot the hinges, however, and when she cautiously cracked open the door, they squealed in protest, a sound the boar mimicked at the rude interruption of his sleep. Fallon didn't wait to see his full reaction. Slipping through the thin slit she'd managed to create when she pulled on the heavy oaken door, she slammed it shut behind her and ran down the corridor."

When she stopped momentarily to catch her breath, she recognized the hallway as the same one Seamus traversed to escape the palace. She took the stairs to her left and the next set upon reaching the landing there. Seeing the door in front of her at what she judged to be ground level, she opened it and stepped out.

Right into another enchanted bubble.

The bubble broke away from the palace and floated to a spot directly above where the battle between the warriors and the rogues raged. Fallon could see her father fighting valiantly beside a huge redheaded warrior who vaguely resembled him. Two other warriors fought with incredible cunning and skill. These two must be Seamus's brother-in-law and his best friend, she thought absently. But where was Seamus?

"Don't try to find him," Griff warned.

"What are you saying? He's hurt." She needed to see him, see the way she could help him.

"Siobhan has disguised his whereabouts from the goddesses—for now. If you discover him from your new prison, you'll reveal him to Maeve, and we can start all over, only she'll have the advantage of knowing how you work and use it against you. Trust me on this, Fallon."

She heard an unfamiliar voice and like before when she heard that voice, a warm glow suffused her body. *"You have done well, my dear, rescuing your warrior and saving yourself from Maeve's beast. But you are not finished yet. The story is not over."*

"Who are you?" She gazed all around her but saw nothing but air.

"Brighid, patron goddess of bards. Like Scathach, I have an interest in the mortals who show the most potential in their destined capacities. We have not seen a bard in nearly a century. To have one come along who can tell her stories without training shows great aptitude indeed. Yet your test is not over."

Movement below her floating bubble redirected her attention to the battle raging on the shoreline.

"You changed the story, played the role of Diarmuid and escaped his fate in the cave with the boar. However, my sister goddess does not play by the rules, and she has poisoned your lover all the same.

You must also play a better version of the part of Fionn and save him with your hands."

She pushed against the membrane entrapping her and cried out in frustration and fear. *"How can I do that when I'm trapped in this floating cage?"*

"You'll need a powerful story. Think about it, but don't take too long. Seamus is in trouble."

The warm glow disappeared into the searing glare of the sun parting the clouds.

"Uncle Griff, you helped me once already. Can you help me again?"

"In the story of Naoise and Deirdre, Conchobar overwhelmed Naoise and his brothers with sheer numbers. It appears Morgan and Maeve are attempting the same tactic with Seamus and his friends and family. Perhaps you can start there," Griff suggested.

Directing her attention to the battle raging on the beach, she could see that the rogues materialized from behind a boulder near the trail to the lake. The warriors fighting insane odds were tiring. Wherever Siobhan had hidden Seamus, he would sense his friends' peril and insist on coming to their aid. His loyalty was too strong to do otherwise. When he reengaged in the battle, he'd die. She had to change the story.

If Morgan could call zombie giants and Maeve could call zombie monsters from the past, perhaps she could call up some champions. The thought led her to an even bigger idea:

"The warriors Scathach personally trained fought valiantly against never-ending odds. Their training rendered them superior fighters to the onslaught of rogues, but like legendary Naoise and his brothers, the sheer numbers of rogues neared overwhelming. The din of battle awoke the great Irish hero Finn MacCool from a long dream on a nearby mountaintop. Seeing an opportunity to right old wrongs, he joined the warriors to even the odds of the battle, taking on the rogues as they emerged from their hiding place behind the boulder beside the trail. Those rogues already engaged with the warriors he left to their fates, knowing his fellow fighters would not appreciate his interference in their pitched battles, but those were the only battles they needed to finish on this day.

"Once Finn took on the first score of rogues, the others disappeared, risking the Morrigan's wrath by visualizing themselves elsewhere. Finn smiled at their cowardice in the face of his superior size and skill before turning his attention to the last of the fighting between the Graham family and friends and the rogues unlucky enough to have entered the fray before his appearance.

"Once the last of the rogues met the fate to which their poor choices in life had led them, Finn saluted his fellow warriors and ambled off into the mountains to resume his long slumber where he dreamed of battles won and ladies loved and gods appeased."

Fallon had closed her eyes as she told her story, trusting the events she wove into her truth were indeed true events. When she opened her eyes and looked down at the beach, she saw four warriors catching their breaths from the battle they'd fought. All around them lay the dead and dying rogues Morgan had called to fight them. In the distance, across a meadow beyond the forest framing the lake, she glimpsed a tall blond figure loping away toward the mountains, and she smiled to herself.

Inside her enchanted bubble, Fallon continued her story:

"While the warriors rested on the beach, Siobhan Lochlann MacManus tended her injured brother. She chanted over him and dressed his wound with herbal salve, drawing the poison to the surface where it bubbled and festered. Though she worked feverishly to scrape away the poison, the goddess had planned well. After every pass Siobhan made over Seamus's injury, more poison surfaced. Fearing her brother's wound would finish what the goddess's torture had begun, she redoubled her efforts. Still, Seamus, who fought this battle as valiantly as he fought every battle, couldn't stop himself from slipping into a faint from the poison drawing up out of his body. Maeve's determination to exact revenge for his escape from her bed reflected her terrifying evil.

"Siobhan had sent Keela Walsh for more water, but it wasn't Keela who returned to her with clear mountain water from the creek roaring nearby. An auburn-haired woman appeared before her with a small quantity of water cupped in her hands. Siobhan wanted to protest, but her brother groaned deep, a pain-filled sound that tore at her heart, and she had no choice but to let this stranger take a chance at saving her beloved brother."

☙

While the battle for Seamus raged, Maeve's floating apparition changed once again, this time taking on the form of a medieval fortress with round towers anchoring the four corners of the curtain wall. Inside the wall rose a tall keep from where Maeve and Morgan watched the battle.

"Can anyone explain to me what just happened down there? Where in hell did Finn MacCool come from? Scathach does not have the power to bring back heroes from the past," Maeve seethed as she paced before the window of her enchanted castle. "And Arawn would never let them go voluntarily." She narrowed her eyes at her sister.

Lounging on a low divan, Morgan yawned, stretched, and stood up in a fluid motion. With a measured, graceful posture, she glided over to the window to survey the damage to her army of rogues. "You are correct. She does not have that power, but someone involved in this battle has it." The placid expression on Morgan's face did nothing for Maeve's temper. Nor did her next words. "Yet, all is not wasted. I shall have a lovely trip across the ford tonight. A fitting way to spend Midsummer Night, in an orgasmic walk thigh deep in the blood of warriors."

"None of the dead is powerful or worthy," Maeve retorted waspishly. That she had had only one orgasm during the course of the day's events while her sister goddess looked to spend several hours privately amused grated on her. The claws of jealousy scraped her insides and heightened her pique.

"Tsk, tsk, sister. You had your opportunity. You were a little too cocky, if you will pardon the pun." The smile accompanying Morgan's words did not reach her eyes.

Maeve sneered at her. "You are doing without too, you know. The blood you will wade in comes from nothing but rogues, so it is only half as satisfying as the orgasm Seamus gave me." She closed her eyes to enjoy the memory. "Which was on par with those Taranis gives me."

Morgan lifted a skeptical eyebrow at Maeve's reckless comment, and a tiny flutter leaped in her belly. No telling where Taranis might be lurking at any given moment, especially with the way he and she had parted earlier. Regretting her rash words, she rushed to change the topic. "Of course, there is the price you will have to pay for bringing a Fomorian back to life."

"I believe you will be paying that price since I brought along the Fomorian in service to you. However, I am not happy about Bolster's end." Morgan frowned. "Doubtless, I will have need of him in the future, and I can only bring the Nephilim back so many times before there is nothing left to recall."

Maeve rolled her eyes. The Nephilim were the least of her worries at present.

"Besides, I may be wading in a warrior's blood after all if your little prisoner does not figure out how to free herself before the poison we introduced into Seamus's body finishes what the battle began." She ghosted a hand over herself, her half smile infuriating Maeve.

"Grrrr! I do not know which I want to happen less—losing Seamus to you or watching that freak-of-nature *bard*"—spittle landed on her lip—"rescue him. I truly cannot understand what Danu and the Dagda were thinking when they dreamed up the idea of bards. No mere mortal should have the power to change the story."

She caught her reflection in the window and saw that her red hair glowed with her displeasure, and her eyes shot purple-black sparks. Good.

"Careful, sister, or you are going to lose your palace before its appointed expiration." Morgan blinked when light like a sunburst flashed into the room. "What is that ring around Fallon's cage?" She all but pressed her nose to the window.

"What ring? What are you talking about?" Maeve elbowed Morgan away from the glass. "Her bubble is iridescent like a raindrop since I know Taranis cannot resist anything related to a storm. I devised her prison deliberately to bait him so that he and I could enjoy this particular warrior pair together. You know that."

"I *do* know that, but it does not change the fact of the golden aura encircling Fallon's cage."

The room expanded with Maeve's tantrum. "How dare she interfere here? Dealing with Scathach is too much. Now we deal with Brighid as well? This is ridiculous. I did not target a Sheridan this time. What is Seamus Lochlann to them?" She threw herself onto a low divan and pouted. "Truly, such goody-goodies should be locked away in Ireland on Tara with Danu and the Dagda and leave us to our own devices."

"Are you giving up? You are not going to fight to take Seamus back? To watch as Taranis enjoys Fallon as you planned?" Morgan paced in front of her. "I thought you had more drive than that. Brighid is no more powerful than Scathach."

Maeve slanted her a look. "That is to say, the two of them together are no more powerful than we are." If anything, her pout intensified. "But they have heroes, and we have rogues and zombies. The playing field is not exactly even, especially with the introduction of a bard."

"Then we will have to use her to draw out the warriors, especially Seamus in his weakened condition."

She huffed in frustration. "I thought I made myself clear. I do not wish to give him to you when I barely had a chance to enjoy him."

"When we draw him out, you will take him again," Morgan said, her tone wheedling. "But time is running out on this floating mirage. Perhaps we should take Fallon back to your stronghold in southern California and finish this business there."

"Have you forgotten that both Seamus Lochlann and Rowan Sheridan have been inside my Los Angeles home, as has Alyssa Sheridan? They could visualize themselves inside my fortress quite easily and cause all sorts of difficulties." She summoned a cup of ambrosia, deliberately choosing not to summon another for Morgan.

Either Morgan didn't notice the slight or didn't care about it as she continued to devise plans. "Or we could use their knowledge against them, set traps for them there, and take all four of them. Perhaps you could even enjoy Rowan Sheridan a time or two before freeing him to face opponents of my choosing."

Maeve saw that if she allowed it, Morgan would take over the entire game, and once again, she would do without in service to her sister. "We have more control of the situation here. I will have to sweet-talk Taranis into sending a mist to reinforce this mirage."

"Good luck with that," Morgan said waspishly.

A wicked smile licked over her lips. "Do not be like that Morgan," Maeve said. "You know quite well Taranis cannot resist my charms. He will do this or risk a long banishment from my bed, a circumstance he would never want."

"Normally, I would agree with you. But not today. Midsummer belongs to mortals, daylight superseding night, and Taranis usually honors it with clear weather. Besides, you insulted him when you made it clear how much Seamus Lochlann pleased you.

You do not truly think your comment will go unnoticed—and unpunished—do you?" Morgan drawled.

"He knows I was only baiting him," Maeve hedged.

"Does he, now? Then how do you explain that?"

CHAPTER TWENTY-SIX

FALLON'S BEAUTIFUL CAGE floated away from the anchoring gravity of the enchanted castle. At first, Maeve panicked before she settled down to enjoy the show. "Look at her. She has put herself into some sort of trance. No doubt, she is telling a story about Seamus, one that will bring her close enough to him that we can penetrate whatever charm is hiding him from our view." She sipped ambrosia as she avidly watched the drama unfolding outside the window. "That sad little mortal has saved us the work of devising another ruse to draw out her warrior. This is even more delicious than forcing him out ourselves." Setting her goblet on the golden top of the table beside her divan, she clapped her hands in glee. "When I take him from her this time, she will know his death is her fault."

Morgan's rigid posture, arms crossed tightly over her chest, eyes glowing vermillion, threatened to ruin Maeve's lovely mood. "You have failed to notice how the golden aura surrounding the talisman's bubble cage thickens, intensifying, almost as though it's becoming something else." She squinted into the light over the lake. "That bubble is starting to resemble a tiny floating sun illuminating the darkness of our desires." She tapped her foot impatiently against the flagstone floor, an irritating staccato rhythm. "Like us, Brighid too has intense appetites. Perhaps she has made Taranis a better offer."

Maeve paced to the window to see what Morgan was on about while her sister continued to needle her. "Or perhaps Taranis, in his usual mercurial fashion, has decided to play for the other team now. Perhaps Brighid and Scathach made him an offer he cannot refuse."

She glared at the sight before her as much as she did at Morgan's words. "I, for one, would be much happier if there were not so many variables."

Rowan hazarded a glance at the castle while the others watched in wonder as Fallon's bubble made its way across the lake. The sight did nothing for his peace of mind. The round towers anchoring the curtain wall glowed red while something resembling thick blood oozed down the walls of the high circular keep in the middle of the fortress. The spectacle made him uneasy as hell.

Beside him, Alaisdair Graham also checked out the ethereal edifice. "There's somethin' evil afoot with her fortress oozin' blood like that," he said.

Clancy Graham joined them. "Pure superstition. That's the work of the druids you've been staying with over the years. Nothing else to it. The whole thing's a mirage. Giving it any credence shows your lack of good sense."

It was all Rowan could do to stop himself from decking Fallon's father right there on the beach. The man's stupid talking only confirmed how little he knew—and how little tuned in he was to the other warriors' mood. "Druids foster unnecessary superstitions to remain in power. When people call them out on this practice, they cease to have any power. You're both warriors. You should know that."

Alaisdair didn't hold back. "Even after everythin' that's happened here taeday, ye still harbor yer ridiculous prejudices. Yer daughter is trapped, and she's goin' tae need a druid's help tae get free." He scrubbed a hand over his face. "Yet ye continue tae hold on tae the belief that our common ancestor aided the death o' her first husband so she could take the second one."

Alaisdair stared hard at Clancy who gave no ground.

"If my wife were of a mind tae be gracious tae the likes o' ye, she could invite ye tae the family manor in Scotland where ye could read the true story o' Fianna Conlan and her two husbands and families. In yer state o' mind, though, I doubt like hell ye would believe yer own eyes."

A smarter man would have backed down after hearing Alaisdair's disgust. Clancy Graham was not a smart man. "Our side of the family is quite well versed in our history." He stared down his nose at Alaisdair. "Fianna Conlan didn't save her first husband because theirs was an unnatural alliance—like my sister's marriage, which her druid"—he spat the word—"engineered when he didn't properly advise the warrior he was assigned to help. Druids are a self-serving, superstitious lot. A warrior should never trust them."

"That mirage ye're seein' wasnae built by a druid. The terrible goddesses who are usin' it are givin' us a sign or somethin', and we'd be wise tae pay attention," Alaisdair said before he turned on his heel and walked over to Duncan, who, Rowan noticed, had kept his distance from Clancy during most of the fighting.

Rowan glared at Clancy, spun on his heel, and joined the others, leaving the man alone to wallow in his prejudice.

⤳

"I think your ruse worked a little too well, sister," Maeve said pointedly. "Brighid has left Fallon unattended for the moment, but she left before the talisman could disclose Seamus's location to us. You did say you would lure him out so I could take him again, did you not?"

Morgan heaved a long-suffering sigh. "Yes, Maeve."

She noted her sister didn't meet her eyes.

"Something is not right here, Morgan. You are up to something." Maeve stood before her, silently demanding Morgan look at her. "We had a deal. You better not go back on it."

"As I recall, we had a deal when I needed your help in Scotland at Samhain too, *sister*."

The nails scraping Morgan's voice gave Maeve momentary pause before she flew into a rage. "Are you saying you are going to take Seamus from me in retaliation for Samhain? You cannot be serious, not if you ever wish for my help again."

"I will take Seamus without giving you another turn with him if that is the only option left to us. At the moment, he still lives, and his talisman has a chance to lure him away from whatever enchantments hide him from us at the moment."

Maeve allowed her purple and black aura to subside. Changing tactics, she asked, "What have you done to pull Brighid away and why?"

"I might have mentioned to her that Taranis is put out with you, which would give her an opportunity to spend time with him. After all, he is a great favorite with many of the goddesses on Tara, and you have him to yourself far too much."

"You set up a tryst between Brighid and Taranis?" She bristled. "How does that help me get Seamus back? How does that help me share Fallon and Seamus with Taranis?" Pacing the flagstones of her enchanted space, she didn't bother to hide her frustration. "I only asked you here for the battles. You have overstepped yourself by involving yourself in my plans with another god," she ranted. Outside, the blood oozing down the castle's walls turned a deep purple-black, reflecting her anger and frustration.

"Once you have Seamus again, you will forget about Taranis, dear. We both know that. With Brighid out of the way for now, you can plant visions in both Seamus's and Fallon's minds, visions that will encourage them to give us what we want," Morgan coaxed.

"What I want, you mean," Maeve reminded her. "You escort them across the ford only after I have finished with them. That was our agreement."

"That is exactly what I have been trying to do, darling."

Morgan's change of tone didn't fool Maeve in the slightest. She wouldn't put it past her sister goddess to devise some vicious revenge for her lack of aid with the events in Scotland on Samhain, a revenge involving Maeve watching powerlessly as Morgan escorted Maeve's prizes across the ford on summer solstice.

She was torn between forcing Morgan to tell her everything about Taranis and taking advantage of Brighid's sudden absence to wreak havoc in Fallon's mind. Her unrequited desire for Seamus Lochlann won out, and she concentrated her efforts on his talisman in the hopes she would reveal his hiding place.

Fallon knew the conclusion to her story. She could see the perfect ending, yet she couldn't seem to create the details to reach it. She blinked open her eyes to survey the scene beneath her on the shoreline and saw it hadn't changed. The warriors squatted beside the water refreshing themselves and washing away the blood of their enemies. She could see no talismans anywhere, but she didn't expect to. Smart talismans didn't show themselves on a battlefield.

Yet she couldn't locate Seamus. His sister's enchantments were obviously powerful. Perhaps Siobhan panicked when the story started to change and pushed Fallon away? Somehow, she doubted that, but what could this interruption in her story mean? She shivered. The golden glow that had settled over her as she wove Seamus's story had disappeared. Why would the patroness of bards abandon her at so crucial a time? Racking her brain, she searched for answers. What had she done to cause such profound anger in Brighid that the goddess would leave her alone when she was so close to changing Seamus's story and saving his life?

Though she tried not to give in to despair, she sensed Seamus didn't have long to live without her intervention. Somehow, she needed to breach Siobhan's enchantments to let him see she lived, to give him a reason to keep fighting. Desperately, she reached out to him telepathically, but his formidable shield held firm against her. She couldn't understand why he wouldn't let her in, and she pushed and punched and kicked at the membranous structure of her prison until she had no energy left. Curling up in a tight ball, she hugged herself as black misery cloaked itself around her, visions of Seamus dying and walking with Morgan across the ford undulating through her mind.

The blackness enveloping her as she lost control of Seamus's story intensified as she suddenly found herself inside Seamus's shield. For some reason she couldn't understand, she could hear his thoughts, but she couldn't communicate hers with him. Her deep subconscious struggled to tell her this circumstance couldn't exist, but the pictures swirling in her head stole her breath away.

He dreamed, his dreams filled with the auburn-haired goddess who desired him, body and soul. In his dreams, Maeve came to him in beauty and grace. She seduced rather than demanded, and he wanted to give her everything she asked. Fallon called out to him, begging him not to surrender, but he merely looked at her, or maybe through her, and continued to undress himself and the goddess.

Deliberately, he led the goddess to bed where he lay her down slowly and worshipped her body with his hands and his mouth. It was a scene right out Seamus's bedroom at the cabin only she had been the woman in his bed then. Intellectually, Fallon understood Maeve invaded their minds and stole their memories to use against them in her own sadistic way. Still, she couldn't help but suffer betrayal as intense as a hot knife stabbing deep into her heart at the sight of Seamus making love to a goddess who meant to use him up before she turned him over to her sister to lead across the river of blood and into the mists in shame.

"Seamus! Please stop! It's not real. She's not real," Fallon pleaded. *"It's the poison working in you. Please, love. Don't let her take you. Don't let her win. I love you so much. Stay with me."*

He showed no sign he heard her.

When he took the goddess's mouth in a devouring kiss, Maeve turned on him, flipping him over onto his back. The sight of her big warrior so weak under the power of the goddess tore at Fallon's soul, and she cried out in abject misery. Reaching a point where she couldn't discern which pain was worse, Seamus's or her own, she turtled down into the haven of Seamus's shirt. Yet even the scent of him on his sweatshirt covering her body wasn't enough to overcome the visions she witnessed in his dreamscape.

It had been one thing to experience those visions herself. Experiencing them through him transcended any torture she had yet to experience. Physical pain on a medieval rack would have been a cakewalk compared to watching her fated warrior, the only man she knew she would ever love, give himself willingly to a shameful death at the hands of a goddess whose sole intention was to steal away his dignity and his life for her own amusement.

Griff could feel Fallon giving up, but he couldn't understand why. One minute she remade Seamus's story, aiding Siobhan as she worked to save her brother's life, and the next minute, she abandoned the story and closed in on herself, her life force slipping away. Feverishly, he tried to breach her shield, but she'd trained too well. Nothing he tried allowed him inside her head. Her lack of druidic training manifested itself in her inability to change her own story, something Maeve must have figured out somehow and used to her advantage. At a loss for how to help his niece, Griff cried out to the goddess who heard him over the conversation into which she had been unexpectedly invited.

"Lady, we need your help. I don't know what Fallon did to earn your displeasure and renunciation at this critical juncture, but please reconsider. She never had the opportunity for proper training beyond basic battle skills as a talisman. She was never allowed to discover that she is a bard. Please, milady, give her another chance to prove herself," he pleaded.

From some distant place, he overheard a conversation he couldn't understand.

"You lured me here on purpose. You are in collusion with two of the evil triplets who delight in taking warriors purely for their own amusement. How dare you, Taranis." Brighid's cold anger vibrated intensely in her rich alto voice. "Storm god, you are a handsome devil, but you align yourself with the wrong side of the pantheon. I do not desire you in my bed that much."

"Brighid, darling, you have it all wrong. While I did heed Morgan's suggestion to pursue you, my interest has everything to do with your golden beauty and how much spending time with you will irritate Maeve with whom I am exceptionally put out. I harbor no desire to help Morgan and Maeve in their unnatural lust for mortals." His voice sounded like distant rolling thunder. "Quite honestly, I have grown rather bored with the two of them and their obsessions with the warriors Scathach favors with her training," Taranis said, the thunder of his voice quieting to a rumble. "Maeve deserves some time alone after her remarks about a mortal warrior's prowess in bed approximating my own."

Griff shook his head. What kind of magic was this? Still, he could hear the gods talking.

"If you are truly honest, you can prove it and find yourself pleasurably occupied in my bed this solstice by helping my favored mortal escape the prison into which Maeve has placed her."

"That would serve me well," Taranis said. "Of course, I expect you will involve yourself with this talisman's warrior. I would like him to have no memory of his time in Maeve's bed after his talisman rescues him with her story."

Griff could hear the smile in Brighid's voice as she agreed to Taranis's terms, and he allowed himself to breathe. Now if the gods would only choose to act in mortal time before it was too late.

⁓

Giving in to the blackness would be so easy, Fallon thought vaguely. She didn't know how to regain her story—if she ever had control of it in the first place. Seamus's anguish and despair overwhelmed her to the point of inertia. In her membranous chamber, she acquiesced quietly to Maeve's desires and hoped her death would come quickly.

From somewhere outside her dreams, she heard a voice.

"Fallon, wake up. Transcend Maeve's enchantment to save your warrior. It is your duty to tell his story. Wake up," the voice demanded. "The poison overwhelms him. He needs your story to cleanse him. Take care of your warrior. It is your duty."

She thought her mother scolded her. Her mother was always scolding her. "Do your chores, Fallon. It is your duty to the family. Do not read that drivel. Druids peddle nothing but superstition. Do your duty. Train to be a talisman." All she wanted to do was finish the story, but she couldn't tell her mother that, for then she'd face a terrible punishment. As usual, she couldn't please her parents and meet her own needs. As usual, duty always won.

"Finish your story, Fallon. You know how it ends. Cleanse your warrior of the poison coursing through his veins. Rescue him from his unnatural fate," the voice directed.

Staring up at the thick golden shield around her bubble prison, she marveled at its intensity and brightness and power. The humming pulse and warmth radiating around her roused her, and she sat up, shielding her eyes with her hand.

Nearby, the floating mirage serving as Maeve's home base for her most recent games oozed black, poisoned blood.

❧

Maeve paced and raged. "Taranis must not be able to keep Brighid satisfied, which I find extremely difficult to believe. See how she interferes with the talisman?"

With a languid gesture, Morgan said, "Perhaps his offer did not please her, or she did not believe him when he told her he had grown bored with you." She plucked a grape from a bowl resting on the table beside her. "Launching into a tantrum will serve no purpose. At times like these, I do not envy you your intense passions." After popping the grape into her mouth, chewing, and swallowing it, she added, "At times like these, a cool head better serves the purpose."

"I imagine you are plotting your next move?" Maeve's heaving chest gave her away, but she didn't care.

"Hmmm?"

"Are you listening to me?"

"How could I not with you screaming your displeasure in my ear?" Morgan snapped.

Maeve stared out the window at the talisman in her bubble prison and saw to her great consternation that Brighid had resurrected her golden halo around it. "I thought you said Taranis was helping us by distracting Brighid," she said, the accusation reverberating through the room.

"I thought so too. In another couple of minutes, you would have had the talisman exactly where you wanted her. Would you like me to find Taranis, ask him what he knows?"

"Oh, you would love to leave me now, wouldn't you? Perhaps

that was your plan all along. Allow things to move along to the point that I give up my claim to the warrior, and you can swoop in and take him for yourself. See if I let that happen." She summoned her purple-black cloak around her shoulders.

Morgan continued to infuriate her. Rather than taking the bait, she casually snacked on fruit and inspected her nails for a moment. "You forget. You had him at your mercy, tied to your bed, completely unable to deny you your pleasure, and you lost him to the talisman Brighid has decided to protect. That was none of my doing, so do not attack me with your accusations." When she looked up, banked coals shone from her eyes.

Maeve seethed. "You have been plotting your own game all along. I asked you to stage a battle to keep Seamus's friends occupied while I enjoyed him. You lost your mind and called forward a Fomorian and the Nephilim, neither of which I asked you to send." Her cape swirled around her as she paced. "You called up hordes of rogues, effectively challenging Seamus's talisman to do something about them. On the side, you are making deals with Taranis and who knows who else. For an ally, you leave much to be desired."

Maeve had worked herself into a state, her chest heaving, eyes flashing purple fire with her agitation.

"I think I understand why Taranis enjoys baiting you so much. When you work yourself into such a towering passion, you are truly magnificent."

The smile playing at the corners of Morgan's mouth infuriated Maeve even more.

"Do not even suggest a tryst," her low voice sounded like a growl. "I have lusted after Seamus Lochlann since I first saw him last winter, and even a goddess of your prowess would be a poor substitute for him at the moment."

Morgan quirked a brow and ate another grape.

CHAPTER TWENTY-SEVEN

ROM SOMEWHERE FAR away, Fallon heard Seamus groan in pain, and she bolted upright, losing her balance as her prison wobbled in the air. Her time had come. If ever she would prove herself a worthy talisman for this magnificent warrior who had stolen her heart in the space of a day, it was now. She could succumb to the blackness easily if she knew Seamus lived. All that mattered was saving his life.

Her story surged back in a rush:

"'I have come to save your brother. You must trust me. Remove your hands from Seamus's wound so I may bathe it in sacred water.'

"Siobhan squatted beside her patient and watched as the auburn-haired woman trickled water into her brother's black wound. As the water pooled in the open gash, Siobhan watched transfixed as the poison began to flow directly into the water. Seamus flinched, and black water oozed from his wound.

"'You'll want to sop that up as it exits his body to stop further infection both of Seamus and of the earth on which the poisoned drops fall,' the woman said.

"Siobhan glanced beneath her brother's arm and saw to her astonishment that in the few places where droplets of poisoned water had fallen, the vegetation withered and died instantaneously. She gasped and pulled a soft cloth from her bag of simples to catch the poison as it exited his body.

"Meanwhile, the woman walked away toward the clear waters of the nearby creek to gather more life-giving water. When she returned with another handful to trickle into Seamus's wound, Siobhan asked, 'Why do you bring the water only by the handful? His wound is long and deep and full of black poison.' Her agitation sounded as the notes of her voice climbed higher. 'Surely you need some sort of vessel to bring enough water to cleanse and save him before the poison can finish the job it started. Look how pale he is, how shallowly he breathes. He needs more than a handful of water at a time!'

"The woman smiled sadly at the druid before reminding her of the story of Diarmuid and Grainne. 'The only way Diarmuid could have survived the boar's poison was if Fionn delivered the life-giving water with his own hands. Seamus's story mirrors Diarmuid's. This means his cure must arrive in a natural, living vessel. It's the only way.' The woman poured another handful of water over Seamus's wound.

"'Then we must move him closer to the stream so you can deliver more water faster,' Siobhan insisted.

"'How shall we do that with the two of us women and he such a massive warrior? We will kill him in the attempt. He is safe here under the protections of your enchantments. If we move him, the goddess will see where he is and take him back for herself. Surely, you know this,' the woman reminded her.

"A single tear slipped down Siobhan's face as she acknowledged the reality of her brother's dire situation. Arguing with the woman only wasted precious time he didn't have. She nodded and went back to catching the drops of poisoned water as they bubbled up out of Seamus's skin.

"The woman made ten trips to the stream, each one careful and deliberate. When she returned with the eleventh handful of water, Siobhan noted with something akin to hope that the water pooling in her brother's wound no longer flowed black. When she turned his arm to let the water roll into the cloth, it was now a light pink as though Seamus's body might win the battle with the poison. He still hadn't awakened from his faint, but he rested more easily, and his color appeared less ashen.

"The woman made two more trips to the stream. After the twelfth trip, clear water flowed from Seamus's wound. After the thirteenth trip, the wound began to knit miraculously on its own. Siobhan stared at the woman who healed her brother's wound so assiduously and discovered the woman had been silently weeping throughout her treks to and from the stream for the water necessary to heal him. An astonishing thought occurred to her—the water the woman brought from the stream didn't originate there. The water came from the woman's tears. What was it she'd said? The water must come from a living vessel?

"When the woman saw the success of her efforts to heal Seamus, she collapsed beside him and fell into a deep slumber, her energy completely expended in her attempt to save her warrior. Siobhan wept in gratitude for the woman's sacrifice and worried about how much she'd given to save Seamus. It was then that Griffin Walsh reappeared from his place of concealment to chant over the exhausted woman."

Fallon had no idea where she was in the story. She didn't know if she lay beside her healing warrior or if she floated in Maeve's iridescent prison. It didn't matter. She'd done her duty to her warrior, changed his story, saved his life.

◾

By giving the druids roles in healing her fallen warrior, something she did without thinking, Fallon pleased her goddess beyond measure. For not only was Brighid the patron goddess of bards, but also the patron of the healing arts.

Yet the bard still floated in her beautiful, imprisoning raindrop. Other than Maeve herself, the only deity who could free her was Taranis. To prove himself to Brighid and thus encourage her to wipe away Seamus's memories of his time in Maeve's bed, Taranis would have to free the talisman. A talent such as Fallon Graham's could not be lost to the world before Brighid had a chance to train her. Maeve wanted the warrior, mistakenly thinking him to be the prize, but the true prize lay in enervated unconsciousness on the floor of her iridescent bubble. If Taranis hoped to gain Brighid's favor—and her bed—he would see to freeing Fallon when Seamus healed enough to spirit her away from the goddess watching from the mirage palace hovering above the lake.

⚜

"I believe the talisman has won our skirmish, sister," Morgan said as she stared out the window of Maeve's floating palace. "But I think you may yet have a chance at another tryst with her warrior before you give them to me to enjoy."

"What makes you say that?"

"See how she lays in her prison? She is not fighting it the way she fought it earlier, nor does she seem distressed. Brighid's glow keeps you out of Fallon's head. Pulling together all those observations, my conclusion is she has succeeded in telling a story to save her warrior's life, which is actually good."

"Why?" Suspicion narrowed Maeve's violet eyes.

"Because the day is far from over, so I have more opportunities to take warriors, not the least of whom is your prize."

Maeve hissed in a breath.

"After you have exhausted his possibilities, of course."

Morgan's calmness alarmed her. "What are you planning?"

"If you must know, I think I have devised a way to involve Milesians in our little war here, a way that will send to me those four delectable warriors catching their breaths on the beach without drawing them into a larger battle over which I have no control."

"*Milesians!*" Maeve gasped. "Are you utterly crazy? The reason Danu and the Dagda rule their kingdom from *beneath* the mound at Tara is because the Milesians drove them there. Our escape to wreak havoc in the mortal world is only due to the assimilation of the Milesians into the mortal world where their powers have diminished, as ours would have done, ironically, had we won the war." She grabbed her sister by the shoulders, determined to stop her from executing such a terrifying idea. "You wish to resurrect those powerful Greek entities who defeated our race and drove us underground?" Her purple and black aura radiated her anger—and her fear. "Not even another round with the delectable Seamus Lochlann is worth such a risk."

Morgan stomped her foot. "I want Rowan Sheridan." Jerking away from Maeve's grasp, she paced across the room and back again. "I have always wanted the Sheridans. At one time, you did too." She huffed out a breath. "If I bring in Milesians, the entire Sheridan clan will have no choice but to come to Rowan's aid, and I will take them all at once. The orgasm I will experience when I lead them across the ford will transcend myth."

To Maeve's ears, the triumph in Morgan's voice bordered on hysteria. Toning down her anger, she attempted reason, the irony of their role reversal not lost on her. "You wish to have only one prolonged orgasm? What will you do when it is over? Who will be worthy of your pursuit then?"

"I enact my plan on the summer solstice, the longest day of the year. My pleasure will last and last," Morgan enthused, oblivious to the fine details on which Maeve chose to focus.

"Danu will imprison you in the deepest halls of Tara for eternity if you survive the battle at all. The Milesians are our sworn enemies, not those of the warriors or even civilians. In fact, warriors are indirectly descended from the Milesians. It's what gives them their supernatural abilities. You have completely lost your mind." She waved a hand in disgust, but it was an act. Morgan's plan terrified her. If Morgan successfully called up Milesians, surely Danu and the Dagda would blame her lust for Seamus Lochlann as the cause and imprison her as well. Such a fate would ensure she'd do without any male companionship whatsoever. She had to stop Morgan.

Deliberately, she walked to the window and glanced out at the bubble floating outside it. "I think it is time I took on the bard directly. She has interfered in my plans enough."

Her spontaneous departure from her enchanted chamber no doubt surprised her fellow goddess. Maeve never acted completely on her own. She always needed Morgan's help in some way, which she understood was the way Morgan preferred things to proceed. But the supreme war goddess had overstepped herself when she announced her new plans.

Hazarding a glance back at the window, she saw to her satisfaction that Morgan watched as she took on the talisman directly. Hovering on a purple and black cloud that announced her poisonous nature, she stood before Fallon in her iridescent cage and commanded her to awaken.

"For all of your unnatural ability, you are still a mortal. You will do as I command, Fallon Graham. Give me Seamus Lochlann."

The woman struggled to stand in her unstable cage to meet the goddess's challenge. Maeve watched with satisfaction as Fallon dropped back to her knees before she slowly stood to face her enemy.

"You are a goddess, powerful enough to bend time and space, powerful enough to conjure monsters from the past, powerful enough to erect an ever-changing floating fortress, powerful enough to bend an unwilling warrior to your will. So, if you want him, you're going to have to take him yourself."

The talisman's insolence enraged her, and she roared her anger at the talisman's stupidity—or courage—to challenge her. Her aura took on the appearance of a purple and black storm cloud floating beside the bubble prison. To her consternation, her display of power had no effect on the mortal.

"Surely, as such an all-powerful goddess, you're capable of taking what you want," Fallon taunted.

Maeve banked her anger. "I would rather you gave him to me. I will enjoy him so much more as a gift from you," she coaxed. She wasn't above seducing a woman as much as a man. One saved playing hardball for when one truly needed it.

"Seamus has suffered enough in pleasuring you. We both have," Fallon said, gathering more courage the longer Maeve allowed the charade to continue. "If you want him, you'll have to take him."

"You can give him to me, or he can watch you suffer from wherever he hides his cowardly self. Hiding behind a woman hardly seems worthy of a warrior." Maeve pitched her words to echo through the valley.

To Maeve's dismay, Fallon didn't rise to the bait and open her shield to her warrior, allowing Maeve to pinpoint where his infuriating druid sister kept him hidden from her.

"You lured him into your enchanted fun house once. Why must you resort to using me to draw him in again? Are your seductive powers diminishing somehow? Are you losing your allure?" The infuriating woman mimicked Maeve's coaxing voice.

"How dare you! You are nothing but a mortal. You cannot think to aspire to be a god! You will give me what I want because I command it of you. And you will give him to me now!" Maeve raged.

⁓

"What d'ye make of it?" Alaisdair asked Rowan as they watched the goddess confront their friend's talisman, purple-black clouds roiling in the air above the lake.

"I think if we all come out of this alive, we're going to have a powerful ally on our side. Your cousin has the courage of a warrior to stand up to the goddess like that," Rowan said in wonder.

"I heard yer talisman stood up tae a god once on yer behalf."

"Which is why I strive to make her as happy as possible. I hope Seamus is as wise," Rowan said with a wink before sobering as he gazed again at the ominous scene in the sky. "I wish we could see what is happening. Maeve is obscuring our view on purpose."

"Must be a good sign. She wouldnae want us tae see Fallon beatin' her at her own game."

Clancy Graham rudely interrupted them. "For the last time, stop with the omens and signs. That druid bullshit is what put my little girl in danger in the first place."

Rowan rounded on the other man. "You are on my last nerve, old man. Your *prejudices* are what put Fallon in this precarious situation." Rowan flexed his fists. "If she'd been trained properly, she wouldn't have had to learn on the fly, putting herself, her warrior, and the rest of us in mortal danger. Did you even notice that Finn MacCool only showed up to even the odds after Fallon floated above the battle?" He got right in Clancy's face. "You disgust me. If you weren't Fallon's father, I'd kick your ass. You may fight beside us, but you are not one of us." He stalked away before he gave in to his intense desire to knock some sense into Clancy Graham.

⁓

Above the lake, Maeve reasserted herself. "Seamus Lochlann is mine. He has always been mine. Since I first set eyes on him last winter when he came to Rowan Sheridan's aid against my sister, I have desired him. He would have come to me willingly if you had not interfered." The purple aura surrounding the goddess deepened nearly to black in her rage.

"Seamus is an honorable warrior. He would *never* have given himself to you willingly. He would never suffer the disgrace of dying in your bed rather than dying in battle," Fallon said and wondered at the temerity of her tone.

The goddess changed her tactics, drawing Fallon's attention to her impressive assets. "He is mortal. Once he has pleasured a goddess, he will always want one. You will never again satisfy him. Save yourself the humiliation of failing Seamus in bed and give him to me."

For a second, Fallon's resolve—and her bravado—faltered before the warmth of her patroness penetrated her thoughts as she sensed Brighid's golden shield intensifying around her bubble prison.

Maeve went for the kill. "I saw how you pleasured Seamus. I saw how much he enjoyed your skills, and I used that knowledge to take his body to places no mortal has ever dreamed. When he comes back to me, he will crave me, especially when he thinks he's with you—at first." Her eyes flashed purple fire. "Once he realizes he is mine, he will give me everything I want and more. He is the most magnificent warrior I have ever had. I will make sure to tell him that before he gives me his honor—and his soul."

The smile she turned on Fallon as she described Seamus's end would have sent a lesser mortal to an early grave. In that instant, she saw the portals of hell behind Maeve's gnashing teeth and purple-black eyes. Greek mythology described harpies or sirens as beautiful women until they opened their gaping jaws, revealing rows of teeth fit to eat a man whole. Maeve, too, resembled a harpy as she bared her tortured warlike essence to an opponent who had demonstrated abilities nearly on a level with the gods.

Fallon almost fainted at the sight, dropping her shield and revealing to the goddess what she wanted to know. But Brighid guarded her. When Fallon staggered in the face of Maeve's revelations, Brighid steadied her. *"Danu gave you a power to change the outcome of the story. Maeve knows this and hates you for it, for she cannot interfere with the story you weave in the moment. Fight back. Tell her a story."*

Sucking in a breath, she followed her patroness's directive. "You seek to use raw power to overwhelm me. You had to tie Seamus to your bed in order to hold him. You're not as strong as you'd like me to believe."

The goddess's purple and black aura pulsed angrily around her, a crackle of electricity that edged the sound barrier.

Fallon held firm. "Let me tell you a story about a powerful warrior who walked away from a goddess's bed because he loved a mortal. The love he shared with his talisman was so strong it gave them the strength to escape the goddess's traps.

"You see, the goddess, being a warmonger, had never known love. She couldn't understand love's incredible power, so she had no weapons to fight it. When the warrior discovered all he had to do was trust in his love, he relaxed and stopped fighting the goddess's bonds. The bonds loosened and dropped away from him when the tension of his fear no longer gave them power.

"The goddess, momentarily distracted by the idea of more warriors filling her bed as she watched them battle insurmountable odds, didn't notice as the warrior dressed and calmly walked away from her bed. Now she rages against her own folly and fights against a foe she can never defeat. For the warrior will carry his love with him even into death."

At the conclusion of Fallon's story, the goddess's rage exploded with a thunderclap of black lightning, the cloud on which she rode roiling in pent-up energy, glowing purple and black and obscuring the sun from the lake and forest below. Fallon flinched as she watched the energy loosed by the lightning knock the warriors and talismans standing on the beach flat to the ground.

Thunder echoed through the mountains for miles, generating a shock wave that resonated deep in the earth. The warriors scrambled to their feet and raced for higher ground as a massive wave formed in the middle of the lake, building strength as it rolled menacingly toward its crashing destiny with the shore. In the recesses of her mind, Fallon feared for her warrior, her family, and her friends. But she showed no fear to the goddess, instinctively knowing all their lives depended on her remaining strong no matter the outcome of Maeve's tumultuous tantrum.

"I imprisoned you, and only I can free you. We will see how long your warrior 'loves' you when he can only touch you in his dreams," Maeve snarled. In a burst of purple and black smoke, the goddess disappeared.

Chapter Twenty-Eight

FALLON COLLAPSED IN a heap, the membranous cage sagging momentarily beneath her before rebounding into its perfect bubble shape. She'd won the battle and saved her warrior, saved her clan. The cost, however, would be dear. The enormity of Maeve's curse weighed on her like stone slabs piled on her chest. She struggled to breathe as she contemplated the terrible loss of never experiencing Seamus's touch again. He loved women, had vast experience with them. That much was clear from the way he made love to her at his cabin. How long before he moved on from the brief memories they'd made? Would he leave her for another? She'd proved she could serve him as his talisman quite well from inside the confines of her enchanted prison. But she couldn't take care of his other needs from inside her pretty bubble. Maeve's curse brought on a despair that threatened to overwhelm her.

In horror, she watched as Maeve's floating mirage evanesced, the towers and turrets, followed by the curtain walls lost color and substance until at last, there was nothing left but red, purple, and black glitter in the air. All at once, the glitter seemed to lose its battle with gravity and dropped like acid rain into the now-calm mirror of the lake below. A faint sulfurous scent wafted on the breeze, the last vestige of Maeve's evil magic.

Unable to control her debilitating sorrow, Fallon gave way to racking sobs.

On the shore of the lake below her, Seamus burst from the edge of the forest and raced recklessly to the lakeshore, his fear for her contorting his features. As Fallon had battled the goddess for him, Siobhan had finished her ritual chanting over him to ensure he healed properly, something Siobhan had communicated to her somewhere during the middle of Maeve's tortures.

Expressions of pity and fear on the faces of his family and friends greeted him as he confronted the reality of his talisman's sacrifice.

"Fallon! What have you done? What did you trade the goddess for me?" he shouted as he ran into the icy waters of the lake to stand exactly beneath her floating cage.

"You're alive! You're safe and you're alive." She smiled bleakly through her tears. "That's all that matters."

"What has she done, Fallon? Where is Maeve, and why are you still imprisoned?"

"I told her a love story. Like Conchobar with Naoise and Fionn with Diarmuid, she couldn't allow me to win. But you're alive, and you're safe, so we changed part of the story." She pushed her hand into the membrane of her enchanted prison, the closest she would ever come to touching him again. "Love has won," she whispered as tears trickled down her face.

She had to remain brave, find the courage to face the worst part of Maeve's sentence. Somehow, she'd have to be strong enough to watch Seamus with other women, to know she could never be to him what the promise of their time together at the cabin had hinted. Desperately, she fought for control of her emotions because she couldn't run. She couldn't hide. Her anguish was on display for all to see. Vaguely, she wondered how Maeve meant to keep her alive in her beautiful prison then thought perhaps the goddess would eventually have mercy on her and kill her.

The lustful goddess of war had no mercy. It was all Fallon could do not to burst out in hysterical laughter at her own folly. The goddess had devised the ultimate torture for Fallon's impudence at defying her. Eventually, she'd lose her mind and be of no use to anyone. The power the gods gave to her as a bard would be lost to the world while Maeve waited patiently for another chance at her warrior. Even a lustful goddess had the gift of patience. Immortality afforded her that.

"Fallon, we'll figure out how to release you. Please, Fireworks, don't give up now," Seamus pleaded.

"Are you happy now?" Griff dragged her attention to her uncle and her father standing on the beach.

"What are you talking about?" Clancy asked.

"Your prejudices have brought us to this impasse. If Fallon had been trained properly in the druidic aspects of her gift, Maeve probably wouldn't have been able to imprison her, or Fallon would already have devised a way out of her enchanted snare. As it is, none of us knows how to free her." Griff glared at her father who seemed to shrink away from him.

"You got your wish. Her destiny was to join a powerful warrior clan, but she can't do that when she remains under Maeve's power. After the way Fallon rescued her warrior from the goddess's clutches, I doubt the goddess will feel charitable about freeing her—ever," Griff said.

Hearing the enormity of her desperate situation stated so baldly did nothing to ease her sorrow. Her heart clenched at the fearful way both of her parents looked at each other as her mother joined her father at the edge of the lake.

"How could we know, Griff? She showed such unnatural tendencies from such an early age we despaired of her becoming the talisman we knew she had to be," Ivori said.

"*Unnatural tendencies?*" Griff roared. "There is nothing unnatural about being a druid. The warrior community depends on druids in every aspect of it." He faced them toe to toe. "Without druids, there is no healing. Without druids, there is no justice. Without druids, there are no stories, no immortality. Without druids, warriors suffer. Did you learn *nothing* in your training?"

Fallon cringed when her dad didn't back down, all the old childhood hurts compounding her pain.

"Our long-ago ancestor, Fianna Conlan, gave up her warrior for a druid. She let her warrior die to have her real love. Every Graham knows that," he said, a defense Fallon had heard her entire life.

"Not so, cousin," the tall, auburn-haired man Fallon had noticed earlier said. "If ye actually read the history o' the family, ye would see that she did everythin' in her considerable power tae save her warrior husband. He was the love o' her life, and she mourned him every day until she died. Her second husband knew and understood her great love fer her warrior, accepted it as part o' her, and loved her devotedly anyway." He paused for a beat to let his words sink in. "Because o' Fianna Conlan's exceptional capacity fer love, yer side and my side o' the Conlan-Graham clan is alive tae come taegether in the person o' yer daughter." He glanced up at her floating involuntarily above them. "She's a powerful being, and we need tae stop fightin' about ancient history and figure out how tae help her warrior save her."

Seamus stared up at Fallon in her iridescent prison and pleaded. "Tell a story, Fireworks. Tell the story of how you overcame the lustful war goddess and freed yourself from your prison."

"I can't Seamus. She cursed me to remain in this prison for eternity. I don't have a story for that."

Seamus staggered under the weight of the goddess's curse. "There must be some way to beat her." He looked to the others. "Siobhan, Griff, some help here."

Without hesitation, they waded into the water to join him

beneath her bubble prison. "She needs a story or an enchantment to escape Maeve's curse and this taunting prison in which Maeve keeps her. What do you suggest?" he asked.

"I wish I knew." Siobhan's shoulders slumped in dejection.

"Griff?" Seamus sounded desperate. "Somehow, we have to find a way to save her."

The unshed tears in his voice tore at Fallon's heart. Worse, she could do nothing to soothe him, couldn't touch him or hold him. Her knees buckled under the weight of the terrible ache she harbored for her warrior.

Griff's sad expression hardened into determination as he stared up at her. "Siobhan and I melded our minds before the end of the first battle. We've been working together throughout the day to help the two of you. In everything we've done since Maeve took you, Seamus, Fallon has had a hand." He smiled up at her. "But since she had no druidic or bardic training, her well of stories isn't complete. I appealed to Brighid once during the battle, and she returned to Fallon. She's our only recourse now."

A red and gold shimmer materialized into Scathach who strolled through the gathered party. "You are correct, druid. I am glad to see you have the good sense to revere and rely on the gods. You must be patient. Another goddess has a plan for delivering your bard to you, Seamus. But you must understand, Fallon's delivery comes with a price."

Seamus nodded. "Whatever the price, you know I'll pay it."

Tears poured unchecked down Fallon's face as she listened to her warrior once again offer to trade his life for hers.

"You will be expected to train even more often and more diligently both with Brighid and with me for the rest of your lives. The two of you together are our most formidable team in our never-ending battles with Morgan and Maeve."

From her position on her hands and knees inside her iridescent cage, she stared at the goddess, a tiny flame of hope flickering to life in her heart.

"After this little escapade, I expect Macha will lend her considerable might to Morgan's and Maeve's battles in the future, and the two of you will be asked to do battle often. You must understand this, Seamus."

"Whatever it takes to return Fallon to me, milady." He shot her a grin before he returned his attention to the goddess. "Ever since you brought me in to train with the Sheridans, you know I've never backed down from a fight."

"Well said, warrior. Very well said." She nodded with satisfaction. "The sun will slip behind the mountains soon, followed by the long twilight of Midsummer Night." The goddess glanced around at the gathered warriors. "The rest of you must leave this place. Leave your gear at the cabin and visualize yourselves back to your homes. Fallon and Seamus need time alone."

"But what about our daughter? How will he free her?" Ivori Graham cried as she ran to the edge of the water near the goddess, the druids, and Seamus.

"That is none of your concern, talisman. Your prejudices are the reason my sister goddess must be involved in your daughter's rescue. Your prejudices are the reason Fallon will need such intense training. You have done enough damage."

Ivori started to protest, and Fallon held her breath as she watched Scathach's red and gold aura intensify. "I insist you return to your home now. When you have shown you have learned something about your unnatural relationship to your community, I may decide to allow you to see your daughter again." Scathach's tone left nothing to argument, and her mom collapsed in tears on the shore. Her father gathered her mother into his arms and stared sorrowfully up at her. Her parents' anguish tore at her heart, but the goddess had spoken. There was nothing else to be said. With one hand braced against the membrane of her bubble and the other over her heart, she watched her parents hold each other.

Keela walked over to them and set her hand lightly on Clancy's shoulder. "Whenever you're interested in reconciliation, brother, you have only to let me know. We'll meet with you and try to mend the past twelve years."

Griff nodded in agreement.

"Your family is not at fault here, yet they are the first to reach out to you. Think on that as well in your isolation," Scathach said to Fallon's parents. "Now that I know how the two of you have hidden from your duties all these years, I will expect your help in future skirmishes where civilian lives are in danger. There will be no argument." Turning her back on them, she dismissed them.

"As usual, Rowan, Duncan, and Alaisdair, you to do. Now, do as I command and give your friend and his talisman their privacy."

"Of course, milady," the man Alaisdair replied with a bow before reaching out to a beautiful blond woman who must have been his talisman. Holding hands, the two of them disappeared as they visualized themselves from the battlefield.

Rowan grasped Seamus's arm in the age-old way of warriors before pulling him in for a one-armed embrace. "Good luck, buddy. I'll be seeing you soon, I hope."

Seamus nodded in acknowledgment of his friend's comment, but his eyes stayed on Fallon.

She surmised that the small, black-haired woman who walked into Rowan's embrace must be Alyssa. The two of them disappeared as they followed their goddess's directive, confirming Fallon's observation.

Once again, Scathach turned her wrathful gaze on Fallon's parents who hung their heads. Holding her grieving mom in his arms, her dad glanced one last time at Fallon, whispered something to her mom, and the two of them disappeared as the goddess commanded.

Siobhan and Duncan and Keela and Griff remained on the

shore near Seamus. "You know how to find us if you need us, brother," Duncan said.

Tears shining in her eyes, Siobhan stepped over and hugged Seamus close before she joined her husband.

"Yes." Still, Seamus didn't take his eyes off Fallon.

"We will always be with you, Fallon. You have only to call us when you need us," Keela said in a gentle tone before she slipped her arm around Griff.

"I knew you were special the first time we met, Fallon. I prayed to Brighid for guidance when I made your bracelet. After being a part of your story, I can see now how she guided me. She is your greatest asset, my dear. Rely on her," Griff said. Then he winked.

Simultaneously, he and Keela visualized themselves away, but his parting gesture gave Fallon hope.

"The sun is setting. Keep your eyes on Fallon, Seamus. Do not let her out of your sight," Scathach commanded before she too disappeared, leaving behind a red and gold shimmer in the air.

They were alone but unable to touch each other outside of their minds. Silent tears flowed down her face as she tried to figure out what to do to return to her warrior.

"Seamus. You know she'll never give up, exactly like her sister has never given up on the Sheridans."

"We're a team, Fallon. We work together." His voice softened. "Besides, you heard Scathach. We can expect some help."

As he spoke, the sun slipped to the jagged horizon of the surrounding mountains, and a single beam of sunlight shot out, momentarily blinding them as it pierced Fallon's raindrop prison. A scream rent the air, and he looked up in perfect time to catch Fallon as she fell out of the sky.

"Hello, Fireworks. That was quite a dramatic escape," he said with a grin before he covered her mouth with his own, his desperate kiss consuming her.

As they traded breath, each of them seeking to kiss the other so deep they melded into one, Seamus gently allowed Fallon to slide down the length of his body until they touched from shoulders to knees, her arms wrapped around him like a vine, while his arms banded around her.

Their kiss went on until the last of the day's light rested on the ridges of the mountains surrounding them.

Long minutes passed until Fallon, standing thigh-deep in a frigid mountain lake, shivered, and she tore her mouth from Seamus. Only then did they notice they'd been standing in the water through the entirety of sundown during the long twilight of summer solstice.

"Shall we return to the cabin, Fallon? I have some ideas about bonding I'd like to run by you," he said with a smile.

"After everything we've been through today, that's what's on your mind? Bonding?" She tried to appear indignant, but she couldn't keep the smile off her lips. Her warrior wanted her, not some goddess imitation of her.

Seamus sobered. "I think you should open your mind to mine so we visualize ourselves to the same room in the cabin. I just got you back, and I have no intention of losing you again, Fallon."

She peered at him from beneath her lashes. "I don't need telepathy to know exactly which room we're going to, Seamus."

"It's unfinished business, Fireworks. We have an obligation to the gods and to each other to finish bonding. Even in your limited training, you learned that." He slanted her a look, but his eyes twinkled.

Her laugh rang across the water. "I'm holding on, warrior. Go wherever you want. I'll be with you."

They opened their shields to each other and discovered they both envisioned the big bed in the master bedroom of the cabin. Their proximity to their destination made their trip there exceptionally short.

CHAPTER TWENTY-NINE

ARANIS DID *WHAT*?" Maeve raged as she paced a path in the exquisite Oriental carpet of her stronghold in the warehouse district of Southeast Los Angeles.

Morgan waved a hand in the air. "I believe he freed the talisman," she said as she gazed at Maeve with undisguised delight. "After we decamped and your mirage ran its course. You instructed him to dispose of the last vestiges of your floating palace, and he went a bit further and sent a sunbeam straight through the raindrop in which you imprisoned the talisman."

"That was not the plan at all! If anything, she was Taranis's to enjoy and then to give to you once her warrior came to her rescue and I took him again for myself. I thought I made the plan clear to Taranis." She stomped her foot as her purple and black aura pulsed around her.

Settling herself comfortably in one of the deep leather chairs by the window in Maeve's great room, Morgan said, "Perhaps Brighid made him a better offer."

Maeve wanted to scream.

Morgan shrugged. "Of course, his behavior might have

something to do with your comments concerning a certain warrior's prowess matching Taranis's in your bed."

"Taranis would know I was only baiting him. I was not serious." She attempted to sound more confident than she felt about Taranis's state of mind.

"To my ears, you sounded like you meant what you said. Perhaps Taranis thought that as well."

She stomped across the room, stopping directly in front of her sister goddess. "You are behind this, are you not? You encouraged Taranis to go to Brighid and steal the talisman from the special prison I constructed to lure Taranis into my scheme." She crossed her arms over her chest. "You are still angry about what happened at Samhain. Your actions are petty, even for you."

"If you recall, you asked me to send Taranis to Brighid to distract her from aiding the talisman," Morgan said with a sniff. "Now you want to change the story. How very convenient and typical of you, blaming others for your mistakes and the disruptions of your plans."

"You do not sound at all like the peacock calling the bird of paradise a show off," she sniped.

Morgan waved her off. "Once again, we have been thwarted by the warrior class. I, for one, am heartily sick of the way they have delivered blows to our coveted plans. At least at Samhain, I took one of them, though he was old and tired. Still, his blood swirled sweetly around my legs." A brief smile ghosted her mouth before the banked coals of her eyes glowed red. "This time, we are left with nothing."

"At I least enjoyed Seamus's skills for a time." Maeve sighed. "I did not come away empty-handed," she said, her memories of Seamus Lochlann at her mercy in bed small recompense for the lengths to which she had gone to deliver him there.

"We must devise a better strategy if we are going to take the Sheridans and their friends in the future. I believe I will repair to my apartments in New York to ponder about what to do next. Your pique at the moment impedes my thinking."

"What are you saying?" Maeve asked, but she talked to the air. The only vestige of her sister's presence was a shimmering cloud of black glitter hanging in the space where Morgan had been. Devoid of even a sounding board for her rants, Maeve dropped heavily onto her chaise lounge to brood about the loss of her prize and the turn of events that returned him to that nuisance of a bard who had no natural place in the order of things.

During the long twilight of summer solstice, Fallon and Seamus undressed each other slowly. With feather-light strokes, they skimmed their fingertips everywhere over each other. Long sweeping caresses led to kneading and palming and testing each other's bodies. They delighted in each other, marveling they were alive and together.

When they tumbled into bed, they wrestled over who would kiss whose body from head to toe and back again. Seamus won the battle with sheer strength while Fallon stole kisses on his shoulders, arms, chest, neck, face—anywhere she could reach as he fired her blood with his hands and his mouth. As she glided her hands over his skin, he tongued a trail along the column of her throat when each abruptly stopped. A glimpse of her branded wrist reminded them of his sign. They stared deeply into each other's eyes, knowing what the other was thinking even without using their telepathy. With his tongue, he traced his sign on her breasts as she slipped her hand between them to trace it along his taut belly, moving lower until he grabbed her hand and held it captive. He pulled one turgid nipple into his mouth and sucked hard.

Beneath him, she bucked, and he laughed before he blazed a path of his sign along the silky skin of her torso until he reached her sex. She held her breath in anticipation of his next move.

When he expertly tongued his sign over her swollen clit, she screamed his name as he brought her instantly to rapture. While she rocketed through the stratosphere, he shifted his body over hers and entered her with one glorious thrust. As he joined them together, she knew in this moment she was alive for the first time in her life.

Seamus waited, probably out of reflex, but Fallon opened her mind to him, showing him her delight in his lovemaking. Soon, she was beyond thinking. Her body took charge of her mind and ultimately took over his body too, her inner muscles tightening around him, pulling him more deeply inside her. He shuddered against her and started moving, having no choice in the face of their mutual desire for each other. They soared together far beyond anything either had ever experienced before.

An eternity later, their bodies still quivered and pulsed with the power of their loving. Seamus lay atop her as Fallon drew lazy halves of trinity knots over the muscles of his broad back.

"I love you, Seamus Lochlann," she whispered.

Fallon awoke the next morning to shafts of sunshine warming a swath across the middle of the bed. When she tried to sit up and stretch, a heavy arm tightened across her waist and pulled her toward the hard muscles of a powerful chest.

"You weren't thinking about leaving this bed, were you?" Seamus's voice rumbled in his chest beneath her cheek.

"Open your eyes. It's a beautiful day in the neighborhood. We should go out and enjoy it," she said as she rolled over in his arms.

"It's a beautiful day right here in this bed. And I most definitely plan to enjoy it," he growled into her neck as he nudged her hair aside to plant an openmouthed kiss on the sensitive skin behind her ear. She shifted to allow him his goal, which he took as encouragement for doing other things.

His hand slid up to cup her breast while he rubbed the full length of his arousal along the cleft of her ass. His movements told her of his intentions, and she smiled and pushed herself against him.

"I'm not sure what all happened during various parts of our ordeal yesterday, but I like the way you aren't holding back anymore," he said as he shifted to push her onto her back.

"I've discovered I have a weakness."

He jacked an eyebrow.

"It's your sign. All you need to do is touch me once with it, and I'm overwhelmed with desire for you. Of course, my response might also have to do with what I discovered about myself yesterday…"

"Yeah? What was that?" He lightly traced his sign in the hollow of her shoulder, smiling at the way she writhed and shifted at his touch.

"I've fallen in love with you. I know that's one of the goals the gods have for bonding between warrior pairs, but it doesn't always happen, as you know."

Seamus stilled his finger on her skin.

"There were times yesterday when Maeve tried to make me believe it wouldn't happen for us, but she was too late. I knew when you left the cabin to go help your friends that I'd already fallen for you."

His midnight blue eyes darkened as he stared deeply into hers. "Fallon, in a couple of short days, you've become my whole world. When I saw you in that floating cage, my heart stopped. I'd rather die than lose you."

"Another success for the gods then," she said with a laugh as she traced his sign over the skin covering his impressive pecs.

"So it appears, Fireworks."

A sobering thought intruded. "Scathach said there would be

a price for our happiness. How soon do you expect she'll want us to begin paying it?"

"Once again, Morgan and Maeve have lost a significant battle. When they realize the prize they sought wasn't what they should have been pursuing, they'll be even more furious than usual. Who knows what despicable plan they'll dial up, but I have no doubt they'll come after you."

In spite of lying safe in Seamus's arms, Fallon shuddered.

He brushed a kiss over her lips. "Until that time comes, we can breathe. Scathach is a disciplined and exacting teacher. If Brighid is her ally, which it appears she is, we can expect the same from her. But Scathach wants her warriors strong and happy. And married."

Fallon blinked up at him.

"We need to see to that part sooner rather than later."

"Did you just propose to me?"

"Not yet."

"Oh." She tried to hide her dismay. Tough to do with him flattening her to the mattress.

"Not that there's any doubt about where our relationship is headed, my beautiful bard. A warrior is only half a man without his talisman, and I can't live without you, Fallon. Let me show you."

With one slow stroke, he joined their bodies, kissing her deeply as he did so and not stopping his pleasurable pursuits until she had no idea where she ended and he began.

⸻

"How much bonding time do you think Seamus and Fallon will need before we can start her training?" Griff asked Rowan as the group of warriors and talismans, minus Fallon's parents, gathered the following afternoon at Rowan and Alyssa's home.

"It would be nice to give them at least a week—standard

honeymoon time," Rowan responded with a grin before he exchanged a secret look with his wife. Their honeymoon had had to be postponed while Morgan and Maeve kept them separated. He understood acutely how much Seamus and Fallon needed some alone time together.

Pacing back across the room, Griff said, "If we knew what Maeve and Morgan planned to do next—and when—we could be more confident about Fallon's safety."

"I understand yer concern fer yer niece, but ye have tae let nature take its course." Alaisdair Graham winked at Rowan as he walked into the great room from the back porch where he'd been playing with Shadow, Alyssa's Great Pyrenees. "If Fallon doesnae bond completely with her warrior, naethin' in yer trainin' will compensate. Besides, they're safe inside the Lochlanns' enchanted cabin. Ye need tae let them get on with it."

Griff walked his empty coffee cup over to the sink and stared out the window above it. "I feel unsettled, like something ominous is awaiting us."

"Somethin' ominous is always awaitin' us when the likes o' Maeve and Morgan are operatin' in the world." Alaisdair settled himself onto the barstool Griff had vacated earlier. "We have tae live our lives the best we can during the times they're leavin' us alone. Thanks," he said as Rowan handed him a cup of coffee.

"Is that what you do? Ignore them until they make you pay attention?" Griff asked.

"Nothing else we can do. Morgan has had a vendetta against my family for a millennium. Now we can expect Seamus has a mortal enemy in Maeve." Rowan sat down beside Alaisdair at the island separating the kitchen from the living room. "However, now that we've established Fallon's relationship to the Conlan line, we probably should contact my brother Rio and his wife Ceri. See about sending all of you to Conlan Manor in Scotland when you start Fallon's bardic training. As a Conlan relative, she now has some additional protections thanks to my brother and his wife." He slanted Alaisdair a look over the rim of his coffee cup.

"No wonder Morgan has targeted you Sheridans. It seems you have a knack for thwarting her worst plans for the warrior class." Griff laughed. "The thought of Fallon having additional protections beyond those Siobhan and I can give her cheers me more than I can tell you."

Shanley Graham entered the room from the hallway and stood directly behind her husband, resting her hands on his shoulders. "Perhaps Seamus and Fallon would like to marry at Conlan Manor. I'm sure my niece wouldn't mind," she said.

Alaisdair glanced up at his wife. "A trip home tae Scotland is exactly what I need, lass," he said, his face beaming.

"Great idea, Shanley," Rowan chimed in. "Then maybe Seamus can get over his pout about not joining us there for the party at Samhain."

He and Alaisdair exchanged a smirk.

Alyssa, who had been seated on the love seat reading, rose and stood beside him. "Now that we've made their wedding plans for them, what's next?" She slanted him a look.

"Now we return to our homes and wait for Seamus and Fallon to let us know what *their* plans are," Duncan said from a chair in the living room where he sat with his wife on his lap.

"Good idea. I think we could all use some private time tae recharge our batteries, if ye know what I mean," Alaisdair said with a twinkle in his eye as he stared at his wife who colored prettily at his suggestion.

"Are warriors always like this?" Keela asked Alyssa in an undertone from across the island where she leaned against the kitchen counter.

"No."

Rowan grinned at her.

"Sometimes they're worse." Alyssa laughed at his pout. "You'll have to get used to it if you're going to associate with this lot."

"Depends on what you mean by worse," Rowan said as he turned around on his stool and wrapped his wife in his arms. "Alaisdair is still new to all the bonding that goes on between a warrior and his talisman, having waited *extra* long before he found her."

"Clearly, teasing Alaisdair about his timing of finding me last Samhain is about to become a new favorite pastime for a certain element of the Sheridan family," Shanley said as her husband chuckled. "But Duncan's right. We should return to our homes. That was Scathach's last directive when she sent us from the battlefield."

"You'll let me know when Seamus contacts you?" Griff asked Siobhan.

"Of course. You'll do the same when Fallon contacts you?"

"Together, we can train Fallon to become the premiere bard of our time," Griff said.

"As long as she's the best talisman for my brother, the rest doesn't matter," Siobhan reminded him.

Rowan waited for the explosion. Instead, Griff bowed to Siobhan.

"You're right. In the end, she'll tell her own story, and that's the most important part of her training."

If he wasn't mistaken, Rowan detected a collective sigh of relief from the warriors and talismans in the room.

Chapter Thirty

ALLON SAT UP in bed and stretched. She couldn't remember a time when she'd felt so at peace, so safe and loved for who she was. Bonding with her warrior without the immediate threat of attack from a vicious goddess had been nothing short of magical. The gods indeed had smiled on her when they gave her Seamus Lochlann.

Chilly air stole over her, and she shivered. Not only was she alone, but Seamus's pillow was cold to the touch. She bailed out of bed and grabbed his shirt, the one she'd been using as a night-shirt since the battle with Maeve, and slipped it over her head before she stepped into a pair of lacy panties and padded out of the bedroom in search of her warrior.

When she didn't find him in the cabin, she slid her bare feet into her hiking boots and wandered out onto the porch. The thwack of metal on wood startled her before she steadied herself and listened carefully. After a minute, she could discern in the odd ricocheting echoes of the forest where Seamus was splitting wood.

Stripped to the waist, he swung a huge ax, splitting half a log in one smooth motion. A fine sheen of sweat covered the bunched muscles of his magnificent shoulders and back. Her mouth watered at the sight of him.

"Hey," she said softly from the edge of the little clearing where he worked.

"Good morning, Fireworks. Sleep well?" he asked with feigned innocence. In reality, the only actual sleep she'd experienced occurred in the hours after dawn.

"Very. Have you not been getting enough exercise?" She peeked at him from beneath her lashes.

"I'm working out to maintain my stamina," he deadpanned.

"Be serious, Seamus. Why are you splitting wood? The weather has been balmy these last few days. We haven't needed a fire at all."

"It's not for us. Well, it might be if we're the next ones to use the cabin. Anyway, my family has a rule about leaving a substantial pile of wood stacked on the porch for the next occupants to use. Since we went through a bunch while Taranis was having his tantrum, I thought I'd better replenish the supply before we return to civilization."

Her mouth turned down. "When will that be?"

Since the day after their escape from Maeve's clutches, Seamus had shown her in many pleasurable ways that he was her warrior, but he hadn't returned to the subject of marriage. Nor had he ever said he loved her even after she declared her feelings for him. When they returned to the real world, what would their relationship be like?

He leaned on the head of his ax and pulled his T-shirt from his back pocket to wipe the sweat from his brow. "We'll need to hike out tomorrow to get back in time to return to work on Monday." He grinned. "My boss is pretty forgiving about my absences from the job when certain cosmic forces intrude on my life." His smile faded. "I'm not so sure you have the same luxury."

She winced at the thought of returning to work and her insufferable boss.

"That bad, huh? You didn't seem unhappy that day I met you in your office."

"I was trying not to let on that I'd seen you before."

He took a step toward her. "You don't like your job?"

She wrapped her arms around her waist. "I like my job fine. It's my boss who's the problem. You're right about him lacking understanding—of anything. My being a talisman and being called away from work at a moment's notice is probably going to get me fired the first time it happens."

"Besides selling season passes for the football team, what else do you do?"

"Marketing for the athletic department."

His questions reminded her how little they knew of each other inside their roles in the civilian world. Another worry he didn't seem to share.

"Are you the brains behind those awesome web ads that drew me in for those football tickets?"

She smiled, her heart singing with her warrior's praise.

"I take that as a yes." He lifted a hand and pushed a strand of hair behind her shoulder. "Listen, I'm not the boss, so I can't offer you a job."

She quirked a brow.

"But I know Rowan's dad has been looking at expanding the business with a stronger presence on the web. Seems to me Security Consultants Unlimited could use your skills. Plus, working for a warrior would mean more flexibility for you when the nasty ladies come calling again."

"What are you saying?"

"If you're interested in a change, I think I know how to solve several problems at once. You can work for a warrior who always allows time off when the world beyond the mists demands our attention, and your boss will be a man who won't make you cringe when you think about him."

Unable to help herself, she swayed a little into him. "Would we be working together?"

Her hair fascinated him as he wound strands around and through his fingers. "We'd likely be based out of the same office, but I don't spend much time there. My job takes me out into the field most of the time."

"Like into a certain pompous congressman's house?" She couldn't help but smirk at the memory of the story he'd told her their first night together.

"Exactly."

She sighed. "I'd very much like to work with you and the Sheridans."

"Well, then, you might want to add some clothes to your very sexy ensemble"—he eyed her from her hiking boots to the hem of his shirt, which ended at midthigh, and up to her face—"and help me carry this wood up to the porch. The sooner we return to town, the sooner we can start on your career change—among other things."

"What other things?" she asked suspiciously.

"House hunting. Now go get dressed."

She opened her mouth, but nothing came out. He motioned for her to return to the cabin and her clothes. Stunned, she silently obeyed.

House hunting? Does he mean we're moving in together? she wondered as she walked the short path back to the cabin.

"That's exactly what I mean, Fallon. Married people generally do live together."

She stood stock-still on the path and turned to look at her warrior who chose that moment to resume splitting wood. With a secret smile, she returned to the cabin to dress.

Chapter Thirty-One

ALLON PINCHED HERSELF again. She could hardly believe the radical way her life had changed in the short month since she'd met Seamus Lochlann. They discovered their fated connection, battled and bested a pair of powerful goddesses, fell in love—though Seamus had yet to say that part out loud—and were now moving into the darling little house in which her new friend Alyssa Sheridan had grown up.

Additionally, she'd started her challenging yet wonderful new job marketing Securities Consultants Unlimited following a miserable final two weeks after giving her notice at her old job. She'd hated saying goodbye to Dorthea Jones, but she certainly didn't miss Alan Tremaine. Seamus had been right about Owen Sheridan, her new boss. From the moment he'd hired her, Owen valued her as an integral member of the team.

The balmy summer weather lingering after the terrible storms in June bolstered her mood. As she loaded the last of her belongings into the U-Haul trailer hooked up to Seamus's pickup truck, she laughed aloud at the way her life was turning out.

"That it?" he asked as he came around the back of the trailer.

"Yeah. I need to lock the door and leave the key in the mailbox. My landlady said she'll come by for it later today."

"Great. With all the help waiting for us at the house, we should be completely moved in by supper. I've already called my favorite pizzeria and ordered a dozen pizzas and a case of their finest imported beer as payment for the help. Hopefully, they'll be too exhausted to stay past dinner," he said in reference to all the family and friends who had shown up to help them move into their new home.

"Griff and Siobhan will stay for a while. They already told you that. Something about the two of us needing to be there when they enchant the house."

"Yeah, but I've watched Siobhan do that before. They need us inside the house and everyone else outside, so that part actually works in our favor." He loosely wrapped his arms around her waist and smiled into her eyes.

"What do you mean?"

"I mean that I have plans for our first night together in our new house. Plans that don't include company." To reiterate his point, he pulled her into a tight embrace and kissed her to within an inch of her life.

"Oh," she managed when at last he let her up for air.

Later that evening as twilight set in, Siobhan and Griff started their enchantments over Seamus and Fallon's new home. Duncan and Keela helped with the ritual while Seamus and Fallon watched from the front room window. If she let her eyes go out of focus, Fallon thought she saw a fine golden net form and fall over the entire house and yard. The glow from the enchantments warmed her soul, and she felt more at peace than at any time in her life except for the few moments when Brighid had touched her while she floated in her prison above the lake on summer solstice.

The thought of Brighid focused Fallon's eyes as she saw the goddess herself standing in the front yard approving the work of the druids who chanted to protect them. Then she noticed something else. On the sidewalk across the street stood her parents. While Siobhan and Griff finished the last of their enchantments, Keela walked over to Clancy and Ivori Graham and spoke to them. She saw her father shake his head and her mother gaze at the house with longing before the two of them climbed into their car and drove away.

Her sorrow reached her goddess who explained to her: *"Your parents have much to learn to overcome the prejudices that put your life and your warrior's life in such peril. They must serve a penance. You watched the second part of it. The first is separation from you until they are ready to admit their failures. The second was to see a druidic enchantment in all its splendor. The third part will include not being allowed to attend your wedding."*

She gasped at the goddess's last pronouncement.

"It is necessary, Fallon, to make them see the error of their thinking. In time, they will come around. Your mother is almost there. Your father, unfortunately, is more stubborn. Do not despair. Your wedding day will be glorious. Trust me."

The goddess disappeared in a shimmering golden mist.

Seamus, who held his talisman throughout the enchantment, tightened his arms around her. "I caught most of that, Fallon. I'm sorry your parents won't be at our wedding. But Brighid's right. There has to be some punishment for the choices they made in your training and education, choices that nearly cost us everything. Griff told me if you'd been properly trained, Maeve couldn't have kept you trapped in that bubble the way she did."

"They made a lot of mistakes, and I often felt out of place in my own home, but they are my parents, Seamus."

"I know." He rested his chin on her hair. "Brighid also said she'll make our day glorious. Focus on that."

"Except there aren't any wedding plans, are there? You've talked about our wedding like it's a foregone conclusion, but you have yet to ask me to marry you. And I have yet to accept."

She tried to pull away from him, but he swept her up into his arms. With a shriek, she wrapped her arms tight around his neck. Mischief played over his features as he carried her down the hall to the master bedroom. Before he stepped across the threshold, he commanded her to close her eyes. Dutifully, she did as he asked, and he started moving again.

"Keep your eyes closed," he said as he slowly lowered her feet to the floor. Momentarily, he left her.

"Open your eyes, Fallon."

She blinked at the fairy tale before her. Lit candles glowing on the windowsill reflected in the mirror atop the dresser and illuminated the turned-down bed. The bed had been beautifully made up with a white eyelet quilt, a white fleece blanket, and fine white sheets. Fluffy pillows lined the heavy mahogany headboard. The whole scene invited her to bed. Seamus knelt on the floor in front of her.

After giving her a chance to take in the room, he took her hand. "I love you, Fallon Graham. More than anything in the world. I want to spend the rest of my life with you."

Tears shimmered on her eyelashes as she stared into the midnight depths of his eyes and saw his love shining there.

"The first time we met, I knew you were someone special, someone I couldn't get out of my head. When you showed up on the doorstep of my cabin one rainy night, I thought I'd conjured you up because I'd wanted to see you again so bad. Then wonder of wonders… turns out you were my fate, and I couldn't believe I could be so lucky."

She gifted him with a watery smile.

"Fallon, this ring belonged to my Grandmother Lochlann. She wanted me to give it to my talisman when I asked for her hand. This is my pledge. I will love you every day of my life. Will you do me the honor of marrying me?"

Her heart swelled with love, and she needed a minute before she could speak over the lump in her throat.

"Yes, Seamus. There is nothing in the world I want so much as to marry you. I've loved you since I met you in my dreams."

Seamus stood and took her in his arms, his kiss promising her all the delights of their love for the rest of their lives.

Thank you so much for reading *Bard*. Turn the page to read an excerpt from *Druid*, Book Five in the Talisman Series.
Coming September 2020

PROLOGUE

RIPPLE IN THE cosmos jolted Davy Sutherland. Actually, the cosmos grabbed him by the scruff of the neck, shook him like a rag doll, and shot a bolt of electricity straight through him. The surge of sexual heat staggered him. Fearing the worst, he looked around for the goddess. Sensing himself alone, he drew in a deep breath. *Maeve prefers warriors, old son. Ye're safe enough from the likes o' her.* Still, he thought it best to return to the safety of Conlan Manor.

Powering up the motor, he turned his skiff toward shore. He'd been feeling restless lately. Something was off, but damned if he knew what. An early morning outing on Loch Broom had seemed a fine idea. The beauty of high summer reflecting in the smooth surface of the loch seized him by his guts and dragged him out onto it. As he absently wove stories in his mind, he'd drifted much farther from shore than he'd intended. The simultaneous jolts, like a punch to his solar plexus coupled with his sudden erection, woke him out of his reverie in a rush. The sixth sense he'd honed over years of druidic training made his exceptional communion with the natural world second nature. He knew better than to ignore a warning.

As the skiff skimmed across the loch, he kept a wary eye out for signs of the triple goddess. The Morrigan, Morgan as she preferred to be called these days, and Maeve, two powerful entities of the goddess of war, had taken a series of beatings at the hands of the Sheridan clan and their friends recently. The third member of the terrible trio, Macha, usually confined her activities to warriors in Ireland, but Davy understood that even though he was a druid rather than a warrior, he still had to be careful. His connection as a resident druid to the powerful Conlan and Sheridan clans could—and probably would—make him a target of the deities sooner or later. Better not to be caught out alone on open water with his guts roiling like they were.

As he neared the tiny village of Ullapool on the shores of Loch Broom, he thought he saw his friend Hamish Buchanan dancing a little jig on the pier. Steering his boat closer to shore, he noted Hamish indeed jumped up and down in a manner clearly indicating he wanted Davy's attention. Looking around to see if there was something dangerous in the water, he spotted what had Hamish in such a state. Directly behind him, something huge and fast, something creating a wake sending waves crashing ahead of it bore down on him.

Davy ramped up the skiff's motor and tore across the loch. When he reached the pier, he wrenched the rudder, sending the boat into a precarious slide that nearly capsized it. Simultaneously, he cut the engine and bumped the small craft roughly against the wood planking. Hamish wasted no time reaching into the skiff to link his arm around Davy's bicep and yank him from the boat. For a man of indeterminate age, Hamish demonstrated incredible strength and power as he jerked Davy to safety.

Right as the two men jumped back onto the dock, a kelpie leapt from the water. Its flashing hooves crashed down in the middle of the skiff, smashing it to splinters with a ferocious crack. From somewhere above them, Davy heard the otherworldly cackling of a vengeful goddess, the first salvo in yet another battle in the ongoing struggle between the goddesses of war and the warrior class they never left in peace.

CHAPTER ONE

Six weeks later: Conlan Manor, Ullapool, Scotland

AVY TRIED TO sleep, but the swirling tattoo on his left bicep was giving him fits again. No doubt the design he'd felt weirdly compelled to have inked on himself on a trip to Glasgow right after *Lughnasadh* had some sort of supernatural power. He couldn't decide if the omens were benign or not, but the intense sexual heat and the erection accompanying the throbbing in his tattoo definitely meant something. He knew about the war goddesses' lust for warriors. Some legends said Maeve could only be satisfied if she had thirty warriors a day. Warriors. Surely as a druid, he was safe, right? Maeve—and her sisters—had to have little interest in him.

Or maybe Maeve wasn't behind the omens at all. Perhaps the signs meant something else. Though the heir to Conlan Manor, the beautiful Ceri Sheridan had rebuffed his advances—rightfully too as it turned out—perhaps there was another woman nearby who would succumb to the power of his stories and welcome spending the rest of her life listening to them. He sighed. Not for the first time did he wish he'd been born a warrior whose mate the gods preordained for him. Taking himself in hand, he eased the throbbing both in his arm and in his groin. A sense of peace washed over him as he indulged his favorite fantasy—being a warrior worthy of his fated talisman. Afterward, for another blessed hour or two, he slept with a smile on his face.

✠

"The bard this clan produced will wed her warrior here in a fortnight on the autumnal equinox. That means we need tae prepare fer a whoppin' big *ceilidh* tae honor her and her warrior," Hamish said, his face alight with glee. Seated around the scarred kitchen table for breakfast were Hamish's cousin Ceri Ross Sheridan, her warrior husband Rio Sheridan, and Davy, who tried to hold back a grin as he watched the usual byplay between Rio and Hamish.

Rio glared at the old druid. "I suppose there are some especially nasty members of the Celtic pantheon we need to invite along with the assorted neighboring civilians you just can't leave out," he grumbled.

Everyone at the table knew exactly what Rio referred to. Rio and Ceri's bonding as a warrior pair included the rather harrowing experience of hosting a large ceilidh on the previous *Samhain*. A ceilidh for Celtic New Year at Conlan Manor necessitated extending an invitation to Taranis, the thunder god who tried to steal Ceri and her best friend Alyssa Sheridan. With some coaxing, he'd contented himself with two unsuspecting civilians who washed up on the shores of Loch Broom the following morning after a squall the god had visited on the loch. Usually, Hamish also invited Morgan, but since she'd especially targeted Rio and had an eye toward killing Ceri as well, Hamish didn't invite her to the last Samhain ceilidh. She had attended anyway with an army of rogue warriors and zombie champions who nearly succeeded in sending Rio over the ford and into the mists forever.

"Och, lad, dae ye still take it as a personal affront that we follow the auld ways in the auld country?" Hamish teased.

Rio remained silent.

Preferring some peace, Davy inserted himself into the conversation. "Since the autumnal equinox is a low feast day, we have nae obligation tae invite any deities tae the party."

Rio sat back and crossed his massive arms over his equally massive chest.

Undeterred, Davy continued. "However, as I understand it from yer Aunt Shanley, Fallon Graham's patron goddess Brighid was pretty handy in rescuing her from Maeve's nasty prison on summer solstice. Perhaps it would be wise tae invite her tae the party and ask her blessing on this pair."

"Good idea, lad, since Brighid is our patroness tae. I knew I trained ye well. Invitin' the mistress o' stories would be a mighty fine gesture." Hamish saluted him with his mug of tea before taking a sip.

"And Scathach. We must invite her. Since Seamus is so close to Rio's family, she's trained him almost as much as she's trained the Sheridan warriors," Ceri reminded them.

Rio smiled at his wife's suggestion. "Scathach and Brighid will be welcome additions to the guest list," he said before adding with a pout, "Wish they were the only two we had to invite on Samhain this year."

Hamish chuckled. "Samhain belongs tae Morgan and Taranis. I'll be sure tae be the one serving 'em their drams o' my finest whisky and a draught o' my special mead this year. They expect it."

"Uh-huh. Last year, I believe Taranis demanded a slice of Alyssa's birthday cake served by my wife and Alyssa herself." Rio's raised brow mirrored the skepticism in his voice.

"That was a test, and our Ceri and Alyssa passed with flyin' colors. This year will be different," Hamish insisted. "But first, we need tae take care o' the party celebratin' yer friends' weddin' and the autumnal equinox. How many are comin' over from America did ye say?"

Ceri named off their guests. "All the Sheridans, Seamus and Fallon of course, Aunt Shanley and Alaisdair who suggested having the wedding here, Fallon's aunt and uncle, and Fallon's friend Sloane." She blew out a breath. "I think that's it."

Rio slipped his arm around her, a reassuring gesture.

Ignoring the wave of longing that came with watching them together, Davy said, "Maybe we should make a point o' invitin' Druantia, our druid patroness tae this little shindig as well."

"Another good idea, lad. Ye dae an old man proud, ye dae." Hamish beamed. "That's settled. We'll invite some o' our particular favorite deities along with some other folks"—he grinned mischievously at Rio—"and enjoy a lovely party. O' course, we'll have tae dae some extra chantin' around this auld pile before the big day."

"I suppose that means you'll be wearing out my wife again, old man." Had Rio been a druid, he might have turned Hamish to dust with his suggestion.

"Och, lad, right when I think ye're makin' progress, ye get all ornery on me." Hamish sounded innocent, but Davy didn't miss the glint in his eyes. "Ceri understands the requirements her role as mistress o' Conlan Manor demands. Ye could make it easier on her by participatin' yerself. If Davy and ye took the upstairs and Ceri and I took the downstairs, we could enchant this place in half the time with half the strain on yer lovely talisman. How 'bout that?"

"If I didn't know better, Hamish, I'd think you led me deliberately to this point where if I refuse your suggestion, I'm a hypocrite and a terrible husband, but if I accept it, I'm a willing participant in your druid activities against my principles. Caught between a rock and a hard place." Rio scowled.

"Admit it, Rio. Ye have a soft spot for the auld man. Or he's been working especially hard on yer dinner," Davy said with a smirk. "Either way, ye know ye're going tae help me with my part o' enchanting this place against the very deities ye despise the most."

Ceri leaned into her husband. "Hey, warrior," she said softly, "you've come a long way in overcoming your prejudices against the druids in our community. Besides, helping these two with the enchantments over our home adds layers of protections to *you*, and after what happened to Seamus's friends, I want you to have as many additional protections as you can get." She punctuated her words with a soft kiss on Rio's mouth, and when she pulled away, he sighed.

Inwardly, Davy sighed too. Watching the two of them often left him wishing he could compose a story wherein he could be a warrior with the privilege of experiencing bonding with a talisman.

"Fine. I'll help but only because you asked me so nicely," Rio said with a smile for his wife before he sent a scowl Hamish's way.

Hamish and Davy burst out laughing while Ceri secretly winked at them.

As Sloane MacIntosh packed her bags for the trip to Fallon's wedding in Scotland, she tried to think happy thoughts about what an adventure it was going to be to see a new country and have the opportunity to meet new people and try new things. At their insistence, she'd stayed with Seamus and Fallon for a week following her warrior's death. But watching them fall in love with each other more and more every day only increased her sadness and sense of loss for what she would never have herself.

As she'd grown up, she'd understood there was always the possibility her warrior would never find her at all, and she would live alone as she awaited him. However, having found and lost him in the space of an evening created a whole new dimension to being alone, a dimension centered on grief. Her friends were great, but they couldn't keep their eyes—and usually their hands—off each other. Then they'd apologize and try not to show how much they meant to each other whenever she was around. At last, she knew she needed to give them the freedom to have what the gods had fated for them without the audience of a talisman who'd been widowed before she'd ever had the chance to become a bride. Before she'd even had the chance to bond with her warrior.

Fallon's powerful druid friends Siobhan MacManus and Griffin Walsh added enchantments to Sloane's home, and she'd felt relatively safe there in the month since she'd returned to it. The murder of crows taking up residence in the trees of her neighbor's yard across the street the last couple of days worried her though. Leaving town seemed a good idea both for boosting her mood and for giving her some peace from Macha's dark reminders of her loss.

The birds made her remember the night before she'd met Gavin. She'd witnessed a blood moon and had been so excited so see such an event. The pulsing of a russet shadow across the face of the moon and the illusion of the full moon shrinking in size as the earth eclipsed it intrigued her. The silver sliver of light emerging on the edge of the moon before it widened across the face, restoring it to a bright silver-white disk in the western sky awed, enchanted, and, oddly, frightened her. The ancients saw a full lunar eclipse as a portentous moment, an occurrence provoking fear and wonder. In the weeks following the events of Lughnasadh, Sloane mirrored their atavistic response. She'd forever associate the coming of an ominous event with a blood moon.

When Fallon and Seamus arrived to pick her up for the trip to the airport, they discovered her on her front step with her packed bags beside her as she contemplated the squawking cacophony deliberately irritating the neighborhood and her. As a goddess, Macha could be anywhere at any time. Sloane knew this. However, she thought Macha sent the crows to torture her rather than to impart evil intent. In any case, she was glad to be leaving home for a few weeks.

"Should you be taking a chance sitting out on your porch with that bunch watching you from across the street?" Seamus asked as he bounded up the sidewalk toward her.

"I don't think they signal any harm to me other than emotional. I think Macha wants me to remember what she took from me. What bothers me is why she won't let up. Honestly, it'll be good to have something much more hopeful to think about," she said as she followed Seamus, who carried her two small suitcases, to his truck.

"For a two-week stay in Scotland, you packed light. You sure you have everything you'll need?" Fallon asked as she stepped out of Seamus's truck.

"Apparently, some women don't think they need to pack every outfit they own," Seamus said in a long-suffering tone as he slid Sloane's bags into the bed of his truck beside the myriad pieces of luggage already riding there.

"I did have to bring along a wedding dress, you know," Fallon said with a huff.

"Not on my account. My favorite outfit of yours is the one you came with." A wicked grin spread over his features.

"You want me to marry you naked?" Fallon asked, her eyes dancing.

"Hey, hey Fireworks. I didn't say that—"

"Oh, I guess I misunderstood. So, there's actually no problem with my luggage then?" she asked sweetly.

"None whatsoever," Seamus said with an eye roll he ruined with a smirk as he hauled himself into the driver's seat of his truck.

Sloane sighed wistfully as she watched their exchange before Fallon caught her eye, the little smile on her friend's lips turning upside down.

"For the last time, Fallon, don't apologize in any way for

finding and falling for your warrior. You didn't steal mine and leave me alone," Sloane said as she buckled herself into the back seat. "We're off to celebrate the joyous occasion of your wedding, and we're all going to have a great time. Agreed?"

Fallon leaned over the front seat, grabbed Sloane's hand, and squeezed it. "Agreed.

"Let's get this show on the road, ladies. The sooner we arrive in Scotland, the sooner you become Mrs. Seamus Lochlann"—he squeezed Fallon's knee—"and I've waited long enough for that," Seamus declared as he put the truck in gear and sped toward the airport.

A word about the Phantom Isle:

As part of my research for the Talisman Series, I read Bob Curran's *An Encyclopedia of Celtic Mythology*. In a sidebar in the chapter on "The Otherworld," he shares an especially intriguing story that inspired the major scenes in the battle for Seamus Lochlann.

In July 1866, a mirage appeared above the waters along the coast at Inishowen, Ireland. The event, reported in *The Coleraine Chronicle* on July 21, 1866, apparently went on for two hours and was seen by several hundred people. People saw castles, a manor house, an entire village—including special mention of a church—and the changing of the landscape below where the mirage hovered over the peninsula and the Inishowen Hills. The story gave me the idea for the place where Maeve could enact her special tortures of Seamus and Fallon.

Sometimes truth is stranger than fiction.

Thank you for reading *Bard*.
Tam

ACKNOWLEDGEMENTS

When I wrote the first couple of drafts of *Talisman*, the first book in this series, I had no intention of taking the story beyond one book. I asked a few people for feedback, and they not only encouraged me to keep going with *Talisman*, but they also asked when they were going to have the chance to read Seamus Lochlann's story.

Huh?

Guess I needed to sit down and write Seamus's story. In *Talisman*, he's a fun guy with a thing or two to say, but when I wanted him to tell me his story, he was decidedly reticent about it. Luckily for me, Rio Sheridan couldn't wait to tell his story, so I wrote *Warrior*. Still, Seamus wasn't talking, but Alaisdair Graham wanted to join the party, which led me to write *Prophetess*. Apparently, Seamus figured out I'd just keep writing other characters' stories, so he decided to open up and let me tell his.

I realize I'm talking about these characters as though they're walking, talking, breathing human beings. In my mind, they are. Hopefully, they come to you, dear Reader, that way too.

Thanks so much Coleene Torgerson and Dodo Rosling for

encouraging me to keep going with this series. These characters live because you loved them as much as I do.

Thank you, Sue Ellen Turnbull for answering my last minute call to give *Bard* one more read before I sent the manuscript out for publication. I truly needed your eyes on this one, and I appreciate your help more than I can say, especially considering your circumstances at the time. Your generosity is awe-inspiring, and I am forever grateful.

Janet Langworthy, Patty Brus, Bri Brasher, Lori Hodges, Anita Daubert, Joni Blood, Jackie DeRudder, and Erin Allen—thank you all for being such big fans of this series. That you enjoy these books so much means the world to me. Thank you, Erin Stahl and Madison Smith-Cox for giving me more ideas. I thought the series would be done at five books, but maybe not. =)

As always, I'm indebted to my incredible editor, Nikki Busch, for giving my words the polish they need to shine. If not for you, I would never have had the courage to put this series out into the world. Your expertise makes these books happen. Thank you.

Maria at Steamy Designs and Chrissy at Damonza, once again, you've made my words look good. I'm lucky to be able to work with such talented designers. Thank you.

As always, thank you Grady, the warrior of my heart. Your love and belief in me mean everything.

Most of all, thank you, Reader, for taking a chance on me and reading this book. I appreciate your time and your feedback. Reviews help authors find more readers. I would be grateful for a review wherever you like to review books. You can find me on Amazon, GoodReads, and BookBub. You can also follow me on Instagram @tamstales32, on Facebook at Tam DeRudder Jackson, on my website at *www.tamderudderjackson.com* –where you can also sign up for my newsletter—and on my blog: Try Thirty New Things on Word Press. Let's grow together.

Tam DeRudder Jackson is the author of the Talisman Series. In her previous career, Tam was an award-winning high school English teacher. Today, she's living her dream of writing novels. When she's not writing, she's reading all the books or carving turns on the ski runs in the mountains near her home in northwest Wyoming or traveling to places on her ever-expanding bucket list. Her two grown sons are the joys of her life, and she likes supporting her husband's old car habit. If you ever see her holding a map, do her a favor and point her in the right direction. Navigation has never been her strong suit.

www.ingramcontent.com/pod-product-compliance
Lightning Source LLC
Chambersburg PA
CBHW050903130726
47900CB00015B/1968